Toggle

Wyon Stansfeld

ISBN-10:1494442175
ISBN-13:978-1494442170

DEDICATION

This book is dedicated to my friend Philip Rogers, who died in 2011. Philip lived life adventurously, thoughtfully, and with a burning desire for inner transformation.

He wrote a book entitled 'Do you feel loved by me?'—which pointed out that we can only love effectively if we listen properly to others about the effects that we are really having in their lives. Bland statements of affection aren't enough, and we often assume incorrectly that we know what is appreciated.

Towards the end of his life he was remarkable in how he handled being very ill. At one point he said "I will find the best in cancer even if it be the death of me." He kept a blog that charted his humour, honesty, and raw courage, trying to do this. Cancer *was* the death of him, but he found his best in the process.

A few days before he died, a daughter brought him an early birthday present: the rights to name a star. It is half way between Orion and Gemini. He named it 'Love is the answer'. When I heard about this I wondered if there might be a species far more advanced than us, living by that star, and how they might respond if they found out about the name Philip had given their home sun; or for that matter how any species might try to make contact…

All of this helped inspire this book.

PROLOGUE

A green circle arrives at an oasis, in the Sahara desert. The buildings there are terracotta mud fortresses against stinging winds of sand. Within seconds a grain of sand blows onto the circle.

Simultaneously another green circle arrives in Oxford, England, in a park overlooking the towers and spires. A passing wind-borne seed has floated up above the surrounding emergency fences and security personnel. Unnoticed and unremarkable, it is an almost weightless fleck, intricately attached to a spherical birth-cradle of a thousand slender hairs. It drifts gently down and settles briefly on the shining circle, receiving, as it does so, a view of the crystal kingdom of the grain of sand, of a subatomic miniature cosmos, and of pointers to a long stretch of history going back to the stars.

PART 1

1

It is before dawn outside a remote monastery in Tibet. The air is thin and icy. Chinpa Dorje is walking carefully, his maroon robes tightly wrapped around him; the path he is on is narrow, treacherous—and familiar. He is aware, though he cannot see them, of mountains all around, steep and immensely present in the silent blackness.

The path leads to a small cave carved out of solid rock. It is here, every day, that he undertakes his unusual meditation. He's done it without interruption for years, and has vowed to continue until he dies. The purpose of his effort is to benefit all beings.

Reaching the cave he bows to the simple shrine, lights some incense and a small butter lamp, adjusts the line of his meditation mat, fluffs up his meditation cushion. He takes his time. There is no end point to get to, no absolute state. There is only this moment, and this, and this.

He settles himself carefully on the cushion adjusting his body into a lotus position, his back straight, alert, and relaxed. He breathes in the fresh mountain air and then, for some time, follows his breathing, allowing his mind to settle. He is preparing for the practice.

Now there is just an awareness of all that is around; the distant sound of yak bells coming up from the village below the monastery; the rise and fall of a chest; the fresh air entering, past a cool nose tip, down a throat, filling lungs, then coming back out, warmer now, releasing back through the nose. Then new cool air entering again;

the rustle of wind through trees… a thought construction arises, inviting distraction, then dissipates back into emptiness and the rise and fall of the breath.

It is time. Time for the Tonglen practice.

Today he has identified Lungrik Kechok from the monastery as his starting point. Lungrik is critically ill. Chinpa Dorje has selected him many times as his starting point. He pictures him now, lying on his bed, tossing in pain, deep furrows on his wet brow, trying not to cry out. The cancer is very advanced, Lungrik can't walk, and is doubly incontinent, his body is emaciated—skin falling in useless folds over his bony, twisting frame. Recently his throat has begun to bubble noisily.

Chinpa Dorje draws in a deep breath: 'may this in-breath be your cancer, may I take your cancer from you'. The breath seems thick and toxic, oily with disease. He holds it in his lungs, then releases.

'And may this out breath give you all my health. This is my gift to you'.

Then he does it again with new words 'let this in breath take your suffering, brother' He lines his lungs with the suffering. 'With this outbreath I give you wellbeing and vitality'.

And again: 'Give me your difficult breathing, I gladly take it from you... here take my good lungs and clear breathing'.

And again: 'Let me take your pain, go on, go on. Here's my joy in exchange, take it, *take it!*

And again, and again.

'Give me your cancer, brother, I will manage this for you.'

And now he broadens it out. One by one he pictures the different monks calling them to mind in turn by walking around the monastery in his imagination and visiting each of their rooms. He draws their sufferings inside with each inhalation:

'I'll take that confusion from you—here have my clarity'.

'Let me hold your grief for you—have my openness to new friendships.'

'Give me your self-hatred—here, have my capacity to love myself'

He continues until he has connected with every monk in the monastery. Then he contemplates the local neighbourhood beginning with a woman he knows is being beaten by her husband.

'Let *my* body take those beatings, sister. Let me take your hurting—take my relief and happiness in return.'

Then he moves to her husband. 'You have violent urges? Give them to me! Let me swallow them. Here take my security and peace of mind.'

He reaches out to all those that he knows in the neighbourhood, then to all those he doesn't. 'Let me have your suffering, all of you, let me have your weakness, let me have your fear, your doubts, your depression, your despair, your envy, your hatred, give it all to me, and here, have all my goodness, it's freely given.

He expands the neighbourhood to the whole of Tibet, welcoming the suffering of Chinese and ethnic Tibetans alike. From Tibet he expands to other countries, to the world, to all beings, to the universe. He allows himself to imagine all the suffering of the universe, of all time, entering him and all his goodness and healing pouring out.

The practice takes about an hour. Usually at some stage he feels frightened. Years ago, when he was just starting, he expressed his fears to the Abbot: "What if I really become ill, or full of hatred, or despairing, what then?"

"Why then the practice is working!" Came the prompt reply.

Over the years he has found many ways of handling his fear. Bypassing it, walking around it, confronting, ignoring, tricking, transcending...allowing. Each way has only worked for a while, like a single stroke of oars from a raft crossing a river. He has learnt the need for freshness. He has needed to be ever creative, to keep finding new doors to softness and receptivity, new words, new lines to keep his openness alive, and the oars moving through the water.

Slowly, with a progressive opening of his heart to the suffering and the horror, the territory on the opposite bank of the river has begun to reveal itself to him. He hasn't, in fact, become ill, or contaminated in any way; but his own suffering has become less particular to himself, his own salvation less significant.

He has finished the practice for today. He dedicates any merit arising from it to all beings, and begins treading softly back to the monastery aware of each footstep on the path. Overhead the stars are fading, and the sky is slightly lighter above the high mountain tops. Morning unfolds slowly here.

2

Quick, kneeling position!

That had to be Muhindo, the unmistakable squeaks of his creeping boots on the floorboards above—floorboards that served as both his ceiling and the floor of the room above. Frenziedly he forced his body to kneel below the hatch.

Don't forget to smile, SMILE!

It was hard to get into kneeling position. He was in a small cramped area, about four feet long, two and a half feet wide, and four feet high, in total darkness. A gap below the floorboards that stank of excrement, vomit, and urine. There wasn't enough space to stand up, or stretch out. The only entrance was the locked hatchway in the floorboards above.

Get the bucket and the cup!

With a swollen hand he felt for the small plastic bucket and the cup. He was supposed to use the bucket as a toilet, it had a long handle. Once a day he passed it out to the guards who would empty it and without cleaning it put in his meagre food rations for the day—just enough to keep him alive. Perhaps this was what Muhindo wanted now.

In the darkness next to the bucket he could feel also the small metal mug which they usually filled with water, but sometimes filled with their own urine—as a 'treat'. Apart from the mug and the bucket, there was nothing else but his wounded, naked, body and his raw fear.

He'd lost track of precisely how long he'd been here. It was hundreds of days. The only difference between day and night was that the days were too hot and the nights too cold.

Above was a guard room. There was always someone there. Hour after hour he could hear their hard military boots pounding on the floor above, and occasional bursts of raucous laughter, or the cheers and groans as they watched football on television. Behind that, in the distance, were frequent screams.

He was often taken out himself for 'questioning'. Muhindo usually did this...

Smile.

Whenever he opened the hatch, Muhindo expected him to be kneeling respectfully just below the entrance, a smile on his face. If he wasn't ready then he would fly into a rage and whack him from above with his baton or a dangling kick through the hole. Once he went further: jumping down through the hole directly onto his stomach and genitals. Sometimes he'd opened the hatch only to squat and defecate over his head.

Having to be ready and kneeling was one of his greatest torments. It made it hard to sleep, impossible to rest. He was always alert for the hatch. Waiting for the next session, not knowing what to expect but turning over and over in his mind what had happened so far and the threats. Waiting was as bad as being 'questioned'. At least then there was a return to the present, the pain bringing a kind of release, and sometimes the relief of unconsciousness.

The interrogators, with Muhindo as their chief source of creative sadism, had used many means to try and extract the information they said they were certain he knew. Sometimes they would become so concentrated on breaking him down that they forgot to ask their questions.

He was in position now, his body shaking with effort and fear.

Smile!

The hatch was being unlocked above him— maybe this would be the end—a release into death at last.

Don't dare think it.

It was best not to hope for anything. Hope was dangerous. He was nothing any more, no-one. He was broken, finished...and smiling.

The hatch was thrown back and blinding light flooded down.

"Ah, the shithead kneels" snarled Muhindo from above. "Move shithead. I have a very special treat for you."

3

On the morning of the day the world was offered transformation, Brian was woken by a small hand pulling on his big toe.

"Daddy, quick, it's snowing!"

Reluctantly he opened his eyes as Tilly clambered up his body with a gappy smile.

"Quick, get up. GET UP."

"Shh, you'll wake mummy." He glanced over at Michelle's head, now turning resolutely towards the pillow and wondered why his daughter couldn't have gone to her instead.

"P..L..EEase.."

"Shh!"

But already he had one pyjama-d leg out of the bed. "OK, OK." He managed a wan smile and squinted out of the window.

Snow was indeed falling, fast and silent, the snowflakes huge through the misty glass. An overnight spell had taken all the dark. The tarmac, the roofs of the houses opposite, the roof of his cab parked below them—all now a dazzling white.

Tilly tugged at his sleeve. "Daddy, please…"

He looked down at her shining upturned face. "What?"

"I want to go out." This time he grinned at her.

As Tilly rushed downstairs and began searching for her red plastic mac and pink glitter gloves Brian looked in briefly on Rowan, his tiger-suited son—still fast asleep in a disarray of quilt.

In the porch he found Tilly's wellies and helped her put them on— never an easy task. Then back upstairs to get Humphrey and

Kimberly, without whom he knew she wouldn't go anywhere. Humphrey was her small much-chewed teddy—so named because if she had 'a hump' she only had to cuddle him to become 'hump-free' and Kimberly, her black plastic doll, dressed in red, yellow and green, her enormous eyes now staring, ever wakeful, with permanently jammed eyelids.

Brian hadn't wanted them to buy Kimberly. It was pushing political correctness a ratchet too far, he felt. Perhaps it would give his daughter misplaced ideas later in life. But Tilly had been so insistent in the shop and when Michelle had said "what's the problem?" he hadn't known how to respond.

Taking Tilly's gloved hand he guided her onto the road—less slippery than the pavement—minding the cars that slithered past unpredictably. As they tottered towards the Heath he delighted in her immersion in the freshly magical world. Clutching Humphrey and Kimberly tightly, she lifted her feet precariously up over the snow ridges and plunged them one at a time into the drifts beyond as if negotiating a high altitude pass.

The Heath was covered in the footprints of people and dogs who'd come before them and they decided to look for other tracks. In a wild part near the rail tracks and allotments, they found the cloven tracks of muntjac deer. There were also fox tracks with their tear shaped feet and brush marks, and the spread-eagled claws of badgers. Brian was glad to teach his daughter the differences. She liked best the squirrel tracks—little clumps of four paws at a time as they jumped, half flying through the air, then landed into a cluster, then bounced off again, each paw mark a perfect relief of tiny nails and pads.

They had to leave some of Humphrey's tracks, of course, and Kimberly's were also very clear, her tiny black feet a startling contrast with the white as she pressed them alternately into the snow.

Back at work, later that day, Brian pulled up in Tavistock Square for a rest. This was one of the things he liked about being a cab driver—you could pace yourself, working when you wanted, stopping when you wanted; and this was a favourite haunt, a haven of tranquillity in the midst of crowded Bloomsbury. He locked the cab and walked into the park, aware of his polished shoes scuffing the melting snow to expose the grass beneath.

In the centre of the park the statue of Gandhi, frozen in meditation, looked benignly down at him with its permanent composed smile, and full heavy-lidded eyes. Around his half-naked body Gandhi's khadi, presumably home spun, now had snow in its folds as it wrapped around his waist and up over one shoulder before sweeping down over his bare wet back. Brian gazed upwards for several moments. Gandhi was certainly impressive, there was something about him, a modest greatness. Even if he *had* fought for India's independence from Britain and even if he *was* Indian, he thought of him as somehow 'honorary British', come home to sit in a park, in central London.

Brian loved statues and had researched all the ones in London at the same time that he'd studied for 'The Knowledge'. He'd seen them all and learnt when each was made, who made it, who commissioned it and why. But most of all he was interested in the stories they told: of generals, explorers and deep thinkers; of battles won and lost, freedoms secured, ideas overturned; of heroism in one form or another. Statues, he reflected, were like the animal tracks he'd just shown Tilly: time capsules of information crossing over from the past into the present. They reminded him of his heritage, of what had been achieved, kept him proud of being British.

These weren't the sort of things he discussed with his customers, of course. As often as not they expected taxi drivers to be thick. Why else would you be a taxi driver? They didn't realise you needed a brilliant memory to qualify, that you had to learn tens of thousands of streets, landmarks and places of interest, that it took years. But all of that was changing these days, of course. Black cabs were being replaced by mini-cabs, whose drivers just relied on sat-navs and their control-offices to get from A to B. It wasn't as good, and most of the drivers were immigrants who didn't know a thing about London and couldn't advise on basic stuff like where to find a good cheap hotel or an open MacDonalds at 3 am. Not that he was racist of course. It was just that too many were being let in. There should be an honest debate about it. People were scared now even to *talk* about people's skin colour least they be labelled racist.

Brian took a deep breath and got back in the cab. He turned on the radio and his 'For Hire' sign and looked out through the steaming windows at the frosty streets and tall heavily dripping trees around the edge of the park. The low, spring sun was dappling the new leaf buds with slanting rays and one of his favourite songs, 'We are the champions' had just come on the radio. Things weren't so bad.

"We are the champions - my friends
And we'll keep on fighting
Till the end
We are the champions
We are the champions…"

Suddenly the song was interrupted:

"Greetings to all people of earth. This message is sent to you in peace."

Brian grunted with irritation. He wished they wouldn't mess around with good songs and put in silly adverts—and right at the start as well.

"There is no need to be frightened."

He wasn't frightened! They were having a joke. Could they please just get back to the music?

"This contact is made in order to offer you transformation opportunities".

OK, OK, he was standing by for the sales pitch… But the voice was soft, crystal, genderless and he was thinking now that it was *quite* a good scam. They'd do anything to get your attention though.

"There is no obligation to accept what is offered, nor any penalty, or offence taken, if any person, or nation, does not take up the offer. There is no military or technological advantage in making use of these opportunities…"

Now he had *no idea* what the ad was referring to—but that's how it was these days. Maybe it was a plug for a new film he hadn't heard about…

"More information will be broadcast in exactly a week's time on the following frequency..." (there followed some figures).

Then the song came back as if nothing had happened:

"… No time for losers
'Cos we are the champions…of the…World."

Brian looked out of the window at a nearby plane tree. The bark was peeling off in country shaped pieces leaving a multi coloured map on the trunk—yellow, grey-green, brown, ochre, cream…

And then there was a young man with long hair knocking on his window wanting a ride. So, it was off with the radio and he was out of the cab in a trice easing in the man's suitcase.

As he drove off into the traffic on Euston Road and down towards Kings Cross, he didn't notice at first how many cars had pulled over.

4

He pushed himself up with great effort so that his head appeared through the hatch and out into the blinding light of the guard room. As his eyes adjusted he could just make out Muhindo's boots on the floor in front of him and all around the locked trapdoors to other cells of misery.

Careful now, keep smiling.

He was worst when you stopped smiling.

The next stage of heaving himself out of the hole was always tricky, one slip or cowering movement could be met with a blow to the head or a stamp on the hand. On occasion he'd made half a dozen attempts to get himself out, each time being met with a contemptuous attack for a faltering move, and a fall back down, until at last, crumpled and defeated he would need to be manually hauled out, which meant further punishments for the trouble he'd caused.

Today though, he managed to haul himself out successfully and stood up shakily by the side of the hatch. It seemed that there were no other guards in the guard room. He was alone with Muhindo.

Alone with him is dangerous. Could be he wants sexual relief.

"This way shithead" Muhindo shoved him towards a door at the side of the room. This was not the door to the room where he was normally 'questioned' but opened into a narrow window-less corridor he hadn't been in before. He groped forwards, eyes stinging, towards a large door.

When they reached the door Muhindo bent down suddenly so that his face and curling smile were within inches and he smelt the familiar rank stench of his breath. "This is bye-bye from me shithead".

Careful, it's a new trick.

Don't look him in the eye.

He'd learnt long ago never to do that.

Never look anyone in the eye.

Think of yourself as nothing, already dead.

Keep smiling.

He tried to keep his body from shaking as Muhindo unlocked the door with a large key and it let in a blinding shaft of light and a hot gust of outside air.

"Move shithead, move!"

Muhindo swung his baton into the back of his head so that he lost balance and fell forwards through the door, which slammed shut behind.

5

Theo Chaldrike sat fully concentrated in the recreation room at the NCTC, (the National Counterterrorism Center), stroking the tips of his velvet moustache, and staring at a game of Akron. His opponent, a PhD mathematics prodigy, had just made an unexpected move, delicately removing one of his golf ball sized spheres from the bottom corner of a pyramid to send four other spheres tripping down, along the edge of the pyramid, in a gentle cascade. It looked like a stupid move but Theo knew better than to rush a reply, even though his clock showed less than two minutes remaining. Always expect the worst from your opponent—then there are less surprises.

He was so absorbed in the enjoyable, familiar, and almost painful tension, of grappling mentally at the edge of what was understandable, that at first he didn't notice the low alerting noise, and the blinking light, of the intercom in one corner of the room. Until, that is, it gained in frequency and strength, forcing him to look up reluctantly and notice his flashing name.

"Excuse me one moment," he whispered to his opponent. Briefly he considered pausing the clock, but deciding against, rose to press a button on the nearest intercom: "Theo, hello?"

"It's Wilkins. Sorry to interrupt you, but a most unusual message has come in."

"And?"

"And it claims not to originate from earth."

The tips of Theo's moustache twitched fractionally sideways. Wilkins, his PA, had a tendency to make practical jokes. At least that is what he used to do, though lately he'd largely given up, having realised, finally, how much it pissed him off.

"Wilkins, you inchoate imbecile, that's a pathetic attempt."

There was a short pause on the line. "Sir, I'm not kidding. Reports are coming in that the message was heard all over earth."

"All over the earth, huh?" He kept his voice deliberately flat.

"Yes, in many languages, and on many frequencies."

Theo glanced longingly back down at the shining pyramids of coloured glass spheres on the table.

"And it purports to be from extra-terrestrials?"

"Yes"

"Have they got green heads?"

"...Sir, we think this is serious, you need to hear the message!"

"Don't be puerile, Wilkins." The man had no finesse. He ended the conversation and sat back down at the table, glancing at the clock—thirty seconds to go—that should up the ante somewhat. With uncharacteristic impulsiveness he placed one of his spare spheres on the top of four others forming a nest at the summit of a pyramid, but the moment he pressed the end of turn button on the clock, he realised he'd made a mistake. His opponent pulled away a piece from the side of a pyramid, and another line of spheres tripped into place, securing a three-dimensional connecting win.

"Darn!" Theo managed a tight lipped grin at his astonished opponent.

Losing was rare, and not something he relished. However it did offer some compensatory solace, dispelling—temporarily at least—a nagging feeling that he was either freakishly abnormal in his brilliance, or that the rest of the species were complete idiots, or both. But losing usually only happened when he gave his opponent a large handicap, or, as in this case, more time. In such cases his relief was undercut by a knowledge that he couldn't quite shrug off, that it hadn't really been a fair match. He was about to offer a return game when his name flashed up again.

It was Wilkins—and this time he was reluctantly persuaded to at least listen to the so-called extra-terrestrial message: "You can go off people, Wilkins. This had better not be another fatuous attempt at a joke."

He strode up the stairs to his minimalist paper-free office, bare except for a lap top on a comfortable 'L' shaped sofa, a huge computer screen taking up all of one wall—and the 'play' arrow that Wilkins had lined up for him:

"Greetings to all people of earth. This message is sent to you in peace……"

He listened right through. Then he listened again. Then he listened with raised eyebrows in Hindi, Arabic, and Mandarin, three of the languages he spoke fluently. Afterwards he sat, in silence, for several minutes, staring into space. There was something unusual under the surface of the message, in all its translations, that he couldn't quite place, but that he knew was there. Something aside from its content—to do with the structure of the message. It was fascinating. He loved not quite understanding something, loved to have a mystery to work on. But in parallel to this he could also feel the acid arrival of raw fear in his stomach. This much *unknown* was terrifying.

He focused back on the computer screen and began to speed-read his emails. They had flooded in from the moment the message was broadcast. There were preliminary statements and impressions from all the in-house representatives of external departments—the Departments of Defence, State, Energy, Treasury, Homeland Security, Justice, and of course the CIA and the FBI. Bringing the last two together had been one of the principal aims of forming an interagency counter-terrorism organisation in the first place, after 9-11.

There was a broad consensus, beginning with the Director of the NCTC, that this was unlikely to be an alien message, and that they should treat it, initially at least, as either an elaborate hoax or a potentially dangerous terrorist threat.

But it had quickly become apparent that there were serious shortfalls in intelligence. No-one understood *how* exactly the message had been broadcast, and in so many frequencies and languages. Attempts to trace its origin had so far manifestly failed. It appeared that there was neither a single source for the message, nor a single means of transfer. There were reports of it coming through in many frequencies: on radio, TV, Hi Fi, computer speakers, telephone lines, even on the tannoy at baseball matches. Lou Rimey, representing the Department of Defence, renowned normally for his narrow minded conservatism, had gone so far as to say that the message appeared to be '*omnipresent*' in its transmission.

'It used a technology beyond the comprehension of my department. We just don't get it. We couldn't do that. We've never seen anything like this. If we had this type of technology we'd have used it. Millions of people around the earth must have heard the message first time, and billions by now must have heard recordings. Imagine the propaganda advantage of being able to control all frequencies, everywhere, with whatever you wanted to say...'

After that, and in the absence of anyone contradicting Lou's email, the Director classified the matter as a priority one alert: 'Technology we don't understand threatens our national security.'

The emails that followed agreed, and then a discussion began around the languages used. Copeland, from the CIA, noted that there were reports so far of *thirty one* different languages having been simultaneously broadcast. 'Not only that, it looks like the translations are high quality. In every case we've looked at so far, the message was grammatically precise and beautifully pronounced. This is a remarkable achievement. To produce that many translations of such high quality would have required considerable expertise and a team of people from many different countries working together. So we could be dealing with an international organisation here, or a national one with relevant in-house skills, such as one that needs the languages for espionage...'

Carterton, from the FBI, noted that the research into the distribution of language spoken around America also appeared phenomenally accurate. The message appeared to have been broadcast in whatever language was most popularly spoken in any particular area, not just English.

'We've discovered that in American cities where there are pockets of residents who don't speak English as their first language, that the broadcast was made in their language, *the language most spoken in that particular area.* They've gone to a lot of trouble to maximise the number of people understanding the broadcast. This is a high level, democratic, announcement and must have taken extensive and sophisticated research and resources to implement.'

Following this several people commented that this was an immense amount of trouble to go to for a hoax—which added weight to the possibility that it wasn't a hoax at all, but some kind of conspiracy.

Theo turned off the computer screen and sat back in his sofa for several minutes, staring at the wall and now feeling a flood of anxiety. As leader of the team of hypothesis agents, identifying conspiracies and helping to defuse them was his responsibility and one he took very seriously. But there seemed so little to go on. If the message originated from earth then they could perhaps begin by looking for unusual behaviours arising from key players within the communication technology industry, those specialising in translations and language. But while this might identify potential culprits it still didn't establish motive. Who would want to pose as an alien race, and why? The only people he could think of was SETI, the Search for Extra Terrestrial Intelligence. They could *just* have a motive. Perhaps they had engineered this whole thing to raise public consciousness around the possibility of extra-terrestrial contact, and to attract funding. But then again, surely they didn't have the technology, know-how, or resources to do this. Plus it would have been a foolish and risky strategy, bound to back fire badly if they were discovered. It all seemed way too implausible.

Which left the possibility that the message might really be extra-terrestrial, in which case there was still the problem of motive. Why would an alien species be approaching them and what exactly were the 'transformational opportunities' they were offering? He had nothing to go on but wild speculation. Perhaps it would turn out to be some form of brainwashing, or contamination. Perhaps they were looking for a way to invade.

Chasing a sudden idea he turned the computer back on and scrolled through his work diary, day by day. Today's date was unusual in not being a religious festival, or a significant day, for any country, or religion, *in the entire world.* He made it his business to be aware of such things. It could be a coincidence, of course. A handful of other days across the year fell into the same category. But the odds...it was either quite a coincidence, or it was deliberate. It did look like whoever had choreographed this message had gone to extraordinary lengths to maximise the number of people hearing it and, through their choice of date and their command of the different languages, to appear non-partisan in the process. Clearly they'd wanted to appeal to, and convince, all humanity. They were deliberately targeting *the entire species* for whatever sinister purpose they had in mind; and he had to believe that it *was* sinister.

6

The force of Muhindo's blow sent him flying head first, down some steps, slamming him into the pavement. Immediately hands were on him, from either side, and he found himself dangling between two men, their hands under his bare armpits. It was familiar being handled in this way. His body treated like a carcass of meat.

Carried from the torture room. My head rolling, semi-conscious. Pain like glass beneath the skin.

They threw him into the back of a car, where a woman was waiting. "Shut up, keep down", she hissed, pushing him to the floor and covering him with a blanket.

Darkness. Always back to darkness. Darkness in Makindye barracks. Darkness in the safe house. Tight darkness, squeezing away my breath.

As the car sped off he could hear the familiar sounds of the motorcycle boda-bodas and hooting buses from the Kampalan streets all around them. The rough un-tarmacked roads tossed him painfully up and down in his dusty constricted area on the floor and there was a familiar smell of exhaust fumes.

Makindye barracks to the safe house. Tossed in the army vehicle.

After a few minutes, the woman, whose feet were next to his head, lifted a corner of the blanket: "Here, put these on. Keep down. Keep quiet".

She threw him a Mobil T-shirt and some frayed tracksuit bottoms. He noticed her shoes—dark blue leather, broad high heels. He hadn't worn clothes since he was first captured. Awkwardly he started to dress. His hands, badly swollen—like blown up rubber gloves—the skin stretched and splitting.

Hands strapped in the electric water.

Cramped into the gully it was hard to get the clothes on as the car kept stopping and starting on bumpy roads. Slowly he pulled the tracksuit bottom over his lower half. But it left him coughing and exhausted. He reached for the shirt.

"Leave it" hissed the woman, pressing his wrist against the seat with her ankle, "Later". She pulled the blanket back over his head.

The car speeded up and now seemed to be on a better road. He judged they must be on the outskirts of Kampala somewhere. The two men in the front were talking about English football teams. Every so often the car would brake suddenly or rattle with the effort of overtaking. Once or twice he felt it swerve sharply, followed by curses from the driver. Silently he vomited into a corner under the blanket.

Suddenly the car was slowing down and the woman adjusted the blanket firmly around him: "shh—roadblock—*not a sound*."

He tried to breathe silently, aware of the rough wool on his bare upper torso.

The car halted and he could hear a brief conversation through the window, presumably with an armed traffic policeman. Then they were on the move again.

Half an hour later the car stopped again. The woman said: "Stay there, don't move". She got out of the car. The two men were also getting out. He heard them rustling about in the boot and wondered if this was his next destination.

Run? Run!

But he felt too weak, and the woman was back now.

"Sit up and put your shirt on". He pulled it over his head as quickly as he could, noticing out of the corner of his eye that the woman was smartly dressed, with a pleated navy blue skirt and plain white top—civilian clothing!

Don't let her see you looking.

"I need to blindfold you", she said, tying a tight scarf around the upper half of his head. "But it won't be for long."

Why is she saying it won't be for long?

She led him out of the car into a building, then up several flights of winding steps, pressing him to hurry. He hadn't walked so far for months and stumbled frequently. Finally they stopped. A door was opened and then locked behind them, and then she untied his blindfold.

7

As Brian waited for his next ride Glenda from the control centre was shouting over the intercom. She always shouted.

"Any of you guys hear that broadcast? Looks like it came through on quite a few frequencies and my boyfriend just phoned to say that it came through on the telly too! He flicked between all the channels and it was on every one. The pictures were all frozen! Weird."

Well, that put a different complexion on things. He couldn't think what it meant but it was certainly different.

He picked up a hugely overweight man whose luggage was fat too—half a dozen bright, bulging, tartan suitcases that had to be shoehorned into the boot and the front. Once he'd got him settled, which took a while, the man said "you guys in the taxi service are not the only ones taking us for a ride…" and they had a short snigger at that.

"It's a hoax, it has to be" he added.

"Yeah, could be."

"Sure it is. Someone's having a laugh". The man paused, gathering his breath. "Mind you it must have cost a fortune—so I reckon it was Richard Branson or that Microsoft guy—what's his name—maybe they were doing it in cahoots with Stephen Spielberg or someone like that. You remember when they first broadcast that HG Wells story about the Martian invasion—people thought it was really happening."

"Yeah, I heard about that."

"I think this is the same, only deliberate. Like some kind of modern psycho-drama where they don't tell people they're manipulating them straight away so they can see what happens—a hyped up reality TV experiment to check out how people would react if there really was an invasion.

"Not the genuine article then?"

"No way José".

He dropped the man off and tuned in again to the control office. Glenda was at such high pitch the radio unit rattled: everyone listening to any media had heard the broadcast. No-one could explain it. It was being discussed on every news channel. This whole thing was gathering momentum.

He picked up a middle-aged man with thin purplish lips, jet black hair, a dark grey suit and a leather briefcase polished to a high sheen. He sat bolt upright in a stiff silence.

"You alright buddy?" He liked to coax his clients into talking. Most people didn't need much encouragement and people seemed to like talking to him. Perhaps it was because they never expected to see him again—and that thought can liberate a tongue. Once the tongue had started to move it was his job to keep it flapping.

The man looked in the mirror, as if noticing Brian for the first time. "Ach yah. I am just so fromped with this media madness"

"About the broadcast?"

"Yah! So nonsense". He pronounced the word 'nornsense' as if it was coming out of his nose.

"You don't think it's aliens then?"

"Hah! You think so! You must be joking!"

"Well, I…"

"This is so garbage! Where would they come from these people? Not from this sun system, that's nonsense—we would know by now if there was clever life near us. Nach, they would have to come from a planet around another sun! But the nearest sun is over forty tri-llion, tri-llion, ki-lo-me-ters away."

He was emphasising every syllable now.

"It takes more than four years just for light alone to reach us from there! For heaven's sake—think about it. *Think*. Even supposing that there is life on a planet around that star even if you assume that—but this is not a sensible assumption—even if you assume that—a ship would take a *huge* amount of time to reach us. Pah! Only idiot would believe."

He stopped momentarily to wipe some saliva from his lower lip then plunged on:

"Or if you say they haven't come in ships but they sent this message to us from more than *four light years away*—then that would take *years* to reach us—but then they are saying that they will send another message next week—which means that they must have already sent it at least four years ago! And how do you think they are going to have a conversation with us if there is a four year gap? *Four years*. That's eight years for one question and answer. But even if you assume they somehow miraculously could—and you cannot assume this—then why would they do this? Why? It makes not toothpick of sense. Why would they waste their time on us—a stupid animal bent on killing ourselves and our planet? This is so nonsense—it make me want to spit." And with that he breathed out another deep sigh of disgust.

Brian waited a little before saying anything. He was pre-occupied with a large articulated lorry that was pushing in in front of them and slowed down to give it some slack. When things were safely settled again, and for sheer mischief, he gave the man another prompt: "you don't think they might want to help us then?"

The man's eyes bulged with contempt: "Hah! You think so? You must be joking!"

That phrase again. Brian sat back and listened with secret delight as he gently negotiated the rush hour traffic. People were starting to turn on their headlights.

Twenty minutes later the man was still in full frothing flow when he dropped him off at Hillingdon underground. It was a relief by then. He was probably right of course, but Brian realised that, as well as finding the man amusing, he also felt disappointed. Aliens were a much more interesting explanation.

A young woman with cut-off shorts and orange trainers hailed him. She had red streaks in her hair and a lopsided top exposing a bra strap so thin it made her shiny exposed shoulder look like cracked china. But it was her eyes that really took his breath away—they were an intense blue like the brightest summer sky. As he lifted her red suitcase for her and held open the door he noticed she smelt exotically of oranges and incense. She settled herself on the back seat as if she'd been there many times before.

"Where can I take you Ma'am?"

She laughed. "That's cute. Don't often get called 'Ma'am'"

"Mademoiselle?"

She giggled. "Nor that neither." She gave him an address.

"It's my sis'. I've come to stay with her." Her voice was soft felt, older than her years.

"Welcome to London then." As he drove off he was aware of her looking at him in the mirror and something about her smile just set his heart racing.

"D'you hear the message?" He nodded at the mirror.

"What d'you reckon then? Her voice sounded excited.

He didn't normally express his own views early on with a new passenger. It could freeze things up. People are put off talking if you're opinionated. "Dunno, I've heard a couple of strong views…"

"Yeah." She was still smiling and looking so relaxed and familiar—as if they'd been driving for hours.

"I think we have to wait and see," he said, glancing up again into the mirror to check her response. Bright blue eyes were waiting for him. "But I guess I'd quite like it to be another species…" he ventured, tentatively, "it might wake us all up a little."

She came alive: "It'll be another level, man, and I'm sure it *is* another species! I've just been listening to the message, right, over and over…"

Surely they couldn't be talking like this. It couldn't actually be...

"...and, like, don't you just want some...of what they're offering? They could've offered us time travel, or cold fusion, or trade, but instead they offer us, like, '*transformation*'. These guys are cool, man, and *respectful,* yeah. See what ends they went to not to offend or impose. You know what? I reckon we're dealing with a species a great deal more evolved than us."

She couldn't be serious...yet she looked like she was. "But if it's aliens what do they mean by 'transformation'?" He asked, doubtfully.

She looked at him quizzically. "Don't you know? Haven't you ever experienced it?"

The directness of her question took him by surprise. Had he? He wasn't sure. Passing 'the knowledge' to become a cab driver had felt *significant*, marrying Michelle, having Tilly and Rowan...those were all significant but also at the same time *ordinary*, they were things that just happened to people: getting a job, getting married, having kids...

"Not sure Ma'am." he said bashfully. Significant things have happened, of course, but I wouldn't call them 'transforming'. I don't think I ever thought about that really..." His voice trailed off and he glanced up at the mirror to check if she was still watching him. She was. She seemed to be drinking him in. "I'm not even sure I know what 'transformation' means." He added, candidly, looking back down at the road.

There was a pause. "Hey man, that makes me sad."

Brian felt suddenly confused. This woman, girl really, hardly knew him yet he felt peeled open in front of her as if her amazing eyes were staring into the back of his head and seeing something he didn't even know was there. Why was she sad for him? Was there something missing in his life? He'd never thought of his life as lacking. You were born, you work, you earn money, you look after your family, you do your best, you die...What more was there?

"You don't need to feel sad for me Ma'am." He said through a constricted throat.

"No, but I do. It's OK." She was smiling again. How come she was smiling? Was she mocking him now?

"I just felt sad you said you hadn't had any transformation experiences, 'specially after you'd said you hoped the message might wake us up, right?"

She wasn't mocking. She'd been listening carefully. Perhaps she was genuinely interested.

"What do you want to wake up from Mr Taxi-driver?

Wha-ow. So fast, and close. He kept his eyes locked on the road.

"Well, I…I wasn't really thinking of myself when I said that." He managed at last, keeping his eyes off the mirror.

"Oh…"

Another pause. Was that disappointment in her voice? Surprise? Doubt? Again he felt confused. He thought *he* was a good communicator but this young woman was in a different league…and her questions disorientating. He needed to shift the focus.

"What about you, have you had 'transformation experiences'? He risked a look into the mirror. Her eyes narrowed, momentarily, before her smile spread into a mass of wrinkles at the top of her nose. She knows I'm changing the subject, he thought.

"Yeah man, course. I feed off them. It's what I live for. Don't do drugs though, or compulsive sex. Just do *change*. Like last year I gave away everything and went to live in this wacky community on an island off Scotland…left my boyfriend and a job in the media, took a leap…"

"Did it work out?" It was a relief to be asking the questions.

She pondered for a moment then continued in a leisurely way: "Sure man, it was random… actually there was a lot of shit…but I asked for it. I learnt if you think the world owes you, you get nothing. You only get back what you put in. So now I'm ready for the next thing. Hit me with it! 'Alien transformational opportunity'." She laughed. "…you got to believe."

"You make lots of changes then?" He had her going now.

"Sure. I get into a new situation and everything's cool for a bit, and I'm learning, and happy, and… free. Then, little by little, it starts to glue over and I start to think about life being so short..."

She looked down at her black-tighted knees.

"Here's the thing: I've tried to hang with these periods, like wait patiently for a new dawn, but something I've learnt, right, is that new dawns don't just toddle along. You have to call for them, and the thing is…." she took a breath. "...the thing is, it always seems too hard, right: like the leap's too big, too risky, there's always like people who judge or who might be hurt, or you think there's too much to lose. Something's always trying to hold you back, right. But you can't let it. That way you don't live and you can't respect yourself proper. So, I've learnt *there's always a choice* and you have to just, kind of, leap."

"And you think that aliens are asking us to leap?"

She looked again into the mirror: "Well yes, but I think that 'transformation' probably refers to what's in our heads, that they might be offering us opportunities to change things there."

She'd lost him now. "What d'you mean?"

"Seeing things different, finding a new frame, realising your old frame was…too, like, *tight*."

He stopped to allow an old woman to step onto a zebra crossing.

"Doesn't that worry you?"

"Look, no man, that's the point, it *excites* me." Again her intoxicating smile.

"You aren't frightened, then, that this message might actually be from aliens?" They were nearing her destination and it felt oddly urgent to hear more from her.

She paused, as if checking this out with herself for the first time "not by another intelligent species, no. Man that would be cool. But I am frightened of *us*, how *we* might receive *them*. Maybe we won't rise to it. Maybe we'll see them as a threat, right. Maybe we'll be, like, the hostile ones and turn down what they're offering."

They'd arrived. He pulled to a gentle stop outside the address, and lifted out the red suitcase, regretting the ride hadn't been longer. He felt captivated by her raw enthusiasm and something he didn't quite understand had triggered inside him.

Outside she paid, but didn't move, and stood looking at him directly, relaxed. My, her eyes were blue. "Good talking to you, Mr Taxi-driver, can I call you for other lifts?"

"Of course." He gave her his card.

Why was he so ridiculously pleased and relieved? He'd only known her a few minutes, she was just another customer.

8

As she took off his blindfold he opened his eyes.

Don't look up.

There was a thin dusty carpet on the floor with a pattern of red and orange swirls. It was a long time since he'd seen a carpet.

"Sit" said the woman, gesturing a sofa. He did as he was told. The sofa was frayed, patches of yellow foam stuffing were moulting onto the floor. He could hear the two men talking in another room. He watched the blue shoes walking away from him and stole a glance around the room. It was about fifteen foot square with a single bed in the corner and a large wardrobe next to it. There was a kitchenette along one wall, where the woman was filling a saucepan from a tin. The windows were covered in black dustbin liners and a single bare bulb, hanging on a frayed wire, glowed dimly. The walls were covered in stains, patches of damp and marks where mosquitoes had been killed.

The woman turned to face him and for the first time their eyes met. He looked down hastily. She was about thirty five, with skin the same shade of black as his. A necklace with gold and turquoise beads traced along the top of her blouse.

"You'd better go and wash" she said pointing with a tin-opener to one of the doors. " There's a towel in there and fresh clothes. Don't put the clothes on until you are completely clean. They're all we've got."

He rose stiffly from the sofa and hobbled into a small room with a shower in one corner. The shower was surrounded on two sides by a plastic curtain coming off its rails. At first he didn't know if he should close the door behind him and was relieved when nothing happened when he did. He was alone! In a shower! He caught sight of his reflection in a small cracked mirror and stepped backwards in shock. He scarcely recognised himself. He was so much thinner, older, his eyes were red, there was a recent bruise under one eye and his face looked terrified.

He undressed as quickly as he could, his body covered in scars. On a small duckboard to one side of the room was a fresh dry towel and some smart looking clothes. There was even some underwear.

Half an hour later he emerged back into the room wearing black trousers and a light blue shirt. He allowed himself to look up. The woman was appraising him.

"That's better." Standing in front of her he felt suddenly dizzy and his knees collapsed beneath him.

He came round on the sofa. The men were back, sitting on the bed sorting papers. The woman was watching him. She said: "Sit up, I've made you some soup."

He sat up slowly, head spinning.

"Here." She placed a large mug of steaming soup on the carpet beside him. Suddenly he was sobbing uncontrollably.

Stop it, you fool, they'll hit you.

But no blows came, and the sobbing got worse. He tried desperately to suppress it.

Get yourself under control.

Painfully he managed to sip some soup, fighting back his nausea. The woman came over again. "We're going to put you in the wardrobe now until morning. Don't try to get out." She continued "It's in case someone comes."

Who is this someone, what does she mean?

He climbed into the wardrobe and she locked him in. There wasn't room to lie, but it was large and relatively comfortable with a small rug at the bottom. It was also dark apart from a thin strip of light along one side of the door. He heard the men and the woman talking and the front door opening and closing, then what sounded like just one person moving around the room, then the strip of light disappeared and there was silence.

Darkness at the safe house, under the floorboards. Nothing has changed.

A few hours later he heard an alarm clock ring. Then footsteps. Then a key turning in the wardrobe lock.

Quick, get into kneeling position.

The door opened and the woman peered in at him. Seeing that he had one knee on the floor she raised an eyebrow. "Get out." He stumbled out, tripping on the strip of wood at the bottom of the door. She looked into the wardrobe as he came out and sighed. He had vomited in the night.

"OK," she said slowly, "there's a razor over there. I want you to shave in the shower. Don't cut yourself. It's really important that you keep your clothes clean. Then there's some breakfast for you on the side." He smelt toast but his stomach revolted, he had no appetite. His insides were stinging.

Head clamped, funnel pushed into my mouth, nose pegged, they pour the foul smelling liquid down my throat. Swallow, you have to swallow.

In the shower as he shaved he recoiled once more at his image in the mirror and thought of all the uses for a razor blade.

Back in the room the woman told him to sit diagonally opposite her on the corner of the bed. She was holding a pair of scissors.

It's going to start.

He froze, wondering what was coming. She looked at him with widening eyes: "We are here to help you! I need to *cut your hair*."

She cut efficiently, clipping down his thick curly hair to a uniform half inch. She'd done this before. He wondered why she was doing it now. He sat very still trying not to flinch when she touched him directly to adjust his head position or to hold away the edge of an ear. He felt a sudden urge to cry.

Control yourself!

There were several unhealed scars on his scalp and twice he winced as the blunted ends of the scissors made contact.

After she'd finished the woman took his photograph.

Is this for their files, after I'm dead? Make me look OK then take my photo…

The rest of the day, and another night, followed uneventfully. He spent most of the time in the wardrobe. Several times the men came and spoke quietly with the woman, then left. They brought him medication—pain killers and something to stop him vomiting.

On the second evening they told him to put on some black shoes that pinched at the heels. Then they blindfolded him again.

This is it, they've got me ready. Now they're going to kill me.

9

When Brian got home that evening his wife was unloading Tesco carrier bags in the kitchen, a saucepan of beans was bubbling on the cooker and bread was toasting under the grill.

"Hi Mich. You OK?"

She scarcely looked up. "Yeah, you?"

"Good thanks. Hear the news?"

"What news?" She pierced a plastic bag of apples so that they tumbled into the fruit bowl, then pressed past him to stir the beans "..scuse me."

"You know. The announcement. The thing that could be aliens."

"Oh that. Not really…" Still stirring the beans with one hand she pulled out the grill pan of browning toast with the other. "You couldn't do me a favour could you?

"Sure…"

"Get Tilly. She's in the garden, she needs to come in for her tea before her hands freeze."

Tilly, wearing her spangly wellies and her plastic mac, was trying unsuccessfully to make a snowman out of the last slushy streaks on the lawn.

"You need to come in now, love, Mummy's made your tea."

"Na-oooooh, I don't want to"

"Your hands will freeze."

"No they won't."

"They will, I promise, and it hurts.

Tilly looked at him uncertainly then backed down the garden.

"It's beans on toast." She stopped.

"We can give Humphrey some."

"And Kimberly?"

"And Kimberly, yes, of course." He held out his hand. Reluctantly she stepped forward and took it.

Back in the kitchen he settled her on a high stool by the breakfast bar with Humphrey and Kimberly. Michelle brought over a plate of beans on toast and two small saucers then chucked the saucepan into a full suddy sink. She stretched up to put a bag of rice on a high shelf.

Brian looked around the kitchen not knowing quite where to put himself. Laptop their cat, so named because of her tendency to sit on laptops, as well as laps, was munching contentedly through a glistening plate of disgusting looking cat food in one corner.

"Where's Rowan?"

"In his bedroom, probably playing Xbox, you couldn't coax him to do some homework could you?"

"Sure." He left the kitchen, on autopilot to look for Rowan.

After homework, and supper, and washing up, and clearing up, and once the kids had been bathed and their teeth cleaned and they'd been read to sleep, he insisted on watching the news. But Michelle lost interest and drowsed off almost immediately in front of the telly "It has to be a hoax dear". He watched on for long enough to know that they still hadn't found any explanation for the broadcasts then helped his wife into bed and joined her. Doubtless it would become clearer tomorrow.

But as Michelle slept quietly beside him he lay on his back, wide awake, thinking about the unbelievable broadcast and about what the girl with red streaks in her hair had asked him about transformation. What would it take to transform things around here, for things not to carry on the same as ever? A terminal illness? An actual alien invasion? His wife was probably right of course, it was a hoax, it had to be. But still, was it a crime to wish for a change, for something radically different? His wife was a rare gem:

pragmatic, hard-working, a great mother. She was the sort of woman who would cook hot breakfasts for twenty kids in a campsite blizzard. Without her a lot of stuff round here just wouldn't get done...

But just then he wished that, once in a while, she could ease up, just a little. All evening he'd been willing the chores to end so that she might sit with him at last, so that they could watch the news coming in together. Maybe they could share an excitement. The girl with red streaks had been excited.

And he remembered how they'd started off all those years ago, as teenage lovers, before the kids were born. Those times seemed golden now. They used to lie in bed making love until late afternoon, or spend a trouble-free day together in the park, with a bottle of wine, smelling the grass and feeling the sun on their faces, talking about ideas, or just, well, relaxing together.

There never seemed to be enough time for any of that these days.

He missed those early days. He really did.

Still, you couldn't roll the clock back…

10

A week after the broadcast the BBC had set things up as if for an election night. A big open plan studio, a news desk, a panel of experts, and two specially made wall-high, maps—one of the world, and one of the UK. Viewers had been told that there were also reporters, on standby, around the world—to gauge the reactions of people in different countries, and to get expert views. The crew behind the scenes were exhausted.

On the viewer's screens an electronic clock was counting down to the next message. 1 minute and 32 seconds to go.

The host, Henry Oakenby, was dressed impeccably in a light blue suit, white shirt, and a thick brightly-coloured silk tie that he had had specially tailored and that contrasted nicely with the formality of the rest of his clothes. He was lightly made up, groomed and oozing with confidence. That morning, as he gave his teeth an extra polish, he had reflected that this might be the most important broadcast of his lifetime.

"…just reminding viewers that the message you are about to hear will be live—if it comes through at all—on the frequency specified for the UK. We are tracking the frequencies given to other countries too, and will let you know about those, as soon as we can."

He alertly scrutinised the clock: "OK, 12 seconds to go—give or take a few—we are about to find out if this will be a seminal point in the history of our species, or," he added, with a flourish, "the biggest anti-climax ever known." Either way it was a winner.

An excited silence followed. The camera focused on the clock.

Then the clear, ethereal, voice was heard, once again. Fresh water in a high mountain stream:

"People of the United Kingdom, thank you for tuning in. This message will finish with a list of coordinates for sites where transformational opportunities will be made available in the UK. Sites will be marked with a green circle—there will be no lasting damage to surrounding vegetation or the environment. To use a site any person just needs to touch the circle. The transformation then occurs instantaneously. There will be no danger to physical health. Other effects will be variable—but those that make use of the circles should be aware that their experience afterwards may not be entirely pleasurable and that they will never be the same again. The experience will probably take time to adjust to, and there is no guarantee that it will be helpful to all—though a significant benefit, and togetherness, is intended, over time.

Please note also that any circle that is not touched by any person within the first week of its arrival will be removed. Sites that are used within a week will remain activated for one year. These are your coordinates…"

A list of coordinates followed. After the first few had been heard the volume gradually turned down, and the camera focused back on Henry, whose voice could be heard over the top:

"Well it seems that that is the end of the message, apart from the coordinates, but we will keep track of the entire message and let you know if there is anything else added at the end, once the list is finished." He paused, pressing his earphone into his ear: "…reports are coming in that other messages around the world have been very similar—though in many different languages. Oh and, yes, it looks as though some of the transmissions in the smaller countries have already finished. Early reports are that Liechtenstein has been given just one set of coordinates, and their message has finished with no other information. But many other messages are still continuing. Let's go over to our panel of experts and ask for their first reactions." He walked briskly across the brightly coloured studio carpet to the panel.

"Mr Montgomery, you're an astro-physicist. What's your reaction to this? Do you really think it could be a message from an alien species?"

Mr Montgomery, a balding man with a thick pink open-necked shirt and half-moon spectacles looked straight into the camera, as he had been told to do beforehand. "We do not currently understand, scientifically, how an extra-terrestrial life-form could be communicating in this way." He said, in a slightly strained voice, as if his words weren't getting enough air. "On the other hand we also have no idea how the message is being sent using means local to our planet. However it is early d.."

"So you're on the fence then?" Without waiting for an answer Henry turned to the conservative politician sitting next to him. "Well, Foreign Secretary, what do you think?"

Ruth Stait had stiffly styled dark brown hair, like horse-hair matting, stretched in a wad over the top of her head, a thin pearl necklace—presumably real—and bright red lipstick. "I think we would be naïve not to prepare very seriously for the possibility that this really is an alien species." She said slowly, articulating each word carefully. Her voice was unexpectedly low and resonant, with a slightly piqued undercurrent. "We have to consider all possibilities. Of course it may be a hoax. But if it is then it's a hoax being undertaken in a way we do not currently understand, and that too is alarming.."

"So you're on the fence too." cut in Henry. Ruth Stait looked annoyed. "What about you, George Smith, deputy leader of the Labour Party?"

"Oh, I agree with Ruth, I think we have to be enormously cautious about…"

"Yes but do you think that this is an alien message?"

"As I was saying, I think we should be enormously cautious before jumping to premature conclusions—this…"

"OK I'm going to stop you there because we've just heard that the message to the UK has finished and we're getting reports that a number of other countries have also finished receiving their messages. Over to Lucille at the news desk."

The camera focused on Lucille, mid-thirties, wearing a dark red jacket over a frothy blue blouse with a white collar and sitting at a large oval glass desk with a laptop in front of her. She was smiling broadly, straight into the camera.

"Thanks Henry, these are exciting times! Yes, the transmission to the UK has indeed finished—with seventy-five locations specified. A number of other messages around the world have also now finished. You already heard about Liechtenstein which was given only one location, other countries that have received only one location include Monaco, Nauru, San Marino, the Marshall Islands, the Seychelles, Paulau… the smallest countries in fact. We're still waiting to hear from the Vatican and don't know yet if it's been given a location.

Let's go over now to Adam with our studio maps."

The camera flicked over to where Adam, a thin, man with a disjointed looking body spaciously accommodated in a light grey suit, was holding a laser pointer and standing to one side of the maps.

"Thanks Lucille. Well, the first surprise is that the coordinates for the UK are not all located where we might expect! He pointed to a flashing light. For instance one is for Pitcairn, a remote island in the Pacific with less than a hundred inhabitants! This is still under the jurisdiction of the UK. Others include Anguilla, Bermuda, the Falklands, Montserrat, altogether 12 overseas territories." 12 lights flashed on and off. "Moving over, now, to the map of Britain we can see that most locations are in areas of high population density. London, for example, has 11, and there are very few up in Scotland."

He pointed to a new screen: "…And here you can see the breakdown of locations between countries" Adam paused, digesting the information, "So, we can see that China is leading the table with 1,362 sites, with India in second place with 1,240. Then as we look down the list…" he pointed his laser, "we can see the US here with

330 sites, and Indonesia with 260, ourselves with 75, and a lot of smaller countries below us. Over now to Lucille for a summary of the news so far..."

Lucille was waiting with her broad smile at the camera.

"Thanks Adam, yes, to summarise, messages have been received by 183 countries with a few more expected. Our analysts are telling us that the number of locations sent to each country appears to be proportional to population with approximately one site per million of population, though some allowances have been made for large countries with lower populations—with extra sites going to isolated regions.

So far the locations appear to be in public parks. Let's go over now to our reporter Vince Carpenter who has just arrived at the location in Hyde Park, London."

Vince Carpenter, looking breathless, appeared on the big screen behind Lucille wearing an orange anorak and a purple patterned scarf. Behind him some oak trees, a park bench, a litter bin and a small crowd of about twenty people. Other people were approaching in groups. A few hundred yards away the curving white top of Marble Arch was just visible against a metallic sky.

"Thanks Lucille, yes, apparently within a few minutes of the first coordinates being received, people immediately began to assemble at them and I am actually standing on one of them." The camera focused on Vince's polished brown shoes, and his finger pointing to a non-descript patch of grass.

"There appears to be nothing particularly unusual about this spot. It's just yards from a public path, near the entrance to Hyde Park, and close to Speakers Corner. Let's talk to one of the crowd: this young man here says he was the first to get here." Vince held a large microphone towards a man in a grey hoodie.

"How did you locate this spot?"

"We been listening to the message on the radio, yeah, and our car was really near, yeah. So we thought we'd come here, for a laugh..."

"But how did you *locate* it?"

"Easy, man,—you just stick the coordinates in your phone, yeah, and there are sites that tell you where it is on the map, yeah."

"And who do you think *sent* these messages?"

"Oh it's aliens, man! Has to be. It's awesome, yeah. But I don't think they're coming to get us, that's all our fear, man. These guys are offering us something, and we want to be here and waiting when it comes. And I'm wondering why they'd pick here rather than anywhere else, yeah? Maybe we should dig up the ground and see if there's something. Perhaps there's a transmitter."

A man raced towards them, pushed his way to the front of the crowd and grabbed the mike. "This is disgusting. I just heard all the locations are going to be cordoned off. They're not allowing people to stay! Look, see there—here come the police." The camera followed his pointing finger to some flashing blue lights at the edge of the park and a line of police. "They're trying to stop us!" he shouted hoarsely above the sound of sirens "This park is ours, it belongs to the public. If we want to receive, whatever it is, they shouldn't try to stop us..."

11

The aliens are here. They're inside his brain, which is an abstract board game. The game is laid out in a vast three dimensional array of synapses, suspended in cerebral tissue. He cannot see them, but he can *feel* their presence through the absences they are creating within his mind, as they place their green circular pieces onto key synaptic junctions. Their pieces have razor edges and placing them inside him slices through his axons and dendrites, reducing his action potentials, severing his live thoughts. His brain is awash with misdirected neurotransmitters. They already have control of his ventral tegmental area and are advancing fast throughout the entire limbic region. They want complete control.

Several times he has fought back. Each time he thought he had their tactics fathomed, and the circles appeared to be receding, but then he found them suddenly revealed again, in a different region of his brain, in fortified regroupings, pinpointing their advances with surgical precision, undercutting his analysis.

His options are receding, they are limiting his capacity to think, dumbing down his thought process—and now they are mounting an assault on his sound centre. They have found a way to turn up the volume, the drumming noise is too loud to think through. They have his alarm. His alarm. His alarm is ringing...

Theo jerked awake, slammed off the alarm and lay back for a moment, staring at the ceiling with a pounding headache and a cold sweat. Another nightmare. One of many over the past few days.

You didn't have to be Jung or Freud to understand what was going on here, he reflected, as he rubbed the corners of his eyes, then swung his legs out of bed and walked shakily over to his underwear drawer and began dressing. No time to shower.

The past nine days had been a continuous nightmare, a steady slide, out of control, into uncertainty and fear. His fears had first started to escalate, he recalled, after their early attempts to classify the contact, and reduce it to something knowable and manageable, had so manifestly failed. After that, everyone at NCTC, had reached an astonished and reluctant consensus. It had become clear that, yes, they must really be dealing with some kind of extra-terrestrial interference. Aliens, with a technology *beyond comprehension.*

Since then he'd had no time to hypothesise on what might be happening, in any case he had so little to go on, just some vague un-crystallised thoughts about the use of language. Together with his colleagues at the NCTC, and the various state departments that they represented, he'd had to focus on damage limitation. For the first week they'd concentrated on alerting the public—both Americans and the world at large—to the immense danger.

He pulled on some brightly coloured bottom-of-the-drawer socks from his younger days, and began hunting for a clean pair of underpants. There hadn't even been time to do the laundry; his bachelor flat was in chaos.

After the second message they'd focused on surrounding all the sites and sealing them off, 'neutralising' they were calling it. If no one accessed the circles for a week after they arrived, then they'd said they would take them away. That might limit the harm.

At first he'd thought it would be a relatively straightforward, at least in America. Every available service man and woman had been mobilised to construct enclosures around every site, and these were now well underway. But he hadn't predicted the public reaction. A 'Free the Circles Campaign' had sprung up from nowhere and was campaigning to keep the sites open. So far there had been over a hundred arrests, and though all the US sites were now under control, with 24/7 surveillance, people had gathered outside them and were camping overnight. There were now 5000 people demonstrating outside a site in New York. Lemmings. The world was full of lemmings.

He found a pair of underpants in the dryer in the kitchen, returned to his bedroom and started pulling on yesterday's clothes—maroon corduroy trousers and a white open-necked silk shirt.

The rest of the world had been even more complicated. They'd been working around the clock with the diplomatic service, and their forces overseas, to minimise the number of sites that remained active after a week, trying to limit the unknown. That was like his dream, attempting to hold back a synaptic invasion. He walked over to the mirror, turned on his razor and ran it over the stubble on his chin, carefully trimming around his moustache.

The smaller countries were more dependent economically, so it was easier to bring pressure to bear on them. Monaco for instance had been brought in line by France; San Marino from Italy; Nauru from Australia, and so on.

He looked over at a row of hooks by the mirror where he kept his religious symbols and selected a silver fish medallion. He liked to do it as impulsively as possible, a different symbol each day, trying to keep it random. Sometimes he gave it a miss and wore no symbol at all. Then he was atheist, or agnostic. He liked to keep people guessing as to his real beliefs. If people had too much information about you, you could become a target. If they noticed that he kept changing, as they sometimes did, he just told them he did it out of respect for all beliefs, which was a lie, of course.

Religion, he reflected, had at least helped them. After the Vatican had discovered that it had not been given a location, the Pope had issued a statement, within a surprisingly short time, giving a lengthy warning against entering the circles. He said that 'only God can provide transformational opportunities, so these circles must be the work of the devil, and touching a circle would be sinful'. It was just what they needed—lots of countries were Catholic. Similarly many of the Muslim countries were resisting keeping sites active on their soil. As with Catholicism, many of the

Islamic leaders had been appalled by the possibility that 'transformation'—whatever that was—might be made available in a non-orthodox way.

Theo splashed his face with cold water and looked at his dripping reflection in the mirror. The glistening lines beneath his eyes looked deeper grooved than usual. He looked tired and *worried.*

He *was* worried. It was clear that they weren't going to do it. Most of the western countries were in line—and most of the others were seeing sense, but a few, such as India, weren't. The debate in the Indian government looked like it would never resolve. They were *still* deciding. And whilst they procrastinated large numbers of tourists, religious pilgrims, and others, had begun to congregate at the coordinates, as if waiting for a second coming. The site at Varanasi had tens of thousands of people milling around it, the largest crowd of any site on earth. They hadn't done enough to keep it secure, and this was just the worst of over a thousand sites in India...

He frowned into the mirror: No, *they weren't going to do it*! Out of over 7,000 sites around the world, perhaps 6,500 would be neutralised, the rest just wouldn't be secured in time. And *surrounding* the sites was only part of the solution. They also had to get other countries to agree that no one should be authorised to touch the green circles, if they arrived. And that had all been made much harder by that quintessential imbecile at SETI. What was his name? O'Donnel, Fergus O'Donnel.

O'Donnel had been making public speeches every day, in front of growing rallies. YouTube clips of him were going viral, and his Green Circles Facebook group was busting all records. He was at the forefront of a world-wide campaign for the circles to be tested with animals as quickly as possible after they arrived. If that went OK, he argued, they should allow humans to touch them to keep them active. That way they'd remain available to all humanity. He said there was no evidence that the aliens were hostile. Maybe the 'transformational opportunities' were just what was written on the tin. Maybe there was something profoundly useful on offer, and if that was the case, and not enough circles survived, then not everyone who wanted to would be able to make use of them within the allocated year. And that, he said, was 'a contravention of human rights'. The man had a bloody soap box, but he was dangerous, he was attracting a lot of support.

Theo looked out of the window. Rain was slashing almost horizontally against the glass. It had been rotten weather all week, all along the east coast. He put on his overcoat and pounded towards the door. He'd grab a café latte at the office for breakfast. Then he'd see what could be done about Mr Fergus O'Donnel.

12

They led him, blindfolded, down the stairs into the outside air where he heard the sound of a car running and its door opening.

"Get in the back with your head bent forwards to hide the blind," the woman commanded.

Why are they hiding the blind? Why are they making me wear it? Something terrible is about to happen…

He felt his way onto the back seat and sat, doubled forwards. She closed the door behind him then walked around the car and got in herself beside him. "Let's go." The car moved off immediately. Again he heard sounds of the busy streets around them.

Minutes later the woman untied the scarf: "You can open your eyes now." He opened his eyes into bright evening light. The same two men were in the front. The car was moving in slow flowing traffic along a busy street. In the gutter at the side of the road a man was wheeling a bicycle loaded impossibly high with bunches of green bananas. The pavement bustled with pedestrians, a narrow alleyway led off the main road to a market stall covered in tomatoes and buzzing with flies. Bicycles and boda-bodas twisted and turned between the cars and taxis. It was all deeply familiar and at the same time almost beyond recall. Perhaps, he reflected, they are trying to help me.

Don't be a fool! I am dressed for my execution.

The car turned onto a major tarmacked road with a sign saying 'Entebbe airport'. Minutes later they were in the car park beside it.

The woman got out of the car, opened the door on his side, "get out". The driver and the other man stayed put with the engine running. She handed him a small bag with a few items of clothing in it, then led him to where a white woman aged about thirty, smartly dressed in a tan suit, was leaning on the long handle of a small leather suitcase on wheels, reading a book. "Hello, Jane, here he is, and good luck." The white woman looked up, keeping her finger on her place in the book. She had subtle, carefully applied make up, and neatly brushed hair. "Thanks."

The woman who had been with him up until now thrust a plastic folder into the hands of the white woman and turned to him: "I have to go now. This woman is going to take you to a safe place. Just do everything she says and you'll be fine". She twirled around and walked with clipped pace back to the waiting car, leaving him alone with the white stranger.

"Hi Mohammed, my name is Jane."

It sounded strange to hear his name spoken, after all this time, and by a white woman. He'd almost forgotten he had a name. It came from a time before the darkness.

13

The SETI Institute, Mountain View, California. Fergus read again the message he'd been handed by his Director:

Will Mr Fergus O'Donnel, please make himself available at 10.00 a.m. for a video interview with Mr Theo Chaldrike from the National Counterterrorism Center.

Ten o'clock, that was ten minutes from now. He wondered what it could be about. There'd been many messages for him the last few days, but mostly from journalists, or people organising events. He'd never had anything to do with an anti-terrorist organisation. He felt a brief tremor of fear, then reminding himself there was nothing to worry about, walked over to the window to look again at the crowds.

They were here already, thronging Bernado Avenue in the bright blue Californian morning and pressed together in the dappled shadows under the trees around the Institute. It was reassuring to look at them: confirmation that this was all really happening. It wasn't a dream.

Ever since the first message the crowds had assembled, thirsty for new information. But it was after the second message that their numbers had mushroomed. Most of them hoped to be chosen to touch the circles once they arrived. There were so many they'd had to call in the police. Public announcements that they weren't processing applications, and that the American government was still deciding if they should, had had no effect. The switchboard had jammed with non-stop calls, new emails scrolled past alarmingly, and the post now arrived in several large sack loads each day. SETI was being gently sieged.

Not that he was complaining. As the principal person in charge of Education and Public Outreach at SETI he couldn't have asked for more. But it wasn't so much the crowds that had set him ablaze with wonder and excitement; it was the fact of the contact itself. In less than two weeks everything had changed. They had contact! Unbelievably the thing that he had yearned for all his life, had happened, and in such an unexpected way.

Even as a small boy he remembered being unable to settle at night if the sky was clear. Long after his parents said goodnight he would lie in bed, wide awake, nervously checking that no clouds had come, waiting for the darkness he loved. Then, when at last it came, he would creep across the floor, settle himself by the window, and stare, transfixed, at the diamonds of light.

His parents were mostly unaware of this. On one occasion his mother rebuked him sternly when, long after midnight, she found him sitting by the window, his head resting sideways on the window sill, staring upwards, apparently oblivious of her presence and the fact that he was shivering in his pyjamas. After that he learnt to listen for her footsteps on the stair and to tiptoe swiftly back into bed, feigning sleep, guarding with firmly shut eyes against the bright V of light from the crack of the opened doorway, and creeping back, after she was gone, to stare, wide eyed again, at the majestically revolving heavens.

He learnt to watch for Venus and Mercury near where the sun had set, and for the other planets on the plane of the ecliptic, marvelling at the rusty glow of Mars and the bright clarity of Jupiter. He learnt to distinguish the planets from the stars and was surprised to discover how few people, including his parents, knew the difference. On special nights when the sky was extra black and the moon new, or thin as a toe nail clipping, he delighted to find the two galaxies he could see with his naked eye— Andromeda and Omega Centauri.

He spent all his pocket money on astronomy magazines and, at the age of 11, on his first small telescope. He learnt the names of the constellations and some of the stars by heart, repetitively rolling the syllables around his tongue and delighting in their foreignness: Sirius, Rigel Kentauris, Pyxidis, Sadal Melik, Arcturus, Rukbat, Antares, Zuben El Genubi…

But on the occasions that he had shared his enthusiasm with his mother and sister he'd been stunned into silence by their profound lack of interest. It was only with his father that he was able to find a measure of understanding and connection.

Before his alcoholism made it impossible, his father had been a sailor skippering yachts owned by wealthy business-men on a series of lavish island hopping cruises around the globe. He had some polished anecdotes to relate and had delighted the boy with his tales of adventure at sea. It was in the pause following one such anecdote that Fergus had said quietly that he understood his dad wanting to meet other peoples and visit new lands. He also wanted to do that.

"Well you can do the same boy."

Fergus had been encouraged by his father's response but it wasn't exactly what he'd meant: "I want to go further Dad," he ventured timidly.

"You do?" His father looked at him with the rough frozen smile he always had when he'd been drinking.

"Yes, I…I want to discover something different. Something we can't imagine: another species, an intelligent species. *That's* why I'm interested in the stars."

"Well then, go for it, my lad. Never let the land lock up your hopes."

For once he hadn't been ridiculed, or ignored. He stored the words in his soul: *never let the land lock up your hopes.*

This one small encouragement had been sufficient to keep him on a trajectory that culminated, after years of study, with the offer of a job at SETI. For a spell he'd been euphoric, but this gave way to a progressive and tenacious gloom. In his first few years at SETI he had had the exclusive brief of developing mathematical algorithms to sift through the vast amounts of data being received from space. This mostly consisted of endless lists of numbers. Numbers referring to electromagnetic waves from space, which, by the time they reached him were, well, just numbers.

Focusing on how to process the stream of numbers, day after day, it had been difficult to preserve his sense of purpose. On a handful of occasions he'd allowed himself to believe that SETI might actually have found something non-random in the stream. But the need for proper scientific scrutiny and analysis had always culminated in further disappointment, made all the worse for the renewed hope that preceded it. Over time he'd begun to admit to himself that the chance of making contact with intelligent life elsewhere was vanishingly small, and he'd even begun to question whether it was worth looking.

He was, to a small extent, saved from this crisis of meaning by a series of quick promotions within SETI, culminating in his current post. But, ultimately, even these new roles had failed to raise his spirits in an underlying context of *no alien contact achieved.* There remained a widening gap between the calling he had found as a boy, and the work that he actually did. The kudos of having a senior position in such an unusual and, some would say, glamorous organisation, failed to compensate for his overwhelming feeling that he had lost his way. This wasn't how he'd imagined it to be. He'd wanted the unknown. He'd wanted to connect across the frontiers of space, to engage with the truly alien, he had wanted to rekindle the awe and hopefulness he'd had as a child…

It was into this context that the messages of the past few days had come, flying straight in the face of his austere training at SETI in the application of doubt in the face of hope. Not surprisingly his internal sceptic had immediately activated—the message made no sense given the immense distances involved, and he had long believed that any contact would be in code—extra-terrestrial life would identify itself by listing prime numbers, or describing the atomic table, or some other such device. It couldn't be speaking so clearly, in virtually every language currently spoken by man.

And yet, despite his acquired scepticism, tiny shards of belief had begun to break through unbidden, as if directly reaching through from his childhood. The naïve boy that he once was, had felt up inside him to touch the heart of the cynical man he'd become.

The past week had been revelatory in reinforcing this process, particularly the second message a few days ago, which had followed the first so reliably, and remained so wonderfully inexplicable. He'd found himself lying awake at night in an excited anticipation reminiscent of the one that he'd had as a small boy waiting for darkness. He felt younger, fitter, rejuvenated, and increasingly exultant. Affirmed, despite everything, in his original vision.

And now here was thickly moustached, Theo Chaldrike, filling up his computer screen from the opposite coast of America. He was wearing an open-necked shirt with a strange fish medallion, yet despite this casual dress he looked gravely serious.

"Mr O'Donnel?" His voice terse.

"Yes, hi, you must be Theo. What can I do for you?"

Theo stared at him darkly, frowning. Below his moustache his chin pressed forwards and upwards, so that his lips were almost concealed:

"You can stop campaigning for people to be allowed to touch circles."

Straight to business then. Fergus was caught off balance by the man's directness. "I'm campaigning for that *possibility* to be kept open. But I want us to test the circles first. I only think people should be allowed to touch circles if the tests prove OK."

"But Mr O'Donnel..."

"Please, call me Fergus…."

"Mr O'Donnel, what makes you think that the tests will show us anything? Maybe the circles are specifically aimed at us, as a species. Maybe they won't affect other animals."

"Yes, perhaps you're right. But we don't know yet what they'll reveal."

"And maybe the circles will be dangerous."

"I don't think so."

Theo gave him a withering look. "You don't *think* so. That's not enough. We have no idea what we're dealing with here, these circles could contaminate us with a plague that will wipe out our species; or they may be a means to invade us, or a means to brainwash us...or something we cannot even imagine. We have no way of knowing that we won't all be dead in four days' time. We need to be extremely careful. It's madness to risk touching them."

Fergus had already heard these arguments: "But surely, if they intended to invade us, or brainwash us, or contaminate us, they'd already have done that. Why give advance warning if they want to wipe us out?"

"Let me ask the questions, Mr O'Donnel."

Fergus felt suddenly incensed. The man had a nerve: "On what authority?"

"On the authority of the American government which is invested in me. We have a duty to identify and disable all threats to our security."

"And you think I'm a threat?"

"The circles are a threat, and you're akin to a domestic terrorist. Your speeches and campaign has made our job of protecting the American people immeasurably harder. Your *contribution,"* he spat the word, 'has threatened the future, not just of the American people but of the *entire human species*."

Fergus sucked in a breath. "So you want me to stop campaigning? That's why you have contacted me?"

"Partly."

"Partly, and what else?"

"Mr O'Donnel, as I said, *I* am doing the questioning here." Theo glanced at a pile of papers by the side of his computer. "I understand that SETI has funding difficulties?"

"Yes, but I hardly see why that's relevant."

"It was relevant to you having to put your most important telescope—the Allen Telescope Array, into hibernation. Correct?"

"Yeah, but we've been able to start that up again."

"You have, but still in its most reduced form, and you have prohibitively expensive plans to expand it further, do you not?

"Yes, well, not prohibitive, but I..."

"And the telescope is unusual in being able to *simultaneously* monitor a wide range of frequencies. Let me see," he glanced down again, "goodness, from 0.5—11.5 gigahertz. Quite an impressive range."

"Yes that's right, but…."

"So if you can simultaneously *receive* signals on a huge range of frequencies then you could simultaneously *broadcast* a signal on a range of frequencies."

Fergus stared at him: "You're *not* implying..."

A brief smile flickered over Theo's lips: "No, I'm not implying anything Mr O'Donnel, though broadcasting a signal that sounded alien would certainly attract a massive interest in SETI, perhaps even bring in funding…"

Fergus swallowed: "But the ATA isn't able to transmit signals."

"Well, I would have to take your word for that." Theo was speaking very slowly now: "Only, taking people's word for things isn't something we do easily at the National Counterterrorism Center—I suppose we could require SETI to be closed down whilst we investigate..."

Fergus felt a cold shiver down his back. "What are you suggesting, exactly?"

"I'm not *suggesting* anything. I'm just exchanging pleasantries. Of course, if I were you, I might like to think very carefully about my approach and start speaking out *against* allowing access to the circles, given the huge risks involved."

Fergus stared at the screen in silence. He'd only been talking to this man for a few minutes, yet already he felt interrogated and threatened. He had also started to feel outraged: "Mr Chaldrike, you've got the wrong man." Theo raised his eyebrows. "You can threaten all you like, but I'm not going to change what I believe, or stop expressing my beliefs. I don' think the aliens are a threat. It seems far more likely to me that they're benevolent. Take the fact that they've taken so much trouble to research our languages, and where to locate the circles, the fact that they've found out about all the countries in the world, the tone of the message, the reassurances that they've given us, the voluntary nature of what they're offering, and their care in describing it. They've gone out of their way to make their contact as non-threatening as possible."

Theo glowered at him: "That could all be *tactical*, lulling us into a false sense of security in order to have their way."

Fergus looked towards the window. Shafts of morning sunshine were making bright lines of contrast on the floor of his office. He could hear muffled sounds from the crowd outside. "There's something else. Something I haven't said to anyone."

"There is?"

"Yes, something else makes me think we're dealing with benevolence here, and a highly advanced version of it. Something about the use of language"

Theo's eyes widened. "What do you mean?"

"Pronouns."

"*What?*"

"Or rather the lack of them: there were no pronouns for the message sender in either of the two messages. Not a single 'I' or 'We'. Not in English, or in any of the other languages that I've been able to check. They used no pronouns to describe themselves so we don't even know if 'they' are a 'they' or an "I". That's quite hard to do, you know. It's hard, for example, to say that you intend to send someone something without allocating a pronoun to the 'you' part of the sentence. It's hard in English, harder still in some of the other languages, I imagine, but it appears to have been achieved throughout." Fergus stared at the screen, expecting to be ridiculed and already regretting having blurted out something that he'd so far kept to himself. It seemed so tenuous.

Yet Theo looked interested, impressed even. Momentarily his guard was down. There was a long pause.

"You're right, Mr O'Donnel. I have to admit that that's a missing piece I've been looking for myself. I *knew* there was something strange about the language of the messages, I just couldn't place it." He looked like he was thinking hard, perhaps re-playing the message in his head, then the frown returned. "But I still don't see why that makes you think that they, I mean *this*, if it is a 'this', is benevolent."

"Because it is advanced enough to think beyond 'I' and 'me' and 'we'. Isn't that what all the spiritual traditions tell us? If this was an invading alien species, only out to conquer us, then *they* would be full of *themselves*, and *their* own importance. It wouldn't occur to them not to use pronouns. Similarly a single individual, a malicious individual, would be egoistic, the 'I's would flow naturally, and whichever it was—organisation or individual—they would have no reason to keep things ambiguous. That's what convinced me that, whatever this is, it isn't malicious."

Theo was still frowning: "This is too thin an argument, though I grant you it's subtle. Moreover your conclusion is faulty. It could mean we're dealing with a machine, a machine without a sense of its identity, precisely because *it's a machine*. Or maybe manipulating languages is part of their convoluted tactics; and isn't it interesting that this little piece of the jigsaw has just been told to me by someone in the very organisation with the capacity to have sent out the messages in the first place?" His tone was impatient now. "No, that was a nice try, and for a moment there you had me impressed, but everything that I've already said, still stands. I see no reason to be reassured by these adumbrative communications, even if they are pronoun-free." He looked at Fergus sternly: "So I now expect you to cooperate fully. We'll be watching you closely, O'Donnel. I'm sure, once you've had time to think, you'll see reason. The risks of not doing so are... far ranging". He cut their connection.

14

Brian was delighted to get a call from the girl with red streaks. He recognised her felty voice immediately. "Hey, Mr Taxi-man, can you take me to the protestors?"

"Sure." He tried not to sound elated.

Half an hour later he picked her up. She was wearing a bright red dress with blue frills and a matching blue and red headband. As she passed him into the cab he noticed again her smell of oranges and incense.

"Settling in OK with your sister?"

"My, your memory's total."

"Except for things like laundry and washing up."

She laughed easily, already settled in the back. "…I did, thanks, it's well good being with her again."

"Where do you want to go?"

"What d'you reckon? Where are the most protestors?

"There's a lot round Hyde Park, but I think the biggest crowd's by Victoria station. They've been jamming up the traffic there for days."

"Cool. Let's go Victoria then."

As he drove off he glanced in the mirror. Her startling blue eyes were waiting.

"Why do you want to see the protestors?"

"To, like, join them." Still that excitement in her voice.

"You mean the ones in favour of letting people touch the circles, if they come, or those against."

She laughed. "Haven't you guessed? The ones in favour, innit? Why man? D'you disagree?"

"Well no, I…" Truth was he hadn't given it a huge amount of thought. Life changing events appeared to be happening yet most people, himself included, were carrying on as normal, as if nothing had happened. Weird that.

"…I—don't know yet—I..."

"You haven't really thought about it, have you?"

Brian gulped. How did she know that? "No." Now he felt foolish.

"That's cool, man, I read you. It's so much to take in."

He risked another look in the mirror, she was smiling warmly, with the nice wrinkles on her nose—she wasn't judging him. And she was wearing lip gloss today. He forced his eyes back to the road ahead and had to brake hastily, a pedestrian had stepped out, alarmingly close.

"Hey, even I had difficultly letting it in. But isn't it awesome?"

"Well, yes…" His foot eased off the brake with relief, there was room to spare.

"And I'm sure it's, like, cool."

"What makes you so sure?"

"Just from the vibe, like I know in my heart."

Well this was nonsense, of course. But he envied her conviction. He glanced again into the mirror. She was so vital and pretty.

At Victoria Station he parked behind the taxi rank and got out to open the door.

"Nice to meet you again Ma'am."

"hey, not Ma'am again!" She laughed. "Please, my name's Minty."

"*Minty*?"

"Yeah, short for Cinnaminta, my parents were, like, *hippies*"

Weird name, but it seemed to fit.

"Suits you, it's pretty." He regretted saying this immediately, too forward. You shouldn't flirt with customers; there were codes of conduct...

"Thanks man." She smiled radiantly. "And you're Brian aren't you?"

She'd read his card. Surely she didn't really care. "Yes."

She held out her hand. "Sweet to meet, Brian…won't you join me for a bit, with the protestors?

He took her hand, noticing her bright blue nail varnish. "Well, no, I…"

"Go on, I need to know where to go, anyway…" She widened her eyes and gave his hand a squeeze.

"Oh, OK..." He said it without thinking—but he shouldn't be agreeing to this—and she didn't need to be shown. They could both hear the protestors. It was obvious where they were.

He led her the short distance to Grosvenor Gardens. The park was closed and completely surrounded by crowds of people shouting slogans. Police were standing by warily, their hands in black leather gloves, radios on, truncheons dangling. A couple of riot vans were parked nearby with perforated metal guards over their windscreens.

A group of protestors were holding placards and waving white flags with green circles on them. Brian read a few captions. 'Free all Circles', 'Trust in Transformation' and a hand written one: 'Unlock the parks. Unlock the sites. Unlock your minds.'

Another group, carefully separated by the police had an image of a green circle with a red cross through it and slogans like "No to alien invasion", "No site in Victoria". There didn't seem to be much difference between the groups. The second group were perhaps less vocal, but there were more of them. Maybe the first had slightly younger people, but there were young and old in both. People were spilling off the pavements onto the street and the tension was palpable.

Brian led them through the crowds to a statue he knew of Marshall Foch on a horse. Not that he liked the statue, it had little merit, and Foch was French, so it ought to be in France. But he knew that the railings around the statue made an indent into the park and he thought they might be able to peer through them. He was right.

Inside the park a high makeshift enclosure with razor wire at the top enclosed an area where a circle was expected. The grass had been trampled into mud. There was a portacabin, a tardis toilet, generators and machinery everywhere and nervous looking soldiers with rifles. Minty pulled away with a gasp and held his elbow. "Isn't it gross?"

"Yeah, I guess…"

She looked at him, serious now. "C'mon Brian…it's gross! We've been offered…*transformation* and these guys…are trying to, like, stop it. We have to *do something*." She looked into his eyes and dropped his elbow. "Well I'm going to join in…" She turned away.

Then turned back, almost immediately, her shining smile back. Gad she was gorgeous. "…Wanna join me?"

15

The white woman looked him up and down slowly. "I'm taking you somewhere safe but you have to follow instructions. Just do everything that I say and you'll be OK. But you mustn't do *any* of the talking. Do you understand?"

He nodded. He'd never been alone with a white person before.

She looks official, she could be involved with the government.

"We're going on a plane together. Just try to act normal, keep your eyes looking ahead, don't look around and *don't say anything*. OK?"

He nodded. He was used to saying nothing.

In the airport the woman took a small maroon coloured booklet from the folder she'd been given and combined it with one of her own from a compartment in her suitcase. Then she led them to a ticket counter where a man in a uniform took the booklets from her and looked at them distractedly. He weighed their small bags, gave Jane some pieces of printed card, passed everything back to her and waved them through.

They waited for about an hour without speaking. As Jane read her book, Mohammed glanced furtively about, his head throbbing. He'd never been inside an airport. Outside a huge window next to them was a plane with 'Kenyan Airlines' written on it. Were they flying to Kenya? Surely not…but what if she was really trying to help?

Don't be a fool. If she was really helping she'd tell you what was happening.

Following an announcement, the woman, who was wearing expensive perfume, indicated to Mohammed to join the queue and board the plane with her. "Don't talk to me on the flight." On the plane she indicated his seat by a window then sat directly in front of him.

Every seat on the plane was taken, and there were quite a few white people. Next to him was a large Ugandan businessman in a flashy suit. Mohammed looked away, staring out of the window as the steps to the plane were removed.

The plane taxied briefly on the tiny airport strip then took off with a roar. He was intensely aware of the sound of the engines, and of being pushed back into his seat. The plane seemed to be at an alarmingly steep angle. Looking through the elliptical window he saw small islands on Lake Victoria beneath them. They were already so high! He'd never left Uganda before and had no idea what was ahead. His life was being left behind. He pulled the plastic shield over the window, clutched the arm rests on either side of him, and closed his eyes, pretending to sleep.

An hour later the plane landed in Nairobi and he followed the woman down the gangway. Neither spoke. At the airport she guided them through another check point. Then they were in another room waiting for another aeroplane. When there was no one within earshot the woman lent towards him and whispered: "I'm taking you to England, you'll be safe there."

This was unbelievable. How could they be going to England? He tried to control his mind and think, but it was hard. Despite the medication he'd been given, he still had a splitting headache, and he felt hungry and nauseous in equal measure. Suddenly he was coughing violently—he was going to be sick again. He placed his hand over his mouth and bent forwards swallowing hard. The woman carried on steadfastly reading her book, as if she wasn't with him. After a while the nausea subsided and he wiped his mouth and hand with a small tissue, phlegm streaked with red.

You are going to die.

Hours later on the plane, which was larger than the first, they sat, as before, in seats by the window, with the woman in front. Again they didn't speak. It was late into the night. Surely they weren't going to be flying at night. How could an aircraft do that? But the plane took off and one by one the passengers around Mohammed fell asleep. He stayed awake for the long journey, alert to every tremor in the aircraft's flight. Once again he pulled the plastic screen over the window, too frightened to look out, trying to think.

He knew no-one in England. He had no family there, or friends. He had left his family behind, perhaps for ever. He had no money, no contacts, he was completely reliant on this white woman whom he'd only just met. He knew nothing about her and had no idea about her motivation. His head throbbed with the confusion and terror of it all. He'd been a dead man. Now he didn't know what he was, but *still* he was being treated like baggage, shifted from place to place without his consent and as if he was nothing. And why should he trust this woman?

Don't trust her. Don't trust anyone. Expect the worst.

And why were they going to England? Would there be further interrogation there, further imprisonment? Uganda was, after all, an ex-British colony, and Muhindo had said it would be a 'special treat'. He knew about Muhindo's treats.

As the plane droned on into a slow sky dawn he thought about his family back home in Mbarara—his widowed mother, his younger brother and his two sisters,. He should be there supporting them. Now that his father was dead it was his responsibility. But he'd been imprisoned so long. His sisters, and perhaps also his brother, would have had to leave school to look for whatever work they could find. Everything had to be paid for, even the dirty water at their local tap. Without schooling they couldn't progress. He wondered if they'd even have enough to eat. He hadn't seen them for….how long was it? He didn't know what date it was…it must be years, and now he was being flown far away.

An hour before they were due to land the air hostess brought a meal. The food was unfamiliar. He managed to eat a small piece of bread and to drink a little tea. He'd heard the English drank a lot of tea. He'd also heard that Museveni, the president in Uganda, was allies with the British, that he'd somehow persuaded them that his regime in Uganda was good and democratic.

It's all linked up—Britain and Uganda are working together.

At Heathrow he followed the woman down long busy corridors, both of them carrying their small bags. He was having difficulty walking because of injuries in his hip. At one point they joined a bouncing rubber pavement that was also moving forwards. Eventually they reached the back of a long queue of people waiting to have their documents checked. The airport felt cold, and huge. The woman was holding the maroon booklets again, and again she warned him not to speak.

At the desk a man behind a Perspex screen looked at them closely. He asked Mohammed a question but he looked away and the woman answered instead. He didn't know what he'd been asked. His English was reasonable but the man had spoken fast. He understood though when the woman explained that he couldn't speak English. The man asked the woman another question and looked sternly at them both as she answered—something about visiting Mohammed's family. Then he stamped the booklets and handed them back into the woman's waiting hand.

They passed through an enclosure where people holding signs with names on them, stared at them from behind barriers. The woman led him outside. The pilot had said it was late morning but it felt absolutely freezing. A line of taxis were waiting with 'for hire' lights on. Mohammed had never seen so many smart looking cars together. The woman spoke through a window to the driver at the front of the queue and immediately he got out and stood beside them. He was about forty and seemed to be scrutinising him. Mohammed looked away down at the ground. The man had polished black shoes. The woman said "Please take this man to the Croydon Immigration Centre—it's called Lunar House".

The man sucked in a breath. "I know it Ma'am…" He sounded annoyed. "Lunar House and Electric House, they're near each other in Croydon."

The woman looked relieved. "Take him to the reception at Lunar House. Here"— she handed him a couple of bank notes— "and please *give him any change*." She turned to Mohammed with her hand outstretched. He held his hand out apprehensively.

"Just go with this man. When you get to Lunar House, go in and ask for help. You're going to be OK now. Do you understand?" She squeezed his hand and he winced, unable to speak. "Do you understand?" She repeated, casting a quick glance about her. Mohammed kept his eyes on the ground.

"*Do you understand?*" She was sounding exasperated now.

Answer the question, you need to say 'yes'.

"Yes." It was the first time he had spoken since leaving prison.

She turned and walked briskly back into the airport.

16

Brian watched, fascinated, as Minty mingled with the protestors from the 'Free the Circles Campaign'. She was phenomenal, working the crowd like an experienced politician, talking to everyone, smiling, getting views, giving her own, swapping emails, never getting trapped with anyone, moving on through without leaving people feeling rejected. Her warmth and enthusiasm was infectious. Everyone seemed mellow in her presence. There were people there he'd have avoided himself, but she seemed equally comfortable and interested in everyone, from hoodies with their underpants showing to the elderly, the upper class, even out and out nutters.

He followed her, a few steps behind, feeling alternately awestruck and despondent. She was captivating, but he wanted her to himself. Yet each time he was about to give up and leave, she turned again, with her smile, and spoke to him as if she'd known him forever, and his hopes soared once more. It was like taking tiny spaced out sips of a vintage port.

Finally, after nearly an hour he tore himself away. "I have to go now, Minty, get back to work, thanks ever so..."

"Ohw! So soon?" She looked him in the eye checking his resolve. "...OK then. Awesome getting to know you better Brian. Let's hang together again...*soon.*" She paused, momentarily, "...I nearly forgot, I owe you for the ride..."

"That's on me...it's such a good cause." His sudden offer took him by surprise. Was he out of his mind? He never let customers ride for free.

"Brian!" She pulled him towards her and kissed him full on the lips, then held him about a foot away, smiling radiantly. "Thanks man…you're *so* sweet!"

Walking back to Victoria, with her kiss playing on his lips, and the smell of oranges and incense, he regretted not making a firm arrangement to meet her again. She'd kissed him, after all. She might have agreed. This might really develop. But another voice inside him told him not to be a fool. 'She's like this with everyone, and you're a middle aged man, not even her type, and she's half your age. And what was that about it being "*such a good cause*". That wasn't why you let her off the fee!'

'Well it *is* a good cause,' responded his first voice.

'Bullshit.'

'And I wanted to help her, I like her'

'Bullshit again. Let's be honest with ourself here, Brian. You didn't follow her around like a mesmerised bloodhound because you wanted to help her. You don't even know if you agree with the cause. You were after one thing...'

Sighing heavily Brian got back in the cab and reluctantly joined the queue to wait for another customer. At the front a man in his early thirties, handsome and with slick brown hair, rushed up and tapped on the window. He looked breathless and urgent.

Brian rolled down his window: "Where're you off to, buddy?"

"Heathrow, can you do it? I have to catch a plane, don't want to miss it for anything." The man clambered in.

Brian drove into Victoria Street and the top end of Grosvenor Gardens, giving the pavement a wide berth to avoid demonstrators and police. He looked for Minty's red dress in the crowd but couldn't see her.

At the top of Grosvenor Park he caught a fleeting glimpse of the 'Lioness and the Lesser Kudu', one of his favourite sculptures. The lioness is chasing a lesser kudu. Both have tendons strained in a moment of reckoning. Is it the moment the kudu is captured, or will it escape? You can't be sure by looking.

He forced himself to concentrate on his passenger. "Where are you flying to then?"

The man smiled gleefully, clearly pleased to be asked, "Mangareva in French Polynesia."

"Sounds exciting. You going as a tourist?"

"Nope, just as far as I can get by plane. I'm leading a mission to Pitcairn island."

"A *mission*?"

"Yup, me and two other Marines. We've been ordered to guard the green circle at Pitcairn once it arrives, and make sure no-one touches it for a week. That way it doesn't have to be guarded for a year. First we fly to Mangareva where we get kitted out and get our weapons and so on. Then we take a fancy yacht to Pitcairn. That takes about three days in itself, but it's the only way to get there. Pitcairn's about as remote as it gets—a tiny sub-tropical island—one mile by two, half way between Peru and New Zealand."

Brian resisted the temptation to say that he knew where Pitcairn was, and quite a bit besides about the island's florid history. He took the turning towards Hyde Park. The traffic was worse than usual on account of the demonstrations. "You looking forward to it?"

"You betya. Adventure of a life time."

"Aren't you frightened the locals might resist not being allowed to keep their circle?"

The man looked at him as if he had not really thought of that possibility: "Not really. In any case, most people think these things will be really dangerous."

"Yes, a lot of my customers seem worried about that—and most now agree that they really *are* being sent by aliens."

"Well, I think that too," the man said, "in the absence of other explanations. But we have to be very careful we don't get hurt, or infected, 'transformation' could mean all kinds of things. It could be appalling. "

Brian turned off Knightsbridge onto Brompton Road. "I had a little boy in the cab yesterday" he said, trying to lighten things: "He must have been seven or eight. He'd muddled up 'transformation' with 'transformer'. He thought that the green circles would be places where we could all become transformers—able to turn into robots and lorries and cars and the like! He was very keen to try it…"

But the young man seemed distracted and didn't find this amusing. Brian imagined he was having pleasant fantasies about palm beaches and girls in bark skirts and decided to leave him to it, returning compulsively to his own inner dialogue about Minty. Just past Hammersmith he joined the M4, then on to Heathrow. But as they entered the airport he couldn't resist checking out his guess. "So might you be hoping for an encounter with a Polynesian woman?" The question was uncharacteristically clumsy. Perhaps it had arisen from his own preoccupations.

The man looked up, startled, and then smiled bashfully. "If only! I never seem to have much luck with women, and I just finished a relationship that was in a rut. Trouble is we won't be there long, and I'll have a job of work to do. But if something came my way..." His voice trailed off.

Brian helped him out with his suitcase. "Well, good luck mate, I hope it meets your expectations." He watched enviously as the man ran off, then queued for 'Arrivals'.

A woman in an executive suit approached with a shifty looking black man. She asked him to take the man to Lunar House in Croydon. Must be another goddamn immigrant.

17

Judge Oliver Surret looked down into frightened eyes. This was in no way remarkable. Fear was so endemic to the workings of the court that it was as if it had infected the fabric of the building and saturated the magnolia covered walls. From long experience he knew too that it took many forms. It could render people speechless or incoherent, or make them sullen, or defiant. Most commonly they became obsequious. The Kenyan man before him hadn't yet shown how he was going to react, but already his wide forehead was covered in beads of sweat.

Oliver didn't consider it part of his role, however, to be influenced by the man's fear or whatever feelings he might have. He could be frightened for many reasons. It could be a genuine fear of being returned to Kenya, or it could just be a fear of authority, or that his lies—if there were any—might be exposed. Whatever the reason for the man's fear, it was his job to remain impartial so that he could to chisel down to the truth and be influenced only by that.

The man before him, Jacubu Macunu, was tall and beautifully proportioned with a broad chest and an intelligent face. He was wearing a cheap navy blue suit, probably bought straight off the peg. His barrister, whom Oliver knew, was standing six feet away from her client. She was a fraught, slightly overweight woman in her late forties and looked ill at ease, and constricted, in her pin-striped suit.

She'd just finished making her presentation, explaining that Mr Macunu had first arrived in the UK eight years before, having fled from Kenya. He claimed he had been captured by a group called the

Kaya Bombo, who had tortured him to extract information about the Mungiki. Her client, she said, was a member of the Mungiki, a group hostile to the Kaya Bombo. After getting the information they wanted they'd left him for dead. But he had survived and escaped to the UK.

Arriving in the UK, she said, he'd applied for asylum but this had been refused, as had his appeal. He later made a fresh claim, but this too was refused and he was now appealing against that decision. During the eight years that he'd been hoping for a successful outcome, she admitted that he'd committed two criminal offences, for which, she said, he was extremely remorseful. One of these was for using fake documents in order to try and secure a national insurance number and the other for driving without a licence.

Now she asked the court to uphold his appeal. She said that if Mr Macunu was returned he would, in all likelihood, be attacked by the Mungiki for revealing secrets about them, and possibly killed. It wasn't safe for him to return without risk of persecution, he should be granted refugee status.

Although the case was far from unusual Oliver had listened closely to the barrister's account and taken careful notes. This was the work he enjoyed doing and he liked to do it to the best of his ability. He loved the complex and subtle protocol of the court, the elevation of good manners, courtesy, and breeding. But he also took the work very seriously. For ten years now he'd worked as a judge; he knew his judgements had often been of monumental importance to the person standing before him, and nowhere was this truer than in his current work, as an immigration judge. Here the stakes were higher than in any other field of jurisdiction.

It was a responsibility he'd worked hard for. Ever since the Honourable Society of the Middle Temple had first called him to the bar, aged only 24, he'd worked for this. He remembered with pride the moment, after many years of hard graft, when he'd finally been appointed as a judge and taken his judicial oath: *'To do right to all manner of people after the laws and usages of this realm without fear or favour, affection or ill-will'.* The words still sent shivers up his spine.

And now one more person faced him with fearful eyes. It was solely up to him to see that justice was done. The least he could do was listen carefully.

Jacubu Macunu had also listened carefully to his barrister, and with great anxiety. He'd had little time to speak to her when they'd first met fifteen minutes previously in a tiny office behind the court. Without acknowledging the fact that she was forty-five minutes late, she'd gestured him to sit directly in front of her, whilst she skimmed through his thick file, focusing on his solicitor's case summary at the front and scarcely glancing up. As she read, Jacubu had noted with dismay her hurry and fluster. It had been as if she was revising for an exam she hadn't prepared for and had only just remembered about.

After asking a couple of small clarifying questions, which exposed further how little she knew, she had told him that, in view of his extreme nervousness, it would be better if he said as little as possible. She'd do the talking. At first he'd been relieved at this. She was better educated than him. Being English, and an important legal official, she should understand the process. His solicitor had also reassured him beforehand that this barrister was right for the job.

But listening to her in court, he'd regretted that he'd somehow allowed himself to become silenced by the process. There was so much more than the bare bones she'd outlined. Ten years of his life had been condensed into two minutes. And his story went back much further than that! His story was so long that it was difficult to know where to start it, and how to tell it in a way that white people might listen…for he knew they soon lost interest, they didn't want to make the effort to know, not really. His story was also much longer than the one lost in the fat file in front of his barrister.

His story went back before his birth, before the British left Kenya, before they first arrived. It went back to his ancestors, to the first people, to the beginning of time. There was no other way to tell it really. It was a story to tell in a shady spot, under a large tree, with an uncluttered day ahead for the telling. And it was a story cut with tribal violence that interwove loyalty and betrayal, love and revenge, toil, greed, fresh hopes, new despairs, and the soil and smells he knew so well—and children laughing in the sun; threads that had been inter-weaving for generations.

But if she'd needed to start in the middle of his story she could at least have started with the day his village had been destroyed without warning by the Kaya Bombo. A day carved into his memories.

In a carnival of laughter and derision they'd swarmed the village setting light to the huts, spearing and shooting the villagers, then riding off, shouting abuse, and warning that if anyone remained when they returned again soon, they'd be for it too.

Hearing the screams he'd run home from the field, to a scene of total devastation. Their huts were burning! All around were cries, roaring wood crackles, smoke stench. His family's hut was burning. And there, by the entrance, his younger brother lay motionless, face down. Jacubu turned him over, flinching at the warm blood that flooded onto his hands. His brother was dead.

Heaving with dismay, he'd plunged into the blazing hut. He saw his father's outline through the thick smoke, lying on the floor and dragged him out with bursting lungs, laying him next to his brother's body. Then, with a huge breath he plunged back into the hut. It was too hot. Burning thatching was falling through the air and was alight all over the floor. A beam from the roof hung down precariously. A furious wave of flame engulfed him. Wildly, and stooping low, he rushed around the hut, searching, then out again to gasp the air.

It was impossible to go in again. Coughing and wheezing, he bent imploringly over his father's blackened face and wide eyes: "Maitu" (mother?). "Jata? Mukami?" (his sister's names). But his father continued staring into space, eyes empty, already in another world.

In just a few minutes they'd cut out his heart. His brother was dead. His father beyond reach. His mother and sisters had disappeared. How do you communicate such things in a way that people will understand and believe? He'd tried to tell his solicitor, but some things are too horrific to account. You can say the words, but few can really hear them.

He had held his father's unresponsive head in his lap, stroking his hair and forehead, desperately trying to reach him through his vacant eyes. The smoke had badly damaged his father's lungs. But worse: his will to live had burnt in the flames. His breathing became increasingly intermittent. Then it stopped.

Later that night he buried his father and brother, side by side, in a shallow grave, banging together a cross from two charred beams. Then he searched for his mother and sisters. A small boy who'd hidden in a gully, had seen some of the women and girls being beaten with sticks and forced, screaming, onto a waiting truck. But Jacubu hoprf he might still find them, perhaps they'd escaped, perhaps they were lying somewhere wounded. Late into the night he stumbled through the undergrowth calling their names into the darkness.

Eventually a surviving elder brought him sharply out of his trance. There was no time to lose—the Kaya Bombo had said they'd return: their own lives were seriously at risk. *They had to make a move.* But where could they move to? No place was home now. Nor could it ever be.

Over the next few weeks, and months, he went on the run, staying first with relatives in a nearby village then, after further raids by the Kaya Bombo, retreating to Mathare slum in Nairobi.

Why the Kaya Bombo believed that this part of Kenya was rightfully theirs was part of the bigger story, the one mixed up with the British, the one that goes right back, the one he'd been told as a child, that he'd heard was told differently by different tribes, each with their own axe to grind, each believing they were right. A story too complex to tell to this court.

In Nairobi, he joined a powerful quasi-religious political group called the Mungiki. They controlled everything in and around the slum—the toilets, water, electricity, the modes of transport, the people themselves. Every household in the slum had to pay them 'protection' money—or face the consequences. They were renowned for their brutality. They were also effective and organised, their influence far-ranging.

It was this that made them attractive. They offered to help him take back the land of his ancestors. In exchange for loyalty they offered hope, purpose, identity. He joined willingly, partaking a secret oathing ceremony in which he, and other entrants, became ritually drunk from a brew of sugar cane and honey, then drank warm goat blood to become 'blood brothers', swearing life-long allegiance to the Mungiki.

He was inducted into a small local platoon, one of five such platoons making up a local cell. It all ran efficiently and secretly, a military operation. There was a vast organisation beyond and above his local cell of which he was given only the sketchiest of detail. There were rigid rules and heavy punishments for defection, disobeying orders, or revealing information. Beheadings were common. But he wasn't concerned about that. He'd committed himself fully. It was unthinkable that he could ever leave or betray. This was his identity, his route back into life and justice. They made him secretary of his cell group.

But he longed to return to his village and wondered if, by some miracle, his mother and sisters might still be alive, perhaps in hiding, desperate for his assistance, aware he'd escaped and feeling abandoned. He wondered what had happened to the village, what it would be like now. He wanted to see once more the Mukinduri tree, with its high twisted canopy, beneath which he'd played as a small boy, whilst the elders had sat and talked. He wanted to visit the stream where they'd collected water and which he'd swum in as a boy. He decided to return.

Trekking back he kept a low profile. He stayed for a few days with a relative, a day's walk from the village, and made cautious enquiries about his mother and sisters. No one had heard. He was warned to be careful. The Kaya Bombo were now dominant, with informers everywhere and no-one could be trusted. Informing was sometimes rewarded with favour…

Having learnt as much as he could, he rose early and set out on foot towards his home village, avoiding the beaten track. He knew the terrain well, and by evening had reached the back of a hill overlooking his village. He crept carefully around the side of the hill, near its summit, and dropped into a thin dark crack in the rocks, only a few feet wide, that he remembered from his childhood. From there, concealed by twilight, he looked down on the village, three hundred yards away.

He saw again the Mukinduri tree, and the stream. But he also noted some new huts, different in style to his tribe's. He could make out little else, and saw no-one. As the light faded in a fast African sunset he concealed himself carefully in the crack and fell eventually into a fitful sleep.

The next morning he woke early, shivering with cold. He knew that his wisest course was to return the way he'd come but he was consumed with a desire to take one last, closer, look. It was, after all, still almost dark and he figured no one in the village would be up this early. It was an ideal opportunity to find out more, and to revisit his former life. He crept carefully down the hill towards the village, moving slowly and stopping frequently, peering through bushes. He could see now the brand new huts with fresh thatching. There was little trace of their old huts, though he thought he made out a couple of charred circular remains.

Just outside the village he spied the strip of land which his family had cultivated and where he'd buried his father and brother. It seemed to have fallen into disuse. He knew that if he could make it there he would be in a good position to look down on the village. He'd also be able to visit the grave. He crawled forward, keeping low in the thick vegetation, scarcely aware that it had grown light.

Arriving at the site he reached the place where he'd buried his father and brother he fell onto his knees. It was overgrown and the cross broken, with only a broken stump remaining. He found the top half just a few feet away. The memory of all that had happened just a year previously welled up within him. The violence and horror, his father's unseeing eyes. He rose and picked up the cross, held it to his chest, and silently wept. Then he turned, intending to plant the cross once again in the grave.

But this was not to be. Silently standing, just a few yards away, were three men, and one of them was pointing a rifle at him. "Mr Macunu," he said "we've been expecting you."

They held him at gunpoint in the back of a pick-up truck and drove to a small disused out-building at the edge of a nearby farm. There they removed his trousers, tied him to a broken chair, and started asking him questions about the Mungiki: What were their plans? What did he know? Who could he name in his group?

When he refused to answer their questions they tied a piece of string tightly around his testicles and penis and began to tighten. A little more with each successive refusal. The pain was soon excruciating and he began to scream. Several times he fainted only to be revived by heavy slaps across his face. Long after he'd told them all that he knew about the Mungiki they continued to tighten and tighten the string, firing questions at him. But there was nothing left to say and the pain was so overwhelming he could no longer even scream. Satisfied that they'd extracted all the information they could, the men laid into him, clubbing his head and toppling him over onto the ground, still tied to the chair. There they left him for dead.

Many hours later he came to in a pool of his own blood and for a long time lay semi-conscious before eventually releasing himself and crawling to the nearest occupied dwelling. As luck would have it, it was the house of a wealthy man who had been friendly with his father. After hearing what had happened he smuggled Jacubu to another location where other friends of the family kept him hidden for several weeks, tending his injuries.

It was apparent to everyone that it would no longer be possible for him to remain in Kenya. If the Mungiki found out about his betrayal, as they undoubtedly would, then his execution was certain. The family worked together, bought him a passport and a ticket, and, as soon as he was well enough, dispatched him on a plane to Paris. From there he travelled to Calais and took a boat to Dover.

But reaching the UK hadn't marked the end of his troubles. For eight years he'd tried unsuccessfully to gain permission to remain. No amount of explaining ever seemed to persuade the authorities. Nobody listened. Officials fogged over at the mention of the Kaya Bombo, or the Mungiki, or his own group of tribes: the Kiguyu. No-one seemed able, or willing, to listen long enough to allay their suspicions.

He had not been allowed to work, or receive benefits. They'd offered him reduced benefits, but only if he signed a form agreeing to be returned to Kenya voluntarily. That would have been like signing his own death warrant. If he returned there'd be nowhere to hide from the Mungiki. He had no future in Kenya. Everything there revolved around identity and connections, without this there was no protection, no life.

Reluctantly, but out of necessity, he'd eked out a living doing illegal work –causal labour in farms and restaurants, and as a security guard. It was intermittent and poorly paid. He found a driving job but had been caught and prosecuted for not having a driving licence. It hadn't been possible to apply legitimately for a driving licence. Following that offence he was imprisoned for a year at a detention centre. On release he got a job with a promise of payment at the end of a month. But he was dismissed without reason, or payment, the day before pay-day. That had been the camel's straw. He paid for a fake national insurance number—but this too backfired. Now he wanted no more of it, no more of the deception. All he wanted, all he had ever wanted, was legitimacy, and the chance to live, and work, without fear.

He looked up into the judge's eyes, trying to read them. At least the man seemed to be listening carefully. Was it too much to hope that he might be able to respond positively to the short summary of his story that his barrister had now completed?

A serious looking man in a brown suit, with horn-rimmed glasses and a sheaf of papers now rose briskly to his feet. Jacubu knew that this was the Home Office lawyer. He braced himself. The cross questioning was about to begin.

18

Brian held the door of his cab open but the black man just stood there awkwardly. He was five and a half feet tall, thin as a rake and had a phoney smile.

"Get in."

The man climbed in, taking forever, then sat bent forwards, clutching his tiny bag and staring at the floor. He had one of the roundest faces Brian had ever seen, high cheek bones and huge well-spaced, bloodshot, eyes, with wide open, dark brown, pupils. Not that he was making eye contact.

Brian shut the door and got in himself. There was a long pause.

"You need to put your seat belt on."

The man looked down in alarm and began to fumble with the belt. He was shaking like a leaf. Must be the cold, he's probably never been in a cold country, thought Brian. He waited whilst the man fastened his belt, watching him in the mirror. It was taking an age. Probably never worn one before, maybe they don't have them in Africa. Then he noticed his hands. Massive they were, each knuckle swollen huge, his wrists too, like he had elephantiasis or something.

He drove out of Heathrow into lunch time traffic. The sky was grey and sombre. He'd get some lunch after he'd finished with this one.

They sat in silence for five minutes. The man wasn't a speaker and Brian had no real inclination to talk to him, but the journey was going to take a while and he was curious to find out a little more. "Been to London before?"

The man continued staring at the floor, without answering. Then, just as Brian was starting to get irritated, he mouthed the word "No". It was almost inaudible.

Brian pressed on. "Just over for a visit then?"

The man leant further forwards, as if he'd been punched in the stomach.

"I don't know" he whispered.

"You *don't know*?"

"No."

"But how come you're here?"

"That woman," he rasped, "she brought me, in the plane"

"Is she your friend?"

"No."

"No?"

"No, I just—I only just met her."

"So how come she brought you here?

"I don't know."

Brian joined the ring road going west. This conversation wasn't progressing, the man was probably being deliberately obscure. "So where did you come from then?"

"Uganda."

Brian thought for a moment. He didn't know much about Uganda. He remembered Idi Amin of course. But that was a long time ago and probably things had improved since then.

At the roundabout for the M4 he glancing in the mirror and noticed the man looking up for the first time—just a quick flick with his eyes. Eyes that looked defeated, and there was a big bruise under one of them.

"How did you get the shiner?" He asked with a slight smile.

There was a long pause. "I…don't understand"

Brian pointed to the place on his own face, "the bruise, under your eye."

The man studied the floor, then whispered "…the men did it, in the safe house."

"Safe house?" What the hell was he talking about?

"… two days ago I was in a safe house…I thought they'd kill me"

"A *safe house…?* Why would they kill you in a *safe house?*"

There was a long pause. "Safe house is little prison"

Brian was trying to merge with the motorway and a big lorry in the slow lane wasn't giving way. He slowed down and tucked in behind him.

"So you've just been in prison?"

"Yes."

"And they just released you?"

"No…yes…I don't know."

"Well they must have, you're here aren't you?" These people made up such rubbish stories to stay in this country.

The man began coughing violently, doubled up. Brian waited for him to recover, then tried again. "But how come they just released you and put you on a plane?"

"I don't…know…the… guard…pushed me out…then some people put me on the plane."

Brian grunted. It was clear he was telling porkies. He drove on in silence. The man kept coughing in the back. After a while his small raspy voice asked "Electric house, what is it?"

"We're not going there. That woman asked me to take you to *Lunar* house. *Electric* house is nearby, same people though."

There was a long pause, "what do they do to you in Electric House?"

"No idea, mate. Things they do with asylum seekers."

There was another burst of violent coughing. Brian nearly pulled the cab over, but it was awkward—they were on the M4 and gathering speed.

Eventually the coughing subsided. "Am I a slime seeker?"

Brian didn't know what he meant at first, then it dawned on him. "*A-sy-lum* seeker. I don't know, you tell me. Why are you here?" Another long pause. Perhaps he wasn't going to answer.

"I don't know."

"How can you possibly not know?" Now he was exasperated.

The man began coughing again. It sounded even worse this time, like he was coughing his guts up. Between coughs he said "I... need to…be…sick."

Brian sighed heavily, put on the hazard lights and pulled over onto the hard shoulder. It wouldn't be the first time someone had been sick in the cab, it happened more often than he cared to recall, and it was a pain to clear up, even with the rubber matting, the cab would stink for days. Goodness this guy had a nerve. If he was so sick he shouldn't have got in in the first place.

He got out of the cab and went around to the back. The man was coughing ominously and struggling to unfasten his seat belt then a sudden pulse of vomit spurted over his shirt. There wasn't much of it but there were unmistakable streaks of blood. Brian backed away in alarm, "Jeez!" Maybe he was infectious.

Leaving him still coughing he went round to the boot where he kept his provisions. A lorry thundered past, horn blaring. God this was inconvenient.

When he got back with a box of tissues and a bottle of water the man had finally got his seat belt off was sitting forwards staring at the floor alternately sobbing and coughing. Brian held a tissue at arm's length "Here take this…and you'll need to get that shirt off."

The man took the tissue but didn't move.

"…You can't keep that shirt on or it will stink the place out, I've got a plastic bag in the boot, we can put it in there." The man still didn't do anything. He was visibly shaking.

"C'mon take your shirt off! We're not going any place 'til you take your shirt off and we get all this cleared up." Why did this have to happen just before lunch?

Very slowly the man began to unbutton his shirt. Brian watched, then gasped in a horrified suck of acrid air. Front and back the man's body was a mass of scars, wheals, gashes and bruises —some old, others much newer—bright pink against his black skin. All over his arms and chest were raised rings about an inch across with blackened centres, and there was a mass of criss-crossing lines all over his back, wounds on top of wounds. His whole upper torso was festering and swollen.

Brian held onto the side of the cab, his head swirling. He'd never seen anything like this. He squinted up his eyes scarcely able to look and finding it hard to breathe. "What the…?"

Their eyes met. It was the first time they'd made direct eye contact. "what the…what happened to you?"

He waited, suddenly patient, dreading the answer. This was no tropical disease. Someone had done this deliberately.

The man said slowly. "…in the safe house."

Again their eyes met and Brian felt his own watering. "You need to see a doctor, mate" he said quietly, handing him the bottle of water and taking his shirt. "I'll be right back." He stumbled back to the boot to get a plastic bag but faltered and stood for a while, propped up against the cab, in a cold sweat, with his knees shaking. How could anyone do such things?

When he returned the man was struggling to pull a yellow Mobil T shirt over his head. Brian thought he heard a muffled sob.

The man's head emerged. Again they looked at each other. The man's eyes were dark pools of terror.

"It's all right, mate, I'll get you sorted" Brian said, then added "I'm not going to hurt you." Somehow it had felt necessary to say that.

The man stared back at the floor, then in a small rasping voice he said "Please, don't take me to Electric House,"

"I'm not taking you to Electric House" Brian repeated softly. "We're going to Lunar House, like the woman said…but why are you so frightened of Electric House?"

The man looked at him silently as if struggling for words, then thrust forward his swollen hands. At first Brian didn't get it, then suddenly, with another wave of revulsion, he understood.

He found himself gently touching the man's shoulder. "No mate, they don't give people electric shocks in this country."

Back on the motorway they sat in silence, Brian's head whirling. Without a word he turned off the fare meter. The M4 became the A4 and then they were on Earls Court Road, getting near. "When we get to Lunar House I can come in, if you like" he said into the mirror "and explain that you need help—would you like that?" The man nodded, almost imperceptibly, still staring down, still shaking

"First off, you need a doctor. But I'm sure they'll take care of that once we get there."

The rest of the trip they remained in silence. Brian no longer wanted to ask questions. He was too busy thinking about what he'd just seen.

At Lunar House he opened the back, squatting so that he was on the same level, and said, quietly, "Here we are, buddy, this is Lunar House, let me help you with that." Leaning over to unfasten the man's seat belt he smelt the unmistakable rank smell of raw fear. "…I'll take you to reception, but first here's my card and some money." He placed his card, the notes the woman had given him, and £40 of his own, into the man's bloated hands.

"My name's Brian Johnson by the way" he pointing to it on the card. Give me a call, if you need to, it's a Freephone, let me know how you get on…and what's your name by the way?"

He didn't normally ask customers their names. All the rules were getting broken today.

"Mohammed….Mohammed Marimbey"

"Well Mohammed, glad to meet you." He nearly offered to shake his hand then changed his mind. "I hope you get sorted soon, let's see what we can do."

Mohammed eased Brian's card, and the money, delicately into his pocket, like he was reaching into a bed of nettles, then climbed slowly out of the cab and limped alongside as they walked to Lunar House.

A few people were outside the building, pacing up and down, some of them talking in small groups. The steps up were studded with cigarette butts. They entered a tiny reception area with a uniformed officer sitting behind a high screen to one side. He was wearing a white shirt with some kind of emblem of rank on his shoulder. Brian spoke into the microphone: "Hello, good day." Always best to be polite.

"G'day." The man waited for Brian to continue.

"I'm a cab driver, I just brought this man from Heathrow Airport. I think he needs to claim asylum. But first he needs to see a doctor, he was sick on the way."

The man behind the counter looked at Brian impassively then passed a ticket under the glass. "Tell him to go through these doors." He indicated an inner set of glass doors, behind which was another guard and a turnstile.

"But he needs to see a doctor, urgently."

"He'll have to wait in the queue like everyone else, and we may not get to him today."

"Oh…" Brian pushed open the glass doors, gesturing Mohammed to follow him.

"*You* can't go in." Growled the guard.

"Why not?"

"It's aliens only."

"*Aliens*?"

"Yes, and we've enough to do without this extra lot from outer space."

Brian ignored the attempted joke. "But, this man needs help. He's desperate, there was blood, I.."

"Aliens only."

Brian wondered whether to argue, then decided against, it was clearly hopeless, the man was a jobs-worth. He gave Mohammed the ticket and said "Goodbye then mate. Go through there." Mohammed flashed an alarmed look at him and Brian nodded, trying to look reassuring, but his stomach was shrinking. "Give me a call if you need to, you've got my number…"

Without looking at Brian again, Mohammed went through the glass doors which swung closed behind him. Brain watched as the guard on the other side took the ticket he'd only just been given and began routing through his bag. Beyond him was a turnstile and beyond that he could see people standing in a long queue edged by tight metal barriers, like in a pig pen.

"*You* can't stay here," barked the guard behind the window.

Brian turned, walked out into the freezing air, and stood with his eyes closed at the top of the steps. An after-image of Mohammed's naked upper body screamed at him from the inner red skin of his eyelids.

19

"Mr Macunu, you say that prior to arriving in this country you had been a member of the Mungiki, is that correct?"

"Jacubu looked at the prosecuting solicitor. "Yes sir." His barrister had told him to talk directly to the judge not the prosecutor but this was hard, and it didn't seem polite.

"And when you arrived in this country you made a statement in which you said that you'd been a secretary of the Mungiki, is that correct?"

"Yes sir"

"And one of the tasks that you were responsible for was the recruitment and induction of new members was it not?"

"Yes sir". He had certainly been involved in recruiting a few new members for his local cell.

"An important task to have undertaken was it not?"

"Yes sir"

"Being secretary of the Mungiki is quite a high office is it not?"

He hesitated, not quite knowing how to answer. He had been *a* secretary not *the* secretary. But he didn't wish to suggest that he was too minor a person in the organisation to matter. Such an admission might be interpreted as implying that the Mungiki would have no reason to persecute him if he was returned and people in the UK didn't understand how powerful the Mungiki was and how extensive its reach. "Yes sir" he replied throatily. His arm pits were soaking wet.

The lawyer ploughed on: "So, as secretary to the Mungiki, and of such high office, you would be savvy to the inner workings of the Mungiki would you not?"

Jacubu didn't answer.

"You do understand my question, do you not?" pressed the lawyer.

"No sir". But he knew there was no way out.

"You must say if you don't understand"

"Yes sir"

"Let me try again. So, it's true you were the secretary of the Mungiki?"

"Yes sir" again he felt cornered, not knowing how to answer differently now, without backtracking. He had a sudden familiar flash-back to when he was being dragged out of the pick-up truck to the farm out building.

"And as secretary to the Mungiki you'd know a lot about them wouldn't you?"

"Yes sir, I suppose so"

"You *suppose* so! Mr Macunu! Would a secretary of the Mungiki know about the organisation that they hold such high office in or not? Yes or no?"

"Yes sir." Now he could feel the rope being tied around him. They were tying him to the chair, preparing him for questions about his involvement with the Mungiki.

"For instance you would know basic matters like the fact that they condone female circumcision?"

"Yes sir"

"And you would know when they were formed?"

"Yes sir"

"And how many members they had?" Jacubu stayed silent. He understood that a trap was being set, but there was now no way to break free.

"Answer my question Mr Macunu." The lawyer's tone was rising in severity now and Jacubu suddenly felt like running out of the court. It was as if he was about to be tortured.

"The secretary of the Mungiki, being of a very high up position in that organisation, would surely know how many members there were in the organisation would they not?"

"Yes sir."

"So how many members were there?" The rope was being twisted. He gripped the sides of the wooden table in front of him. He had no idea.

"There were rumours there were 500,000."

"*Rumours?,* Mr Macunu."

"Yes sir."

"And 500,000 is a very round number is it not. Half a million exactly. A number with 5 zeros at the end."

"Yes sir."

"And yet by your own admission, Mr Macunu, you should, as secretary, have known this most basic piece of information. But instead you know only *rumours.* Surely you should know to a far greater accuracy how many members there were, should you not?" Jacubu fell silent now, not knowing what to say, aware of the twisting.

"Answer the question Mr Macunu: should you, or should you not, have known the number of members of an organisation in which you were so instrumentally involved to a greater accuracy than units of 100,000?"

The silence that followed was eventually interrupted by the judge, coming in with a more conciliatory tone:

"Mr Macunu, you do need to answer the question here."

"Yes sir."

"Do you, or do you not, have a more accurate recollection how many members the Mungiki had?" There was another pause, then: "You *must* answer the question Mr Macunu."

Jacubu, who had been staring down at his feet now looked up.

"I'm not sure, sir, I don't know exactly."

"Surprising that," said the Home Office lawyer severely. "So, tell us, at least, when the Mungiki first formed?"

Another twist of the rope. "uh.. I think sometime in the late 1980s"

"You *think*?"

"Yes sir"

"You *think* but you don't know"

"Yes sir"

"As an ex-secretary to the Mungiki you don't *know* when the organisation was formed, the organisation you had joined and were involved in so instrumentally?"

"No sir, I am not quite sure."

"You are not *quite* sure?"

"No sir."

"You're not sure when they were formed, you have only the vaguest of ideas as to the number of members they had, yet by your own admission these are the sort of facts that you ought to know, isn't that true?"

"Yes sir." He felt hopeless now.

"Mr Macunu I put it to you that you don't know, and you are not sure, because *you never knew*. I put it to you that you never knew because you were never a secretary of the Mungiki. Had you been secretary you could have easily answered these simple questions. I put it to you that you're a liar and that you've deliberately told a false story in order to try and stay within this country." He paused for a hiatus few seconds, glaring at Jacubu, then sat down with affected finality. "No more questions your Honour."

The judge now turned to Jacubu's barrister. "Do you wish to question the appellant further yourself?"

She stood up hesitatingly. "Er, no your Honour."

"And do you, Mr Macunu have anything further to say?"

But Jacubu had been rendered speechless by the process. How could he fit his story into the small opening now being offered to him? There was still the entire story of his life to tell, and now he felt emasculated, depleted of the necessary resources with which to tell it. There was everything still to say, and no way of saying it.

"Mr Macunu, do you understand my question?

"Yes sir," the words came out strained and high pitched.

"And do you have anything further to say?

"No sir." He had nothing further to say. He needed the twisting to stop.

"Well then, as no one has anything to add, that ends today's hearing. Mr Macunu, you will be advised of the decision of this court within the next two weeks. Court dismissed."

Judge Oliver Surret retired to his chambers to consider his verdict. It was, he reflected, pretty straight-forward really. It had been clear from early on that the man had the slimmest of arguments. To be granted permission to remain he needed to have demonstrated, following the 1951 UN Convention for Refugees, that he had a 'well-founded fear of persecution' if he was returned to Kenya. But he'd clearly not achieved this.

The clincher of course had been the exposure of his lie. The Home Office solicitor had done a good job there. He'd wasted no time at all with his direct, no fuss, line of questioning. He must remember to congratulate him the next time they went for a drink.

No, Mr Macunu had surely been lying, and with the exposure of that lie the credibility of his entire testimony had collapsed. Could they even be sure that he'd ever been a member of the Mungiki? Or, if he had, how could there be any justification for the fact that he'd chosen in the first place to join an organisation that condoned female circumcision—how contemptible was that? If people chose of their own free will to join such organisations then surely they should, by the same token, take responsibility for the consequences of doing so.

And yet, also, he felt slightly uneasy. As ever he was being asked to pass judgement on a situation in a country thousands of miles away, about which you could never know everything. He'd read up about the different countries of course, and prided himself on the fact that he probably did this more than most of his colleagues, staying awake late into the night after Marjorie had gone to bed. By most accounts Kenya was low down on the list of dangerous regimes…No, there needed to be more evidence of danger than this. He'd have to turn him down.

He wrote a few sentences justifying his decision. Mr Macunu should now be returned to Kenya. So much time had elapsed since his alleged escape that it would surely be safe now for him to return, and he should settle in a different part of the country, perhaps under an assumed name, where there could be no threat.

But as he marked the final full stop, Oliver felt another surge of unease. Was this really true? Would the man really be safe? Just how extensively had he lied?

Momentarily he considered changing his mind, then thought better of it. His unease could be due to any number of things—possibly it wasn't connected with Mr Macunu at all. He knew he was worried about the alien messages for instance. Something momentous was about to happen and he didn't like the threat to the status quo that was hanging over them all. Or maybe his unease had to do with Marjorie, there'd been something odd about her at breakfast that he couldn't quite place. She probably didn't think he'd noticed.

Yes, many things could account for his unease. And, anyhow, certainty wasn't possible. He had to be pragmatic and do his best within the confines of a necessarily imperfect system. He pushed the signed papers into his 'out tray', and out of his mind.

Just as he was leaving, his secretary phoned through. "A call for you, sir: Hattie Taylor". Marjorie's sister. What could she possibly want?

"Hello Hattie, this is an unexpected pleasure." It was a lie of course. He didn't find it easy talking to Hattie at the best of times. She was always so irrational and emotional, so different from Marjorie.

He heard a whimper on the line—she was crying! "Oliver…it's…"

"Yes?"

"It's…"

He began to feel impatient.

"It's about…Marjorie. She's at the Royal Infirmary. There's been a terrible, terrible, *accident*."

20

Early that morning, when the sky had been navy-black through the kitchen windows, Marjorie had listened to the news on Radio 4, as she prepared breakfast.

'… Opinions still differ about whether or not these really are alien messages, and many have dismissed the idea as ludicrous. Nonetheless in the past few hours, as the deadline approaches, huge crowds have assembled at every location.

In a carefully worded message the Prime Minister avoided stating his own view and cautioned against premature conclusions: "We don't know yet what we're dealing with but you may rest assured that we're working round the clock and doing everything we can to prepare for every eventuality. Meanwhile it is important that we all stay calm…"'

Oliver would be down any moment, but she was pretty much ready. Her granite work surfaces were gleaming under their concealed spot lights and the smell of toast and freshly ground coffee filled the air. She went through to check the dining room.

As always she had laid the table meticulously, the previous evening, before retiring to bed. Each had their designated place. Marjorie at the end of the table nearest to the kitchen, so that she could serve more easily, Oliver opposite her, a good six feet of ironed pink table cloth between them. Each had a pristine breakfast plate and bowl with glinting silver cutlery laid correctly beside. Their serviettes matched the table cloth—and were carefully rolled up and held in place by individual napkin rings: hers a delicate inter-weaving spiral that looked like it had been fashioned out of lace; his broader, smooth and slightly concave, polished shiny as a mirror and holding miniature reflections of the room. In the middle of the table a cut glass vase filled with pink roses diffracted light, from the chandelier above, in all directions. She could still hear the radio in the kitchen.

'...Mr Theo Chaldrike from the US National Counter Terrorism Center has been much more alarmist "This is beyond red alert. This is far and away the greatest threat our species has experienced in its long history. Global warming is a walk in the park without sun-cream compared to this and nuclear war a kids fireworks display. Unless we act decisively, as a species, we will no longer be a species..."'

To one side of the table on an antique dresser was an ornate tray, with a silver coffee pot, surrounded by a matching hot water jug, a creamer in the shape of a cow—its open mouth a spout for the cream, and a sugar bowl with eagle claw sugar tongs. She always put out the multi coloured sugar cubes, even though neither of them now took sugar in their coffee. It was too much a part of the set to be separated.

'...But Mr Fergus O'Donnel from SETI advised otherwise "Let's all try and keep our heads here. Nothing we've been told suggests hostility or that we're being offering anything other than help. Far from being the demise of our species this could be its most seminal moment. We would be foolish to turn away from this extra-ordinary opportunity, an opportunity to..."'

She heard a slight creak from the ancient floorboards above her. Oliver was moving about upstairs. He must have finished shaving, she thought, and would be browsing his walk-in wardrobe in the master bedroom, selecting his shirt and tie for today's session in court. She turned the radio off. He wouldn't have it on over breakfast.

She walked over to the ornate mirror at one side of the room and looked at her profile sideways, sucking in her stomach while she pressed it with a flat hand and sighed. She had on one of her favourite dresses. A colourful pattern of red and green flowers, on a white background, set off by a wide matching belt pulled as tight as possible around her waist.

She was a tall, nicely proportioned woman with a clear brow, full lips and a determined nose. As she looked herself over now, however, she had eyes only for the blemishes, a tiny spot on her right cheek was just peeking through her carefully placed concealing make-up and her bright red lipstick had over run one corner of her mouth, 'and my eyebrows need plucking'.

As she tucked in a couple of loose strands of hair she heard Oliver's steady footsteps coming down the staircase and quickly corrected the lipstick smear with the tip of her finger and moved away from the mirror towards the table, pretending to be making some adjustment.

"Good morning, dear". His voice was deep and resonant behind her. She turned around, looking him up and down. He was wearing one of his dark grey suits, with a crisp faintly striped light blue shirt and a dark grey tie, tied in a careful Windsor knot. A light blue triangle of silken handkerchief peeped out from his suit breast pocket, matching his shirt. On his feet were hand-made shoes, with laces carefully tied in double bows.

"Good morning". She looked up at his clean-shaven face with its familiar wide jaw and his short hair brushed neatly away from its straight parting. His small, penetrating, eyes looked back at her, from behind almost invisible half-moon glasses. "Did you sleep OK?" she asked.

"Yes, thank you, although I woke up thinking about this strange alien business." He took his seat at the table as Marjorie poured their coffees.

"Do you still think it's genuine then?" she said, placing the china cup and saucer carefully beside him, then carrying her own over to the other side of the table. "I mean genuinely *alien*?"

"Yes." He unfolded his serviette and placed it neatly in his lap, "I think we've got to trust the scientists. But it's still incredibly hard to believe."

"Then what do you think can be meant by 'transformational opportunities'?" she asked, anxious to keep him talking before he picked up the copy of the Financial Times that waited, neatly folded on the corner of the table. Breakfast was usually her best window of opportunity to talk to him. He worked long hours in court and would often return home late in the evening, only to spend more time preparing for the next day. No-one could say he wasn't diligent.

He was pouring muesli into his bowl now, organically produced at his insistence, and for a moment she thought he hadn't heard. This was common enough, he was often distracted by his own thoughts; but he looked up at her. "I can't think, Marjorie, I can't imagine what is meant." He returned the china muesli container back to its place. She noticed the back of his hand as he did so, comfortably in control of the object it was holding, his flat nails trimmed to perfection, curling effortlessly around the edge of the china, each nail with a clear half-moon showing. It was as if, she reflected, his body remained perfectly groomed without need of attention, as if his nails and hair, having reached their requisite length, had stopped growing and remained perfectly in place, as if he were stuck, frozen, in a moment in time. In the twenty five years she'd known him he'd hardly aged at all. He was exactly the man she'd married, his body almost identical to how it had been when it confidently waited for her by the altar.

"The thing is," he continued, "we don't have any precedents for thinking about it. In law there are always precedents to refer back to. This is the context. You can follow the precedents or adjust them slightly. You can even, rarely, and perilously, reverse the precedents completely, and take a step in a new direction. But there's always a context from the past. With this we have nothing to go by. *We are in the unknown.*"

She hated when he talked about the law and looked down to focus on her own breakfast—a hemisphere of blood grapefruit—

plunging her special, pointed, silver spoon into the pink pre-cut flesh and negotiating the first segment past her lipstick. The tiny pith-wrapped capsules of juice burst onto her tongue disturbing the traces of toothpaste there with a cool blast of bitterness.

"Would you want it though?" she said, as soon as her mouth was empty.

He looked at her quizzically

"Would I want what?"

"Would you want to take a *transformational opportunity* if you were able to?"

She had his attention now. He looked at her, his lips thinly stretched into a slight smile.

"You mean without knowing what would happen?"

"Yes."

His smile subsided. "Of course not." He took a spoonful of muesli. She wondered if her question had slightly disturbed him. Was that a ripple on the tranquil pond? But once his mouth was clear he continued with unruffled assurance: "Why would I want to transform things? I have everything I want—the perfect job, the perfect house in Willow View, the perfect children" he looked at her "and the perfect wife" his smile was back in its thin stretch. "Why would I want to change such perfection?"

The compliment had been delivered with practised ease. She was used to this way he expressed his appreciation of her—so fluent and apparently sincere; except that is, for the fact that they both understood the implicit irony: nothing was perfect, and she wasn't, of course. Nobody was. Often she'd allowed such speeches to reach her, re-playing them afterwards in the long periods of time she spent alone. But today it was as if his words had crossed the table towards her, past the vase of roses, only to flounder, gasping for oxygen, on a bare expanse of pink table cloth, just before reaching her.

He looked at her levelly now, assessing her response, and apparently expecting her to make some compliment back. Such was the form that they had established. Now she should use a line like:

"And I have the perfect husband." This would have met the call of politeness and pattern completion. But she looked down, studying her grapefruit, as if she hadn't heard, and took another spoonful of bitter-sweet flesh.

Later she listened at the door as the sound of Oliver's BMW receded on their gravel driveway, then disappeared completely. Now there was only the sound of the distant motorway, like tinnitus. He'd insisted on buying a house near a motorway: 'So that I can commute easily, wherever I'm needed'.

She started to clear the breakfast table, carrying the home made marmalade, quince and strawberry jams into the larder. She'd return with a tray. It was cool in the larder with its marble floor and tiny high up slit of a window. It smelt of rice and herbs. She put away the jars and automatically reached behind the bread bin for the bottle. The transparent, innocuous-looking liquid was lower down than she remembered. But there was an inexhaustible supply in the cellar. Oliver didn't scrutinise the bills. She untwisted the white cap, circled her lips around the hard glass neck, sucked deeply through her nose, and slowly gulped down a long fierce spear of vodka. It started lancing cool in her throat, then soon gave way to spreading heat. She carefully wiped the bottle clean of lipstick, screwed the cap back on, replaced it behind the bread bin and helped herself to an extra-strong mint from a nearby bowl. That should set up the day nicely.

Forgetting the tray she returned to the table and finished clearing away the breakfast, making a dozen short journeys to and fro to the kitchen. There was a tiny stain of coffee on the table cloth, close to where Oliver had been sitting. She pulled the cloth into a bundle, keeping the stain visible, then applied a chemical stain remover to the offending mark and bundled the whole tablecloth into her industrial-sized washing machine, setting the temperature high.

There was a lot to be done in the day that stretched out before her. Her sister had arranged to visit for elevenses. She needed to bake some ginger snaps for that—Hattie's favourites. She would need to do her Pilates exercises of course. It was important to keep going with them, she'd lapsed for a few days already and if she didn't start up again today she was bound to get fatter still. There was also a dinner party the following evening to prepare for. Oliver had invited colleagues to come and discuss the Government changes in respect to legal aid. A table cloth would need ironing for that, the silver polishing and new flowers cut from the garden and arranged. And the house would need a thorough clean.

They'd bought Willow View twenty years ago. It had meant suspending her career as an actress because the company was too far away. Stopping acting had seemed a pity at the time. She'd had to turn down a role as Lady Macbeth, a part she'd always wanted to play, a part for a woman with some depth to it. But life's like that, you have to make sacrifices. And the house had six bedrooms. It would be perfect for the large family that she decided she wanted to have.

In the event they'd only had two children, and now, with one of the boys safely established at Cambridge, and the other in his last year at Rugby, there was even less need for a house so big. But over the years each room had become a separate shrine to the goddess of interior decoration and a showcase for her artistic talents. The garden, an exacting study of mature shrubs and manicured trees, overlooked splendid views of a valley and a winding brook, with willows on either side. It was all much too precious to consider leaving now. Besides they had no financial need to, they owned the house outright. The mortgage had been paid off early. This was the time that they'd been looking forward to.

She thought that she might start off today by preparing the soup in advance. She would need to do a big shop for groceries—so that meant she needed to finalise the menu. And she would need to decide what she was going to wear. Then there was the lining on an upstairs curtain that needed repairing, and she needed to get a man in about a loose tile on an outhouse roof. She'd have to get three quotes—Oliver always insisted on that, and how right he was. There was also a lunch time meeting tomorrow of the church spire fund-raising committee, and this year's holiday to think about (something that would never occur to Oliver to do). Yes, there was a lot.

Outside a robin was singing, faint through the double glazing but she could clearly make out its flurry of tiny notes…there it was again! She remembered that she needed to fill up the seeds in the bird feeders and change the water in the mosaic bird bath. She could start with that...

Back in the larder again she found the container of Niger seeds. They were for the goldfinches, and some peanuts for the tits, and she picked out a fresh fat ball to provide energy—it being a difficult time of the year for birds, she felt, being so close to winter. And then, yes, well, why not, just one more little swig of vodka for herself.

She carried within her, in a sealed capsule, the knowledge that this was a difficult habit she'd acquired. The capsule was like an unwanted friend—never quite getting the message that it wasn't welcome. It stayed in contact, inside her, unheeding of the implied rejection of her silence. She did not respond to its one-way correspondence or encourage it in any way. But she always knew it was there, trying to get through, waiting for her to renew contact. And, now and again, it would turn up, unannounced, barging its way more forcefully into her life, and expect to stay, not just for a day, or a week, but for life. She could not countenance that.

Over the years there had been several occasions when matters had come to a head, and she had walked a few shaky steps along a path of sobriety. The last time was only a few months previously. Oliver had returned home, unexpectedly, to find her stretched out on the Chesterfield, an empty bottle of Chablis beside her. It had been intensely embarrassing. She had felt so inadequate, and faulted, alongside his perfect negotiation of life. She was normally so careful, but must have drowsed off; she hadn't heard his tyres on the gravel. She had leapt to her feet, scooping up the bottle, and muttering something about friends having visited earlier and getting him some tea. Then keeping her head low she walked past him into the kitchen, and quickly masticated a mint, before returning apologetically to join with him in their usual greeting kiss. To her surprise, and relief, he didn't seem to have noticed.

After that she'd waged another faltering war of attrition, alarming herself that it was indeed much harder than she had led herself to expect; then persuading herself that she needed to break herself in gradually because of this; before finally resealing the capsule inside her and succumbing to the slide.

The fact that she had failed on this, and all previous attempts, had thickened the coating on the capsule. But she consoled herself, that although, yes, she had failed to give up completely, she was in fact able to keep things under control. Willow View was immaculate; there wasn't a crack to be seen in the plaster, anywhere. She continued to prepare an endless round of cordon bleu meals. The freezer was stuffed with neatly packed double portions of delicious home-made desserts. There was hardly a weed in the garden. There was a neat stack of beautifully ironed and folded shirts for Oliver in the wardrobe. Even his underpants were ironed. He wanted for nothing. Anyone could see she was coping. Not that these were the sorts of things that Oliver noted of course. He took it all for granted, just like he had with his mother.

She took the bird food out into the garden and filled up the dispensers. The sun had risen now, but far down in the valley there was still a thin mist, hanging low, and the garden was wet with glistening dew. A mass of dusky pink violets were swinging gently in unison from side to side, their petals freshly opened to the sun. The border led down in a sweeping curve to their lily filled pond. She was momentarily tempted to sit for a while on a nearby garden bench. She ought to be enjoying the violets, she knew she ought, she ought to be savouring this moment. Isn't that what they said, the sages? You need to live in the moment. But there was always so much to do. On her way back to the house she paused to check the laundry that she had hung out the previous day, damp with the mist.

There was much less laundry to do now, of course, now that the boys had left, or as good as. She'd loved handling their dirty clothes when they were little. It was a way to steal insights into their private lives in the wild. Dusty green smears on T-shirts from climbing trees, grass stains on knees, clay splashes from playing by the stream, burrs embedded in jumpers, autumn pockets crammed with acorns, horse chestnuts, and sycamore helicopters. She'd repair, and bleach, and send them out clean the next day, their pristine early morning clothes receptive canvases to the world.

It was six weeks until Harry would be back from school and Bart—she no longer knew when he'd be back. He had a girlfriend now and there was talk of the two looking for a flat together. She didn't approve. Hailey would borrow money for a take-away rather than make an omelette and Bart seemed unable to see beyond her heavy make-up.

She'd been ambivalent about sending the boys to public school but Oliver had insisted: 'It's character building, my dear. It's the very best education in the world and more important than that—it's where tomorrow's leaders are groomed.' But Bart had returned from Rugby evasive of her waiting arms. He was prematurely adult, she felt, his newly broken voice lapsed, all too frequently, into raucous, whooping, laughter and he'd acquired a contempt for all matters homely. Before he'd left, both boys would still sit regularly, puppy-like, in her lap, and cuddle; their outsized bodies pressing her down into the sofa, chins against her neck. But a single term had severed boy from puppy, and Bart had become remote and irritable, avoiding all contact with her except for fleeting appearances to eat. Harry had been quick to follow, abandoning his own sessions in her lap at the first sneering hoot of his brother.

Oliver had tried to reassure. This was only natural—boys needed to separate out from their mothers, he'd had to do exactly the same himself…

Hattie arrived at one o'clock, late as usual. Marjorie had expected this and had prepared a light lunch contingency as well as the ginger snaps. Hattie was five years younger than her, cheese to her chalk, and always late. She arrived in her purple jeep, embracing Marjorie with an effusive flourish and immediately showing her the pair of brightly patterned charity denims she had just acquired "Aren't they *absolutely divine*? I got them for nothing". Her latest hair style was a hot shock of coral curls, well beyond what could conceivably be considered natural, even by a man. On each wrist was a clinking charm bracelet.

"I am *so terribly* sorry I am late my dear, it has been *such* a morning. First I had Nigel on the phone for hours, nearly in tears because of the downturn in the stock market—he does go *on* so. He thinks it will carry on falling for ever and we will all be *ruined.* I told him it won't of course—but he doesn't listen to me. Then I had a sales visit from a dreadful little man from the art supplies store, he kept trying to sell me larger and larger canvasses and I kept saying no. But he wouldn't listen either. It was over an hour before I finally prised him out of the door. I had to buy a canvas just to get rid of him. After that I came straight here…" She sat down on a crafted oak arm chair on the decking—where Marjorie had laid the table for lunch, and stretched out her legs. She was wearing bright green tights and hand-made, soft leather, red and blue sandals.

"Via the charity shop." Marjorie said reactively, before she could stop herself.

Hattie stiffened, drawing her feet back under the chair. "Yes, via the charity shop. What of it Marjie?"

"Well, you said you'd come straight here…"

"Yes, well it was only a brief stop on the way—it only took a few minutes"

"But there isn't a charity shop between your studio and this house."

"OK, O-kay! But what of it?"

"Well you said you'd come straight here and that you were late because of Nigel and the salesman. But actually you were also late because you took a huge detour on the way."

"Christ Marjie, what is this, the Spanish inquisition? I only made a brief detour to visit a charity shop, and I only spent five minutes there, *five minutes.* Is that so terrible?"

"It is when it means you're going to end up two hours late for your appointment with me. You could at least have phoned me Hat."

"But you're my sister Marjie, surely I don't have to be *exactly* on time and *make appointments* with you. You're *family*."

Marjorie looked down the garden into the valley below. She'd wanted this to be a happy time with her sister—a pleasant break in her busy day and, yes, to feel like family. She'd worked hard for this. But within moments of her sister arriving, it was all going terribly wrong. For a split second she saw a way out: she could explain, she could eat humble pie, she could apologise for being so attacking. She could try to make peace...

But she still felt incensed. This was what *always* happened, it was always *her* that made the effort, made allowances, climbed down. She was *not* going to do that again. "That's not good enough Hattie, I need you to be on time or to at least have the decency to phone when you're going to be late, which is pretty much always." She knew with dismay as she was saying this that it was one jab too many, and true to form, Hattie was on her feet.

"Well, thank *you* Mrs Surret" she glared at Marjorie "Mrs too-important-now for her little sister. I shall make sure I am on time the next time I'm lucky enough to be given *an appointment* to see you, if you ever have enough time in your busy schedule that is. I won't be a second late the next time *I* make the effort to come and see *you*..." She grabbed her charity denims and Nepalese shoulder bag and marched towards the jeep, sandals squeaking on the driveway "But it could be some time!" she shouted tremblingly, without turning, as she wrenched the door open, threw in her things and then herself and slammed the door shut.

Marjorie had been sitting inertly through this, and listened now as the jeep engine revved angrily into life. Again she was aware of a tiny window. She could leap to her feet and race out towards the jeep shouting 'Hattie, Hattie, stop, I'm sorry, please, please forgive me—I don't know what came over me. Please Hat...'

She could do that—and was that a slight delay in her sister leaving, was she revving unnecessarily, was she waiting for her? This would certainly be their pattern. Then they would make it up. Then, having crash-landed into intimacy, they would start to talk with the air a bit clearer. She could do that—but for once she felt immobilised, her heart still throbbing with the rage coursing through her. The window closed, and with a sudden lurch the jeep kicked off down the drive way, spitting gravel behind it.

Marjorie stayed sitting. She half expected Hattie to do a U turn at the end of the driveway and come back, apologetic. Then it would all be easier because it was she who would have committed to the first climb down. But the sound of her tyres dwindled away. She'd be on the main road now, heading towards the motorway. It was too late to catch her.

And now the first ripples of guilt started to fret at the edges of her indignation. She sat very still, agitatedly turning it all over, knowing she had to somehow unfasten the angry mantle that now encapsulated her like a restrictive suit of armour. What *had* they been arguing about? She should have bitten her tongue.

She watched miserably as two long tailed tits pecked at the new fat ball, highlighted against the bank of nodding violets behind them. It was hopeless challenging Hattie. She was so quick to become hysterical. She knew this—but Hattie could be *so exasperating.*

She rose half-heartedly and began to clear away the lunch things. She had no appetite for lunch herself now. It would, at least, save another round of washing up. She'd begin by putting the cheese board and the ginger snaps into the larder...

Later, when she'd finished clearing up, she sat down at the kitchen table with a row of vegetables, ready to start making the soup for the next day's dinner party. She liked to have everything lined up first, then chop it all together using the wonderful chopping knife they had bought in Provence the previous summer. She'd decided to make gazpacho soup, one of Oliver's favourites. It was probably too early in the year for a cold soup. Summer was best for it—but she could turn the heating up. She'd bought the large Italian tomatoes that are so much tastier than the perfectly formed supermarket ones that taste only of wet fibre and perfect conditions.

The knife cut down cleanly through the tomatoes as if slicing air. First into halves, then quarters, then eighths, the ripe pips deserting the red curves of skin in fresh glistening piles on the huge chopping board. Now for the red peppers. Normally she enjoyed preparing vegetables, and cooking. Today though, it rankled and her hands were shaking, probably still with rage, she thought. Her sister could come and go as she pleased—but she couldn't. The housework wouldn't do itself. It was an endless round, never to be abandoned. Oliver had no concept of the hours it took her just to keep things ticking over. He must think it all got done by divine intervention. She'd messed up big time with Hattie now. She couldn't forgive herself for that. She'd been *such a bloody idiot.* It would take days of effort and careful diplomacy just to bring back a semblance of peace between them. And now she was already running behind. Oliver would expect there to be wonderful food on the table when he came back from court this evening. There'd better be, or he'd go off her. Lord knows he had plenty of reason to, she was already far too fat. Perhaps he would get attracted to a younger woman. Perhaps he already was. That wouldn't surprise her. He expected to eat at seven, although, sometimes (often actually), he would be late, and they would sit down and eat an overcooked meal that had taken over an hour to prepare and which he would gulp down in fifteen minutes—and then she would need to do the washing up and lay out the breakfast things for the following day…

Her hands were shaking badly now and the end of the knife slipped whilst paring excess pith off the inside of a strip of pepper, and sliced into the end of her thumb. She turned her hand over in exasperation to survey the damage. There was a penny sized piece of flesh hanging loose. Blood was already pumping out onto the sliced tomatoes. Damn! Damn! You idiot! She'd have to get more tomatoes now. She'd have to begin again!

Suddenly, and with a savage purpose, she raised the knife high up above her head and brought it down hard and deliberately—slicing into her waiting wrist.

21

As Jacubu stumbled out of the court his barrister made a half-hearted attempt to re-assure him. Their best policy was to see what the court had to say and then decide what to do next. But he was an intelligent man, he could read the writing on the wall, and this was the end of the line. He thanked her, preserving his politeness, then walked out of the building in a daze, half expecting to be arrested.

It was rush hour and the pavements were crowded by people in smart clothes who'd just left their offices, and shoppers negotiating the bustle, their arms stretched vertical by clusters of carrier bags. In the early evening light the shops seemed extra fluorescent. Light flooded onto the pavements. He passed a window with mannequins dressed in bright clothes—peering out with haughty, chiselled, faces, then an array of marbled cakes and miniature marzipan sculptures; then a bank of flat TVs—elephants splashed in mud on thirty screens.

He walked slowly, his feet brushing the pavement between steps, not knowing what to do. Then abruptly his step picked up and his feet, determined now, set off at pace, towards the station.

At the station he bought a one way ticket to Dover, digging deep into the tiny reserve of money he'd so carefully preserved and that separated him from destitution. He joined a swell of passengers mounting the train and found a seat by the window, squeezing his broad knees under the plastic table.

Throughout the journey he stared out of the window as the world hurtled past. There were bridges of every description, rows of terraced houses with narrow gardens leading down to high fences by the track, villages and village greens, church spires, factories, playgrounds, country mansions, fields with cows and sheep, a canal with holiday makers on narrow-boats. At one point he saw a crowd of people with banners standing around one of the hastily constructed circle enclosures. He'd heard about those, of course, and the green circles that were meant to be arriving. But none of this was for him, this wasn't his world. He had his father's eyes now, and his mind had calmed at last with resolve. He'd been foolish to ever dream of redemption. He'd made one unforgivable mistake—he'd given in to the Kaya Bombo. He should have endured the torture and died then, with honour.

As the train neared Dover the houses grew infrequent and he looked out on farms, and barns, and ploughed fields—the earth scoured in undulating patterns, as if furrowed by a giant comb. The hedges were high here and full of early spring flowers, they twisted and turned, sometimes running parallel, sometimes folding with the countryside, disappearing over the horizon.

He got off at Dover station to the sound of a tinny voice saying "Mind the gap. Mind the gap." then hired a taxi and asked to be driven to a place he remembered from when he'd first arrived in the UK. The driver wanted to talk about the alien messages, but Jacubu was beyond talk, and soon they travelled in silence, hemmed in by stone walls, and hedges. At his destination he gave the driver all his money, more than the fare, and he drove off shrugging into the night.

Jacubu walked steadily up the high path. The sky was clear and a full moon lit his way with cool white light. He was, he reflected incongruously, dressed for the occasion. Better to leave like this, quietly, and on his own terms. Better than what awaited otherwise. It would be a release. He had, in any case, no identity left to lose. He wasn't of this land and never would be. There was no place left that he could ever call home, no place that was safe. No connection with the earth under his feet. It would be a small matter now to leave.

As the path ran parallel to the cliff edge, his heart throbbed rebelliously. Reaching the spot he remembered, he climbed over the safety railings. He could hear the sea crashing on rocks at the bottom of the white cliffs, a sheer drop below. He pressed the back of his legs against the railings and took a deep breath, then ran, as hard as he could, leaping out into the night.

22

Oliver found Hattie in the hospital foyer with smudged mascara and bloated eyes. He shook her hand, glad she wasn't actually crying, particularly in this public place. "Hello Hattie, where is she?" No time for formalities.

"It's OK, no rush, she's calmer now, sedated. I've just spent the last few hours with her. I'll take you to her, then I've *got to* go."

They walked past a row of elderly patients in wheel chairs and into the main corridor of the hospital, stopping by the lifts. On one side was a shop selling flowers, fruit and newspapers.

"Is she OK?" he ventured, wondering if he should buy some flowers.

Hattie hesitated, staring at the indicator lights above the lifts. Both were indicating seven and going up. "They've stitched her up now—she's going to be OK—physically—but there'll always be a scar." Oliver winced. They could easily cancel the dinner tomorrow by saying she was sick. But how was he going to explain the scar on her wrist to his colleagues?

"Has she said why she did it?"

"Not really, Oliver." Hattie paused, debating whether to continue "But I, we, we had an argument..."

Oliver felt relieved at this, it was nothing new, and it offered a welcome explanation. "You did?" he tried to sound neutral, as if arguments were natural and only to be expected. Except that he *never* argued with Marjorie, or with anyone for that matter. It was all rather immature.

"Yes....only a little tiff really, and I went back to apologise. God knows......*god knows* what would have happened if I hadn't..."

"What was the argument about?" Oliver whispered, painfully aware now of a gathering crowd of people assembling by the lifts. Standing very close to them was a surprisingly young man in a white coat with a stethoscope hanging around his neck.

"Oh, nothing really, that's why I don't understand. I can't see why she'd do this. She has everything, *everything*." She was talking much too loudly, Oliver felt, and there was a strained emotional lilt in her voice. The man in the white coat seemed to be listening in.

"Hattie, I—ah—perhaps we should go somewhere quiet to talk?" But Hattie carried on as if she hadn't heard him: "I feel so *terribly* guilty. But you don't expect someone to *cut a wrist* just because you're late, do you?"

Oliver winced at this. Surely people could hear her now, "....you really don't. It is all so...so unexpected. She's always so dependable, predictable."

One of the lifts arrived with a ping-ping and its doors slid open powerfully. They moved towards it, then realised it was going down.

"How high up is the cut?" he asked, keeping his voice low. Hattie looked at him, frowning with incomprehension. "I....don't know: there was so much blood, it had spurted everywhere, I've never seen *anything like it*." She looked down at the polished lino floor "I think it was about *here*...." She pointed to her own wrist. "But why? Why do you want to know *that*?"

"Well I was just wondering how easy it would be to cover it up. Perhaps under a long sleeve or something..." The middle of Hattie's mouth came open and it's corners tightened. The lift was back now and going up. A hospital porter came out pushing an elderly patient on a long trolley, she was staring up at the ceiling, one half of her face distorted. The crowd waited just long enough for them to be out of the way, then surged forwards into the lift. Oliver found himself pressed up against Hattie from his chest downwards, the lower part of his suit against her orange dress. He looked down at the crown of her head and her thick coral curls. She did have a certain bohemian attractiveness...

On the fifth floor Hattie led the way, past an art exhibition by local school children, into a corridor that stretched off into the far distance and smelt of detergent and air freshener. Oliver was conscious of the clipped sound of his shoes and of Hattie's clinking charm bracelets and squeaking sandals beside him. He wondered what lay ahead. He was anxious to get Marjorie home quickly and out of the public eye.

Behind the desk at Ward 56 'Observation and Assessment' a middle-aged nurse was writing slowly and with tiny letters in a large file. Oliver waited for her to look up, but when this didn't seem likely to happen, he said "We've come to see Marjorie Surret"

The nurse appraised him briefly. "And you are?"

"Oliver Surret, her husband."

"One moment please" she turned and took a cardboard file from a trolley behind her and began studiously reading a series of longhand entries.

"I have to go now," said Hattie "Now that you know where you are. I'll be back tomorrow morning. Give her my love"

"Yes, thank you Hattie, hopefully she won't need to stay, I'll let you know". Hattie looked at him, holding his eyes for a few seconds. "No." then she turned and walked back down the corridor.

Oliver watched the nurse studying the file. "Just tell me where she is…I can make my own way."

"One minute sir, please." She carried on reading, then closed the file and replaced it carefully back. "I'd like to have a chat with you first", she said

"OK, if you think it's necessary" He wondered how it possibly could be.

The nurse led him to a room with plastic chairs and a pile of children's toys in a cordoned off corner. "Have a seat", she said closing the door behind them. He sat down, crossing his legs and weaving his manicured hands together.

The nurse settled herself in the chair opposite him and looked up with a strained smile. "Your wife's going to be OK, but she's certainly going to need to stay in hospital. She has seriously damaged her wrist and has needed to have a blood transfusion on account of all the blood she lost. We have her on tranquilisers now, so when you go in she's likely to be a sleepy."

Oliver rose to his feet. But the nurse looked gestured for him to sit down again. "One moment please…your wife did a very serious thing. It was lucky her sister found her so soon, otherwise *she could have died.* Do you know why she did this?"

"Well, I don't really know…her sister said they'd had an argument..."

"I think it must have been more than that," the nurse smiled sparsely "…she was getting on very well with her sister just now. I don't think this one argument can have made her do such a drastic thing. Do you have any idea what else might have upset her?"

"No, I don't," he was genuinely baffled,

"No one close has died recently?"

"No"

"She wasn't worried about money or anything else that you're aware of?"

"No."

"You have children?"

"Yes."

"Are they OK?"

"Absolutely, look I…"

"There isn't something that she might have discovered that might have upset her?"

"No."

"For instance, and I am sorry to ask this Mr Surret, but she couldn't have discovered that you're having an affair, could she?"

Oliver bristled: "Certainly not. I haven't been having an affair."

The nurse looked at him closely. "And you don't think she might have been having an affair herself?"

"No! I don't! Look...nurse...we've been perfectly happy. I don't understand this."

"Do you drink very much?"

"No, certainly not. We have a bottle of wine a few nights a week, and a few spirits, nothing excessive."

"How many units do you think you have a week?"

"Less than the proscribed levels, I'm sure, look I really.."

"And your wife, how much do you think she drinks in an average week?"

"Same as me, nothing remarkable." He had a sudden flash-back to the time he'd discovered Marjorie with the bottle of Chablis. But that had been a one off.

"Does she drink alone to your knowledge?"

"No, of course not. We only drink moderately, and then only some evenings. Look I really don't see the point of your questions."

The nurse lent forward in her seat and said quietly "I think you might be surprised to discover, then, that when your wife came into the hospital she had very high levels of alcohol in her blood."

"You're sure?"

"Yes, we had to examine her blood prior to giving her a transfusion and we checked it for alcohol, we would anyway, routinely. The readings were sky high."

Oliver moved both hands involuntarily to his face and pulled them down so that they covered his mouth. Surely the nurse had something wrong.

"So, we're concerned. As well as a serious suicidal predisposition your wife may also have a longstanding addiction to alcohol."

"Longstanding?"

"Yes, longstanding. There were really high levels in her blood."

"But it may have just been a one off? Something made her drink heavily today."

"But you have no idea what that something might have been?"

"No." Oliver sat back and looked out of the window at the massive car park.

The nurse smoothed her hands across her blue cotton skirt, as if clearing crumbs away. Her knees were close together and turned off to one side. "So I'm sure you understand that we do now need to keep her under observation. If she's been drinking heavily on a regular basis, which is the most likely explanation, and which she's come some way towards admitting, then she'll need to detox. Also we need to get to the bottom of what has caused all this.

"She's admitted it?" He was incredulous.

"Yes. She's admitted drinking today. She's admitted drinking 'most mornings'. She was very distressed when she came in, so we haven't pressed. But you must understand—this is a general hospital, not a psychiatric hospital. She may need to go somewhere where she can be closely cared for and a proper assessment can be undertaken."

"She will be closely cared for at home. *I* will look after her." He wasn't having this. He'd use the full force of his authority to get Marjorie home. She could sign the papers to discharge herself, if necessary.

The nurse narrowed her eyes. "You don't seem to understand. Your wife *could have killed herself*. She could be successful next time. At the moment she isn't safe on her own."

"I want to see her. I want to take her home. I'm sure she'll be fine."

"You can see her, by all means, though only for a few minutes, she's calm now and we don't want her agitated again. But she can't come home yet. If necessary, we will section her."

"*Section her*! On what grounds?" He was indignant now. This would be a gross invasion of his freedom.

"On the grounds that she's a danger to herself and not in her right mind"

"My wife's perfectly sane."

"And yet you have no idea why she's done this thing."

He was momentarily lost for words. It was true, he had no idea. "I'd like to see her now."

"Yes. I'll take you. But we'll need to keep her at least overnight for observation. We can meet again in the morning and talk about what should be done next."

"I have to be in court tomorrow."

The nurse regarded him with raised eyebrows: "You do?"

"Yes, it's my work. I'm a judge."

"Then you might have to take time off work."

"No, I can't do that." It was out of the question.

The nurse blinked, "Then you wouldn't have been able to look after her anyway if she'd come home."

Oliver felt suddenly cold. "Look, can I speak with my wife? You haven't even let me see her yet. *I need to see my wife*."

"Certainly, but let me just check on her first. I'll be back in a few minutes."

The nurse left the room, leaving Oliver staring at the wall. Just before he was about to crack and enquire what could *possibly* be going on, the nurse returned and stood by the door looking very serious. "OK, Marjorie has agreed to see you, for a few minutes."

"She's my *wife*, nurse…of course she's agreed to see me."

The nurse looked at him darkly. "This way please." She led him down a short corridor to a ward with about twenty beds in it. "Your wife is the third on the left" she said, pointing to an area where long plastic curtains had been drawn around a bed. Oliver had expected a private room. Without any further acknowledgement to the nurse he walked with long strides and stepped between the curtains.

Marjorie was propped up with pillows, the bed bent up at an angle behind her. She looked up at him pleadingly as he came in, her face desperate and subservient. He'd never seen her like this, so forlorn and powerless, the life seemed drained out of her. Yet, somehow, despite this, her expression seemed oddly familiar. He couldn't place where from.

"Oliver...I'm so sorry." Silent tears flowed down her cheeks. Oliver stood awkwardly at the side of the bed, not knowing what to do, noticing that her left wrist and thumb were heavily bandaged.

"What is it? What's happened?" But she couldn't speak for crying. Oliver was aware of people all around, just behind the curtains. A man at the other side of the ward was calling repetitively: "Nurse, nurse..."

"What happened?" he asked again. She gestured mutely for him to sit beside the bed with her right hand, weakly searching for a composure that wasn't there. He waited tensely for the crying to stop. This was so...*awkward.*

"I, I don't know what came over me." She said, staring through a slit in the curtains, and avoiding his eye.

"But you *must* know."

"It….just came over me."

"What did?"

"I don't know. It was like a huge urge, an urge to cut down, to cut away, to cut through, to *feel. To feel the pain.*"

Oliver wondered what on earth she could be talking about. This wasn't the Marjorie he knew so well. "But why? Why in god's name? What pain?"

"I don't know. I don't know…" Still she was looking away.

"Was it because you'd argued with Hattie?"

Marjorie shook her head. No way she thought. It had been easy making it up with Hattie. Hattie had been wonderful in the way she'd rescued her from the floor, tying a tight tourniquet around her arm, then racing her to hospital, holding down her horn as she weaved through traffic. Hattie had held her close for hours in the hospital, stroking her hair and crying with her. She had refused to leave when they put in the stitches and afterwards had attended her every need. She had asked her how she was *now* and not focused on what had driven her to this. She had been gentle and sisterly. She'd been superb. There was no difficulty between them, there never had been, really. The issue wasn't Hattie. Their argument felt microscopic and ridiculous now. Marjorie looked up into Oliver's solemn face and his square jaw "No, that was nothing really, not that important."

"Then what was—that important?"

Marjorie stared away again. Nothing felt important now. She was washed up on the bank of a desolate shore. Numb also from the drugs they'd given her. Nothing felt important, except...except perhaps the cutting itself. She'd replayed the moment in her mind, over and over. She didn't know, either, why she'd cut herself. But she did know with lucid vividness that the cutting itself had felt intense and *vital.* For a whole second, before the horror of the situation had flooded over her, she had felt *connected.*

But now it was as if she'd looped back to how she'd been before, when she'd begun chopping the vegetables. She felt almost exactly the same as then, and yet, also, at the same time, everything had changed profoundly. She no longer knew herself. And this man sitting beside her—he was her husband. Yet she no longer knew him. He was demanding an explanation, but his questions came from another domain, another world.

Oliver had been watching intently. She seemed to be receding from him: "Marjorie, can you hear me?"

"Yes, I can hear you, and I can hear the man over there calling for the nurse, and neither of you, nothing, feels important, any more." She paused. "You asked me why I did it, and I've told you. I don't know, *I don't know*. Maybe I was bored. Maybe I wanted to somehow break through, for something to matter. Maybe I wanted….everything….to end."

Oliver looked horrified: "…Is this because you've been drinking?"

She looked at him directly now. "They told you then?"

"Yes, I had no idea…."

"It's not the drink"

"You have been drinking then?"

"Yes, far too much, but it isn't that Oliver. It's much bigger than that."

"Marjorie I don't think you know what you are saying. You're tired and confused. Let me get you out of here, let me take you home…"

"NO!" it was a sudden shout. He was taken aback by the force of her reply. She never raised her voice. Her face was stiff now. "No Oliver, no." she said, quieter now. "I can't come back anymore. Not now."

"Why ever not? I really don't understand. What is it? What's happened to you?"

"There is nothing for me anymore."

The nurse appeared at the slit in the curtains looking concerned. "Is everything OK here?" Neither of them responded. Oliver wanted to punch her.

"Mr Surret, it's time for you to go. It's the end of visiting time, anyway, and your wife's had a long day….haven't you dear?" She looked over to Marjorie who made a single firm nod. "You can come back tomorrow."

"Are you sure Marjorie? You want me to leave?" His voice had become oddly high.

Marjorie looked at him briefly: "Yes! I'm...sorry"

He stood up and bent over the bed meaning to kiss her but she turned away and his lips landed clumsily on her wet cheek. "I'll see you tomorrow…evening then. Take care dear." He turned, as if in a dream, out past the nurse without looking at her, out of the hospital.

It was dark and it took him some time to find his BMW in the car-park. On the road home he switched on the radio. It was full of discussion about the alien contact. People seemed to be talking about little else at the moment—but he couldn't concentrate on this. He knew it was momentous, but there was too much else going on. He turned off the radio and carried on driving in silence, carefully sticking to the speed limits on the motorway. It wouldn't do for a judge to be caught breaking the speed limit. As he turned into Willow View he had an unexpected flashback to Marjorie's face in the hospital when he'd first seen her, and suddenly he realised where else he'd seen that expression. That Kenyan man in court—his expression had been exactly the same: frightened and hopeless, awaiting judgement.

Willow View was dark and cold and the front door still open. There was blood on the carpet in the hallway. In the kitchen, blood and vegetables were mixed up on the chopping board, the table and floor. He looked around for the mop, not knowing where it was stored, eventually finding it under the stairs. Mopping the tiles in the kitchen he found the knife under the table. He took a washing up bowl full of water and detergent to the carpet in the hallway and tried to scrub out the stains there with a J-cloth, but he couldn't make them disappear completely and the bleach seemed to be taking colour out of the carpet. As he stood up some of the water in the bowl slopped over his suit. He carried the bowl back to the kitchen, poured the pink water down the sink, washed his hands and wondered what to eat.

He found some bread and stilton and made a sandwich on the chopping board he'd just cleaned. This would have to do. As he sat down to eat he noticed a line of blood along the edge of the table that he'd failed to see and two hot tears began to roll unexpectedly down his cheeks. He wiped them away quickly with his handkerchief, but more tears followed. It was alarming—his body was silently shaking. Uncontrollable waves of feeling were pushing upwards inside him, like waves of sea riding up the beach, each one trying to pitch higher over dry sand, reaching for the high tide mark. He tried to hold them back, recalling the last time he'd cried.

He'd been 13. He remembered the occasion well. He was newly arrived at his new school, boarding for the first time. He was up by the cricket pitch. An older boy had caught a beetle in the long grass and was slowly pulling away its legs, delighting in showing him. He watched, horrified, not knowing what to do, imagining what it must be like to be alive and thinking, but unable to move. Then, in a flood of indignation, and with tears in his eyes, he had rushed at the boy and tried to snatch the beetle from him. But the boy was much bigger than him and pushed him away with a scornful sneer: "Get away you wet creep."

Later that night, after lights-out in his dormitory, the other boys had chanted 'Blubber, blubber beetle lover' as he lay, in the darkness, tears flowing silently, pretending not to be affected.

The next day he spent some time finding another beetle, then brought it back so that he could demonstrate to his peers just how easily he could pull away its wriggling legs. After that the teasing stopped, and so too had his tears.

Now he leant forwards, put his head in his hands, stared down at the chopping board, and allowed a few more tears.

23

Calvin Broughton scrutinised the Pacific horizon with his high-spec military binoculars; nothing yet. He was in the pilot house of a Nordhavn 68 motor yacht. Beside him, at the helm, Stephen Dexter, the boat's owner, steered them towards Pitcairn. It ought to be coming into view at any moment and Calvin couldn't wait. For 60 hours now they'd been cruising at a steady 8 knots per hour with nothing but sea in every direction, not even another boat, or a plane in the sky. Just blue: clear blue sky, blue sea.

Stephen, a wealthy British expat living in French Polynesia, had agreed to his boat being used in return for certain tax concessions with the British Government—the precise details of which hadn't been revealed to Calvin. His crew were playing poker with the two marines under Calvin's command in the magnificent saloon below. The yacht was a wonder of craftsmanship, exquisitely furnished throughout in high-sheen teak and specialist fittings, a multi-millionaire's toy and a fully functional boat capable of crossing any ocean.

As they travelled Calvin had been in contact with the Mayor of Pitcairn who'd insisted that he would send out a longboat to fetch them when they arrived. "The waters round here are treacherous—better ye let us come for ye than risk going aground on the rocks." He'd also explained that the islanders, of whom there were only 67, had already constructed a fence and lockable gate around the site. "We thought it best to get on with things because ye still be a while off arriving—and by the time ye get here there'll be only hours to spare before the circle arrives. We wanted to make sure that if it does appear, no one can accidentally wander on to it." This all seemed very sensible. It was working out fine. All they'd have to do when they got there was guard the site.

Calvin looked again through the binoculars, and this time, with a rush of excitement, he spotted a tiny shimmering dot through the heat haze on the horizon. This was an adventure unfolding beyond his wildest imaginings. He already had a well-developed image in his mind of what lay ahead. It would be like in the holiday brochures—palm trees, and long beaches, sand soft as brown sugar, coral reefs teeming with brightly coloured fish; beautiful scantily clad young women with flowers in their hair, attending his every need....

Within the hour the ship dropped anchor and a longboat drew alongside. They passed down their bags and equipment to the outstretched hands of the islanders on the boat. In the largest bag a couple of rifles had been carefully concealed so as not to cause offence. They also handed down some containers of diesel, and other provisions the islanders had requested. Then Calvin and his men said goodbye to Stephen, who'd agreed to wait out the week with his crew, and climbed down onto the jostling boat.

Standing shakily as the boat bobbed in the swell they shook hands with the islanders. There were only three. George—a man of about sixty-five dressed in a rather old fashioned frayed tweed jacket, canvas trousers and boots. Luke, a middle aged man with a rough-hewn smoker's face and prematurely greying hair, sitting at the tiller, and Matilda, an attractive woman of about eighteen.

All three were friendly, and welcoming, and Calvin began discussing the arrival of the green circle that they were expecting later that day. But he could not prevent his eyes from straying to Matilda even when she wasn't speaking. It was a relief when she did speak because then he could focus on her without having to disguise his interest.

She was wearing a tight green blouse and a multi-coloured mid-length skirt made from myriad scraps of material all carefully sewn together so that it hugged her hips and waist. Her skin was a deep tan, and her bare feet were propped up casually in front of her, on the seat between them, allowing him occasional glimpses of darkness under the frilly rim of the skirt. She had a relaxed dimpled smile, and the whitest of teeth. The general effect was all set off, unbelievably, by a large red flower tucked casually behind one of her ears. When he looked at her, which was too frequently he feared, she took his breath away.

It was a perfect day, the hot sun reflecting invitingly on the changing colours of the sea. As they approached the island its detail came into focus. They could see a few houses on a narrow plateau about half way up the island, surrounded by vegetation. Higher up and at either end of the island were outcrops of grey and brown rocks. All along the coast steep cliffs swept down, almost vertically, to a white encircling band of breaking waves. Beyond the island in every direction was the immense empty sea.

The longboat docked at Bounty Bay, the only harbour on Pitcairn where a few islanders were waiting for them on the thin landing area. After a round of greetings, their bags were taken, together with the supplies and diesel, and the islanders started climbing energetically up the steepest path that Calvin had ever seen, almost a sheer cliff face. Calvin and his crew followed as best they could, but were soon out of breath. Seeing them struggle, Matilda dropped back slowing her pace to set them at ease.

"This we call the hill of difficulty. Yonder is the edge with Adamstown near behind in Walley. It ain't that far my dears when you're used t'it."

Calvin was entranced by the lilt in her voice. Her accent and manner of phrasing things seemed from a different age.

And now she was climbing alongside him and answering his enquiries about the island. He looked at her out of the corner of his eye and found, to his surprise, that she was already looking at him and held his look without embarrassment. He had time to sip her naked eyes and thick dark eyelashes.

"Ye like a sum whettles?"

"I'm sorry?"

She laughed "Ye like a sum whettles. It means: 'would you like some food'" she added, feigning a posh English accent,

"Oh, sure, that would be wonderful"

"Cooshoo, we've been maken whettles for ye and yower crew! We have Hampus Bumpus for ye."

"Hampus Bumpus?" said Calvin, breathing very heavily..

"It's Pitcarn's speshal dish—made from mashed bananas and manioc. Its cooshoo and delish, and we also have ower own drink for ye to wash it down." She smiled again at him with a bright twinkle in her eye.

"Your own drink?"

"Oh ah. We have ower own still, we make ower own drink." There was a breathless grunt of appreciation from one of the crew behind them.

The path had grown even stepper and they seemed to have arrived at 'the edge'. He watched as Matilda pulled herself effortlessly up a near vertical section of rock, her muscular thighs smooth against the roughness of the rock and her bare feet and hands finding tiny points of purchase. Having eased herself over the edge, she turned and offered her hand to him, grasping him firmly around the wrist and pulling strongly as he scrambled inadequately after her. Arriving at the top, exhausted and panting after the climb, but exhilarated now by his recent physical contact with Matilda, Calvin looked about him and tried to steady his breathing.

They were in a small clearing about three hundred metres long, behind it steep cliffs led upwards into mist. The others in the reception party were nowhere to be seen having gone ahead at pace. Scattered amongst the vegetation were half a dozen brightly decorated timber houses with steep sloping roofs, porches and verandas.

"This be Adamstown," said Matilda "Welcome to ye."

The houses surrounded a village green about thirty metres wide. Dominating the middle of the green was a two metre high circular fence.

“Yonder is where circle is due to arrive” she said, following his gaze. “And the fence we’ve built; and yonder is where the whettles’ll soon be ready.” She pointed to a grove of fruit trees with a line of tables laid out beneath them.

It was an idyllic setting in which to eat. Some of the trees were in bloom and there was a trellis along one side covered in bunches of ripening grapes. A middle-aged woman was hunched over a fire, near the tables, stirring a large cooking pot. She had thick black hair flowing down her bare back. In between the houses were plots of cultivated vegetables, amidst exotic vegetation. A group of children were playing tig, running between adults. It appeared that people were assembling to eat.

“Wa sing yourleg doing now?” said Matilda. “I can take ye to see the site for the circle or settle ye down to wait for the whettles with an iwi drink. What is te be?” Again that glint in her eye and the dazzling dimpled smile.

Calvin spoke briefly with his men to one side. He instructed them to go and wait for the meal whilst he went alone with Matilda to inspect the site. “There’s no need for us all to go, it’s looking good from this distance, and I think our presence here is probably just going to be a formality. I’ll get you if I need you.”

Matilda called over to a couple of young women, who’d been waiting to one side and who now approached, introduced themselves, and began talking to his men. Then she and Calvin started walking to the enclosure.

Calvin asked: “Do you know where our bags have been taken, Matilda?” He was wondering about the rifles hidden in the suitcase.

“Oh ah, I can take ye there if ye wish, youse have a nice cabin, but ‘tis further up the Walley and about a ten minute walk.” She looked at him mischievously “’bout twennie minutes for ye.” She concluded, smiling. “So there and back might make us late for the whettles.” Calvin considered this briefly. The rifles now seemed a ludicrous and embarrassing precaution and he could not think how he could bring them over without causing offence. These people were all so friendly and helpful, there was no need for a heavy display of authority.

"OK, no, that won't be necessary. But perhaps you could take me later?"

"That would be my *pleasure*". Was that a seductive emphasis on her last word, he wondered, and looked away for fear she might too easily read his thoughts.

They had arrived at the circular fencing. The islanders had done a good job. The timber was well sunk into the ground and the fencing looked solid. The circle was about ten metres wide with a single, thick, wooden gate locked by a large old fashioned padlock which looked to Calvin like it might have been salvaged from HMS Bounty, which he knew was the ship that had brought the first settlers to the island—mutineers—who'd arrived several generations before, and from whom the islanders were descended.

"Here's the key" said Matilda, pulling it from a concealed pocket in her skirt. "it's the only one, belongs to the mayor, ye'll meet him later. He said to give it to ye." Calvin took the key which was about 6 inches long and solid iron. He placed it into the lock and it turned easily. The gate swung open and they looked within. Inside was an unremarkable circle of freshly mown grass. All about the edge of the circle, facing towards the centre were make shift-chairs and benches behind a circle of rope fencing.

Calvin stepped over the rope and stood in the middle of the circle. He took out a portable tracker that he'd brought with him and checked the coordinates. After a few seconds he got the reading he was hoping for.

"You guys have done a good job—it should arrive bang in the middle!"

It was all in hand. The coordinates were right. The perimeter was well fortified, the gate strong. His job had been done for him.

"But what are the seats for?"

"Well it's up to ye, but we thought we might watch together when the circle arrives, later on this evenen. If that's OK with ye though..."

Calvin thought briefly. "Well I *think* that should be OK. The seats seem far enough back, people would be behind the rope, and it could be interesting. Do you not think it might be dangerous?"

"I nor believe, and we could keep the little sullens away"

"Little sullens?"

"Children to you."

"Well, OK, I think that should be fine…"

"Cooshoo, thank ye," she smiled at him radiantly. "I'll let the Mayor know then, I think everyone'll be pleased. We didn't want to miss this." She was obviously happy with this outcome and Calvin felt good for having pleased her.

They locked the gate and he pocketed the key. Then they walked back slowly to the tables under the fruit trees. His men were already drinking the local brew and were deep in conversation with the two young women whom, it appeared, had been designated as their hostesses.

The rest of the evening went by like a dream, and very fast. The islanders were attentive to their every need and served a series of sumptuous dishes which they ate by lamplight together, washed down by the intoxicating island brew. Calvin hardly noticed the food however, and hadn't much desire for alcohol. His desires were firmly focused elsewhere. Matilda had chosen to sit next to him and as there wasn't a lot of room he could feel her firm thigh pressed against his under the table.

With half an hour to spare, everyone rose. A few whisked off the children and the rest walked quickly to the site. Calvin unlocked the padlock with the ancient key. Then they all took seats and waited. Again Matilda sat next to him. The other two crew members sat separately, each with their young women.

Calvin and his crew had agreed that, if a circle arrived, they would divide the next seven days into shifts. Every day they'd each take an eight hour stretch to guard the circle from intrusion. Calvin reflected that this was probably now an academic precaution, and he regretted the fact that he'd drawn the short straw for the first shift, overnight. It would have been preferable not to have been bound to remain by the circle—especially as things seemed to be developing so well with Matilda. Or was he imagining this?

As the big event got closer the merriment and nervous anticipation around the circle heightened. The mayor, who'd been introduced to Calvin earlier, and seemed a responsible sort, was keen to make sure that everyone knew to remain in their seats, behind the rope, it might not be safe to be any closer.

With seconds to go they began a countdown, with everyone joining in.

PART 2

1

On time, the circles appeared, flicking silently into existence. Perfectly circular, about a metre wide, impossibly thin, luminous, and flowing out continuously from their middles with intricate fractal patterns in every hue of green. Their arrival was witnessed at every location, mostly by people standing behind secure fencing, with armed guards present.

One arrived in Cappadocia, Turkey, under a hover fly. He was moving his wings with great skill in the shifting air, hoping a female would notice. Left a little, right, up, down—back again. And seconds later back again. And again! Holding true to his precise 3D spot, his point in territory.

As the circle arrived beneath him he connected with a seed in Oxford.

...and revelled in the ease of the seed, its surrender to the flow, the suppleness of its myriad filament wings, its riding of the breeze, and its spiralling inner design.

On Pitcairn, the onlookers went silent, staring open mouthed. The circle definitely seemed of another world—just *so* smooth, so perfectly circular, It had a quality of being both artificially made and somehow organic; and the patterns were enticingly beautiful. Sometimes they were like ferns, or branching trees, sometimes rippling liquid or fish scales, or zebra backs, or finger prints…

For a long time they stared in silence. It was hard to take in, it's foreignness so absolute. How could it possibly have just arrived, from nowhere?

Eventually people began to talk in low whispers. It felt profane to talk loudly in its presence. Then one of the younger men rose from his seat and stepping over the rope moved hesitantly towards it.

"Get back!" barked the Mayor. "It's madness to get closer. We've no idea what its powers may be." The man immediately obeyed, returning bashfully to his seat. Calvin was relieved, the mayor had significant authority here and was doing his job for him.

After a few more minutes the mayor spoke again: "It's time for us to go home, let's not spoil this wonder by doing anything silly. There'll be other opportunities I'm sure, tomorrow and over the next seven days, for us to come again and have a supervised look. "You will allow that, won't you, Calvin?" he asked deferentially.

"Of course."

"So now, friends, let's leave. Calvin is staying to guard the site. We need to file out, carefully, following the fence. Make sure you don't cross the rope."

One by one the villagers rose and walked around the outer perimeter towards the gate, saying goodnight.

Calvin felt Matilda's warm hand slip into his.

"Would ye be liking me to stay with ye for company?" she whispered, close to his ear.

"I would," said Calvin, without hesitation. "Yes, I would."

The Mayor was last to leave the enclosure, he looked down at Matilda and Calvin sitting close together and said quietly: "I'll be leaving ye two then."

As soon as the Mayor had gone, closing the gate behind him, Calvin felt Matilda squeeze his hand. He was only too happy to make a squeeze in return. They sat together in silence watching the patterns, Calvin struggling with his inner desires and not quite knowing what to say or which beauty to focus on – the wondrous circle or the woman beside him. Both seemed impossibly exotic and intoxicating, to express interest in either seemed irreverent to the other.

The sounds of the villagers retiring home gradually receded into silence and the last orange and purple strands of the sunset began to fade into blackness and a panorama of southern stars. But they weren't looking at the sky, they both still continued to gaze at the circle in front of them—its glowing ever-changing patterns becoming more pronounced, in the growing darkness. Now that there were just the two of them, it seemed to have an even stronger presence.

Calvin was intensely aware of Matilda's closeness, her hand warm in his, her wonderful loose limbed body comfortably relaxed beside him, the smell of her fresh young womanhood, and although he had only just met her, and scarcely knew anything about her, he felt as if he had known her all his life. The moment had a wholesome completeness that he wouldn't have imagined possible and was loath to compromise. But at the same time there was now an aching tension in his genitals...

It was Matilda who broke the long silence: "It's darking and I be getting cold." She said in her sweet lilt, and with a slight shiver. "What say ye we make our way up the walley to your hut?"

Calvin's heart raced. Was this a proposal? Could he abandon his watch?

"Ye could lock up here and no one need know—I won't tell." She smiled. "Then I can show ye your hut and we can get ourself warm together, and ye can come back in the early morning afore your watch be ended." She smiled at him conspiratorially and he looked into her dark brown eyes and felt himself falling, as if into a trance. There was now no possible alternative course of action. But still he couldn't speak, consumed by her eyes.

"Would it please ye?" she said simply, still looking at him brightly.

"It would please me very much."

Still holding hands they stood up and passed through the gate which Calvin locked behind them, fumbling with the key. Then they walked quietly along the path, past the place where they'd all eaten. There were one or two lights still on in the houses but it seemed most people had already gone to bed, exhausted from the excitement of the day.

Matilda led them up a narrow track past the last of the houses and up a hill. He could hardly make out anything in the darkness and was finding it difficult to walk with his restricted erection. But Matilda knew exactly where she was going and guided him safely, holding his hand, alerting him to the tricky twists and bumpy sections of the path. They hardly spoke and Calvin was intensely aware of the depth of silence around them. There was only the faint distant sound of the sea, and although he couldn't see it, he sensed that he could feel it stretching out in all directions around them.

Finally, after what seemed like an eternity to Calvin, they arrived at a small hut. In the darkness outside he could just make out a wooden veranda with decorated pillars and, presumably, a vast view of the sea. Matilda pushed open the door, which wasn't locked, and lit a small paraffin lamp at the entrance. The room was simple, with a two person sofa, a small kitchenette, a dining table and large windows on all sides. His bags had been stowed in one corner.

But she didn't pause in the living room. She continued to lead him by the hand into the bedroom, her fingers tightening around his wrist.

"I think ye should take your clothes off now. And be quick about it." She said with a giggle, abandoning his wrist and peeling her blouse upwards in a flourish to reveal her bare breasts, and upstretched arms, and her smiling face.

The shock of this sent a surging wave of lust through Calvin's body. Right in front of him, waiting for him, was the most beautiful woman he'd ever seen. He was entranced by everything about her. Her easy smile and grace, her freedom, her playfulness, her abandon. She stood, arms still high above her head, her glossy black hair tumbling back in bouncing curls, then hurled her blouse off to one side and sat backwards onto the bed.

He fumbled with his shoes, then his trousers and underpants, unable to manipulate his fingers with precision. She was giggling now on the bed, watching him, and holding her dress up for him to see her nakedness beneath and her widening thighs. With his underpants still half down one leg he threw himself clumsily on top of her, relishing at last the feel of her bare skin against his.

She laughed, uninhibitedly, rolled him over onto his back, placed her knees on either side of him pushing his arms outwards and pinning him down with her full weight. Again she looked him straight in the eyes.

"Got ye!"

He was consumed by her beauty and abandon.

"I think ye need to be inside me."

Her head came down and their lips met and her hot tongue penetrated him. And now he could feel the outside of her wet cunt on his straining cock, sliding first up and down, up and down, lubricating him with practised ease, then, at last, encompassing him inside her, her inner warmth tightly sealing around him. She pulled up from his lips, arched her back and rode him, as if she was riding a horse, moving up and down in the saddle, the inside of her thighs gripping the outside of his. Her cunt tightening whenever it was at the base of his cock and then softening and loosening as it rose, only to swallow down again with a squeeze. It was like she was milking him for all his juice, thirsty to suck in his very last drop and keep it deep inside her.

Calvin wrestled momentarily with some notion about trying to make her come with him, before he was spent, then realised this cause was hopeless. He had no hope of exerting any control now against the waves of exquisite pleasure and heightening tension that were flooding through him. He lay back and surrendered at last to the relief on its way, to her quickening plunges, glorying in the musky fragrance in her hair as it tumbled down onto his face and chest, then lifted again, then tumbled, then lifted, then tumbled, then stayed, and now she was all over him, clinging him tight, squealing with delight, their sweating skins shaking, tightly sealed together, their life forces mixing, in an ecstatic, tumultuous, eruption, once and for all.

2

Lou Rimey was in the bath trying to catch a moment's relaxation after a 20 hour day, when Theo rang. His wife held a phone into the fog: "Sorry to disturb you, Lou, it's Theo."

Lou's huge belly rose up through the bubbles like a low tide sand dune. He wiped his hand on a towel and took the phone. "Hi Theo, everything alright?"

"Oh sure thing Lou, Armageddon's just a side-show."

"Well I…"

"Lou, can you do something for us?"

"Uh…yes."

"Get some of your guys from the defence department to dig up a circle so we can examine it. See if bulldozer can lift it onto a lorry. Then take it to a military base so we can have a good look, see what it's made of—we might be able to just destroy these things or move them to safer places…needs to be top secret though."

Lou liked this idea. He'd been thinking along similar lines himself…

Three hours later he called Theo back: "It was unbelievable. We got a bulldozer inside the compound and lined it up alongside the circle. But it scooped into nothing—it went *right through* the circle, leaving it untouched, the patterns just kept moving, totally unaffected. That circle wasn't made of anything! Nothing we know about anyhow. Not solid or liquid, maybe it's anti-matter or something. It's like it wasn't there, and yet there it was—luminescent greens flowing outwards—hanging unscathed in the air, with a scoop of soil missing from underneath it. I don't get it Theo. We tried a few times, but it was hopeless. So we put the soil back to make it look like the circle was resting on the ground, so people wouldn't suspect anything. Weirdest thing I've ever seen..."

3

After Brian left, the guards body-searched Mohammed, and directed him to the back of the long line. Ahead of him the queue twisted from side to side, cordoned between metal barriers until it disappeared through a doorway in the distance.

He looked around, trying to assess the situation. The room was huge and stuffy, with brash strip lighting and grubby walls. There was nowhere to sit. Around the edges of the room, behind the barriers, were uniformed guards.

Don't look any of them in the eye.

Apart from the door he'd just passed through and the door at the end of the queue there were no other doors to the room.

Don't think about escaping.

There were poster instructions on the walls.

'Smoking is forbidden'

'The use of cameras, tape recorders, mobile phones or any other type of audio or visual recording device is forbidden'.

'The UK has a proud tradition of providing a place of safety for genuine refugees. However, we are determined to refuse protection to those who do not need it, and will take steps to remove those who are found to have made false claims.'

'If we have refused to give you permission to stay in the UK and your appeals (if any) against our decision have failed, you must return to the country that you came from. If you do not return voluntarily, we will enforce your removal and we may detain you until we do this.'

High up in one corner of the room a flickering screen was endlessly re-running a video. Each time it came round it was in a different language with different subtitles. He couldn't understand any of the languages but it was the same repeating pictures: and much of the film seemed to be about airports and people signing papers and smiling as they boarded planes. In the credits he read the words 'International Organization for Migration' and 'Voluntary assistance to go home'.

The woman in front was heavily pregnant and clutched grimly onto the metal railing as they shuffled slowly forwards. In front of her was a group of lighter skinned men, with black hair in short crew cuts, leather jackets and two day old beards. Then there was a young girl who looked about fifteen, probably of African origin. She was crying incessantly and appeared alone. Two men behind him were wearing floppy white clothing. One had a red-brown stain along one leg of his baggy trousers. It looked like it was probably dried blood.

Suddenly he was doubled up, coughing again with spasms in his stomach and great rippling heaves coming up his throat. He fell to his knees and the queue on either side of him drew back in alarm. He couldn't stop coughing. The room started to spin. The guards were over him.

He came to on his back in a small bright room.

Get into kneeling position

He tried, but his body didn't respond. A woman in a white coat was leaning over him talking loudly. "...needs medical help—ah he seems to be coming round—you won't be able to question him today though."

Two guards joined the woman peering down at him, their faces upside down. One of them said: "Speak English?"

"Yes" the word somehow bubbled up through his nausea.

Smile!

"Where do you live?"

"Uganda"

The guard gave him an upside down smile "Where in this country?"

"Nowhere."

"Where were you last night then?" He seemed to be frowning now. Mohammed tried to keep smiling.

"On the plane, sir." He started to cough again, his body twisting with the spasms.

"We'd better put him in temporary accommodation for the night. We can question him first thing tomorrow."

The woman was the only one looking at him now. "We're going to put you up for the night and bring you back tomorrow. You'll be able to get medical help where you're going. Then you can apply for asylum tomorrow."

Head still throbbing he was wheeled into the back of a large van, which drove off swiftly.

Perhaps I am going to Electric House

Twenty minutes later the van arrived at a building in a back street. He was led by the guards through a front door, which was immediately locked behind them, past a reception area and down a narrow corridor. Off the corridor he was shown to a small room with just enough space for a bunk bed. A man was lying asleep on the bottom bunk. A barred window looked out onto a high wall. The guards told him they'd be back for him the following morning.

As he climbed into bed he noticed the headline of a paper on the windowsill.

"Alien circles arrive! The world stares in awe."

It made no sense at all, and he had no interest in reading more. This was the first bed that he'd been in for several years and he was beyond exhausted.

4

Pete Flavier paused by the front door, listening keenly. No sound from within other than the steady ticking of the grandfather clock. His parents were still safely asleep. They would be furious when they found out—but it was too late to change his mind now. From the first astonishing moment when the idea came to him, a few days previously, he had gone over and over the plan, and was resolved in his intentions. It would be his claim to fame, perhaps the seminal moment of his life. He closed the door carefully behind him and tiptoed to the garage.

He was excited and fearful now in equal measure—a cocktail of feelings he was familiar with—but this morning it was amplified—his heart pounding and his breathing tight with an adrenaline rush of anticipation and foreboding. Forcing himself to concentrate, he focussed on the panel of electronic numbers that controlled the multiple locks on the reinforced steel door to the garage. One mistake would trigger the alarms.

It was early in the morning with only the faintest suggestion of the sun's presence in the east, far under the horizon. He'd calculated his timing carefully, as early as possible, with just enough light from the rising sun.

The heavy door clicked open and he eased inside, his movement activating the automatic lighting. The garage was superbly equipped with an array of tools. Parked along one side was a white Aston Martin DB6, its beautiful tail curved upwards in a sculptured celebration of power. But for once he scarcely glanced at the car, his focus on something quite different, though no less expensive or powerful. It waited for him on the workbench, freshly primed with hydrogen peroxide, its harness positioned in readiness. He eased it carefully onto his back, tightened the straps around his chest, shoulders and waist and fixed the controls into place in front of him. Then he pulled on his helmet and made for the door.

Outside the garage, he turned and walked as fast as he could towards the park. The launch spot he'd chosen was a small mound three hundred yards from the newly constructed perimeter fence. As he'd hoped, not many people were up. A few had begun to assemble, but their attention was focused on the fencing and the guards surrounding it. He could just make out the glow of cigarettes in the gloom. So far so good—no-one had seen him.

Quickly he turned on the various switches, checked the straps, held onto the two controlling levers sticking out like extra arms in front of him, bent his knees slightly and fired the ignition.

The jetpack burst into life and a torrent of superheated steam blasted vertically downwards behind him in a deafening roar. He took off almost instantly and was dragged forwards, his legs trailing behind him as he headed at speed, downhill, towards the enclosure.

He had a maximum of 33 seconds of fuel and had calculated that the trip would take 28 seconds. This left 5 seconds lee-way, but only if he shifted it. A stopwatch on one of the controls in front of him was already counting down from 33. But there wasn't time to look at that.

Although he was used to the 800 horsepower machine on his back, it nonetheless took his breath away, as ever. Already he was twenty feet up, and gaining speed.

All eyes of course, were now on him—the machine made an immense 150 decibel noise. But whilst it attracted attention the noise also helped to confound. The guards, who were armed, had no time to take in the situation, let alone react, and stood stunned and rooted to the spot as the soles of his boots hurtled above them and over the fence.

Banking and spiralling down on the other side he could see the glowing green circle waiting below like a tiny heliport. One last extra strong braking blast of steam and he was dangling in a hiatus two feet above it.

He took a deep breath then relaxed down gently on the flowing greens. His first adventure of the day was over.

5

Mohammed was woken from a fitful sleep by banging on the door.

Get into kneeling position.

The staff showed him a self-service breakfast area. Cautiously, making sure that it was acceptable, he helped himself to a bowl of tinned fruit and some tea. His hands were shaky and it was hard to swallow. He was about to ask about medical help when a set of guards arrived saying that they had come to take him back to Lunar House. He grabbed his tiny bag.

At Lunar House he was led through a back entrance into a waiting area and, after an hour's wait, called into a room where they took photographs of him.

This is for when I am dead

Then they brought a black pad and told him to press his fingers down onto it.

My hands in the electrified water. They're going to electrocute me.

He hesitated, and the guard laughed. Pushing one of his hands onto the inky screen. "It's to get your fingerprints."

One by one he pressed down his swollen fingers.

Then they escorted him into a small room with two guards sitting behind a desk who motioned him to sit in the high chair in front of them.

"Do you speak English?"

Mohammed nodded

Smile!

"Let's start with your full name then."

This is it, this is where it begins. Always with questions.

"Mohammed Marimbey"

"No middle name?"

"No sir."

One of the guards was asking him questions the other was writing down his answers in long hand. Mohammed watched as he wrote Marimbay rather than Marimbey. He didn't dare correct him—he was already too alarmed at how the interview had begun. Back home you began conversations with courteous remarks, building up slowly and gently to the matter at hand. It was ill-mannered to go straight to business. These men seemed very rude. He kept the smile on his face.

The questions always end in torture

"Where are you from?"

"Uganda"

"And when did you arrive in this country?"

"Yesterday, sir." Didn't they know already?

"How did you get here?"

"By airplane"

"Let me see your passport"

"I don't have one, sir".

"Where is it then?"

"I don't know, sir"

"Did you destroy it?"

"No, sir."

"Do you have *any* documents with your name on?"

"No, sir."

"Then how did you get here?"

"By plane sir."

Smile!

The guard looked at him sternly. "This isn't a joke! How did you get here without documents?"

He's about to flip

The pain in his stomach was back.

"The woman who was…with me… she had them."

"Who was she?"

"I don't know, sir"

"You don't *know*?"

"No sir. She was called Jane."

"So *you do know*—she was called Jane. Jane who?"

"I don't know sir."

"How did she get documents for you?"

"I don't know, sir"

"How did you get past customs?"

"I don't know, sir"

The guard sat back, frowning. "You must know more than that! How come this woman brought you on the plane?"

"I don't know. I was in a safe house and one of the guards threw me out."

"A safe house?"

"Yes. It's a kind of prison, in Uganda" The taxi driver hadn't known that either.

"And a guard threw you out?"

"Yes sir, he made me fall into the street. Then some other men put me in a car and took me to a place, I think it was a hotel. Then the next day, I think it was the next day, they took me to the airport and I met this woman. It was the first time I ever met her, I…"

"Wait a minute. Why did the guard make you 'fall into the street'? Why did he do that?"

"I don't know sir."

"So you don't know how you got out of prison, you don't know how you got to this country, you don't have a passport or identity documents, you don't know the full name of the person who brought you here. Do you have any other information at all?"

It's coming, they are about to begin. Questions, torture.

"No sir"

"You must know more…"

"Yes sir"

Never argue. Smile.

"What else do you know then?"

"Nothing sir."

The guard closed his eyes for a moment. Mohammed looked around the room. No way out.

He's going to shout, then it will all follow. He's like Muhindo.

"So why were you in prison?"

"Because I was in the FDC"

"What's the FDC?"

"The opposition party, in Uganda. They arrested me after a talk I'd given. They locked me up in Makindye Barracks. Then after a few—months—they transferred me to the safe house. Then I came here..."

"And you want to claim asylum?"

"I don't know, sir." At home the asylum was where mad people were locked up. But that taxi driver, he'd said asylum is what happened when people escaped. Did claiming asylum mean going to Electric House?

The guard rolled his eyes. "Do you want to be sent back to Uganda?"

"No sir." They would arrest him at Entebbe Airport.

Back in the dark. I'm no more than the sole of Muhindo's boot.

"Then you want to claim asylum. Since you say you've no documents at all and no other reason to stay here—that's the only way you can stay here."

"Yes sir."

Smile.

The guard who'd been questioning him creased his nose and turned to his colleague: "Get all that down? What little there was?"

"Yes"

"Then give him the form and let's be done with this one." He turned again to Mohammed. "Do you write?"

"Yes sir"

"Then sign here." He passed him the form and a pen, pointing to where he should sign.

Just sign, or there will be trouble.

Mohammed signed. Usually signing meant the end of a session. He was led out into a different waiting area. Two hours later he was on a van with ten other 'asylum seekers'. One of them told him in broken English that they were being sent up north, to somewhere called Sunderland, to await trial, and that they were all lucky not to have been sent straight to a detention centre.

Detention centre—another word for prison. Like Safehouse, Electric house. Makindye.

Four hours later the door was unlocked and they were met by a white woman at the door of a semi-detached house in a long street of similar houses. It had a grey slate roof and a peeling pebbledash exterior. The woman said: "Come in, I'm from the company that owns the house. I'm your key worker."

Key worker, what is this? Does she keep the keys?

The tiny entrance smelt of wet leather and mice. The woman gave them each some vouchers that she said could be spent in a local store. Mohammed asked her if he could see a doctor and she wrote down an address for him. Then she led him along a corridor to a double room, smelling of mould. A man who looked African was sitting in a chair by one of the beds wrapped in a blanket. Mohammed put his bag on the other bed. The woman said goodbye and left. He sat down on the bed, his head throbbing.

The man looked at him: "Where from?"

"Uganda. You?"

"Somalia."

"How long have you been here?"

The man squinted up his eyes: "No Engleesh."

They tried other languages, but found none in common.

None of the other occupants in the house had languages in common with him either. Over the next few hours he managed to piece together a few more details about them, though. There was a Kurdish woman from Turkey, a woman from Eritrea, two men from Sudan, a young boy from Afghanistan who looked fifteen but said he was eighteen, and a man, possibly from Iraq, who didn't speak at all. He learnt that, early that morning, four people who'd been living in the house had been taken off, handcuffed, in a van. No one knew where they'd been taken.

6

Fergus had watched, mesmerised, as the circles arrived, then given a series of interviews culminating in a late night discussion program where he'd argued against 'irrational fears'. He finally got home to bed, exhausted, at 4.00 am. Now what seemed like only minutes later his mobile was already ringing. He flicked open the cover: "Hello."

"Fergus?" It was his boss, the director of SETI.

"Uh yes," he glanced at his watch as the last few days flooded back into consciousness, "You know it's *6.30 am*?"

"Sure, but there've been some developments. Two actually"

"There have?"

"Yeah, first is we just got a strange report through from Toronto about the animals they've been experimenting with."

Fergus sat up in bed: "What did they find?"

"Well there isn't a lot to go on yet. Apparently they tried various animals, including mice. They haven't been able to discern any worrying physical effects on any of them, but the mice have been acting peculiar.

"Peculiar."

"Yeah, peculiar"

"What do you mean?"

"Well it's one mouse, actually."

"What about it?"

"It started jumping."

"Jumping?"

"Yeah, jumping".

"Isn't that what mice do?"

"Yes, but this was unusual amounts of jumping, Fergus. Over and over. Then it jumped right off a lab table. The guy doing the test said he'd never seen anything like it in twenty years of working with mice. Normally they have more sense, apparently."

"Why did it do that?

"I have no idea"

"Was it OK?"

"Well, yes, but that's hardly the point Fergus".

"You're not suggesting it might put a stop to trying out the circles with people?"

"No, I'm not, Fergus, *because that has already happened.* That's the second thing. We've just received a report that an American citizen has entered a circle."

"How did he manage that?"

"He used a jetpack."

"He did? Wow! We didn't expect that."

"No, indeed. Apparently his father's a billionaire and he'd been testing out the jetpack for him. Early this morning he flew over the fence and dropped onto a circle in San Francisco. His name is Pete Flavier"

"What happened?"

"Well, we're not sure. He also seems to be acting strange, and he's been rushed to quarantine. I had instructions directly from the US president to call you. He wants you to visit him, urgently, to assess. Can you do that?

"Yes…but *what*…the *president*? Why me?"

"PR. The president thinks that the Free the Circles Campaign will trust you. He thinks if you do it there won't be bad publicity. People won't think there's been a cover up, or the dangers exaggerated."

"And how has this young man been acting strange?"

"Well, apparently he's fully conscious, and some of the time he seems quite normal. But he also has phases when he has been acting weird. He...er..."

"Yeah?"

"He keeps licking the tip of his nose."

Fergus was unprepared for the high security at the hospital. There were hundreds of police monitoring the entrance and fending off reporters. It took some time to get them to take him seriously. After triple-checking his authorisation and ID, six armed policemen escorted him to a side entrance where he was thoroughly frisked.

Once inside the building he was escorted along several dreary linoleum corridors to the ward for tropical diseases. There he was given a white coat, a mask, a cap for his hair, elasticated covers for his shoes, and rubber gloves. Then he was taken to a tiny room for an interview with a consultant.

The consultant, a man in his mid-sixties, was also wearing protective clothing. His face was almost entirely obscured by his mask but Fergus could see his brow was heavily furrowed and his dark watery eyes, magnified by black horn rimmed spectacles, fixed grimly on Fergus.

"…on no account take off your mask, or get too close to him, and certainly do not interfere with the plastic tent," he said, his voice muffled by the mask. "We've no idea what infections this foolish young man may be carrying. It could be a killer virus, or something we don't even have a name for. It could be enough to see off our species. He's in deep trouble. We're all in deep trouble. If you want my opinion: his crime is akin to stealing the smallpox vaccine..."

Fergus cast his eyes around the room. Bland white walls returned his gaze.

"…You see it's possible that infections are already at large *in this hospital.* In the process of getting him here 23 people—all now in quarantine—were in close contact with him. There are many more outside who had more distant contact. We have a potential pandemic here and are keeping further contact with him to a minimum. If it hadn't been for the president I'd never have agreed to you seeing him—I've spent all morning fending off my colleagues and the press. Moreover, once you're out of the room, we'll need to decontaminate you, then we'll need to quarantine you…"

As Fergus absorbed this the doctor continued to glare at him, as if to check his message had struck home. He felt uneasy and off balance. His earlier excitement at being intimately involved with the first ever alien contact—something that he'd waited for as long as he could remember—was being undermined by this man's catastrophic pessimism.

"OK," he said, reluctantly. It felt strange talking through his mask, as if his capacity to express a view was being artificially restricted. "But how is he?"

The furrows on the doctor's brow deepened.

"Hard to say, and much too early. We've had to keep our tests to a minimum. Physically he *seems*…normal. What tests we have done show no signs of any infection or any physical problem. He was a fit young man in the prime of health."

"Was?"

"Yes, *was*. There's no telling quite what he is now. When he first came in here he seemed possessed, in some sort of dis-associative state. We had to restrain him because he kept struggling to get out of the tent. Then, occasionally, he became quite coherent. But he keeps talking about lights in his head, and sometimes he can't even talk. Just makes odd sounds. Or his words are slurred. Other times we can understand what he's saying but it doesn't make much sense—and he keeps licking his nose."

"Yeah, I heard about that."

"So we think he's delusional, maybe schizophrenic, and we've lined up some Risperidone. He's already on a strong tranquiliser. His records prior to landing on the green circle show no history of any mental issue and his parents, whom we haven't allowed to see him, have told us he's pretty sane, though a bit wild. Apparently his hobby is doing daredevil stuff. So we think the causes of his symptoms must be exogenous. He could be having a psychotic incident or it could be much worse. We're not ruling out anything. He could have been invaded by an alien species."

Fergus felt suddenly irritated. Couldn't anyone see that this might be an opportunity rather than a challenge? Theo was full of fear, the press were full of fear, and now this consultant was more of the same.

"Why haven't you let his parents visit?"

"Because, as I've been trying to tell you, we're trying to limit the spread of infection. It hasn't been *easy* to stop them, though, because they're rich and influential. But this is a matter of national importance."

"But wouldn't they be an extra source of information?"

"We have our biggest source of information strapped to a bed a few feet from this room. There are many more tests we haven't done yet. Only once those are completed will we consider personal visits. We've enough to handle, as it is, without his parents throwing their weight about."

"And why did you put him on tranquillisers?"

"Because he was agitated, what do you think?" The doctor's voice was contemptuous now, and his face redder around his mask.

"And now you're wanting to give him more drugs, and powerful ones at that. How will you know what is due to the effects of drugs and what is due to the circle?"

"We know what the side effects of the drugs are."

"Yes, but we have no idea how a drug may interact with him after this experience. Giving him drugs will just muddy the waters and make it harder to find out what's happened. Why make things more complicated?"

The doctor looked at him in exasperation: "Mr O'Donnel, why don't you do your job and I'll do mine?"

Fergus looked away, collecting his thoughts. The carpet still had zig-zag marks from recent vacuuming. He looked back at the doctor, angry now. "No doctor. I'll do my job and *you will take orders from me*. I'm here under instructions from the *President*. You are not to administer further drugs without my agreement. I can't carry out a proper assessment if his behaviour is complicated by drugs. I also want you to contact his parents immediately and arrange for them to visit, so we can talk to them and they can support him... and now I want you to take me to him."

The consultant's eyeballs bulged behind his conspicuous glasses. There was a long pause. Fergus felt his own anger coursing through him, making space in his chest. It felt good.

"OK, OK, I'll take you to him." The doctor was clearly nonplussed; he hadn't thought Fergus had this in him—having already dismissed him on the basis of the foolish broadcasts he'd been making all over the media. "You can have a few minutes," he added as an afterthought, as they walked out of the room.

"No doctor, I'll take as long as I want."

A few yards down the corridor was a room guarded by three armed policemen. The consultant beckoned him to an observation window.

Inside the room Pete Flavier was lying flat on his back. Around his waist and chest were canvas securing straps. The whole bed was contained in a thick plastic tent. Pete looked about twenty-five with straight brown hair in a low fringe. There were two guards inside the room as well, on either side of the bed, both armed and wearing masks. Pete was looking up at the window but didn't seem to see Fergus.

"OK, you can go in."

Fergus put his head around the door.

"Pete, is it alright if I come in and talk to you?"

Pete came to with a start. He looked alarmed, but didn't say anything.

Fergus tried again: "Do you mind if I come in?"

"N-a-ooh."

Was that a 'no'? Fergus entered the room and stood by the only available chair, some distance from the bed.

The young man stared at him fixedly.

"Mind if I sit down?"

"Sy-ure". The word seemed to have been dragged across a foreign frontier. But he did at least appear to be talking and responding. Fergus settled into the seat.

"I'm Fergus O'Donnel, I've come to talk to you about your experience."

Pete stayed silent. Fergus looked at him through the plastic. He had a handsome face and a nicely ironed dark green shirt. Around his neck was a gold necklace that contrasted pleasantly with the shirt and his tanned skin. But he looked exhausted and frightened.

"Why have you got me tied me up?"

"It isn't me, Pete, it's the hospital. I'm not from the hospital, or from the police. I am from SETI."

"Seti?"

"The Search for Extra Terrestrial Intelligence. I'm here to see if we can start to work out what effect these circles have, I..."

Pete interrupted: "Can you get these straps off?"

"Will you cooperate if we do?"

"Yes!"

Fergus reflected briefly. "OK." He turned to the consultant still standing by the door.

"Take these straps off."

The doctor looked at him with derision. It was bad enough to have his authority undermined by this man privately—far worse in a public context.

"Don't be ridiculous. He could struggle out of the tent."

"You heard him. He says he'll co-operate. I choose to trust him. Take the straps off."

"Well I want it on the record that this is against my express permission…"

"Sure, I take full responsibility. Take the straps off."

Reluctantly the doctor slid his hands into two plastic tubes that led into the tent and ended in rubber gloves. Using the gloves he undid the straps. Fergus and Pete watched silently.

"OK, now leave us alone," said Fergus "and the guards too. You can watch through the window if you have to."

"I hope you know what you are doing."

So do I. Fergus thought to himself. So do I.

7

When Mohammed first surfaced into consciousness he couldn't remember where he was. He couldn't be under the floorboards because there was an orange light filtering through a tattered curtain ...and he was in bed.

Slowly the events of the last few days came back, displacing the dark pit horrors of his dreams and bringing some small relief.

Don't be a fool, there's no hope here.

The man from Somalia was still fast asleep, breathing deeply. Careful, so as not to disturb him, Mohammed swung his legs out of the bed and moved silently to the door and tried the handle. It wasn't locked! He picked up his bag and tiptoed into the corridor, scarcely daring to breathe. The front door wasn't locked either! The keyworker must have forgotten to lock it...this was his chance...

Don't even think it.

He stepped out, closed the door gently behind him and looked up and down the street. A row of lampposts shone in pools of mist and a few of the houses had lights on but mostly the street was dark and there was no one about. It must be early morning. He stepped onto the wet pavement and began walking as fast as he could glancing behind and tucking in his shirt against the bitter cold.

You'll pay for this

At the end of the street was a main road with traffic. He glanced again behind him—no-one was following—then joined the road, aware how grey everything was, grey granite walls and slated roofs, dark grey tarmac on the road, grey pavements. Back home there was more colour, vibrancy. People would stop in the streets to talk and laugh, and they would know your business. But here the few pedestrians he met passed by without a glance. They all seemed so preoccupied here, and purposeful. And most of them were alone inside shiny modern cars, staring ahead. He began to feel hopeful that he might just pass through un-noticed, that he might somehow find a way to disappear and hide somewhere…

But after two hours of walking he began to tire. His leg was hurting badly and there didn't seem to be anywhere to hide. There were buildings and people everywhere and it was bitterly cold. He would need some kind of shelter, and he would need food and money. He had the money the taxi driver had given him, of course, but that wouldn't last for ever. He would have to find some way of making money but how was he going to do that, especially when he still felt so ill?

It's hopeless, you'll never escape.

At the corner of the street he saw a red telephone box like ones he'd seen back home. Perhaps he could phone the taxi driver. Perhaps he would help, maybe he could hide him. He'd seemed hostile at first but then later he'd seemed kinder…

The Johnson breakfast was in full swing when Brian's phone rang. He'd been trying to read about the green circles in the paper in the midst of a cacophony of distractions— Tilly was feeding sloppy spoonful's of honey nut clusters to Humphrey and Kimberly, Rowan, still in his tiger-suit, was demonstrating how many Weetabix he could eat without a sip of milk, Laptop was doing her mal-nourished-cat meow routine and Michelle was rushing about packing Rowan's lunch box and rounding up homework.

He pressed the green button. "Hello."

"Is that Mr….Brian?" It was an African accent.

"Yes...But Brian's my first name. This isn't a sales call is it?"

There was a pause at the other end "It's Mohammed, Mohammed Marimbey." Brian's mind went blank, then the memory of Mohammed's upper torso flooded back.

"Mohammed!…You OK?"

"...No..." It sounded like he was outside, Brian could hear traffic.

"Why, what's up?

"...I ran away"

"Why? Where from?"

"From a house, in Sunderland, I think they're going to send me back, to Uganda."

"Naah, they wouldn't do that mate, not with your injuries." That much was certain. There was a sob at the other end.

"Where are you now?"

"In the street, in a phone box."

"How long ago did you run away?" He gestured to Rowan to keep the noise down. He was dry-munching with exaggeration, like a horse eating gravel.

"Just a couple of hours."

"You weren't... locked up or anything?"

"No...but I think they forgot."

"And you were in an ordinary house?"

"Yeah...I think so." He didn't sound convinced. Brian suddenly remembered the 'safe' houses.

"You'll be fine, mate, just go back. They don't lock people in houses here. They're probably just keeping you there 'till they find something better...whaow, just a minute" He put the phone down to alert Tilly to the fact her bowl was tipping and milk was slopping down her front

"...You still there?"

"...Yes"

Just go back to the house, mate. I'm sure you'll be fine. They won't send you back with your injuries. Have you seen a doctor yet?

"No."

"*What?* Why ever not? *You need to see a doctor mate.* Go back and demand to see a doctor. I'm amazed they haven't arranged that yet..." There was a long pause.

"You need to go back mate, go back to the house and demand to see a doctor…you'll be fine, I promise…we look after people in this country. The system's good here, honest."

There was another long pause then "OK then." and the line went dead. Brian thought to call him back but Rowan had gone red and looked like he was about to explode Weetabix everywhere.

After the kids had been packed off to school, Michelle asked about the phone call. She listened really intently as he explained all about Mohammed and looked sad when he'd finished. "That poor man, do you think he'll be OK?"

"Sure, of course he will, they'll let anyone into this country."

"I hope so… sounds terrible what they did to him in Uganda."

"They will. His injuries were horrendous." Brian picked a fleck of Weetabix off the table. "It's as if I can still see them."

Michelle gave him one of her caring-and-impressed looks. "Well, well done Brian, I wouldn't have thought…I mean… *I'm so glad* you helped him."

8

Pete re-positioned himself on the bed as the guards and medical personnel left the room and breathed a long sigh of relief. "Thanks man—that was driving me nuts."

Fergus smiled. "How long have you been like that?"

"I—not sure—been away some of the time—hard to tell"

"Been away?"

"Sort of. When I'm in the green."

"What green? The green circle?"

"No man, the green light, it's in my head."

"You have a green light in your head?"

"Yeah…its here." Pete pointed to his right temple. "Just behind here. Sometimes it's green, sometimes blue. It's like it's in the corner of my vision—but I think it's inside my head. Can you see a green light over there?" He pointed to the corner of the room.

"No, I can't."

"Then it must be in my head. I thought it must be because it travels whichever way I look"

"When did you first notice this?"

"When I landed on the circle, but I only half noticed it then, cos there was so much else going on." He paused, recalling what happened. "It all happened at once, and it was too much to take in, there were people all around me shouting at me to get off the circle. Then I noticed the green light. Then it turned blue, then it was green. Green, blue, green, blue….I hadn't realised, then, that it changes colour when I focus on it, and that was what I was doing.

So it was flicking backwards and forwards. It's a kind of switch in my head, like a computer toggle button."

"So what happened then?"

"Well then I think I must have got stuck—with the light showing blue…"

"And then?"

"Well, when the light is blue it means I'm in the green and it all goes weird. I don't remember getting off the circle—guess I must have—but I was in another world. Like I was low down on the ground and surrounded by smells. You wouldn't believe the extent of the smells. They're a whole new dimension."

"Are you in the green now?"

"No man, if I was in the green I don't think I could speak. The *light* is green now. That tells me I am in the blue. Blue is normal. Blue is how I always was."

"OK, so can you stay in the blue?"

"I can now— thank god! I only just figured out it's a toggle and I don't have to get stuck, I can toggle it back and forth! That's such a relief."

"What happens when you're in the green, Pete?"

"Well first thing is, once I got over the fear—it's pleasurable. It feels good to be there—kind of makes me feel whole! And it feels normal when you're in it, but real confusing when you come out. It's like I lose touch with being me, like I'm something else. It is harder to come back than it is to go there. That was the hardest bit to learn, coming back, remembering how to focus on the blue. I didn't get it at first. I have to remember to change the blue light back to green then I'm back to being me."

"I'm having difficulty following you here, Pete, just check I understand. You're saying there's a light that toggles between green and blue in your head. When the light is green in your head you are back to being normal, and that is how it is now. When it's blue in your head it's like you're in another world."

"That's it man." He looked relieved to be understood.

"And you've learnt to toggle between the two?"

"Yep, I think so, and I'm getting better—but only just in the past couple of hours. Before that it was *really scary*. It's still a bit scary but I think I have it under control. This thing doesn't come with any instruction manual."

"No". They sat gazing into space for a moment, Fergus aware of the doctor watching them through the surveillance window.

"So what happens, Pete, when you go in the green." Fergus asked gently, holding down his excitement. Could this be the first encounter at last?

"I don't know man, it's hard to describe. It's like I'm entering another world, another being." Pete paused, searching for a way of explaining. "It's a bit like snorkelling? You ever been snorkelling?"

"Yeah, couple of times"

"Then you'll know. It's like that. Hanging over another world, like you're an alien visitor, seeing everything for the first time. You can't breathe the water so you aren't quite of their world, the fish's world, the world of coral and water, you're just an outside visitor looking in. And everything you see is foreign and new, and bright and sparkly. I get that a bit when I'm jet-packing too, the sense of being somewhere new, of looking at the world differently. Then I can feel like a bird." He paused, searching for words to use. "But it's different, too. It's not like anything I've known. It's like I'm *of* a different world as well as in it. I'm a different being. I think differently… I don't have words in my head, I have images. It's like I'm remembering things that have happened, and that are deeply familiar. But they aren't familiar to me as Pete, they're familiar to me as a different being. It's not like I'm watching the fish on the coral—it's like I've become a fish on the coral, I'm not just looking at it, *I am it*." He paused to draw breath, as if hauling himself back from his recollections.

"So what's this other being like?"

"I can't really tell because I can't see myself, but I'm low down to the ground and my eyesight's crap. But the smells are fantastic."

"The smells?"

"Yeah, they're so interesting, man! Like a whole different vocabulary. I can smell things a hundred feet away! I can smell specific objects. I can find them in the long grass. I can find them because I know when a particular smell is getting stronger or fainter as I move around. I can smell when there's an animal around! I know what sort of animal it is from its smell alone. I don't have to see it. I can tell how far away it is. I can tell what sex it is and how old it is and where it's been because I can smell what it's been walking in, and I know the territory all around by the different smells so I know which way it's moving by the other smells it has with it. It's like a huge woven landscape of smells that is constantly changing." Pete looked off distractedly into the mid distance, a half smile on his face. "It's amazing, man. And my own smell, that's pretty important too, and it's like I have always known all this and how to understand it. I get different bits of information from different parts of my nose. Inside my nose, towards the top I get some types of information—like the age of things and how much decay there is. The roof of my mouth tells me other stuff, and the tip of my nose tells me about distant smells and helps me understand new ones..."

"Is that why you keep licking the tip of your nose?"

Pete looked at him slightly aghast.

"Do I? I didn't know that…yeah I guess it must be. You see I don't really know what I'm doing, as me, Pete, when I'm in the green..."

"But where are you when this is happening, Pete?"

"Well, I don't know, I think I'm still here, because I'm still dimly aware of me, Pete, in the background, but it's like I'm tapping into another set of memories. It's like I'm another being remembering things, not a human being."

"So if you're not human what sort of a being are you?"

"Well I'm a being with a good sense of smell, I can run fast. Ah—and yes—there's another seam, I have a memory of being little and of playing with …."

"With?"

"With small… fluffy…animals. We'd play for hours biting each other's necks and rolling around on the ground and—uh—yelping. It was such good fun! Sort of play fighting. There were at least four others. It's like you want to be the one on top holding the other ones neck in your jaws. Then you give him a little bite. Not really strong cos you don't want to really hurt him, just enough to make him yelp a little! Then you do something else like roll over or jump..."

"Why wouldn't you want to hurt him?"

Pete went silent, thinking "Well because, he's a friend, no, because... because he's *family*."

"Family?"

"Yeah, kind of. But that's my word, that's what I'm adding. I don't think in words when I'm him." Pete looked perplexed. "I know it sounds weird man but, wait a minute—there's more..."

"Yes?"

"Yes. I remember being picked up by a bigger animal, with fur. I'm very little, it's a sunny day and she has me in her mouth. I'm intoxicated by the smell of the inside of her mouth, it's rich and all encompassing, I can tell what she's been eating. We're moving through the grass and it's brushing past me, all around."

"Is she hurting you?"

"No! She has me by the back of the neck. I can feel her hot mouth around my neck, but she isn't squeezing hard. I'm real relaxed. I'm looking down at the ground as it whizzes past in a blur. Everything's OK. Then she puts me down. Some of the others are there. I start up play-fighting with them again.

"So what's she like, the one who has been carrying you?"

"Like I've always known her, she smells wonderful, she's musky and damp smelling and it's all mixed up with earth and she has a particular piss smell. God, it's so complex and intricate, the piss smell, I don't know how to describe it properly—but it's wonderful!"

"But what does she look like?"

"Well the smells are much more interesting man, uh, she has long black fur with white patches. Her eyes are all brown, there's no white around her pupils; she has a black and white face with a long nose, with a wet black end to it."

"…Sounds like she's a dog."

"Uh? Yeah, I s'pose…now I translate it all into words…"

Fergus and Pete looked at each other, thinking hard.

Pete was the first to break the silence. "That helps man, I think it's right. When I go in the green it's like I'm remembering a dog's memories."

"So what's it about? Do you think, perhaps, that the aliens are *like* dogs and they're just telling us something about themselves and their world?"

Pete fell into a kind of reverie before responding. His eyes went out of focus and his body limp and twitchy. Then, just as Fergus was starting to get concerned, he came to, and his eyes re-focused. "I—uh—just went in the green again. I wanted to remind myself. What were you asking?"

"I asked if you think the aliens are trying to tell us something about themselves and their world."

Pete gathered his thoughts. "I don't think so man. Just now I was outside *in this world*, somewhere familiar, with paths and shrubs and shit smells. We were by a lake, I was on a little strip of shingle. It smelt of wet rocks, and fish, and of squashed grass, and footprints. And the water smelt reedy with a bit of funny chemicals. There was a litter bin near the beach with fresh—uh—crisp packets in it—jeez that vinegar smell's strong and mixed up! And there was someone mixed in with the shingly smells. It was a woman! She smelt good that day—I think she was having her period!" Pete looked up—suddenly self-conscious.

"How did you know that?"

"…I could smell it. Actually I know the smell anyway." He smiled shyly. "But it was altogether a different experience smelling this woman with my new powers…that smell is exquisite man!

Anyhow, I was watching a big stick she was waving. The stick smelt of dog spit and tar and dead, wet, wood, and of her hand. Next thing I knew it was flying out over me, into the water. I could see its movement in the air but when it landed in the water I couldn't see it against all the water, but that didn't matter because I knew where it was! This was a game I knew well and liked. I was racing off after the stick, paddling through the cool water. My whole body was moving fast, like I was just running, but floating on the water. It felt excellent, man, lots of fun. And my nose was just above the water line smelling for the stick and...

"Yes?"

"..And I was swimming out to get the stick!"

They both let in the full implications of this.

"And then I focused on the blue light, so I could come back and tell you."

"Sounds pretty much like you were just being a dog."

"Hmm…yeah." Pete's half smile subsided to a look of alarm." Do you think I'll be alright?"

Fergus reflected. He didn't want to add to Pete's anxiety, nor did he want to mislead. "I've no idea, Pete, and that's the truth. But I do know you've done an incredibly brave thing." It was a heartfelt reply.

"You think so?" There were tears in his eyes now.

"I *know* so Pete. We are all still trying to make sense of what these circles are—and most people seem to be terribly afraid of the unknown. That much has become clear to me over the last few days. But you…you just went for it!"

After seeing Pete, Fergus was placed in intensive quarantine in a small private ward where an official brought him a laptop with a video conference request from Theo. This was the last person he wanted to talk to. He'd ignored Theo's threats and had hoped that would be the end of the matter.

Reluctantly he opened up the channel and Theo's face filled up the screen. This time he had a lotus flower pendant, and a bright orange cheesecloth shirt, but his severe face looked drawn and closed, exactly as before. Fergus tried to smile, "Hello Theo." Keep it civil.

"O'Donnel, what have you learnt?"

The same brusque rudeness. "What do you mean?"

"From interviewing Mr Jetpack."

"How do you know about that?"

"It's my business to know things, particularly with respect to you. You are one of our chief suspects."

"*Suspects*?"

"Sure, like I told you..."

Fergus took a deep breath. He was *not* going to be intimidated: "Mr Chaldrike, I want to keep this polite, but I'm not prepared to tell you anything further unless you tell me on what basis you think you have a right to know."

Theo looked at him, unblinking, then smiled unexpectedly. "You have quite a nerve O'Donnel, I don't normally meet such opposition."

"I don't wish to *oppose*." Fergus said quietly. "But I need to know what you do for the NCTC, and what your authority is?"

"You've no right to know anything about me."

Fergus didn't reply and rode out a silence. Eventually Theo smiled again. "OK, if you insist. I'm a hypothesis agent, and I head up a team of hypothesis agents at the NCTC. Does that satisfy you?"

"Not really. What do hypothesis agents do?"

Theo scrutinised him as if deciding whether to say more. "We're the guys that link up the dots. There are massive databases on suspected terrorists, and tracking systems on worldwide incidents and atypical events. The information is separately collected by a number of different organisations, including the FBI and the CIA, but it all comes together at NCTC, streams of intelligence data. Most of it is just background noise, so there are significance agents whose job it is to separate out the significant 'dots' from the rest. My job is to watch those dots and hypothesise how they might link up. I look for conspiracy."

"So you're similar to us at SETI in a way—looking out for patterns in apparently random data?"

Theo squinted. "Yes, similar, but unlike you I look out for *sinister* connections. I'm paid to be paranoid, to think like terrorists do, and to fear the worst. Then, when I have a hypothesis I test it out. If it checks out as dangerous, I recommend how to deal with it. It all came about after 9/11. That could have been prevented, you know, the dots were there in abundance. It's just that no-one was bright enough to connect them."

At last the man was talking, Fergus reflected. If only he could keep him going long enough to try and forge a relationship, then things might get easier. "Quite a responsibility you've got Theo, isn't it very stressful?"

Theo's forehead creased: "You've no idea. Most people don't. Most people are oblivious to the dangers all around them and expect others to take responsibility. But I'm not. I'm paid to *think,* and think the worst. Most people won't do this. They don't want to go there."

"So you must be pretty intelligent to do a job like that?"

"Nine languages intelligent, two Phds…I..." Suddenly his face clouded over. "Nice try O'Donnel! Get me off my guard, seduce me with compliments." He winced. "Now tell me about Jetpack."

"So you think I'm a terrorist suspect?"

"I think you're a serious threat to the safety of our species, isn't that enough? Tell me about Jetpack."

Fergus sighed: "His name's Pete."

"Yes. And?"

"And it's kind of confusing"

"What is?"

Fergus took a deep breath. "Well, he seems OK physically but as soon as he touched the circle he acquired a kind of toggling device in his head. He can remain as he was before he landed on the circle, or he can toggle into the memories of another—being. It seems he is able to do this at will..."

"Another *being*?"

"Yeah," Fergus felt his throat go dry, "another being"

"What other being, O'Donnel?"

"Well it has a heightened sense of smell, much more than we have."

"It does?"

"Yeah."

"And?"

"And it seems to be quite low to the ground."

There was a pause. Theo was waiting.

"He can toggle backwards and forwards between himself and this other—uh—being, it seems he can access its memory, it's like he becomes it for a bit, or becomes what it was."

Theo stared at him. "Yes, but *what is this other being*? Is it an alien? Is it trying to communicate?"

"I don't think so."

"Then *what is it*?" His tone was impatient.

"I think it's a dog." There, it was out now.

"A *dog*?"

"A dog."

"An alien dog?"

"No, just a dog."

"A *dog*?"

"Yes, a dog."

Theo's moustache twitched: "Don't joke with me, O'Donnel. I don't like jokes."

"I'm not." There was a long pause whilst Theo stared at him, as if trying to read his mind.

"A *dog*?"

"Yup."

Another long pause.

"How do you know it isn't an alien dog?"

"Well, one of the memories Pete just accessed—he was chasing a stick in some water. A woman threw it for him"

"He was *chasing a stick*?"

"Mm hmm."

"A woman threw it for him?"

"Yes."

"O'Donnel?"

"Yes."

"Jetpack—is he of sound mind?"

"I think so, he seems pretty clear. They've been running tests and haven't found anything. He's just had a pretty awesome experience, of course, which would be hard for anyone to adjust to."

"I'll say. It isn't every day we adjust to becoming a dog." Theo went silent for a few seconds. He liked a mystery but this was off the spectrum. He pulled out that day's single, rationed, cigar from his shirt pocket and lit it carefully, rotating it slowly over a silver lighter. "But O'Donnel, what could possibly be happening here? *Why* would aliens give someone dog memories?"

"I've no idea. That's what I've been trying to work out myself. I think we just have to wait and see what happens, and to study the results of experiments using animals, here and in other countries."

Theo exhaled a large puff of smoke at the screen. "No need. We've already gone way beyond animal tests, O'Donnel. There's a report about a circle not being properly defended in Ethiopia, and one in Christchurch New Zealand got broken into by an angry mob. We don't know how many people touched it before the authorities regained control. But, worst of all, the one at Varanasi, in India, has been *completely overwhelmed.* The government there are complete schmucks. They deployed too few guards and a massive crowd just chased them away, pulled down the barriers, and started taking it in turns to touch the circle. We think hundreds already have, maybe thousands. We are, of course, insisting that the Indian authorities re-surround the site immediately, and quarantine the whole area, but I'm not holding my breath, they haven't a brain cell to share between them." He took a large suck on his cigar.

"So what happened to the people who touched the circle?"

"Early reports are saying they've connected up with *other people.*"

"What, inside themselves?"

"Yes, like Jetpack, but with people."

"Not *alien* people?"

"Nope, ordinary people. They come out with the memories of one other person. We think it's someone who preceded them, not the one directly before them or necessarily from that circle – but someone else who has touched a circle somewhere in the world. Come to think of it, Jetpack may have connected up with a dog used experimentally. We know some circles have been tested with dogs."

"Are the people OK?"

Theo looked at him wildly and took a savage draw on his cigar. "Who can fucking say, O'Donnel? This whole thing's totally out of control. The very thing we've worked to prevent is *happening*. I've had no time to assess the consequences. Worse, and *partly because of you* we now have a strong public lobby to keep the circles here active by putting volunteers through them. There are lots of people out there talking the way you talk, O'Donnel, saying we shouldn't waste the opportunity, that it's about transcendence, that it's a civil right, and other such drivel…"

Theo blew a smoke ring. "And Jetpack hasn't exactly helped by surviving the experience; in fact this whole dog business is only going to exacerbate things. There are plenty of people out there, *dog-lovers* and the like, who would *want* that experience. We have to shift public opinion now or the results could be catastrophic. Probably already are."

He stared at Fergus with sudden ferocity. "I understand you're now in quarantine?"

"Yes."

"And you'll be wanting to get out as quickly as possible?"

"Of course."

"I could probably pull strings with that." Theo smiled slyly. "Though I expect their checks will have to be pretty thorough. There isn't a precedent for this, but I seem to remember the Apollo 11 astronauts had to be quarantined for weeks, remember that? "

Fergus nodded imperceptibly. He was starting to feel nauseous.

"I think they kept them for 3 weeks inside an airtight NASA trailer, just in case they'd brought back germs from the moon. They couldn't touch anyone, not even their families..." Theo blew a few more rings of smoke. He seemed to be enjoying himself. "But there might be a way of avoiding all that. They're going to want to interview you, aren't they, and ask what you think about Jetpack? So you could *emphasise your concerns*—or not, of course."

Fergus replied slowly: "As I said before, you've got the wrong man. I'm not responding to threats."

Theo glowered: "How come you're so unregenerate, O'Donnel? Just think about it…*carefully*." He cut their connection.

Fergus looked at the empty screen as his heart beat returned to normal. Goodness Theo had a nerve. But surely the quarantine wasn't essential. Theo wouldn't have implied he could get him out if it was really important. No, he was bluffing. Well two could play that game. He stood up and walked through the door startling the two uniformed guards sitting just outside. "Can't stop, I'm on instructions from the President." He strode away confidently down the corridor.

9

The day after his arrival in the north of England Mohammed received a letter instructing him to attend another asylum interview, this time in Newcastle. His fear built up as the day approached. He managed to see a doctor and got some medicines, but he was still finding it hard to eat or sleep, was tormented by sounds in one ear, headaches, swollen eyes, and attacks of vomiting… But at least he was able to come and go as he pleased and it was a huge relief to be outside on his own, walking the cold streets. He'd even managed to spend an afternoon by the sea. He'd never seen the sea before. When he was working in Kampala he would sometimes eat his lunch by the wild life park next to Lake Victoria, look across the lake that seemed to have no end at all, and watch the waves lapping along the thin beach. But even on the windiest of days the waves were trifling compared to the huge rolling breakers on the beach at Sunderland which he watched, mesmerised. It was so good to be lifted, however briefly, out of his everyday terrors.

On the morning of the appointment he got up early and caught the bus to Newcastle, spending the last of the money given him by the taxi driver. The bus stopped in the centre of the city and he showed his creased letter to a few people before finding someone who could direct him to a formal looking building, off one of the main streets. He gave his name to the receptionist and took a seat.

After a few minutes a formally dressed black woman came into the room: "Mr Marimbey?"

"Yes."

Don't forget to smile!

"Do you speak Luganda?"

"Yes." He noticed that one of her eyes had a white pupil.

"Good, come this way then." This time she spoke in Luganda. As she led him down the corridor she explained: "I'm your interpreter. From now onwards we'll talk in Luganda, please don't say another word in English. If you don't understand anything, or feel misunderstood, just talk to me direct, but in Luganda."

At last here was someone who spoke his native tongue! The woman led him to an office where a man sat behind a table piled high with papers sipping a mug of coffee. He didn't look up as they entered. The woman indicated Mohammed to sit in a chair facing the man, then sat down herself. "It's OK, he speaks Luganda" she said in English. The man looked up and began talking in English, with the woman interpreting.

"Your name and date of birth?"

Not even a 'hello', this doesn't look good.

"Mohammed Marimbey, February 28th 1982".

"Can you spell out your name please?" Mohammed spelt his name.

The man studied a piece of paper in front of him.

"Why have you spelt your name wrong? It says here your surname is Marimbay with an 'a' at the end."

Mohammed looked down at the floor, unable to speak, his head swimming.

He seems angry. He's going to flip.

"Why have you spelt your name wrong?"

"I—er—got it wrong—at the last interview—it was written down wrong."

"So you're now saying it should be spelt with an 'e'?"

"Yes". The man slowly wrote a couple of sentences.

"Why then did you sign the form in which it was spelt with an 'a'?"

"I didn't think it mattered."

The man looked at him silently, then continued: "When did you arrive in this country?"

"I—don't know. About a week ago. The day before my last interview."

"He says he doesn't know exactly" translated the interpreter.

The man started writing again.

"Are you married?"

"No"

"Children?"

"No"

"OK, I have to read you out a statement", he began reading swiftly, '*you are being interviewed in connection with your asylum application in the UK, this is your opportunity to explain the reasons why you are claiming asylum and an opportunity for us to obtain all the information necessary to make a decision on your application…'* " The interpreter had begun speaking over the top of the man's voice. Mohammed stared at the carpet tiles, trying to concentrate, his head pounding and his ear buzzing. The medication had helped a bit, but it all seemed worse today. The man appeared cold and formal and was reading a long passage in a fast monotonous tone. He tried to place the accent of the woman interpreting. He would have liked to know which part of Uganda she was from. She'd hardly introduced herself.

" '*…credibility, section 8, warning. Your actions since leaving—uh—Uganda—will be taken into account when your claim is considered. If I think that anything you have done makes it hard to believe your claim for asylum, I will give you the chance to explain. It may harm your asylum application if you cannot provide a reasonable explanation for your actions.*' " The man stopped and the woman rounded up her interpretation.

What was that about a warning?

The man waited for her to finish. "OK so now we are starting part B of the asylum interview: Why did you leave Uganda?"

Why are they asking this again?

"I was put on a plane."

"Who put you on the plane?"

"I don't know, some people, the ones who picked me up when I was thrown out of prison…"

"And how did you get documents to get into this country?

"The people, the woman who took me on the plane. She had documents."

"What documents did she have?"

"I don't know. She had two small booklets."

"Did they have photographs in them?

"I didn't see any."

The interpreter translated: "There weren't any photos."

The man cocked an eyebrow. "OK so let's go back to before you left Uganda. Who put you in prison?"

"The Government of Uganda"

"Why?"

"No good reason. I was a member of the opposition party, the FDC"

"What can you tell us about the FDC?"

It's the same question! Over and over they ask about the FDC. This is going to hurt. I don't have any answer they will accept…

"I don't know anything. I can't tell you anything". He watched as the interpreter translated, his heart pounding. The man creased his forehead and carried on with his slow writing.

This is it, brace yourself. Smile.

"When did you become a member of the FDC?"

"2001."

"So, you were in the party for—many years—and yet you can't tell us anything about it?"

"I don't know what you want."

"What does FDC stand for?"

"FDC? Forum for Democratic Change."

"Why did you join the party in 2001?"

Mohammed looked down not knowing what to say. Was this a trap? The interpreter sounded like she might belong to the same tribe as Museveni. Her accent was similar to his. Perhaps the British government was just the same as the government back at home, they were both in league against the FDC. Perhaps they were trying to pin him down. He wondered how to answer. It was difficult to explain.

His decision to join the FDC went back to his father. His father had been in the NRM first, Museveni's party. He'd joined the NRM shortly after Museveni had seized power after five years of guerilla warfare against the Obote and Okello regimes. He'd been attracted by Museveni's fine and intelligent speeches about democracy, freedom and justice. But although his father rose to become an important man in local government, he didn't like what he saw. Despite his fine speeches, Museveni ruled by fear and ruthless cruelty. So he'd defected to the FDC.

A year later he was shot dead when he was walking home by a gun through the window of a passing military vehicle. Mohammed, who'd been working as a mechanic at the time in a garage in Kampala, became the eldest male in the family. He was only 19, but he was now responsible for looking after his mother, his sisters, and his younger brother. There wasn't much money in mechanics. Kampala was packed with tiny garages, under bridges, in hot corrugated-iron huts. He hardly made enough money to feed himself, let alone his family.

After his father was killed he carried on as a mechanic, but signed up to the youth wing of the FDC. He'd already attended their rallies for several years and agreed with what they said. They knew his father had been killed for the cause and respected him for it. At least in the FDC there were good prospects of promotion—particularly for those, like himself, who were willing to be part of the public face of the party. If he could rise fast enough, then his higher profile might protect him. Senior members sometimes survived, and Kizza Besigye, the leader of the party, though occasionally harassed by the police, seemed protected by his position.

Taking risks was, in any case, part of what it meant to be a man. He would stand up for what he believed. He wouldn't be intimidated by his father's murder. He would take on the people who had killed him and if the FDC gained power then his future would be rosy. There'd be a job for him in a new government.

The party had welcomed him, delighted he was following in his father's footsteps. They kitted him out with a uniform and cap, with the letters F D C on every item of clothing, and trained him up as a regional mobiliser. He was given a district in Kampala and threw himself into the work, every day attending campaign meetings at the crowded FDC headquarters and afterwards heading out to give talks. He was a rising star.

It had been easy giving talks. There was so much to improve in Uganda. If the FDC got in, he explained, then they'd introduce a real democracy. People would never again be prevented from voting freely and fairly. There'd be no more threats. The army and the justice system would be separated out at last from the government. Corruption would be stamped out; there'd be no more bribes. Taxes would no longer go into the back pockets of politicians but would be spent improving the infrastructure. The FDC would bring in free education and genuine, universal, health care. They would build new roads. They would provide electricity and water for all. No-one need ever go hungry again.

At the end of the talk, while the crowd was applauding, he would dramatically pull away an FDC flag that had been draped over a pile to the edge of the stage. Beneath it would be a heap of small bags of sugar, or maize flour. 'Here, help yourself, one for each of you! There'll be more if you help us to get in'. The FDC gave him expenses to pay for this. Every party speaker did it, and the crowd expected it. He kept any money left over.

After each talk he'd been surrounded by people, particularly young men, asking questions. They'd been impressed in particular by his uniform and his preparedness to wear it. They were as interested in him as the promises he made. His fearlessness was attractive. His friends at the garage were also impressed and his campaign poster went up on the wall of the garage. He started sending money home.

But all of that was ruined now. He'd had plenty of time to castigate himself for his folly. How could he have been so naïve? He'd been so fluffed up with his own importance and his new-found status. He was no less vulnerable than anyone else. He had said that he could take anything that they threw at him, that the cause was all he cared about. This was what he knew people wanted to hear. It was also what *he* wanted to hear himself say. He'd become like a lion amongst zebra. Whatever happened they could never take his spirit.

But from the moment that they'd first arrested him the fear that he'd staved off so successfully burst free inside him, bubbling up and festering in the darkness. He learnt that his spirit was as finite as the rest of him. It could be snuffed out like an ant under a twisting heel. He would have said anything, done anything, in the torture chamber just to stop the pain. They had surgically removed his spirit. He was living, but the lion inside him was dead. There was no means to re-awaken it now. They'd taken everything—his father, his purpose, his future, his humanity, his very soul.

He looked up. The two other people in the room were staring at him intently: "Mr Marimbey did you understand the question? I'm asking why you joined the FDC?"

He grappled for an answer: "It seemed the only thing to do."

The man wrote down his answer in his ponderous long hand. "Tell me how you were arrested."

Keep answering, it'll be worse if you don't.

"I was in a meeting, outside, I was the leader, there were about ten of us. We were discussing strategy. Some soldiers drove up and asked what we were doing."

"What did you say?"

"We told them the truth. That we were discussing our campaign."

"What happened then?"

"They said we were lying—that they knew we were plotting a coup against the government. I thought about escaping, some of the others were running away. But they shot into the air. That frightened me. They said we were going to explain what we'd been doing. Then they dragged three of us into the vehicle and blindfolded us. They took us to Makindye Barracks and put us in a small cell with 18 others. An officer came in and made me take my clothes off. Then he started hitting me, with his baton, in front of everyone. I fell to the ground, and he started kicking me and stepping on me. He said it was to make me tell the truth. I must have passed out. When I came round at about 4 am he'd gone. I talked to the other prisoners. They were all party activists, rounded up from other meetings."

"What happened next?"

"The next morning they moved me to another cell, it was completely dark, and I was on my own. They used to come...and hit me, with batons. They said I had to tell them the truth or they'd move me somewhere else, somewhere worse. They'd find out one way or another. But I had nothing to tell them, we'd only been talking about the election campaign. They kept me there for months."

"What happened then?"

"They told me that they were taking me to a safe house. They made me dress in a uniform, hand-cuffed me and blindfolded me again. Then they drove me away. They spoke in Swahili and I couldn't understand. Eventually they stopped and took me into a building. Then they put me in a dark place underneath the floor."

All is black.

Trapped for ever, no room to stretch.

Here till I die.

"What happened then?"

"After a few hours they took me out into a room. There were three men. They stripped me naked and hosed me down."

"Hosed you down?"

"Yes, always they started by hosing me down. It was freezing cold."

"And then…"

"Then they beat me. One of them, Muhindo, sat at the back of the room giving instructions and asking questions. He told me that I should tell him the secrets of the FDC. They hit me on the head and in the mouth, and stabbed me with something—I don't know what—on my leg. They kept asking me questions and said that if I didn't tell them the truth, I was going to be killed. They kicked me and forced me to cower in the corner. They made me drink some smelly liquid, that was very bitter. Then they took me back and locked me under the floorboards. As he closed the trap-door Muhindo said he'd be back the next morning and would torture me until I told him the truth.

The next morning they dragged me back again and asked if I'd made up my mind to tell them the truth. They said they knew that the FDC was planning a violent coup and that I knew who was involved. They wanted me to tell them names. I told them that I didn't know anything. I was innocent. They brought a metal trough full of water. They had straps to keep my hands in the water. Then they gave them a long electric shock. That was how my hands have got like this." He held out his hands.

"Please continue."

"They attached some electrodes to my head and down my right side. They sent an electric shock into my body. Since then I have got a loud sound in my ear."

"Did they do anything else to you?"

"Yes, many things. They would tie me up and twist my legs, or they would kick me between the legs. They pointed a gun up my nose and said they'd pull the trigger if I didn't tell them. One time they showed me a freshly severed head. His eyes were still open. They held it—him—by his hair. His neck was like meat. They said that that is what would happen to me if I didn't co-operate. They said it showed that they could do anything to me, that nobody would ever know. They did many, many, things—I lost track of what they were doing to me. They rubbed chillies in my eyes—that's why they're so swollen. For days I couldn't open my eyes at all so I couldn't see exactly what they were doing. Sometimes I lost consciousness. I have scars all over my body. I can show you."

The interviewer looked at him, startled. "That won't be necessary. It wouldn't be appropriate. How long did they keep do this for?"

"I don't know. I lost track of time. I think it was all day the first time."

"What was the room like?"

"What?"

"What was the room like, what did it look like?"

"I couldn't see, it was very dark. The guards shined torches and bright lights in my face, I had chilli in my eyes so I couldn't see around."

"Were there windows in the room?"

"I don't know."

"What happened when they'd finished torturing you?"

"They returned me under the floorboards."

"What was that like?"

"Terrible, it was terrible."

"I mean what was the space like?"

"It was tiny, too small to stretch out. Completely dark."

"What was the floor made of?"

"I don't know what it was covered in, it smelt terrible."

"How long did they keep you there?"

"I don't know, months, years, they'd take me out and torture me then put me back."

"Which? Months, or years?

"I don't know exactly, there was no way of recording time"

"How often did they mistreat you?"

"I don't know, it was so often, I lost count."

"For example once per week, once per month?"

"It wasn't on a daily basis but it didn't have a pattern. It was difficult to keep track."

"How often did they bring you food and drink?"

"Twice a day, the food was usually rotten, and the drink sometimes smelt."

"Did you try to escape?"

"No. There was no way out"

"How did they lock you in?"

"I don't know, it was a trapdoor in the floorboards, over my head"

"How did you know it was locked?"

"Every time they checked me, or brought food, they locked it behind them. I could hear it being locked."

"Did you try to unlock it?"

"No, I told you, there was no way out."

"How did you come to leave that place?"

"Muhindo came and got me. He led me down a corridor. I thought he was going to kill me. They had been constantly telling me that. Then he hit me so I fell out onto the street."

"Why did he do that?"

"I don't know."

"And then you were picked up by some people who arranged for you to come on a plane to this country?"

"Yes."

"And you don't have any idea who arranged that, who they were?"

"No."

"Doesn't that strike you as strange, Mr Marimbey, that some people that you don't know would suddenly arrange for you to come to the UK?

"Yes."

"So, is there something that you're not telling us?"

"NO!"

Never get angry

"I mean—no." He said it gently now, his body shaking.

Back in the room, guard standing over, baton in hand. 'So we're angry now, are we? I'll show you who is angry.'

Three hours later when Mohammed stumbled out again onto the pavement outside the building where he had been questioned, he was surprised to find himself in daylight, free. His head was throbbing, his stomach clamped in an aching spasm of alarm. But as he limped towards the bus station, and the cold began to grip, no one rushed to seize him, no car slowed down on the kerb alongside. Nobody seemed to be following. Indeed, nobody seemed remotely interested in him. They were all just calmly going about their daily business, these white people. Perhaps he was going to be alright.

At 3 a.m. that night the whole household was woken by loud banging on the front door.

Get into kneeling position, smile.

Mohammed exchanged a terrified glance with the Somalian man. There were heavy footsteps in the hallway.

Muhindo's boots on the floorboards above.

Two uniformed men burst into the room. "Mr Mohammed Marimbey?"

He nodded.

One of the men approached him. "Put your hands in front of you."

This is it. I'm a dead man.

He held his hands out and the man locked handcuffs around his swollen wrists. A fresh acrid wave of terror flooded though him.

The other man pulled a letter out of his pocket. "Mr Marimbey we've come to take you into custody. Your application to stay in this country has been refused. This letter explains everything. You'll have plenty of time to read it."

They pulled him out of the room and along the corridor using the chain between his hands, past other residents peeping through door cracks, out of the front door to a white van with small tinted windows and 'Group Four Security' written along its side. Still handcuffed he was locked into a single cubicle in the back of the van with just enough room for a seat. As the van started up and began to pull away the Somalian man ran out of the house, bright in the headlights, waving Mohammed's small bag in the air. He passed the bag to the men and looked up at Mohammed in the window as the van pulled off into the night.

10

"Pete, it's Fergus."

"Fergus! Great to hear from you man!"

"How're you doing?"

"I been wonderful, man, wonderful."

"*Wonderful?*"

"Yeah, no other word for it—*full of wonder.* This is the most amazing trip. Every time I visit Harvey I come back blown apart."

"Harvey?"

There was a chuckle on the other end of the line. "Yeah, Harvey, or Hardy, that's the name of the dog, man. He has difficulty remembering words but it's something like that. He doesn't think in words you see. I've settled on Harvey, 'cause I like it."

"So have you been spending a lot of time…toggling… 'Harvey' then?"

"Sure man, I half live in him—whenever I get a spare moment. Not that there's much time to toggle at present. We've been inundated with press calls and requests for interviews—so it's hard to get time off. I'm used to the press of course from my jet packing, but this has been unbelievable. And I've been spending much more time with my parents—I owe those guys so much, I never realised it properly before but they're really…. just the best. I don't know how they've forgiven me for all the stuff I've done, but they have, somehow, and now...now I feel like I owe it to them to give them time."

"You managed to get out the hospital then?"

"Oh yeah, not long after you. My parents threatened legal action and got me into a private clinic, then later that day they got permission for me to be discharged if I wore an electronic tag, and a mask in public. Lucky I have such rich and powerful parents. I think the mask will be coming off soon though, what with all the other people who've touched circles and been just fine."

"And what do you think about the reports of other people's experiences?"

"Well, we seem to be toggling in the same way. We all seem to be accessing the memory banks of another being. But to tell the truth, I was a bit upset at first—I wanted to be the only one." He was laughing at himself now: "Such an ego! Then I felt jealous so many people were toggling people not animals." More laughter. "Particularly when I found out that you can't do it twice—that people who've touched circles more than once don't get any more beings to toggle. Then my dad told me about Diogenes and it dawned on me how lucky I've been."

"*Diogenes*?"

"Yeah, Diogenes. He was a really cool Greek philosopher. It seems he modelled his life on that of a dog—he more or less lived as a dog for the second half of his life—really anarchic, man. He said other people should model themselves on dogs too—because dogs live in the present you see, without anxieties. They aren't as self-important as people and they don't worry about their reputations, or what they eat, or where they shit, or sleep. Diogenes himself lived in a tub in the market place. He said a dog has a way of distinguishing instinctively between friends and enemies. And I think he was right about that too—there's something about how someone smells that tells you whether or not they're on your side. Anyhow, it felt great learning about Diogenes. After that, the more I toggled Harvey, the more I realised how lucky I am. Don't get me wrong, it must be cool to toggle another human, but going across species is just stupendous, man. Every time I do it I come back with new experiences—whole new perspectives. Harvey's amazing, man. He's so happy and full of spirit, so trusting and joyful. I love being in his skin. He just enjoys himself, no fuss, no anxiety. And he's so loyal. This woman who is his owner, somewhere, he just *loves* her. I'm learning so much whenever I'm being him and it leaves me feeling.... *joyous*. Last night I toggled him and fell asleep. I spent the night dreaming Harvey's dog dreams and woke up thinking I'd been chasing rabbits."

Fergus had been listened to all this with his mind spinning. "Do you know where the real Harvey is Pete?"

"Nope, but I've got some ideas—I'm trying to piece it all together. I think I live in a big house—I mean I think *he* does," Pete chuckled, "and there's plenty of countryside around, and the vegetation isn't hugely different from the vegetation here, and it seems like it's probably the same season because when I access his recent memories the smells there are spring smells. And we've been for some great walks. Thing is though I, he, doesn't look up much, he's more interested in the surrounding smells so I'm not getting much information where he is.

But there's another big clue—he understands 'sit' and 'fetch' and 'down boy' and 'good dog' and 'here boy', so his owner clearly speaks English. A few hours ago I accessed his most recent memory. At least I think it must be the most recent. The woman, his owner, put him in the car. Harvey had his head out of the window when they were driving along. He loves doing that—it's amazing man, you get smells rushing past the tip of your nose in a flood of information. It's fantastic overload! Anyhow they didn't go far—just to a park he recognised because it's near where he lives and he is sometimes taken there for walks. But when he got there, there were also some smells that were new to this park, petrolly ones and ones from the earth having been disturbed, and a lot of recent people smells. His owner let him out of the car on a lead. Lots of people were patting him and his tail was wagging like crazy. Funny how it does that when he's happy, which is most of the time.

Then they took him through a gate in some metal. I think the metal must have been fencing, though when he sniffed it—it seemed to have some really toxic paint stuff on it—and they led him to a circle. I think this must have been a green circle but his colour sense isn't very well defined, so it didn't look quite the same. But it smelt really sweet … like a compound mix of ripe figs in the distance and something else unfamiliar, something unusual, but *friendly*. That's when his owner passed his lead to a man and then walked around the other side of the circle and called: 'here boy, here boy" so he ran onto the circle. He loves to please her you see…. And then the memory stopped. It just went black, suddenly, stopped dead. It's the only time that's happened when I've been toggling, which is why I figure it must be Harvey's most recent memory, and it just came to an end, suddenly. I've run the same memory over and it always stops at exactly the same point."

"So maybe the circle just recorded everything in Harvey's mind and that is what has been downloaded to you. What you remember doesn't go beyond that point because that was where he had got up to when he entered the circle."

"Yeah man, that seems to be it. I've been wondering though what happened to Harvey at that point. Then yesterday I found out that they'd been doing some experiments with dogs in Canada—making them touch a circle there to test what happened. So I think I may be one of them. Harvey may be one of them I mean."

"Well I've heard about that too, and there have also been dogs introduced to other circles around the world, as well as other animals. So it's possible that Harvey could come from another country as well."

"Yeah, but it would need to be somewhere where they speak English and are in pretty much the same season …. I'd like to track him down though".

"I'll see if I can find out anything for you Pete."

"Thanks man, I appreciate that."

There was a pause as they both thought things through. Then Fergus said: "I think I'm jealous of you, Pete."

"You are?"

"Sure. All my life I've wanted what you have now. I've wanted a route out of the everyday into the extraordinary. I've wanted to hear from something alien, a bridge to something absolutely *other*. And that's what you've got."

"Yeah, well, you could have it too, if you want. You might get a dog too—or maybe toggling with a human is just as amazing. Why don't you go for it, Fergie?"

No-one had ever called him Fergie before—Pete had got familiar and friendly so quickly. But it felt right, *Fergie*. "I will Pete, once I can afford the time. But first there's other work to do and that's partly why I'm phoning you. I've been commissioned to get people to visit most of the sites within the week so we don't lose them. The administration only wanted 20 sites activated at first but there's been such a public lobby, and so many other countries are doing it, that they've upped the figure. Now we're going to activate 300 sites. That's almost all of them. Only the ones with substantial local opposition won't be touched."

"That's great man."

"Yeah, it is, but we've been working flat out for 48 hours sorting applications. SETI's been deluged with enquiries, and the process has gone crazy. It was easy at first but then a significant number of people we'd approved pulled out when they realised someone else might later toggle them and get intimate knowledge about them."

"Yeah, *I* had no way of figuring that one out up front." Pete said, with a wry chuckle

"Does it bother you?"

"No, man, not any more. When I first realised it I was bothered for a bit that people might find out about my—uh—masturbatory habits, but that seems rather irrelevant now, alongside some of Harvey's habits..."

Fergus was inwardly impressed with Pete's honesty here and wondered briefly about his own masturbatory habits becoming public knowledge. It wasn't something he'd considered up to now. "Well, it's amazing how many people do have secrets they think are too important. Most of them relate to their personal lives, I reckon, but many people—politicians, business men and so on said that they had organisational secrets that they didn't want public. At least that was the line they took. Lots of people withdrew on that basis. Significant numbers also got second thoughts, it seems, about taking on someone else's suffering. They were worried it might change their lives irreversibly."

"Isn't that the whole point of transformation, it changes you?"

"Well, yeah, sure, but people are frightened. Someone explained it to me with a Sufi myth. In the myth there is a tree of suffering. People are invited to move around the tree and tie up a bundle of all their suffering on a branch of their choice. They all enjoy doing this of course. Then they're told to take back any bundle in exchange. Everyone circles around the tree for a while, thinking, then they all take back their own bundle! It seems we are too attached to our own suffering even to consider changing it for someone else's—let alone taking on someone else's *as well*."

Pete pondered this for a moment "That's a bit weird isn't it? Being attached to your own suffering?"

"Well yeah, it is, I know! People are also just frightened of change. They don't want to take on anything new. A lot of people pulled out straight after that story about the woman in New Zealand who'd toggled a starving child in India. It seems that people don't want to face that kind of thing. I can understand that, I guess. Anyhow, despite all this, we still have thousands of applicants to choose between and we haven't really found a rational basis for selecting people because we've no idea what's really going on here. Most of the people who've touched circles have been linked up with people—though one or two, like you, have had animals that were being experimented with—and someone in Ethiopia has been talking about toggling an English blackbird! Why would an alien species be doing this? Are they choosing what happens and, if so, how do they decide what match to give different people?"

"I can't help you there Fergie, I've no idea."

"Yeah, well, anyhow we've finally chosen 300 people and that's why I'm calling you. I'm wondering if you can help?"

"Of course! I'll do anything for you Fergie. Anything."

"We need someone who can be with people when they touch the circles and help them learn to toggle.

"I'd be delighted, man."

"You sure? You're not going to miss being able to spend more time with Harvey?"

"Of course I'm sure man, of course! Like I said, I'll do anything for you. In any case Harvey's a part of me now. He'll always be with me. And I'll never forget that it was you that got those straps undone, and I heard as well that it was you who told the hospital to let my parents visit. You're my friend Fergie, big time. You always will be. Besides this is important work."

"Well, I'm really grateful Pete, I…."

"Don't mention it man—when can I start?"

"Well...it needs to be straight away, really. We have to do it within the next three days! It's going to be really tight because it means travelling all over America. Obviously you won't be able to do it all yourself, we'll support, but the more you can do the better because you've got the experience, and you seem so positive," he added as an afterthought, "I'm sorry I've left it so late to contact you Pete, there's been so much else going…"

"No worries Fergie—*please*."

"OK, well I'll commission a private jet to pick you up in San Francisco. Then it's a matter of flying from circle to circle, help each volunteer, then fly on to the next."

"Sounds *fun* Fergie! But there's no need for a jet—I can use one of my Dad's helicopters. I think that would be easier than a jet anyway as I'll be able to save time by getting closer to the circles."

"But who will fly it Pete?"

"I will, I can fly, man. Actually no, I'd better just check with my Dad this time. I realised just how disloyal I'd been taking the jet pack without asking, and apologised. I'd been doing all kinds of stuff that worried him sick. We've made so much peace between us now."

Over the next three days Pete flew non-stop around the country, his father not only agreed to lend him a helicopter but joined him in it, together with an employee pilot. The three of them flew from place to place, Pete and the employee alternating flying between them, so they both got a chance to sleep, his father staying in touch with Fergus and other staff at SETI.

First stop was Las Vegas, the circle in San Francisco having been activated by Pete four days previously. Four days that felt like a lifetime.

They touched down close to the circle and Pete was soon shaking the hand of a man aged about sixty, with a neat moustache, reddish complexion and bright startled eyes. His hand was cold and sweaty.

"You must be David?"

"Yes." The word croaked out.

"I think you'll be the second person in America." Pete said with a broad smile, still holding his hand. "Sorry to beat you to the post, man." David didn't even smile. He was clearly frightened and kept staring at the enclosure.

"Sure you want to go through with this, buddy?"

David hesitated, choosing his words carefully. "More than anything, Mr Flavier, though I don't have your natural courage. I'm normally a cautious person. But this—this is the most astonishing thing. We're at the verge of something really extraordinary, as a species I mean—and I want to be part of it—I want to be on the edge of it—to cross the edge. I want to be a part of this with my whole soul. But that doesn't mean it isn't deeply scary…"

Pete took this in for a moment, wondering how to help. "It doesn't hurt, you know" he said gently "and you never have to toggle, if you don't want to."

The man looked at him in surprise. "Oh I want to toggle! I'm ready and open for this." He glanced again towards the enclosure and took a deep breath. "Let's go".

They walked past a line of security personnel and through a large metal gate. Inside the enclosure was a green circle .To one side a couple of chairs had been placed out for them. They both stood still for a long moment, gazing at the circle in awe as it flowed glowing patterns from its centre.

"Well here you go. As soon as you touch the circle you should get a green light in your head. I suggest you don't focus on it at first though, just walk across the circle, and sit down the other side. If you do focus on it accidentally just remember you can always toggle back—its '*blue* for *you*', '*green* for a new *scene*'. That's all you have to remember. Whenever you've had enough –just focus on *blue* for *you* and it'll bring you back. But I'll be here. I'll be by your side mate."

David stood now, a foot short of the circle, preparing himself. Pete noticed that suddenly he seemed calmer, his shoulders had loosened and the staring look had gone out of his eyes. He stepped forward, standing for a moment on the circle, then walked on and sat down. Pete sat beside him and took his hand.

"How're you doing?"

"It's worked! I've got a small green light in the top right hand corner of my vision and I'm trying not to focus on it."

"Excellent! You've got it, man. And when you're ready to toggle it just let me know. If I want you to come back then I'll squeeze your hand. If that happens just focus on the blue, OK?"

"OK". He was breathing evenly now. "I'm ready Pete. I'm going for it." He closed his eyes. Pete waited about thirty seconds, then squeezed his hand. David opened his eyes and smiled for the first time. "Goodness me."

"You OK?"

"Yes—I—I'm just digesting." He looked off into the mid-distance. "He's an Indian man. I know that much already. He's called Gajbaahu. It means 'he who has the strength of an elephant.' He thinks in another language, and I—I understand it! This is unbelievable." He leant forward dropping his head into his hands, his whole body shaking with emotion. "I want to go back."

"It gets to you like that David—it can be addictive. Why don't you go back once more and then come back into you in a few seconds, so I'm sure you're handling the toggling alright. Sound OK?"

"Sure", David closed his eyes again, then reopened them half a minute later: "He's an agricultural labourer. He's got a wife and four children. It's literally like being in someone else's mind! All the things you know about yourself, who you are, what you believe in, where you live, who you know, all the things that are just there, that you take for granted without thinking—all that is just waiting to be accessed in just the same way. Only it's someone else—*someone else's mind*."

"Yep." Pete smiled complicitly. "*Good* isn't it?"

"Good! It's incredible."

"You'll get memories too if you stay in him. Only I've realised that remembering things is not something we can always do consciously. Strange that—memories bubble up in a semi-conscious way, I'd never clocked that before. We can't demand a particular memory. It's the same when we toggle. We can put out a thought cue though and wait to see what happens, then one thing leads to another. So—you have inherited not only his thinking process—but his memories too. There will be years of his story to catch up on. But that's quite easy too. You can learn a lot quite quickly."

David was listening to Pete alertly, but his eyes were also blazing.

"You want to go back don't you?"

"Yeah! But for longer this time. I want to know this guy better. All my life I've been alone with my own thoughts, like everyone, I guess. You think you're separate. But this is telling me what I've always known, intellectually, but never quite let in. I'm not separate. I'm not the centre of the universe. None of us are. And what I think of as *my problems*—that's nothing special. There's so much I can learn from this."

"You ready to be left then David? You comfortable, man, with the toggling side of things?"

David sat up and came to slightly "Yeah, sure. The toggling bit is easy, and *you* have to get on, I know. Thanks for all you've done. This is the most amazing thing—thank you so much."

"Don't thank me David, thank—them—whoever they are—they've given us this gift." He pointed to the circle, standing up as he did so. David also rose to his feet and the two of them hugged, David's body heaving.

Pete looked him in the eye: "We're brothers now David, stay in touch."

Moments later the helicopter was back in the air. They moved on to Salt Lake City where an elderly woman smelling of cheap perfume and with a strong Irish accent had been waiting eagerly for Pete: "Good-day to you sir. I saw you on the telly." She smiled at him, impishly. She was five foot tall with shiny black hair, high cheek bones, hazel coloured eyes and a tiny, brightly lipsticked, mouth.

"Hiya—you must be Caitlin?"

"I am indeed! Why fancy you knowing that! That is my name sir, it is."

Pete gave her instructions on toggling and led her to another glowing circle.

"You know what to do?"

"I do, I understand for sure."

"You ready then?"

"And why wouldn't I be?"

He took her hand, leading her through the circle and onto a waiting chair.

"You've got the green light now?"

"I have that, sir. It's something else indeed."

"Then, when you're ready, try focusing on the green." He waited while she closed her eyes and went inside. Seconds later she was back: "Sweet mother of Jesus—she's a Protestant."

"Is that a problem?"

"Yes, I'm a catholic! I mean no, it's not, of course it's not. I mean yes it is—I mean, I mean, I *don't know*. Here let me get back inside her."

Pete waited. After about a minute Caitlin started to smile. He left her to it. After a few more minutes he squeezed her hand gently: "Time to come back now, Caitlin, focus on the blue…" She came to, smiling broadly, now, and opened her eyes: "She's quite alright, you know. I think I—quite like her!

They moved on through Denver, Albuquerque, and a series of other stops where Pete initiated people. At Houston Texas, he was introduced to James Anderson—a wealthy looking man, with neat waves of polished black hair and a dark suit. James declined to hold Pete's hand as he walked confidently through the circle, sitting down briskly the other side. He'd explained to Pete beforehand that he was hoping to run for Congress and wanted this experience to add to his CV. "I think it might enhance my chances significantly, don't you think? None of the other candidates are doing this."

But he surfaced from his first toggle with the blood drained from his face: "Well, I wasn't expecting *that.*"

"You OK?"

"I think so." He didn't sound convinced.

"Sure?"

He lowered his voice: "Well, no. Can I tell you something *in private?*" He asked looking around nervously.

"Of course." Pete beckoned the surrounding guards: "Can we have a moment on our own please?" Somewhat reluctantly the guards filed out through the gate. Pete waited until they were out of earshot. "So what is it, James?"

James blinked. "She's a Mexican," he whispered.

Pete raised an eyebrow: "Does that bother you?"

"Yes, it does. She regularly crosses the border to work here *illegally*, in Texas. That's something I don't agree with."

Pete's nostrils dilated slightly. "Well you can't swap her back, James. Maybe you could go inside and find out more. Find out *why* she's crossing the border."

James shrugged. "I suppose so, but I'm not sure I want to know that."

"Well, you don't have to go back man, if you don't want to."

James was staring at the ground now. "You're right, I don't *have* to.."

"No."

"But then again, nobody needs to know if I do." He searched Pete's face, as if looking for a clue as to what to do next.

"No."

James looked away nervously: "It was really strange. When I was her, I got a feeling that there was—I don't quite know how to say this—I got a feeling that there was a lot of *room*. There was *space* in her mind."

"Hmm, that sounds interesting." At last here was a straw to catch on to.

"Yes, and she also seemed quite—*happy*"

"Even more interesting!"

James flashed a hostile distrusting look at Pete "No, not really."

"Oh?" This one was a tricky customer. "She's not interesting then?"

James looked at him with his brow furrowed. "Well, yes, she's interesting, but that's not the point. I wanted someone that would progress things for me. Perhaps a foreign diplomat or a business man whose methods I could learn from, or an honest family man, a voter I could say I'd learnt from. Instead I've got a Mexican migrant, a *law breaker*." His voice was scornful now.

Pete looked at the ground. A small bird had landed about six feet from them and was pecking at the grass near to the circle. It put its head on one side, listening. James continued: "And yet—she *was* interesting. It's just that I -" He swallowed heavily, the words seemed disjointed inside him, like the unthreaded beads of a necklace. Pete waited carefully. This was a time to stay silent.

"I realise that I'm not so—happy myself." He pulled a pristine white handkerchief out of his jacket pocket and dabbed his eyes. A short silence ensued. The bird made a sudden jab at the ground and seized a small millipede, which it picked up wriggling in its beak.

"I think I *would* like to go back"

"Do you want to do that now, James, so I can sit with you?"

"Yes."

James sat back and closed his eyes. Pete watched as the bird hopped about on the grass holding the squirming millipede in its beak. Then it flew off into the air, passing low over the circle and up to the top of the enclosure where it settled on a high wire, a black silhouette against the sun. He wondered if the pair might now be able to toggle. Perhaps they were toggling each other. He wondered how *that* would be for them both. Or maybe the millipede was enjoying a final release into something exotically *other.* These two might now have become available for others to toggle. Maybe someone else that he sat with would toggle *this* bird or *this* millipede. It seemed too preposterous—yet he was aware, as ever, of the tiny green light in the corner of his vision. Harvey was there inside him, dormant, waiting to be accessed, as if alive. He couldn't imagine not wanting to return to him.

James opened his eyes with a jolt.

"How're you doing, man?"

"A *bit* better, thanks. She's so—*caring.*" But he still looked disappointed. "She spends more time here in America than she does in Mexico. There are two young white children she looks after here: Jamie, and Annette. She really—*loves*—them. But, she's also got her own children too—Eduardo and Manuel—they're back in Juárez. And she loves them too! She's pulled in two directions. But she's—found a way. She hates leaving her children in Juárez but she really cares about the children she looks after here. So wherever she is there is always this mix of loss and love in her life. And yet, as I said, there's also *happiness*, there's really no other word for it..."

"Do you know why she is crossing the border illegally?"

"Sure, well, it started because she was desperate. The family had no money. Her partner disappeared—she didn't have any money to feed Eduardo and Manuel. She was living in a place with no work. So she left the kids with her mother and came across the border. That was really hard for her, leaving the kids. But she didn't have a choice. She knew it was risky, and she lives in constant fear of being caught and taken back, because then she'd lose her job. She saves up everything; she hardly spends anything on herself."

"But she's also happy?"

"Yes. She's frightened, she doesn't have much freedom, she doesn't think she's important, she works incredibly hard, and she's always missing someone, but she *is* happy. She *likes* to care for people, she cares *deeply*. Her thoughts are full of other people."

"Sounds like you've got a good woman."

"I guess."

"You *guess*?"

"Yeah." James suddenly stiffened. It was as if a black cloud had just blocked the sun. "But she's crossing the border illegally."

"Is that such a bad thing?"

"Of course! *She's breaking the law*!" He looked accusingly at Pete "And we can't have immigrants just coming into our country and scrounging our resources."

"Is that what she's doing?"

"Is *what* what she's doing?" James almost shouted.

"Is she scrounging our resources?"

"Yes! Of course! She *is* scrounging. She has no right to be here. This isn't her country."

Pete brushed an imaginary hair off his jeans. He wondered about reminding James that Texas had once been part of Mexico. But mental challenges wouldn't help here. James had to work things out for himself—or not.

"This must be hard for you, James." Pete said,

"Yeah."

"So you don't have to toggle."

"No." Pete looked up to the wire, where the bird was still sitting. The millipede had gone now. There was a long silence before he said: "OK, well, is it alright to leave you then?" He hated saying it. But there were other circles to activate.

"Ye-eah. Yes of course." James rose quickly to his feet in a kind of auto drive. "Well, er, thanks."

"You're welcome," Pete mustered a smile. "Let me know how you get on"

James followed him to the helicopter and watched glumly as it rose into the air. Then he made his excuses, dodging the press.

Over the next two days Pete, his father, and the pilot, frog-hopped through Texas, completing all twenty seven circles there, then on through Louisiana, along the southern coast and up the East coast, jumping from site to site. Most often the candidate would be waiting expectantly near where the helicopter was due to land, surrounded by personnel and looking like a rabbit caught in the headlights. As soon as they touched the ground Pete would race out under the spinning blades, involuntarily ducking his head. If possible he would embrace the candidate—some resisted this—and then take him or her off to as quiet a place as he could find, to try to calm them down and prepare them.

Most of them relaxed as soon as they met him. It was hard not to be infected by his enthusiasm and excitement. After a few minutes talking he would walk with them to the circle. Almost everyone worked out the toggling side of things quickly. It wasn't difficult—you had to make a deliberate choice to toggle in order for it to happen. Once you knew this there was no danger of getting stuck, or of going backwards and forwards, out of control. Pete soon learnt, though, that the hardest part was helping people to adjust to the new being inside them. As much as time permitted he stayed with them as they began to do this. In most cases, it seemed to develop nicely by the time he left—but with a significant minority, such as James, he wondered how it would all unfold.

There were a number of very memorable stops. A very traditional heterosexual man toggled a gay man. A basket-ball player, whom Pete guessed was probably quite chauvinist in his attitude to women, toggled a woman. A depressed looking woman toggled an Eritrean baby. A young athlete toggled a disabled Angolan man. A Jewish man toggled one of the Arabic guards who'd been minding a circle in Lebanon, and had secretly entered it when his colleagues had left the area during a shift change.

He also witnessed several people toggling animals. Some of these, like Harvey, had been used experimentally on the circles. Others, mostly smaller animals, such as beetles, flies, and birds, and also a mongoose and a cat, appeared to have strayed unnoticed onto circles somewhere. In one of the more remarkable of these encounters he listened as an exhausted looking middle-aged mother of four described with sparkling eyes how she'd toggled an eagle, and could flex the tips of her wings to catch the thermals rising up under the cliff near her waiting chicks.

As the week drew to a close it became clear that all 300 designated American sites would be activated in time. Reports were also coming in that thousands of other sites had been visited around the world, both officially and unofficially.

With half an hour to go before the end of the week Pete reached his last stop, in New York City.

Father Simon, wearing a dog collar, met him. "I'm so grateful you've been able to come," he said after Pete had settled him down and checked he knew the basics.

"You're welcome, Father. It's been my privilege—I've so enjoyed watching people touch the circles, and seeing what they end up toggling, it's been amazing."

"I'm sure it has". The minister spoke in a soft, high voice. "And I imagine you've seen the hand of the Lord at play?"

Pete considered his answer carefully. A few weeks ago he'd been certain that God didn't exist. Now he wasn't so sure. "I don't know, man—but I've certainly seen *something* extraordinary at work. It looks as if people can only be matched to beings—people or animals—who've already entered circles elsewhere, before them. But I don't think it's random—there's deep intelligence involved. Whatever it is—it seems to be matching people up with others who are in some way challengingly different from themselves and most also find, often to their surprise, that they enjoy toggling into this difference."

"Hmm, that's interesting, and what effect has that had do you think?"

"Well, I've witnessed some remarkable changes starting to take place in people—in the way they view others and in their orientation. It's as if the experience offered has been selected individually for each new person."

Father Simon smiled: "That sounds like God's hand," he said simply, his voice sounding like it was echoing in a church. "…and I want to see what he's holding in his hand for me! I've waited all my life for this." Pete noticed him glance upwards, as if to catch sight of the tail of God's robe high above them.

"Have you prayed for this then?"

"Not exactly. But I've prayed for a more direct *connection* to him." Again, he glanced upwards. "I've longed to join with him better, to understand his purpose in me. He made us in his own likeness. Out of all the animals it was us—*people*—whom he gave souls…" His mouth pursed into a small wrinkled ball. "But I don't *feel* like him. I feel so imperfect by comparison. I can't see how I'm like him. How I can serve him best. I long to know how my soul fits his design. I need a sign."

"You're not asking for a lot out of today then?"

Father Simon chuckled: "No...you're right, I should be less vain..."

His confidence seemed so frail. "I think we don't know, man, what's in store for you," said Pete, "but I've begun to understand over the last few days that it should be something that can help you." He glanced at his watch. Fifteen minutes left. "We should go, or the circle will be lost."

They walked together, the minister treading in meditative silence. When he saw the circle for the first time he fell to his knees, gazing at the smooth, flowing greens. "This has to be the work of the Lord." He began to pray out loud: "Oh Lord, I deliver myself into your hands. Show me your way." Then he walked into the circle and stood for some time, before proceeding to a chair.

Pete was waiting for him: "Do you have the green light?"

Father Simon nodded, his eyes wet.

"OK, so when you're ready, toggle the green light, I'll squeeze your hand if I want you back."

Father Simon closed his eyes. After a few seconds his eyebrows raised in astonishment, then a small line appeared between his eyes which developed into a deep frown. Pete squeezed his hand and the minister opened his eyes and sat staring at the circle.

Pete broke the silence: "What was it like?"

Father Simon continued staring, without answering.

"*Father Simon*?"

He came to, half rising in the chair, then sinking back. It was as if he was rousing from a deep sleep.

"Can you hear me OK?"

"Yeah—yes." He looked up and to Pete's relief met his eye.

"Seemed like you were getting stuck there."

"Yeah, I guess. It was so powerful… and there's much more. I'd like to go back."

"Hold on man, just a bit. Let's get clear first what's happened. Who did you toggle?"

"Well, that's just it…" Father Simon seemed to be struggling to find words: "He's not human but then again, he doesn't really seem like an animal."

"No?"

"No, he's so clever, he knows all about the trees and the plants, he knows so much. And he has strong feelings—he's very like us. But he's *so hurt*. He's probably hurting now. I ought to help him…"

"So take me through what happened, take it a step at a time"

Father Simon closed his eyes and began to speak: "I high up."

"You mean *he* was." Pete had got used to this—people associated so closely with the being they were toggling that they sometimes didn't differentiate. It felt important to keep them somehow clear and separate.

"Ye-es, *he* was." Father Simon still had his eyes closed. "*He* was top tree. Knew this tree type strong and tall, good to climb and look from. He look trees all round for good tree with tasty fruit. Then see purple! There it is! There are many, good trees. Purple fruit.

They down wind. Not too far. He make whoop, tell others." The minister's voice had become rougher and deeper.

"Sounds like you're toggling some kind of a primate"

"Yeah, I guess. He has his own thoughts though."

"Well, yeah, man, of course." But the minister looked ill at ease. "So what else did you learn?"

Father Simon closed his eyes again. "We—they—running. Running through trees. Sometimes climbing, swinging. Sometimes on vines. We fast. Run to purple fruit. Suddenly I—he—suddenly..." He stopped abruptly and took a deep breath.

"Yes?"

"Suddenly he upside down. Hanging from branch. Big pain in leg. Bad! Trying to move. Hard vine round ankle. Tight, tighter. Swinging. Pain. Others looking. No help. Long time. They go. Alone now. Pain bad, *bad*, goes black. Then…." Father Simon opened his eyes. He was crying now with great heaving sobs.

Pete put his arm around him and waited until his sobbing subsided. "What happened then?"

"Then he trapped. Somewhere else. Very straight branches, standing up together. Can't lie out. CAN'T GET OUT. Leg pain. And *men*, men give old fruit. Give water in round shiny coconut. Too much shit. Too small. Many sleeps. Leg pain. Want others. Want itch picking. Want trees. Want fruit from branch. Want swing. Want air. Want away. Many sleeps. Men back. Vine again around hands. Tight. Arms stuck. Into black, smooth, moving fast place. Want away. More sleeps. More moving. More sleeps.

New place with stand-up branches. Others here! Others different and sad. All sad. Want away. CAN'T GET OUT. Many sleeps. Sleep, day, sleep, day... Men come. Pull by vine round neck. They PAIN HEAD. Carry back. Sleep day sleep day... Men again. Pain head again. Pain. PAIN. Pain to sleep. Sleep day sleep day…

…Men again. NO PAIN HEAD NO! NO! FIGHT! Pull by vine round neck. NO! Men pull long. New moving fast place. Moving stops. Pull by neck. Outside! Air fresh. Cold. Outside! Want to stay. Pull by neck to round green *hard water*…"

Father Simon sat back in the chair, opening his eyes again. He was crying, silently. "And that's it. That's when it stops.

"Of course, and you will have his whole life up to that point."

Father Simon was on his feet now "Yes, but…. but I want to know what happened to him since he went on the circle. I want to make sure he's OK, that he's being looked after. The men, they don't understand. He's not an—*animal*."

"Isn't he?"

"No….that's just it," he was pacing now. "He isn't. He has feelings! He knows things. He cares." His voice had gone falsetto.

"Sounds important that you've found that out."

Father Simon looked down at him, his cheeks clenched in agitation: "No,—no! This isn't a small thing—this is fundamental."

"Hmm, OK" Pete suddenly felt very tired. It had been such a long few days. He had an overwhelming desire to curl up somewhere by the fire, toggle Harvey and sleep long dog dreams. "What're you going to do now then?"

"Find him of course. I can't let him carry on suffering, or the others."

"I get you there. I feel the same. I want to find the dog I toggle. Not because he is in pain like your…primate…is, but because, I feel, well, responsible."

"Yes that's part of it. *I* feel responsible now. He still has terrible pain in his leg, and I don't know what they're doing to his head in that—I think it's a laboratory. There may not be much time…" He slumped back down on the chair and began rocking backwards and forwards. "But it isn't that. I'll help of course… It's that he's *so like us*."

11

As Calvin waited for the circle to disappear, he was painfully aware that Matilda wasn't with him, or any of the villagers, apart from the Mayor. It was so different than just a week before when things had started off so well.

On the night the circle had arrived he'd made love with Matilda for hours and they had stroked one another, and looked into each other's eyes, listening to the sea. He'd never felt such contentment. It was only marred by the fact that he knew he had to go back to the circle. It felt like an impossible madness to leave her, but an hour before dawn, when she'd finally fallen asleep, he wrenched himself out of bed, searched out his clothes, and cast her a long last look. She was breathing softly into the tousled sheets, her dark hair splayed out around her in luxurious curls.

Outside he stumbled down the narrow path, back past the houses and on to the fortified enclosure. Unlocking the gate with the ancient key he slipped inside. The circle was just as it had been, green-luminous, flowing with its beautiful patterns, and unreal. He spent the rest of his shift, until his replacement arrived, staring into it, replaying his love-making and feeling inwardly exultant.

With dawn in full swing, he walked swiftly back to the hut, past unfolding views of the sea, craving his next encounter...

But she was gone.

The rest of his time on the island was a nightmare. The islanders were still as friendly as before, and there was much to see, but he had no interest in anything but Matilda's return—and she was nowhere. At the end of the first day he summoned up courage to enquire, he hoped casually, if anyone knew where she was. "Ah, that Mattie! She be on fishing trip with men folk." He was told

And that was that. The first day stretched with terrible slowness into the second and the second into the third. Between shifts he searched the island from tip to tip, scanning the horizon for fishing boats—but she was nowhere to be seen. Further enquiries of the villagers were fruitless—most of them said they had no idea, or seemed evasive or non-committal.

"She gets about ya know," or "She has lots to do, Mattie."

With devastating effect he slowly realised that she must be avoiding him. He had read her wrong. The thought was appalling. It wouldn't reconcile with his clear memories of the hours they'd spent together. At night he returned to his cabin where her musky smell still clung to the sheets—a bitter-sweet reminder of his loss, and proof that it hadn't all been an exotic dream.

Surely this had been more than a casual fling to her? For Calvin it had been momentous, life changing. Her absence left him with a hollow ache and a scratched record of memories. Endlessly he replayed their conversations, searching compulsively for any clue to her disappearance, but he found nothing.

On the seventh day he packed up with his men and they readied themselves to leave the following morning when the circle would have disappeared. Their mission would be complete. There would be one less circle needing to be protected and no need to remain.

He asked the villagers if they wished to witness the disappearance, but none were keen. This was hardly surprising, he felt. It would mark the end of an exciting alien presence in their midst.

So now it was just him, the Mayor, and his two men, who waited around the circle, counting down the minutes.

But when the moment came, the circle remained. They checked their watches. It should have gone by now.

"Perhaps they can't take 'em all precisely same time," said the Mayor "Expect it'll disappear soon."

They waited and waited, but the patterns on the circle flowed on defiantly. They checked the radio broadcasts. There'd been a handful of other cases around the world of circles remaining when it was thought they hadn't been touched but almost all that had been protected had now flicked away, instantaneously, just as they'd arrived.

Calvin realised something was amiss. "Perhaps someone climbed over the fence during the week." He ventured.

"But then whoever was on shift would have seen them" said one of his men.

"Well then I guess it must be faulty." he said, "If no-one touched it there's no other explanation."

"Ye be right, it must be faulty," said the Mayor.

The following morning the circle was still there, but they decided to leave anyway. There was no point in staying because no one could predict how much longer they would need to stay and Calvin was reluctant to advise his commanding officer that the circle had remained. In a private discussion with the Mayor he proposed that they'd be foolish to unnecessarily alarm the authorities about the circle having remained. "You wouldn't want a military presence on the island for a whole year."

The mayor readily agreed. He was happy to take responsibility for keeping the site protected, and accepted back the key: "Thank ye. I think it's all for the best."

A handful of villagers turned up to help Calvin and his crew carry their bags over the edge and back down the steep slope to Bounty Bay. At the harbour goodbyes were said and politeness observed, but the atmosphere was reserved…and there was still no Matilda.

As the longboat pulled away Calvin desperately scanned the shoreline looking for her face. Then, when they were about thirty feet out, to his amazement, he saw her standing on a rock, slightly up from the harbour, waving vigorously, and smiling her wonderful smile. Was that for him? She had a fresh flower behind her ear and her hair was blowing back in the sea breeze. She was wearing the same multi-patch skirt. His heart leapt, trying to reach her in the widening gap between them.

But it was too late to turn back now, much too exposing, too inappropriate to his rank. He stood and waved back, appalled at the feelings welling up inside him. The boat chugged on towards the waiting yacht.

12

At the bottom of Martin House's gardens, Marjorie squeezed behind the potting shed through a small gap in the high fencing. On the other side a narrow path of compressed leaf mould led along the side of a wood. Just by the hole in the fence and to one side of the path was a pile of discarded spirit bottles, presumably the hoard of a previous resident. She wondered, briefly, how they'd managed to smuggle them there, even though she'd now resolved firmly to *give up once and for all.* She was relieved to be out of sight of the house for the first time since she'd arrived and beyond the limits of the tightly cultivated garden and the 'therapeutic schedule'. It wasn't that she wanted to escape, just to find time alone.

In fact it had been an immense relief to arrive here, to be searched on the way in, and to learn that she was not the only one, that there was a path forwards, that others had successfully trodden before her. Sobriety *was* possible. She just had to follow the program at all times and *stay honest.* Honesty, was all it took, they said. The one rule. Admit honestly, a day at time, everything that was going on for you. For you cannot actually lie to yourself, they said. Not really.

It had been a relief to admit the extent of her drinking after so many years of pretence. Some of the others had found it much harder, and were still wavering, struggling with their denial at the edge of the group, muttering about the staff and 'the regime' in the corridors, arguing for permission to make trips off the premises. But the nurse at the hospital had convinced her—she had a drink problem. She *was* an alcoholic. She was out of control. That much was plain, at last.

'But can you *own* it fully?'— they'd asked. She felt she could. 'And own what caused it?' That was more complicated but it was beginning now to unravel. There *was* something she'd known for a long time and just hadn't wanted to admit. Something she was now beginning to unpick, to let in, in waves of painful relief. News of the circles too that had been acting like a trigger. She had followed every interview with the people who had touched them, fascinated by their accounts. These people had clearly changed. It *was* possible to change, and for things to transform.

She followed the path as it twisted down a mulchy bank into dark cool woods dripping with bird song. At the bottom was a moss covered, bench, beside an ancient oak whose lowest branches rested on the ground like giant elbows. She sat down, breathing gently. Unexpectedly the sun emerged from behind a cloud and the bank in front of her illumined into a shimmering violet sea. She hadn't noticed them! Bluebells! Bluebells were everywhere! The slope was massed with them. Clusters of bells on stems held high and proud above the dark green shining swirls of their flattened leaves below. Bluebells drunk with sunlight, blending hazy bright in the distance. She sat, mesmerised, sighing deeply, and inhaling the honeyed air. This was it. This was all it took. It was so simple. There was really nothing to do. Looking at the bluebells she connected again with something she'd always known, a transcendent viewpoint emerging as if from a dream, something long lost—yet which she knew had always been with her, waiting patiently for revelation. There was nothing to worry about. *Absolutely nothing.* Nothing was lost and nothing even damaged. She had only forgotten, grown out of connection, failed to stay open. And, as she remembered, it became clear to her what she had to do.

Late that afternoon, in visitors' hour, she led Oliver down the same path into the bluebell wood. He stalled at the gap in the fence, aware that they must be breaking the rules, and reluctant to go with her, even if she was saying she needed to talk. Besides he didn't want any more intense conversations, or any difficulty. The last few days had been fraught with difficulty, not just because of Marjorie's actions and their consequences at home, but because of the wretched circles. Everyone at work was talking about them ad-nauseam, even the asylum seekers. He'd had to do extra shifts when a close colleague had taken time off work, ostensibly for sickness, and one of the court clerks had even phoned in without an excuse—saying the news was too momentous to miss. Meanwhile work was stacking up. He followed his wife apprehensively through the gap.

She sat on the bench indicating for him to sit beside her. He stood awkwardly, then acquiesced, laying out his handkerchief carefully before sitting on it gingerly. They sat silently for a few moments, Marjorie aware of the bluebells dancing in the late sunlight, Oliver wondering what might be coming. Ever since she'd cut her wrist his wife had been acting out of character. On one occasion she'd refused to see him, on another she'd shouted down the phone. He'd bought her, at great expense, and at her insistence, the best rehabilitation treatment in the region. She hadn't even thanked him. This was not the woman he knew so well, who was so consistent and quietly dependable, so upright, so mature.

The sun went behind a cloud and Marjorie took a deep breath:

"I'm not coming back, Oliver."

He looked at her uncomprehendingly. Hearing what she'd said but the words somehow not adding up.

"*What?* What do you mean?"

"I mean I'm not coming—home. I'm leaving."

He scrutinised her closely. She seemed to be avoiding looking at him, her moist eyes looking off into the distance. He noticed the long brown gash on her wrist, out of bandages now.

"I don't understand you. You can't stay here. We can only afford another week, two at the most."

"No, I know that, Oliver. I mean after here. I'm not coming back. I'm leaving you."

Still it made no sense. "Leaving me for what? Where are you going?"

"I don't know yet, I'll stay with Hattie first, then decide."

"But Marjorie, you can't be serious. What about Willow View? What about the boys? You can't just up and go, just like that, you can't…

"I *can,* Oliver." She was looking at him directly now, her face suddenly caring. "I'm serious, I'm leaving. I'm sorry—I have to go"

"You don't *have* to go"

"I'm going Oliver, I'm leaving."

He felt like he was at the edge of a deep pit, staring into darkness. He hadn't even known the pit was there. He had no idea how deep it was. She was asking him to walk over the edge. "Marjorie, please, these couple of weeks have been so stressful, you aren't thinking straight, you're tired, you're not yourself…" His voice trailed off as he looked into her soft eyes. She looked—different—she didn't look tired, she didn't look uncertain. She looked oddly vital, caring. He had a sudden longing to hold her in his arms. But she met his gaze and cut through fiercely: "I'm leaving, Oliver."

This time the words stung. Perhaps he would never hold her in his arms again. He felt suddenly exposed, in a rare vulnerability in front of her—peeled back and bare—and with a pressure building up behind his eyes. "But why?"

She looked away searching for some way of explaining.

"I don't know, I…."

"You must. You must know. *Why*?"

"Oliver, this is so hard, it's so hard to explain, please listen, there's something—missing. I've known it for a long time. I just haven't wanted to admit it. Maybe it's always been missing. I don't feel…connected…to you. I'm sorry"

Connected? What nonsense was this? What could she possibly mean, 'connected'? Of course they were connected, they were man and wife weren't they? They went on holiday together, they'd had children, they had an overlap of interests, they knew each other well, they spent most evenings together. Their lives were intricately inter-connected. "Marjorie, of course we're connected. How could we be more connected?" He felt exasperated now. "And what more could you possibly want?"

She didn't answer straight away, but looked down at the bank of bluebells, no longer in sunlight. She longed for the sunshine to return, and the drench of violet light. "It's not what I need. We have a nice house, we have a nice garden, we have wonderful children—though they are leaving now. But I don't have a purpose. I don't feel *connected.* There's only more of the same to look forwards to. I'm done with dinner parties and soirees and the bloody church spire. I'm done with dressing up for your colleagues. I can't do it anymore. I only managed by drinking. It was my only source of joy, but I turned to it in—in *desperation*, because I couldn't find joy elsewhere, or fulfilment." She looked into his face, imploring him to understand.

"You don't really know me Oliver. You know the woman who always dresses so well, who irons your shirts, who makes polite conversation, who presses flowers. You know the cook, the shopper, the interior decorator, the one who hangs on your every word, who massages your ego. You don't know *me* though—and you can't be blamed for that because I haven't really shown myself to you, I haven't known how to, and I don't think you understand yourself how to make a bridge outside of your own skin. So we've both failed, and in the process I've lost touch with myself. I've been too long in your shadow. But these last few days I've been finding her again, finding myself—and she is so sad, I am so sad. I am sad—and I am angry, because I lost connection, I've no purpose. I gave up too much, and let things drift for too long. There has to be more than what we have and I have to find what it is."

"I didn't imagine," he said after a few moments, wrestling not to react to the stings in her words, "that you were so sad. Why didn't you tell me?"

"Because I didn't know, because I wasn't admitting it, even to myself."

"But if you didn't know why does it matter? And can't you find your purpose without leaving? Why do you need to go to do that? Can't you stay?"

"Because it's over between us, Oliver, don't you see? I could never come back to Willow View, it would kill me. It would stifle me with its—normality. *You* would stifle me. I wouldn't be able to breathe. I would slide back to how I was before, in just a few days, stuck, unconscious—drinking."

"*I* wouldn't stifle you. I don't think you know what you are saying. You'll regret this. You need to think this through, carefully, you need to..."

"*Don't tell me what I need to do!* Don't you see? That's the whole point. *You* don't know what *I* need to do. Only *I* know that, and I *have* thought it through. In a way I've been thinking it through for years."

Her answer reached him. She was serious. He'd never imagined this could happen. He'd known things might be slightly amiss with her, but not this. Had it all been a charade for her then? Was all that had happened between them somehow rendered valueless now? Could he have been so wrong, so out of tune with her, for so long? He felt a sudden despair. "Please Marjorie, don't do this to me." There, he was pleading now. Was that what she wanted?

The sunlight came back, slanting through the fluttering canopy of leaves, lighting an electric swathe of nodding violet bells.

Once more she looked at him squarely, eyes wide, nose resolute, brow smooth, shining. For the first time in years he noticed just how beautiful she was. Why didn't he notice that normally?

"It's no use, Oliver, I'm leaving."

13

Before the raid at 3 am, and against his better judgement, Mohammed had nurtured a tiny seedling of hope. Maybe his health was going to recover. He was coughing less, eating more, his headaches weren't so appalling, his hands were recovering. He'd even been sleeping better. The interviews had been difficult, but perhaps this was because people here just weren't as friendly as back home. And the British were well respected for human rights. Their justice system was acclaimed throughout the world and kept separate from politics. It was obvious that this was a rich country. Back in Uganda, when he'd given talks for the FDC, he'd held up the British system as a paragon of virtue. Maybe he really could stay. Maybe he could begin a new life here, away from his family and his roots, but at least safe. Maybe, maybe, maybe.

But at 3 am that morning, when his stomach churned with fresh horror at seeing the uniformed guards, his tiny seedling of hope felt pinched out routinely, like a weed, not to be tolerated.

It was, he surmised, as if he'd walked through a mirror. This was no different from Uganda. Seamlessly they'd carried on the questioning here, they'd even asked some of the same questions, and showed the same disbelief. Even the handcuffs were the same. And he was locked up again now, this time in a tiny dark compartment in the back of a van with armed guards only feet away, just like when he was under the floorboards.

He tried to imagine what he could possibly have said in his interviews that could have been so damning. Had it been a genuine enquiry or was it just an exercise they went through? Perhaps, like his interrogators in Uganda, they hadn't been interested in truth. Whatever they had been doing it meant he was now being returned to Uganda. He'd be arrested at the airport. They'd want to know how he'd escaped and again he'd have no answers. They'd imprison him again and the punishments would follow.

First day in Makindye barracks, doubled up like an embryo on the floor. Holding my head as long as possible. Initiation. Boots slamming into me, I am being kicked—unconscious.

After a few hours driving, the van pulled off the motorway, and he could just see the guards through a tinted window, as they bought themselves take-away burger meals, at a Wimpy outlet. Propping themselves up against the van they ate their meals under his window, slurping Coca Cola from large polystyrene cups. After they'd eaten he followed the glow of their cigarettes in the half-light. Then one of them opened the side of the van, and unlocked the door to his cubicle.

Muhindo stubbing out a cigarette on my neck. Smile.

The man passed him a drink of water and a slice of bread.

The van drove on and he saw signposts to Heathrow airport. Not long after this they drove through two twenty-foot high metal security fences into the compound of a huge building. The tops of the surrounding fences were swathed in coils of razor wire leaning inwards at an angle. The building was ablaze under floodlights and looked new, with pallid yellow brickwork and rows of narrow barred windows.

Officials at reception removed his hand-cuffs and gave him a thorough body search turning his bag upside down and emptying out its contents onto a shiny metal table. They confiscated a tube of toothpaste.

Once through security he was passed to a towering pear-shaped guard with a massive roll of belly fat that strained against his stretched white shirt in a run-away ellipse. The guard looked him up and down with small red rimmed eyes. "Right, Marimbey, this way," he said, grudgingly, unlocking a door into a small floodlit room just large enough for the two of them. He gestured Mohammed to go ahead then followed, locking the door behind them with a large key on a chain that disappeared under his belly. Then he squeezed past Mohammed and unlocked the next door in front of them. Mohammed, pushed back against one of the walls, noticed an array of CCTV cameras all around them like giant pointing fingers. Escaping would be extremely difficult…

Don't even think it!

Outside the room at a junction of corridors, the guard pointed with a thumb down one of them: "Walk." Mohammed walked in front, the guard pounding at his heels and pushing him from behind whenever his pace slowed.

"Speak English?"

"Yes—a bit." He had to force out the words, his throat had gone dry.

"Good, that's what I like to hear, Marimbey." The guard glanced around swiftly: "I'm supposed to be looking after you," he said, in a lowered voice. "Do as I tell you, and I'm sure you'll be fine. We'll get on like a house on fire" He chuckled slightly and pounded on without saying anything further.

Identical doors punctuated both sides of the corridor, which smelt of toilets and detergent. The guard stopped outside one of the doors, looked around again, his red face suddenly stiff. He gripped a pinch of loose fabric from Mohammed's shirt sleeve between two twisting fingers and pulled him closer, his rough chin scraping the top of Mohammed's head: "Any trouble though—there's always the solitary lock up—do I make myself clear?"

Mohammed froze. He could feel the heat of the guard's breath on his head and the fabric of his shirt tightening in a tourniquet.

Muhindo's breath smells just the same.

"Do I make myself clear?" the guard repeated in an intrusive whisper.

"Yes."

Smile

"Good!" He let go, pushed the door open with his boot and slapped Mohammed firmly on the back so that he staggered through the entrance.

Hit in the back, falling through the open door onto the pavement.

The room was sparsely furnished as a cell for two people with a door leading off—presumably to a toilet. A man was sitting on one of the beds, reading a newspaper. He looked up quizzically as Mohammed staggered into the room. The guard growled from the doorway: "That's it Marimbey, remember what I said". He winked savagely, then turned and pounded down the corridor, leaving the door swinging. The two men listened as the sound of his footsteps faded.

The sound of guards boots on the floor above.

"Welcome to the Ritz", said the man on the bed. Mohammed didn't answer. He couldn't find words. He was a startled animal, trapped away from the herd, not knowing which way to run.

"Such friendly service here, wouldn't you say?" The man smiled at him, closing the door.

Mohammed dropped his bag but stayed standing, awkwardly.

Smile!

The other man surveyed him carefully for the first time then changed his tone. "It's your first stay here isn't it?"

Mohammed nodded. "...That guard?" he ventured in a whisper.

The man smiled. "Don't worry about *him*, he's all bark, no bite. Some of the others are—much friendlier—but I'll point them out so you can avoid them...How long have you been on this lovely island with its tropical clime and friendly citizens?" He brushed back a lock of hair and Mohammed noticed that there were fingers missing from his hand.

"You mean Great Britain?"

"Hmm, yes, *great* Britain."

"Just a few days."

"And where are you from?"

"Uganda."

"Eh!" the man said, with a clipped and delighted falsetto. "Me too—eh!" He held out his good hand, "I'm Zoro." They shook hands, Mohammed also using his left hand. He tried to look friendly but it was alarming to learn that Zoro was from Uganda. Maybe he was in league with the Ugandan government. Such things were common back home, people lured you into their confidence, pretending to be against the regime, then, if you'd agreed with them, they arranged your punishment.

"You speak Luganda?" Zoro said in Luganda.

"Yes..." Mohammed replied, reluctantly, also in Luganda.

"Eh! We can speak in Luganda!" Zoro smiled broadly, "And you've just come from Uganda! Eh!...I haven't been there for seven years."

Mohammed sat backwards onto the other bed, knees caving away beneath him: "*seven years*?"

"Seven years, yes, and *still* I am waiting"

"Waiting? What for?"

"For permission to stay, of course, same as everyone here."

Mohammed looked at him, aghast. This couldn't be true. "How come they haven't sent you back or given you permission in all that time?" He ventured dubiously.

Zoro gave him a concerned look: "You haven't learnt much yet, have you? Some people wait even longer. That's the way it is here. Whatever you do, they won't believe you. I have lots, lots of evidence." He held up his right hand "this hand for instance was courtesy of a Ugandan prison—but they said it could have happened some other way; and I've got a copy of a wanted notice for me that was published in the Sunday Monitor shortly after I escaped. Surely you can't get much better evidence than that? But my solicitor told me not to even use it. He said it would make my case look *worse,* they'd say I'd paid a bribe to put it there." He was laughing now—an infectious belly laugh. "Paid a bribe with *what money*? And the Monitor wouldn't risk taking a bribe. You must know that, Museveni would kill them if he found out." He chuckled dryly. "…Every time I get more evidence the Home Office says I've made it up."

Mohammed recoiled. What could he mean? Was there a home office in Uganda? "The *home* office?"

"The 'Home Office' yes - the people in charge of immigration in *great* Britain as you call it. Don't you know anything?"

Mohammed felt so confused. "…But if they don't believe you why haven't they sent you back?"

Zoro smiled at him indulgently. "Because they're hopelessly inefficient. Because my case is still open. Because I'm still fighting them." He laughed again. "I thought I was a dead man, many times. But the system here is—unbelievable. Some they send home quickly. Others like me are kept hanging on and on, like a slow death. What about you, how come you're here, what's your situation?"

"I don't know what's happening…" Mohammed said with quiet despair.

Zoro smiled softly. "Don't worry, I'll help you. "Did they give you a letter?"

Mohammed remembered the letter and pulled it out from his bag, still unopened. He passed it to Zoro.

Zoro delicately put on some cracked reading glasses—held together at both sides with tape. "Let's see…" He opened the letter expertly, "I do this for a lot of people, there's people here don't understand English, or the system. Not that the system is easy to understand. I think they make it complex on purpose to keep us busy during our stay here—so kind." He read the letter carefully, holding it up to his glasses with his thumb and little finger. "Oh, OK, so you had your second interview in Newcastle and they turned you down. That's where they interviewed me," he glanced up from the letter, "they didn't give you a Lugandan interpreter did they?"

"Yes…"

"What was she like?"

"She had a white eye."

"Uh, she's the same! That's not so good."

"Why?"

"Cos she's messed up lots of people's cases. She distorts things. She knows what will weaken a case and twists your words. And those interviewers don't know anything. They rely on her to interpret not just your words but everything about Uganda. If she says, afterwards, that one little thing you said didn't ring true they'll believe her, not you, and then they'll disbelieve everything. She has a lot of power, that woman. I don't know how she sleeps at night. But then, that goes for a lot of them."

"Why would she do that?" Mohammed was appalled.

"Isn't it obvious? Because she is supported by Museveni's regime, of course. She's helping Museveni preserve his image abroad. Stands to reason, who else would get over to this country in a normal way?"

Mohammed's head was throbbing. "So does that mean they'll send me back?"

Zoro looked back at the letter. "…Nah…not yet anyway. It says here you have ten days to appeal."

Mohammed stiffened. "What do they do when they peel you?"

Zoro raised his eyebrows, then burst into laughter. "*Appeal*—all one word not 'a….peel'. It means you can ask to go to court and try and persuade them to change their minds. You have ten days to request that or they can take you back to Uganda."

"How do I do that, then?"

"Do you have a solicitor?"

"No."

"Then you need to get one. I'd give you the number for mine, but he's hopeless. There's a legal surgery here—so good of them to provide this for their guests, don't you think? But by the time your appointment came up it would be too late. The best bet is to get your own. They let you make one free phone call here—though they don't exactly advertise this right with neon lights. You need to ask someone outside to find you a solicitor."

"But I don't have any money to pay for a solicitor."

"Oh, they pay for it"

"*They* pay for it?" He was so confused.

Zoro smiled knowingly. "Everything is strange here. You need to understand that. This hotel is actually Kafka's Castle. The thing is they get it wrong a lot of the time when they first assess people. So they have to look at it again and—sometimes—they change their minds. You'd think they'd try to get things right in the first place—then they wouldn't have to pay for this hotel, or for your solicitor, but no." He grew suddenly serious: "But the odds aren't good, whatever your evidence. Only about one in three get permission."

Mohammed stood up stiffly and shuffled over to the barred window. Below him, was a compound covered in tarmac and marked out with faded lines. It was surrounded, on all four sides, by tall yellow brick walls, each studded with at least a hundred, identical, barred windows. Guards talked in clusters under bright surveillance lights by the exits of the compound, and in the middle groups of men stood about smoking and talking. A few were mirthlessly kicking around a punctured football. He thought about the taxi driver. That man had persuaded him to go back to the house in Sunderland, and now look where he was, he was back in prison. He turned to Zoro with dismay, "but I don't know anyone outside who could help me".

14

"We've had to fight them every inch, know what I mean?"

"Hmm."

"First, to persuade people that the circles aren't like a terrorist plot or, like, *sinister*." Minty prodded her vegan salad with a disinterested fork.

"Then to push for as many circles as possible to be touched within a week, so they stay."

"Hmm."

"Now to make sure anyone can touch them – not just the chosen few."

"Hmm." Brian used his last chip to wipe his plate clean and looked up at her encouragingly. She was wearing a bright yellow campaign-issue T shirt with a picture of a green circle across her chest over-written with the word 'Quality' and large dangly red earrings. Striking, as ever.

"I've found my calling, Brian, no shit. They can't do this. It isn't up to politicians. The circles belong to the people, right. That's what I told that MP today, it's about personal freedom, yeah?

"Hmm." Brian swilled his mouth out with a sip of tea and listened contentedly. These past few days he'd driven her every day, free of charge, to and from the meetings and rallies of the FCC—the Free the Circles Campaign. She was a leader now, making speeches, organising, meeting officials, representing the younger protestors. She'd risen so fast it was hard to keep up. But after meetings, like today, they would sometimes have a little time together before he drove her home. This was what he enjoyed most, when he had her to himself. There was plenty to talk about. Not that he felt that he had much to say himself, her life was so exciting compared to his; and once he had her started it was easy to keep her going by asking the odd question then sitting back to enjoy watching her.

"It's going to change the world, Brian, if enough people visit them."

"You don't think it might be dangerous for some people then?"

She tossed her red streaks and laughed, at ease with his question. "No Brian. Look, you have to trust, man, it does people good."

"That's not what the papers are saying. There've been several examples recently from the States of it going wrong for people."

She narrowed her eyes. "Look, don't believe all the crap you read. That's because of the FBI raid on the SETI office."

"What?"

"That tosser, Theo Chaldrike, he was behind it, man. I'm not big on conspiracy theories myself, but this guy's unreal. He made the FBI seize all SETI's records of people who'd touched circles, right, so he could trawl through for people he could manipulate to speak against and put the shits up everyone. Can you believe that? But out of over 300 he only found a handful willing to do it…and *they distorted stuff*, like that anorak republican candidate who said he was being tormented by a Mexican immigrant he'd been matched with. What shit, man, he was just stirring it for the fear vote…" She took a sip of carrot juice.

"Besides, no-one promised we wouldn't suffer… and all the stories I've heard of had cool consequences, even if someone did suffer. Sometimes transformation hurts."

"What do you mean?"

Minty raised a forkful of alfalfa and pomegranate pips to her mouth and looked at it without enthusiasm. "…Well take the woman whose talk I just heard, right, she told us that visiting a circle transformed her husband…*but he suffered.*." She chewed for a moment.

"Why? What happened?"

"She said her husband got chosen for a circle because he was powerful enough to pull strings. But she was frightened because she thought he would take it out on her if it didn't go well. That's the kind of guy he was, right, a bully. But he got matched with a woman who had a violent husband just like him! How mental is that? So when he got back he told her he was sorry, right. Well she'd heard that before, like forever. They went round in circles: he'd hit her, she'd threaten to leave, he'd get all sorry and fit, then she'd agree to stay, then it'd all be cool for a while, then he'd start up again, bashing her. And they'd go round and round, know what I mean?"

"Yep, I've heard sections from that cycle a few hundred times on Friday nights in the cab."

"So, anyhow, she said he came back *changed*. For starters he didn't try to touch her. That was nuts, man. He always needed to touch her when he came back. Touch her sexually, like he was a seasoned hyena, or something, marking out his territory. Sometimes he'd insist on having sex too, straight away. She didn't dare say no, right. But this time he left her well alone. He said he knew now he couldn't force her to be cool. In fact he offered to leave— he'd leave for ever, right, if she wanted, and she could have the house..." Minty put down her fork by her half-finished salad.

"She didn't believe, for sure. People don't flip that much. But he was quieter, right. He started sleeping in the spare room and spending loads of time toggling there. Came out looking gutted and saying he was learning, like, *so much*..." Minty pursed her lips and gently dabbed them with a serviette, leaving a kiss shape of lipstick. She glanced up at him, her eyes lapis lazuli blue under thick eyelashes.

"...After a few days she got round to testing him, right. She said she'd take up his offer and wanted him to leave. He went really dark for a couple of minutes, and she waited, shaking like a leaf, right, thinking he'd explode. But he said: 'OK'. He didn't even argue. Then at the door he said—and this was the bit that really shocked her, because he was always so jealous—'Find yourself a man who can love you properly.' She hasn't seen him since. She's had no bother. She said that would never, ever, have happened before, man. She said the woman he'd toggled matched her perfectly. It couldn't have been a coincidence; there was just too much overlap between the other woman's experience and hers, the way they were treated, the brand of violence…"

"So you think the circles deliberately gave her husband someone like her then?"

"Sure, so he could experience what it was like to be on the receiving end of his own type of violence. Like people are matched *intelligently* to the person, or animal, already on record that's most suited for them, and the more people that enter circles the more people will be on record and the more accurate the next matching will be, know what I mean? That's why we have to get as many people as possible to use them. Her husband suffered, sure, but that's how we learn."

"But why do you think they're doing this?"

Minty smiled broadly. "It's so totally cool, man, I think they're trying to teach us. They're matching each person up so they see things different, from someone else's point of view, like wearing someone else's shades."

"And what about her, do you think she'll go back to him?"

"Dunno man. Right now I think she's enjoying the break. The cool part is she's thrown herself into the campaign. She wants everyone to be able to use the circles, says they're like holy gifts, and we mustn't get in the way. We've got loads of people like her campaigning now."

"I know. I've heard a few on TV."

"It's urgent, Brian. We've only got a year, right. This won't happen again so everyone should have the opportunity, total, the elderly, kids, prisoners, the mentally ill… We're running out of time. Someone calculated that if everyone on earth wanted to visit a circle there'd need to be one person touching each circle *every thirty seconds*, right, day and night, throughout the year, and it'll have to get faster if we waste time now…"

"I hear things are happening in Varanasi."

She flashed him another smile. "That's iconic, man"

Later that day Brian got an unexpected call. It was Mohammed.

"Mr Johnson, please, *please*. I need help, can you help me? You're the only person I know on the outside…" His voice sounded distant and doubtful.

"What do you mean, on the outside?"

"…They put me in prison"

"*What*? Whatever for?" Brian was appalled. Hadn't they seen his injuries? Surely he should be in hospital, not prison. He listened, sighing deeply, as Mohammed related his interview and subsequent arrest.

"OK buddy, of course, I'll help."

Mohammed explained about needing a solicitor to make an appeal and also wanting to contact a friend of his in Uganda called Abdul whom he knew would take a message to his mother, but whom he didn't have a number for, just a work address in Kampala.

Brain got straight on with it. He hadn't thought much about Mohammed since he'd been in the cab, but the image of his upper body still haunted him and he was angry now. How could they have put him in prison? It was obvious he was genuine.

It was easy finding a solicitor's firm who said they were experienced in asylum cases. Getting a number for Abdul proved a greater challenge, the work address Mohammed had given for him wasn't on the net, but through a friend of a friend, he tracked down a Ugandan man in the UK who had family in Uganda and who agreed to ask his family to look for Abdul.

A few days later Brian phoned Mohammed back with both numbers. It went quiet on the line. He thought he'd been cut off at first. Then he heard him sobbing with relief.

Thinking about it afterwards, and for the first time ever, he felt ashamed to be British.

15

The crowd had her name. A rapturous whisper that rippled through them in eddies and swirls: Tara. Om Tara, tu tare, ture, svaha…

Tara, whose name means star. It was her.

Tara, Goddess of compassion, green skinned, beautiful, saviour goddess. Ancient Tara, of many religions. She'd come for them! She was here, manifest—a beautiful green circle, subtly radiant, patterned with nature, down by the great Ganges river, near the burning Ghats.

The dusty roads outside Varanasi swarmed with pilgrims converging from many directions. They lined the narrow, temple fringed alleyways down to where she waited for them, packing in tighter together as they got nearer, a vast molten flow, studded with the many colours of their clothes, slowly inching closer. Hindu, Sikh, Muslim, Buddhist, Jain, Christian. Men, women, children, rich and poor. Each waiting for their moment, their union with her, and the tangible sign she would give them.

Guest houses were packed full, bodies squeezed together on roofs and verandas. Food was expensive. Toilets overflowed alarmingly. The air smelt of incense laced with sewage and was peppered by the shouts of children and vendors, the beat of drums, the clang of bells and trumpets.

From dawn until dusk the sun blazed relentlessly, shady fringes at the edges of the alleyways packed tightly with drowsy standing bodies. Water sellers, squeezing through the crowd, jangled bells and passed out thin disposable pottery cups of tepid muddy water, their prices rising in tandem with the sun.

By night, fires were lit to prepare food, and many stayed up, singing and dancing, and smoking ganja. They sang with desire, in ecstasies of devotion. She was here, really here. She was here to save them. Those that attempted to sleep lay in a dovetailed mosaic on the street, arms draped over shoulders, noses pressed to backs. They slept fitfully aware of the stars, Tara's light, shining upon them, waking to shuffle sleepily forwards a few more steps towards her. It was said that it took three days now to reach her, and times were getting longer. But they were patient. This was a one-off. This was celebration, jubilation, *confirmation.*

Amongst the crowd, Marjorie and Hattie, contrasting all too dramatically with their pink skins, expensive clothes, bulging suitcases, and broad hats, now stood, exhausted and exultant, within a few steps from the circle.

It had been Marjorie's idea. After discharging herself from Martin House, she'd gone to live with Hattie, sleeping for several oil-paint infused nights in her art studio amongst her green and gold 'ensembles' of woodland vegetation.

She had astonished her sister by proposing the trip, explaining that she had nothing to lose now, and everything to gain. Who knew when the circles might become available to the public in the UK and what the criteria for visiting them would end up being? Perhaps they would bar those with a history of the mental illness. Perhaps the authorities in India would give way to international pressure and close down the circle at Varanasi. There was no time to lose. She was going, anyway, but would love it if Hattie joined her.

Within days they were flying, first to Delhi, then on to the Lal Bahadur Shastri Airport airport near Varanasi and then as close as they could get by rickshaw. There they joined the throng and were soon funnelled by a fast assembling crowd into a narrow street leading steeply downwards.

Hattie, who'd been to India three times, cast herself in the role of chaperone and cultural advisor to Marjorie, who'd never travelled further than Europe: "Don't accept any food or drink, however tempting. It'll give you the shits, or worse. Don't give any money to anyone—it just encourages them. We can do that later if we want to, just before we leave. Always keep track of all your belongings, keep bags and pockets zipped."

Marjorie listened to her sister's well-meaning advises and indulged her greater experience, but her body bubbled delightfully with scarcely contained excitement and relief. She was running on raw adrenaline now, intoxicated with their situation and a tingling sense of her own aliveness—a feeling she'd long ago forgotten she could access. Contrary to expectations she found herself not at all intimidated by the situation, but brimming over with joy. This was as far as she could get from her life in England with Oliver, and the cul-de-sac bottle behind the bread bin. Only a few weeks ago she'd been so hopeless, so blinkered. She hadn't even been aware of the prison she'd allowed to build around herself. And now she was in India! It felt like another planet! At the same time, it felt oddly familiar, like she'd always known it, as if she was returning home.

They had attracted attention as if they were street performers. The moment they joined the queue children formed an enchanted circle at their feet, content just to stare at them, scarcely blinking their wide dark eyes, as if watching celebrity TV. Vendors, weaving through the crowd, made a beeline for them, the women half covering their bright white smiles in mock embarrassment. Speaking in broken English, they offered jasmine flower necklaces, crafts, ornaments, morsels of food…stealing a stroke of material or a touch of hair as they did so. Young men, too, eyed them longingly, now and again approaching with a proposal:

"Come with me, I take you another route which is quicker. I save you many days."

"Where you sleep tonight? My uncle very good hotel. Good bed, good sleep. I keep your place for you when you sleep."

"Engleesh? Engleesh? I been Lon-don, Leicester. I show you carving factory. They give you chai. Look only—no buy. Good price. You keep place."

It wasn't long before Marjorie's carefully laundered clothes became creased and covered in stains, and her glossy hair thick with dust. She found a wipe in her bag and with particular relish removed her make up. It was a relief to let go.

Over the days and nights that followed they'd grown familiar with the people they were queuing with, and learnt the first name of many of them. One woman in particular, Rupashri, spent long hours discussing with them in broken English the upcoming event. She told them about Tara, surprised that they did not know her. She delighted in demonstrating, with much giggling laughter, how to put on a sari. After that, the conversation broadened out to compare their lives and families, their worries about children and relatives. And Marjorie, to Hattie's dismay, accepted a samosa from Rupashri and gave her a high energy cereal bar in return. After that, food was pooled, and a friendship sealed. 'If I get the shits,' thought Marjorie, 'then so be it.'

Rupashri noticed the scar on her wrist and their eyes met in a silent exchange. Nothing was said, but after that Rupashri grew tender, frequently taking Marjorie's hand in hers and stroking it gently. In the evening she offered to braid her hair, and Marjorie accepted, delighting in the touch of practised hands against her scalp. She returned the compliment with a silver handled hair brush that she'd brought with her, brushing through Rupashri's luxurious black hair. Rupashri liked the brush, and the matching mirror that came with it, and held them afterwards, gazing admiringly for some time at the fine silver craftsmanship.

Rupashri also helped them greatly by negotiating with the beggars, who came relentlessly, pestering with outstretched hands and imploring looks, pointing to their mouths and stomachs. She spoke to them in their own language, firmly, but with tolerant kindness. Most, as soon as they picked up her tone and realised she was with the white people, walked on silently.

In this way they passed time, and slowly grew closer to the circle. What might have been a demanding and desperate experience, in searing heat and discomfort, turned out to be immensely enjoyable. It was as if, Marjorie thought, they had merged into the crowd, and become no longer separate with their individual worries and fears.

As they all grew closer, an infectious anticipation took hold of the crowd. Those who were returning, having touched the circle, could be identified by the green spot that had been painted by the holy men on their right temples, and their bright astonished eyes. They were besieged with questions from the crowd. Most, having had no time to digest their experience, were intent only on pressing their way back up, through the throng. But some spoke of their awe, and of the incontrovertible proof inside them now. Once you'd received her touch, they said, she remained with you, inside you, not as an idea, or a hope, but tangibly, *actually*.

Stories from those who had touched her raced through the crowd, which savoured and embellished every detail of the individual matchings, taking them as yet more confirmation of Tara's great compassion. She was here to transform, to link together those that visited her, to help them break free from the cages of their souls. The links she forged were magical, specific. She put another soul inside you. A soul whose experience you could enter at leisure. You could think their thoughts and relive their memories. You were no longer *alone*. You were connected now for all time. And a copy of your own soul would be left behind for Tara to care for and hand on for another to see. It was a route out of isolation and mortality.

Aware that they would soon be parted, Marjorie wrote out her address for Rupashri. But Rupashri could neither read nor write and although Marjorie tried to copy down phonetically the address she spoke in return it seemed unlikely that they would ever meet again. She pulled her silver brush and mirror from a side pocket in her bag, where she had kept them ready, and pressed them into Rupashri's unwilling hands, holding her fingers around them until she accepted the gift.

By the time they reached the final stretch it was nearly dark and a muggy, rank, breeze was blowing across from the Ganges. All around Tara, lamps and candles were being lit, and she herself was a wondrous moving pool of gentle greens. They had had plenty of time to learn what to do and how to respect her. It was important not to touch her with your foot. That would be considered very offensive—maybe you would be matched with a mosquito as a result! And you needed to take off your shoes and make an offering. You could offer leaves, paper flowers, beads, anything green. But you needed to offer something. Rupee notes didn't offend. The holy men, or sadhus would take the offerings.

Rupashri had brought a piece of green material that she'd hand embroidered, Hattie had a green origami bird she'd bought from a vendor, and Marjorie had decided to give away an emerald broach that she was particularly fond of, and had brought from England, not realising its destiny.

Finally, they were there. Rupashri went first, carefully kneeling at the side of the circle, her glossy hair reflecting the moving green light. Marjorie watched, spellbound, as she pressed her hands worshipfully together and leant forwards, touching her head into the green, then rising, elegant in her sari, and radiantly smiling. Next Hattie did the same, kneeling into the dust then bending, her coral curls falling forwards as her brow made contact with the swirls. As she rose to her feet she gave a startled cry of astonishment.

Now it was Marjorie's turn. She knelt, clasping her hands together, and with a prayer for the future, bowed into Tara.

16

Aware that rush 'hour' in Kampala goes on all day Abdul had got up before dawn to catch the first bus. But only now by mid-morning, had the bus finally shrugged off the hooting carbon monoxide quagmire, reaching an escape velocity of just over walking speed to join the road towards Mbarara—Mohammed's home town.

He knew of course that it would take at least another six hours. The road wasn't tarmacked, except for a brief stretch of four-lane highway near to Museveni's home village.

Once underway the bus negotiated the dusty road at breakneck speed. Thundering past pedestrians on both sides of the road, horn blaring, missing by inches and spitting up a swarm of spinning pebbles into a black exhaust streamer.

Abdul pressed his head against the dusty vibrating window. He'd been amazed to hear that Mohammed was still alive. After he had failed to return from Makindye Barracks, they had given him up for dead. It had been a further shock to discover he was phoning from a prison in the UK.

Mohammed had been a local hero when he was campaigning for the FDC. They all knew the risks he was taking and admired his courage, preferring to take a lower profile themselves. Abdul had watched him with a mixture of respect and concern, never quite able to decide whether his friend was a true visionary, consciously and willingly martyring himself in the name of freedom, or just naïve.

Either way, his friend needed him now, and he had, with some trepidation, agreed to help. It was a significant risk. The government could listen in on mobile calls. They probably knew he was connected with Mohammed. It was hard to know how to make enquiries, and who to trust, and if the authorities found out he had been asking questions then he'd surely be detained himself. But Mohammed was his friend. If their roles had been reversed he'd surely have done the same for him. Perhaps it would be liberating, just for once, to be actively subversive. Or was he being foolish himself?

The bus braked violently behind a slow moving line of traffic. A sign at the side of the road announced the line of the Equator. Tourists were taking photographs at a place you could stand with a foot in both hemispheres and on a newly constructed hoarding, surrounded by armed guards, a notice read:

'Alien Object,
Entry Strictly Forbidden.'

That was another odd thing. Mohammed had only just heard about the green circles, and he didn't really have an opinion one way or another. In the past he would certainly have had an opinion—he had an opinion about everything, he'd have been arguing for everyone to visit them. Mohammed must be in serious trouble if he'd only just found out about the circles, everyone knew from day one.

He found Mohammed's mother's home just off the high street in a smart residential area in Mbarara—a large detached two-floor house with a smartly painted door. A well-dressed middle aged woman answered. But when he asked if she was Mohammed's mother she looked at him with alarm and stared carefully behind him, before disappearing into the house. Several minutes later she emerged with a piece of paper. Again she looked around carefully then leant close and said quietly: "She moved. We bought the house from her. This is where she is now—it isn't far. Take a boda boda."

Back on the high street he found a huddle of boda bodas, in the shade of a large tree, their drivers sitting sideways on the saddles, playing cards and talking. After some discussion about the price, one of them agreed to take him, and drove him out of Mbarara for about ten miles, before turning off abruptly onto a steep undulating muddy track at the edge of a banana plantation. Huts and make-shift shelters were scattered about them. They made enquiries and were eventually directed to a woman, aged about 50, sitting on the ground outside a tiny mud-built shack with a rusty corrugated iron roof. Abdul asked if she was Mohammed's mother. She nodded mutely, remaining seated but shuffled her bare feet and adjusted her faded pink dress. Her face was round, like Mohammed's, with large brown eyes that seemed fearful and exhausted. Abdul sat on the ground beside her, trying to set her at ease. "Mohammed asked me to come and see you. He's my friend."

She looked at him carefully: "I thought he was dead."

"No—he's not dead! I spoke to him on the phone. Only a couple of days ago."

She grasped his arm staring at him with a flash of hope: "Where is he?"

"He's—in England. He escaped there, about two weeks ago."

"Thank God, thank God!" She leant over, sobbing. Abdul waited for her to recover, not knowing if he should reach out. Eventually she raised her head and looked at him again, hungry for reassurance: "You're sure?"

"Yes, I told you, I spoke to him on the phone. He sends you his love. But also..."

"What?"

"Also, he needs to know *how* he escaped. He doesn't understand. They just let him out, put him on a plane."

Now she looked startled. "Why does he need to know this?"

"Because the British authorities—they don't believe him. They won't let him stay—unless he can explain *how* he got out of Uganda."

She sat very still, then turned and faced him, looking directly into his eyes. "Can I trust you?"

"Yes."

She stared at him without smiling for a good minute scrutinising his face for signs of betrayal or deception. He felt like his soul was being tried by her eyes. Finally she whispered slowly: "OK then, but you mustn't tell anyone but him, do you agree?"

"Of course"

She looked off into the distance. "Mohammed was just like my husband. Couldn't stop himself getting involved in politics. My husband was in the NRM, he was high up, then he defected. They shot him for that—you probably heard?" Abdul nodded.

"But he had a close friend in the NRM, I won't tell you his name. He stayed friendly even after my husband joined the FDC. It was very dangerous, they had to meet in secret. After my husband was killed—his friend used to come and see me. He used to come at night, in disguise, sometimes he'd bring me money." She looked down at the ground. "We were very poor, without my husband."

Then when Mohammed disappeared, I asked him if he could find out where he was, if he could do that for me. I didn't see him for several weeks. When he came back he was very serious. He told me Mohammed was in a safe house and that he feared for his life. I begged him to help me get him released. He said we needed to pay a bribe to get him out, and not just out of the safe house but out of the country. He knew someone who could do it, but he needed a lot of money. He said he'd never be safe in this country, and I wouldn't be safe either if he hid with me. I asked him how much it would cost. When he told me I was really upset—it was too much for me.

But I couldn't stop thinking about him, in the safe house. At night I kept imagining what they might be doing to him. So I figured I could raise almost enough by selling my house and that's what I did, six months ago. I gave all the money to my husband's friend and moved here." She pointed to the shed behind her. "This is where I sleep now, this is my home. They let me stay here in exchange for picking bananas.

Abdul looked into the hut, there was a pot in one corner, a frayed mat on the floor, a few clothes hanging up on a hook, and nothing else.

"What happened then? Did you hear from your husband's friend?"

"No, I never heard from him again, I can't tell you any more. I thought he'd betrayed me, just taken the money and done nothing. That is, until today, until you came…" She looked at him now with shining eyes. "Thank you for bringing me this news. At least they won't hurt him in England."

17

It is the strained smile of his wife as she leans over, trying to comfort, that most inflames his rage. Not that there is much of him left to rage. His body thin and skeletal white, already stinks of death. Clear liquid, suspended out of reach, drip feeds him through translucent skin, and beneath the sticky sheet he can feel the tubes draining away his waste to a putrid bag at the side of the bed. He is an expendable link in a circuit of machinery. Clean fluid in, contaminated fluid out. Nothing left in between, nothing of value, anyhow, only a contaminating process. Maybe that's it. Maybe all that's left is this rage, this putrefaction. Rage at the war and his part in it, rage at those he fought and those who made him fight, rage at the world…but most of all rage at his wife for trying to help, for underlining so faithfully his inadequacy, his dependence, his failure, his weakness… And yes, of course, it is really rage at himself. Rage for the waste. He knows that now. Now that it is too late and he is unable to turn without a bloody nurse, now that he can no longer have a drink, or ten, now that he is forced to remain conscious. Surfaced at last from his alcohol sea, he is drowning in air, oppressively conscious with rage…and regret.

Marjorie toggled herself out of Besnik with a shudder. It was almost unbearable to enter his world but she had steeled herself to keep doing it. She looked over at Hattie, asleep at last, with her head juddering against the plastic frame of the oval window, and past her, through the window, she could see the approaching lights of London beneath them. They were coming into land.

Shortly after touching down her phone leapt ominously back to life. There were 15 new texts—all from Oliver.

Seeing the number of messages she feared at first that something might have happened to one of the boys—but they were all about his worries for her. 'Please call me, I don't think you should go through with this ' ,'Are you in India yet? If so please come straight home'; 'Are you OK?'; 'I have been thinking it is unwise for you to visit a circle'; 'Please answer me'; 'Why aren't you responding?'

She waited until she was back in Hattie's studio before reluctantly ringing him. She was weary of trying to explain. Her explanations didn't add up without referring to the emptiness she felt had consumed their relationship but she didn't want to hurt him again by talking about that. 'Emptiness' wasn't the kind of concept he understood anyway. From his perspective their relationship was calm, mature, *efficient*—what more could she want? He wanted tangible explanations. Had she been unfaithful? Was it because she was too embarrassed about her drinking? Did she perhaps need to develop new interests? Should they go on holiday more? Should he be doing more around the house? Endless telephone conversations with questions she couldn't answer.

She couldn't blame him for asking questions of course—he must think she was acting so out of character. Well, she *was* acting out of character—she had always been so reasonable. It was hard enough understanding what had happened herself, but she remained convinced she had made the right decision. The part of her that wanted to separate from him had lain at bay for years, semi-conscious, anaesthetised, but silently gathering a hold in her soul until it had overwhelmed her and locked irreversibly into consciousness. Now that the decision had been taken there was no going back.

She phoned him and arranged to meet, declining to give any detail of her toggling experience, other than that she'd touched a circle, was back, and was OK. He proposed meeting at Willow View, but she couldn't think of anything worse. The house felt more like a place of work than a home, it was stiff with memories. Besides once she was there with him it might be harder to leave. She also declined his suggestion of lunch at the Blue Lagoon—the luxurious fish restaurant where they'd had their first date. Too formal, too full of memories, and he'd try to romanticise it. Reluctantly he agreed to a walk by the river.

She reached the car park slightly late and breathless, having borrowed Hattie's bicycle. As she locked it to the railings she was aware of him standing by his BMW, waiting for her. He was wearing his dark full length coat, his hair unruffled by the wind, an umbrella in one manicured hand. Only his eyes betrayed anything other than affluent self-assurance. They were mournful, wider than usual, appraising her.

"Hello, my dear." She wished he wouldn't refer to her that way.

"Hello Oliver." Awkwardly she held back from touching him and walked through the entrance to the river walk. It was a late spring day and the wind was hurrying dark clouds across the sky. Beside the path, the river flowed slowly in a wide silent curve.

"So, how was it?" asked Oliver, as soon as they were underway.

"Totally extraordinary." She tried to tone down her voice to disguise the mixture of excitement and shock about her experience for fear that he would somehow undermine it.

"India or the toggling?"

"Both—and both have changed my life for ever." She told him selected extracts from her experience—arriving in India, waiting at Varanasi, then arriving at the circle and touching it. Oliver listened without interrupting.

"...and then I touched my head into the green circle and it was just as they said, a green light came on in my head, and it's still here." She touched her temple, suddenly self-conscious under Oliver's wide, astonished, eyes.

"But, who, or what, are you toggling?" asked Oliver.

She took a deep breath: "He's a man, Besnik, a Kosovan man. I was expecting an Indian person, after all most people have been getting Indian people, because you can only toggle someone who has touched a circle somewhere in the world, before you, and I think more people have visited circles in India than anywhere else; but he's from Kosovo." She paused and looked out across the river, its brown surface scuffling into wrinkles in the wind. "He's very ill. He's in hospital with cirrhosis. Being in his body is *hell*—especially in his most recent memories. For most of his life he drank from first thing in the morning until last thing at night." She looked down at the path. "Even I've been amazed how much he drank. His whole life has revolved around drink; he has woken up tipsy, drunk all day and gone to sleep in a stupor—often not even making it to bed. It's been hard to access a lot of his memories because most of them are a booze-induced fog. But I know he was in the fighting and I know he did some—terrible things."

They walked on in silence for a few paces.

"Does he have a wife or children?"

"Yes, he has a wife, whom he seems to hate for no good reason, and two children who won't see him... Her voice was trembling with emotion. Oliver reached across the gap between them and touched her elbow, but she shrugged him off.

"The worst of it is that he's not much older than me and he's going to die soon." They walked on a few more paces. A duck with a raft of ducklings, was drifting slowly down river, keeping close to the reeds by the bank.

"But you said it had been a life-changing experience for you?"

"It has, don't you see—his feelings about his situation are almost unbearable to enter, but this is what awaits *me*—if I don't make changes and face things."

"But it's hardly the same for you, Marjorie. It's not like you haven't been facing up to stuff, other than, perhaps, your drinking."

"Oh but I haven't. That's the point. It is always easier to say it doesn't apply to you, to say that you're different. But now that I have Besnik's situation inside me I can't do that anymore. There are so many internal arguments that he used, rationalisations for drinking for instance, that I recognise in myself, the resemblance is shocking. He's just further down the line."

"But surely you could just avoid toggling into him?"

"I could, it's true, but the thing is when I toggle him I get *insight* and that's useful. I get the place he's arrived at—his terrible despair and regret that it's too late now and he's trapped. So, when I toggle back into myself, I feel relieved. It's not too late for me—I can still make something of my life."

"Haven't you been doing that?"

She looked at him, askance: "No, no I haven't."

"How can you say that, Marjorie? You've successfully brought up the boys, we have a wonderful house—all thanks to you. I couldn't have done my work if it wasn't for you, I..."

"But that's just it, Oliver, it's *your* work.

"But don't you think it's important?"

She felt desperate to explain something to him, but unable to do it in a way that did not devastate him. There *was* something about his work that she didn't agree with. Especially now that she'd visited India, and seen the way that people in poorer countries live; now that she'd met Rupashri; and now that she had Besnik's experience inside her. Besnik, who'd suffered the effects both of war itself, and then of living in a war blighted country. Oliver's work seemed to revolve around keeping people out of Britain, and disadvantaged. She could no longer support this.

"It's your work, Oliver, not mine," she repeated quietly, trying to avoid the issue. "I need my own work, my own meaning..."

"It *is* about my work isn't it?

She might have guessed he wouldn't let it pass. He might be many things but he wasn't stupid. Again she cast her eyes about her, searching for a way to answer. She was struck by how carefully managed the scenery here was. It was so different to India! The trees and bushes were pruned, the path litter free, the smells contained. There was none of the chaotic abandon and charm of India. If this was India there might be rangoli designs drawn in flour on the path, or a shrine to Ganesh, at the base of a tree, with freshly cut flowers beside it. There would certainly be people everywhere—washing in the river or selling their wares beside the path. Here they were completely alone, protected, cocooned.

"Yeah, I guess, it's partly that. I'm not sure that I agree with your work as totally as I once did, I..."

"You're saying it's not important?"

"No, I didn't exactly say that... I said I have to find my own meaningful work. I've changed. Oliver. There is also Hattie's experience to consider..."

"Hattie's experience?"

"Yes, she toggled an Indian child—Nabendu. He's from a slum. He's only seven and he hasn't enough to eat. The boy's had no childhood. He is already selling postcards to tourists. Hattie wants to help him, and I—I want to too. I want to use some of our, *my*, wealth to do that."

"What, just by giving him money?"

"No, not just him and not just by giving money, by getting involved with the charities who are working with all this."

A light drizzle had begun to fall. Oliver undid his umbrella and held it over her. She moved further away from him. "It's OK, I'm alright." Oliver shrugged. "So you want to become a Good Samaritan then?"

"Well, that's one way to put it."

"And my work's no longer good enough for you?"

Suddenly she felt angry. "No, I didn't say that. You're just parodying things."

"So what *are* you saying?"

She felt cornered now. "Look, can we go back?" she asked, turning around without waiting for his consent. They retraced their steps in silence. By the time she spoke again, the rain was drumming harder on Oliver's umbrella.

"…I guess I *am* judging your work in a way. But it isn't just your work. It's all that we stood for: Willow View, the wealth, the advantage, the privilege. Your work is all about protecting that. Not just ours alone but the wealth and advantage of all the people in this country. We only want to prevent foreigners from coming to our country because we want to hold on to our wealth and privilege *as if we are somehow entitled to it.* Yet we're no more entitled to it than Nabendu."

"So what would *you* do my dear? Would you allow anyone to enter this country if they wanted, just throw the borders open?"

She thought for a moment. Trust him to reduce it so incisively to such an extreme. Momentarily she felt thrown off balance; she was a fool, hopelessly idealistic. But then she felt a sudden surge inside her. It wasn't idealism that was the problem, but the lack of it. It was the lack of meaning in Besnik's life that had left him so despairing. And it was the erosion of her idealism over the years that had left *her* feeling so empty, and needing to compensate with alcohol, more and more possessions, and keeping their home like the centre pages of Country Life magazine. Her idealism had been sacrificed on an altar of greed and security. There had to be a better way.

"Yes, that is what I'd do! Throw the borders open! The lines we draw around ourselves, and around all countries, are nothing anyway but lines in wet sand, lines drawn by people, lines that'll soon be washed away by the sea. We don't own this earth, Oliver." She pointed to the wet path beneath them. "The earth owns us...it isn't ours to hand out in the first place." It felt wonderful talking like this.

The rain was now a torrent and Oliver quickened his pace towards the car park. "This is nonsense, my dear. It isn't just about wealth, it's about culture and identity. If we threw our borders open, in the manner that you say, there'd be a huge popular backlash. There's no way we could house and feed all the people who'd want to come here. We'd be inundated.

"Not without sacrificing a large part of our own wealth you mean?"

"Yes, precisely."

"But that's my point. We can't give without losing something. Look, I know the borders aren't going to open fully tomorrow, and I know there would probably be all manner of trouble if they did. But we don't have to think of it in such extreme terms. Can't we at least begin to ease them up a bit? The work that you do seems to be about keeping things as tight as possible. About keeping our borders closed to even the most needy people—the asylum seekers—the people who say they're fleeing persecution."

Oliver sighed with dismay. "But a lot of them are just saying that, my dear. A lot of them just tell lies in order to get here. My job is about deciding which of them are telling lying and which aren't. We have to have some control, you've just more or less admitted that yourself."

She was incensed now: "I haven't admitted it! I still think getting rid of our borders is what we should be aiming for! I only agreed there might be problems if it happened tomorrow—too suddenly. But what worries me is that, if anything, our borders are getting tighter rather than looser. How do you *know*, Oliver, that what you decide in court isn't as much determined by your own defences and denial, than by a genuine desire to open yourself to the truth—which is a painful thing to do? What I've learnt through toggling Besnik is just how easy it is to deny the truth—especially if it is appalling, and if it makes us feel guilty. It's easier to believe someone is lying about, say, being tortured, than to let in a truth that requires us to take action." There she'd said it now, she shook the water out of her hair and glanced over at Oliver, whose square jaw seemed slightly stiffer. These were probably not ideas he could understand, she realised.

"Look, *you* can do what you like," she continued, anxious to finish what she had to say before he could reply "and asylum is just one aspect of it all and, I admit, not really my area. But what's bothering *me* is *my* hypocrisy. We both know that there are starving people all around the world, people suffering from easily prevented diseases, people whose lives have been ruined by natural disasters—yet the fact of the matter is that we only manage to help a minute proportion of those people—and at the same time we enjoy a life of luxury ourselves. It's that hypocrisy *in myself* that I now feel *I* have to change."

"So what do you want to do" Oliver asked wearily, smarting at her attack on his work and anxious to move the subject from himself.

She took a deep breath: "I want us to sell Willow View and use the money to help people."

"You want to *sell our house*?" He was incredulous now.

"Yes, and the shares." She glanced at him. He looked so forlorn.

"You can't be serious. Where would we live?"

"Somewhere cheaper—in bedsits. We don't need a house like Willow View. It's monstrous that we hang on to it with the likes of Nabendu in the world. We don't *need* a house so big. We never did—but it's especially true now the boys have as good as left. We could use the money, we could use it to help."

"So you would make us homeless to satisfy a philanthropic whim?"

"Don't dramatise so, Oliver! I'm not saying we should do it overnight, and this isn't a whim. I've never been so clear about anything."

"Over my dead body," said Oliver quietly and she suddenly felt cold to her bones, she'd feared this would be his reaction.

They walked on swiftly in silence. Oliver already regretting having rebutted her so absolutely. Of course it was ridiculous to sell Willow View, but he shouldn't have expressed it so extremely. He had wanted to win her back today, somehow persuade her to return, and it had all gone horribly wrong.

At the entrance to the car park they had to jump across a run-away stream of floating car park tickets and cigarette ends. The rain was hammering on the roofs of the cars and there were expanding muddy puddles everywhere with bursting raindrop bubbles. Marjorie was shivering and soaked through, her hair hanging in lank rat-tails and her blouse semi-translucent with the wet. Oliver, by contrast, had largely kept dry under his expansive umbrella and thick coat, only his shoes and ankles were splashed.

"Let me take you home, dear." He offered. "We can come back for the bike later."

What did he mean by 'home' she wondered. "No, I..."

"Don't be silly, you'll get soaked."

"No, I have to go." she turned towards Hattie's bicycle and started wrestling with its U lock.

"Come on Marjorie. This is madness"

"No! Just go!" she shouted into the wind, as the lock twisted open in her hands. She backed out the bike and faced it into the squall. She cycled as fast as she could back to Hattie's studio, soaked by the muddy spray that splashed up from passing vehicles, and making no attempt to avoid the puddles, feeling suddenly exhilarated—freed up by the thought that she couldn't get wetter.

18

A loud banging at the back of the court, preceded two men entering—one of them tall, grey suited and beautifully manicured, the other a bustling court official shouting: "all rise."

Brian and the others in the court stood up. The taller man walked with measured paces behind polished wooden panels to a single throne-like chair half way along a separate, raised up, area.

'Be seated'.

They all sat down in the lower area. Brian glanced over at Mohammed who noticed him for the first time and nodded almost imperceptibly. He was wearing the same ill sized T shirt he'd put on in the cab, and sitting on the sharp front edge of his chrome rimmed chair.

The tall man, directly opposite Mohammed, and some twenty feet away, introduced himself as Judge Oliver Surret and began outlining the procedure. He seemed formal and humourless to Brian—but not unpleasant. It was hopeful, at least, that he was making some effort to help Mohammed understand. Surely this was all going to be straight forward with a good outcome. He'd have to be sympathetic in view of Mohammed's injuries. But he also seemed to be routinely reciting a speech he'd made before.

He explained that he was entirely independent of the Home Office and would consider all the arguments of the Home Office, and of Mohammed's lawyer, before deciding between them in a written decision. If there was anything Mohammed didn't understand, he should say so.

Phrase by phrase, the speech was translated for Mohammed by a young male interpreter beside him. Mohammed smiled broadly throughout and nodded frequently but Brian wondered how much he was really understanding. Despite his smile he looked frightened and alone, caught in a nightmare crack in the world. Brian began to regret that he hadn't visited him at his detention centre and got to know him better. He'd only managed to talk to him on the phone on a few occasions in the months that had passed so quickly since he'd picked him up at Heathrow.

Once the judge had finished, a man in a suit with shiny elbows stood up for the defence. He began by asking Mohammed his name and date of birth and then went through various bits of evidence, asking clarifying questions on each—his first statement when he arrived in the country, the longer follow-on interview in Newcastle, a report from a doctor he'd seen in Sunderland, and a recent statement from himself describing his telephone conversations with Abdul and what Abdul had learnt when he'd visited Mohammed's mother in Uganda. It all seemed straightforward enough, though Brian did get the impression that he probably didn't know Mohammed well.

Mohammed blurted out answers to his questions then sat with his frozen smile, as the interpreter translated. The judge listened carefully, taking notes, his face inscrutable. On the wall behind him was a royal coat of arms, a crowned lion and a chained unicorn and the motto: 'Dieu et mon droit'.

After Mohammed's solicitor the judge invited the opposing Home Office lawyer to ask questions. A man in a formal suit with bright contrasting red silk tie leapt to his feet.

"Mr Marimbey, I note that in the screening interview that you had with the Home Office that your name is spelt Marimbay with an 'a' at the end whereas at the second interview it is spelt with an 'e' at the end. Which is correct?"

Mohammed explained (via the interpreter) that his name should have been spelt with an 'e' but that they had spelt it wrong in his first interview.

"Why then, if they spelt it wrong did you not correct them?"

"Because I didn't think it was important enough to correct."

"You didn't think it was important to get something as basic as your own surname correctly spelt?"

"... No, sir."

"And you went ahead and signed a form with your name spelt incorrectly?"

"Yes sir"

"But you expect everything you say here today to be taken as accurate?"

"Yes sir."

The solicitor didn't look up at this response but paused significantly and shuffled through his papers.

"In the same interview you say that you arrived in this country accompanied by someone called Jane, but you did not know anything else about her. Is that correct?

"Yes sir."

"You said that you'd never met her before you met her at the airport in Entebbe, is that correct?

"Yes sir"

"And you also said that this woman, Jane, whom you'd never met before, had documents which she used to get you on a plane is that correct?"

"Yes sir."

"Mr Marimbey, what were those documents?"

"I don't know sir."

"You don't know. Had you ever seen those documents before?"

"No sir."

"And when asked at the interview how this woman had acquired those documents you said that you didn't know that either, is that correct?"

"Yes sir."

So you didn't know who this woman was or how she'd acquired a document for you that would get you past customs or even what the document was—though presumably it was a passport with a photo—is that correct?"

"Yes sir."

"A document that not only got you on the plane in Entebbe, but though passport control in Kenya, and then again through passport control in the UK. Is that correct?

"Yes sir."

"But you had never seen this document before, and have no idea how this woman acquired it?"

"No sir."

"Have you ever applied for a passport?"

"No sir."

"Or gone for a passport photo?"

"No sir."

The solicitor paused to take some notes, his face impassive.

"You also refer in the second interview with the Home Office to having been held in a 'safe house' is that correct?'

"Yes sir"

"How long were you in the safe house?"

Mohammed paused, clearly not sure how to answer. He talked for some time to the interpreter before it was translated: "He says that he isn't sure. He was held in darkness and lost track of the days."

"Mr Marimbey I am not asking for an exact period of time here. Roughly speaking how long were you held at the safe house?"

Again there was a pause as Mohammed talked to his interpreter: "Maybe two years."

Both solicitors, and the judge, copied the answer down in silence.

"And then, one day, you were just released, is that correct?"

"Yes sir."

"Indeed, as you put it, a guard: 'Made me fall out into the street.' Is that correct?"

"Yes sir."

"And you had no idea what was happening."

"No sir."

"Did the guard say why he was releasing you?"

"No sir...he just said he was giving me a special treat."

"A special treat?"

"Yes."

"So one of the guards involved in holding you for approximately two years in the safe house suddenly and without explanation told you that he was going to give you a special treat and 'made you fall out into the street'. Is that correct?"

"Yes sir, but I didn't believe him..."

The solicitor coughed perfunctorily. "No, indeed, it *is* hard to believe." Another silence followed whilst he ruffled documents further, his bright tie glinting.

"OK, so moving on to the reasons that you gave for being arrested in the first place. You said that it was because you were a member of the FDC, is that correct?"

"Yes, I had been holding a campaign meeting."

"When did you first join the FDC, Mr Marimbey?"

"2001."

"So by the time that you were arrested you had already been in the party for many years, is that correct?"

"Yes sir."

"So you should have known a good deal about the party?"

"Yes sir."

"Why then, when you were asked what you knew about the party, did you say and I quote—'I don't know anything. I can't tell you anything'.

"I don't know, I do know about the party. I don't think I said that."

"*You don't know…you do know*. Mr Marimbey it is written clearly in the notes for the interview that you *did* say 'I don't know *anything*, I can't tell you *anything*'. Notes that you signed…"

"Yes sir."

"So, how do you explain that?"

"I don't know sir."

"No—you don't seem to know much about a party you claim to have been in for over a decade."

There was another painful silence. This didn't appear to be going well. Brian glanced up at the Judge and thought he saw a slight, almost imperceptible, shake of his head. Mohammed, sweating profusely now, was squirming in his seat, as if in front of a firing squad. As the Home Office solicitor carried on in his apparently reasonable but subtly menacing way Brian wanted to scream at him. It was as if he was a boxer punching a swinging bag.

"…So coming back to your time in the safe house, Mr Marimbey, you say you

were regularly taken and questioned in another room. Is that correct?"

"Yes sir. They tortured me."

"But according to your testimony, you can't remember how often they did that."

"…No sir."

"Can you describe the room?"

Mohammed stayed silent after his interpreter had translated, his big eyes darting about the court as if looking for a poisonous snake.

"For instance were there any windows in the room?"

"I—don't know." His voice falsetto.

The solicitor looked at his notes.

"Yes, that *is* what you said in the interview." Mohammed looked relieved.

"But how come you didn't know if there were any windows?"

"It was very dark, I guess there must have been windows."

"You guess."

"Yes sir."

"Hmm. And after they finished questioning you, you allege that they returned you to a small space under the floorboards. Is that right?"

"Yes sir."

"And that that place was where you spent all your time when you were in the safe house, apart from when they were questioning you, which was 'about 2 years' is that correct?"

"Yes sir."

"And in the testimony you gave in your second interview you say that you didn't know what the floor of this area was made of, is that correct?"

"Yes sir."

"And that the only way out of it was by a hatch, is that correct?

"Yes sir."

"And that during the time that you were kept in this space you didn't try to open the hatch, is that correct?"

"Yes sir."

"Or try to escape?"

"No sir."

"Hmmm. No more questions your honour." Abruptly he tapped his papers together with brisk finality.

The judge looked over at the other solicitor. "Are there any other questions that you wish to ask arising out of the Home Office examination?

"Yes your honour." Brian breathed with relief. Hopefully Mohammed's solicitor was now going to redress the balance.

"Mr Marimbey… you do now have more information about how you escaped from prison, do you not?"

"Yes sir."

"Do you want to describe to the court what you now know?"

Mohammed looked slightly relieved, "Yes sir, I managed to contact a friend of mine, Abdul, in Uganda who went to see my mother. She told him that she'd paid a bribe to get me out of prison."

"And the bribe also paid for your fare to this country did it not?"

"Yes sir."

"And for a fake passport to be prepared."

"Yes sir, I think so."

"So there's now a perfectly valid explanation of how you got to this country which you didn't have when you came to this country."

"Yes sir."

"And when you did come to this country you had just been held in captivity for a long period of time and had been severely mistreated. Is that not correct?"

"Yes sir."

"So, it's hardly surprising that when you were being asked questions about, for example, how long you had been held in custody, or what you knew about the FDC it was hard for you to answer with any great coherence or accuracy, is that correct?"

"Yes sir"

"You were still traumatised?"

"Yes sir."

"No more questions, your Honour."

The judge spoke slowly. "OK, so Mr Marimbey, both sides have had an opportunity to ask questions, and we will now hear a speech from both solicitors, after which, today's hearing will end and I will make a judgement. We are going to hear first from the Home Office solicitor. Do not worry if he says some things that you may not agree with, because your own solicitor will have a chance to respond immediately afterwards. You are the most important person in this court, so it is very important that if there is anything that you do not understand that you let me know. Is that OK?"

Mohammed nodded and smiled.

The Home Office solicitor rose to his feet. "Thank you, your Honour. I would refer you to the skeleton argument in your notes. Nothing in the appellant's replies to the questions he's been asked today leads me to wish to revise what was argued there. We don't know how Mr Marimbey secured his transit to this country, how he secured a passport, and air tickets, or how he escaped from prison. We don't know precisely how long he was held in prison—we don't know these things because the appellant himself was unable to give this information when he came to this country. We only have a much later account from the appellant of a phone call he *says* he made to his friend, uh, Abdul, in Uganda. However I submit that the appellant's report of this phone call, if indeed it ever took place, hardly constitutes proof. It's a convenient explanation, is it not, but one secured long after the event, and, given the importance of this explanation, is it not surprising that the defendant did not secure it earlier? Moreover we have only the appellant's word for the content of his phone call with his friend. There's no other separate or independent evidence to substantiate this account—a fact which, in the view of the Home Office, seriously undermines its acceptability. I would also refer you to the report by the GP from Sunderland who examined Mr Marimbey." He held up the report with an outstretched arm, a disparaging look on his face. "In that report she describes a number of injuries and states that in her opinion, and I quote, 'these injuries are *probably* the result of tortures received whilst in Uganda.' In this respect I would draw your attention both to the use of the adjective '*probably*' and also the fact that the doctor who examined Mr Marimbey was a *general practitioner*—not in any way an expert in diagnosing the effects of torture or qualified to comment with authority on the *cause* of these—ah—injuries." He threw the report back onto the table and took a sip from a glass of water.

"Your honour, I submit that the appellant's case is completely implausible. Beginning with the misspelling of his own name there are many points in his narrative where his testimony lacks robustness and reliable detail. He claims to have been involved with the FDC, but then also said, during an interview with the Home Office, that he couldn't say anything about this organisation. He claims to have escaped from prison, but had no idea initially how this was achieved, and still has no idea how a fake passport was secured for him, with a photograph of him, without him knowing about it. He conveniently didn't have the passport at the point that he claimed asylum, and yet we know that he must have had a passport in order to come into this country. He claims he is Mohammed Marimbey from Uganda, but in the absence of a passport or any other identity papers, we can have no confidence even of this. He claims that he was kept in a safe house and tortured, but he's been unable to furnish us with the most basic details about this experience, such as whether the torture room had windows—surely one of the first things that you'd notice if you were being tortured—you'd be alert to any possible means of escape. He claims to have been kept in a small space under some floorboards, yet despite the alleged intolerability of his conditions he made no attempt to escape from this area and on no occasion attempted to open the hatch above him. He claims that he was kept in these conditions for a period of time that he can't quite remember but thinks it was years. Yet despite being held there for a long, though unspecific, period he didn't even know what the floor of the area he was kept in was made of!

"Your honour, the appellant claims a great deal, but his testimony is thin on content, lacks supportive evidence of any validity, and frankly isn't credible. It is our submission that it is a *complete fabrication* devised for the cynical purposes of securing admission to the UK. It's true that there is some non-expert medical evidence of injuries sustained prior to the point of application for asylum, but in the absence of any proof that they occurred as a result of persecution, we submit that they are insufficient in themselves.

"Your honour, not only is it the view of the Home Office that the appellant's case lacks credibility, we would also argue that *even if he was telling the truth* there would be no danger of persecution in returning him to Uganda. The events that he claims took place prior to his escape to this country, took place several years ago and by his own admission he was not a prominent figure within the FDC, an organisation about which he knows very little. We have no reason to believe, therefore, that if he was returned to Uganda, the authorities would either recognise him or connect him with the FDC. Further if he really fears being recognised, we submit that there is nothing to stop him from re-locating, to a different part of the country, where he could live without any fear of recognition or danger."

The solicitor looked about the court room—everywhere except Mohammed—with a slight smile on his face. "Your honour, I rest my case."

Brian had listened to this speech with some dismay. It was as if the solicitor was talking about someone who wasn't actually in the room. But he also had to admit, for the first time, a small disillusioned, voice inside himself. Some of what had been said he hadn't known about, and was quite convincing. Maybe Mohammed was just another lying immigrant, trying to deceive his way into the country, there were plenty of others who did. Maybe he'd been hopelessly naïve. He closed his eyes in dismay…and there, etched on the inside of his eyelids, was an image of Mohammed's wounded torso in the cab.

Mohammed's solicitor, a tall black man with sloping shoulders, rose to his feet, slightly hesitantly, and began to speak. Brian couldn't see his face from where he was sitting but he noticed several white stains on the back of his suit jacket, and a bulging, badly scuffed briefcase by his feet.

"Your Honour, I hope also to elaborate on our skeleton argument which you will find in your bundle." He paused and took a sip of water. "It is our contention, your honour, that the appellant would be under serious risk of persecution if he was returned to Uganda. We do not accept that the appellant has failed to provide a credible account either of his escape or of the time that he spent in custody. At the point that he arrived in this country he had no possessions with him and so could not be expected to provide immediate proof. But at the first opportunity he did manage to ascertain an explanation of the means of his escape—I refer you to the testimony of his friend Abdul—which is entirely plausible. I would also draw your attention to the fact that the Home Office were unable to interview him on the day of his first application due to his poor physical health. Ill health directly caused by his period of incarceration and torture, which has been confirmed by the medical report in your bundle. It is totally plausible too, in our view, given the degree of the appellant's traumatisation on arriving in this country, that he would not have been able to give a coherent, and detailed, account of his period in captivity or his involvement with the FDC prior to this."

He had been speaking very fast and now took a short pause, as if to gather breath.

"With respect to the medical report we would submit that it is unreasonable to have expected the appellant to have been able to commission a medical report from an expert in the area. Such experts can be hard to find, and require large fees, so wouldn't have been within the means of the defendant…"

"Why then did he not apply for legal aid for this?" interrupted the judge with steely levity.

"Because, your Honour, at that point he didn't have legal representation."

The judge raised an eyebrow. "Why then did your firm, not commission an expert report?"

"With respect, your honour, it isn't my firm—I've been recruited to represent them, and I"— he rustled his papers some more—"I think that they didn't do this because they didn't have sufficient legal aid, your honour."

"Why then didn't they apply for more legal aid?"

"I—I'm not sure your honour—it has become much harder—."

"But the firm that has commissioned you today didn't even try?"

There was a long pause as the solicitor continued to look through the papers in front of him then: "No, your honour, it would appear that they didn't."

The judge looked irritated. "OK, proceed with the rest of your argument, please."

"Yes, thank you your honour. I—ah—we also contend that it would be unsafe to return the appellant to Uganda. I refer you to the document with the blue ribbon— the report from the UK Border Agency itself concerning the conditions in Uganda. As you will have seen, they quote many reports, from sources *they themselves have assessed as reliable*, of the detention, torture and execution of Ugandan citizens for their involvement in political activities. There are references there to unregulated prisons run by semi-official organisations within the country that seem to be operating with impunity and..."

"Yes, yes. I've read the report," interrupted the judge impatiently.

Mohammed's lawyer looked winded by this interruption: "Yes, thank you, your Honour. I didn't wish to imply, of course, that you hadn't. Of course you have. So, ah, our point is that because of the conditions outlined in the UK Border Agency report, it isn't safe for the appellant to be returned without risk of persecution." He stopped abruptly, off balance. Even after the interpreter had finished there was an agonising pause.

"Anything further to add?" asked the judge with a high frown.

"No, your honour, that will be all."

There was another long pause. The judge looked over at Mohammed. "Is there anything you wish to add yourself, Mr Marimbey?"

Mohammed looked shocked at being questioned directly.

"No sir."

"Or anything you did not understand?"

For a split second he seemed to hesitate: "No sir."

"Right then, well thank you to everyone for your submissions. As I explained earlier I will now consider the arguments that we've heard today and will let you know my decision in writing. Court dismissed."

"All rise". They all stood up.

As the judge went out the back of the court, Mohammed was led away past Brian through a side entrance. Their eyes met, momentarily. He looked like he was being led to the gallows.

PART 3

1

From early June a rare British heat wave swept away the spring mists and the sharp chill miraculously disappeared, along with Brian's thermal underwear. With the arrival of the school holidays Rowan, a confounding two inches taller than in the spring, abandoned his Xbox to play with his mates on the Heath terrorising pedestrians with machine gun water pistols. Back at the house Tilly invited all her friends to their giant paddling pool and played long hours of happy families with Humphrey, Kimberly and a pack of plastic yellow ducks. For days there was no hot water left and the lawn had become mud city.

Not that Brian was complaining. He loved the summer and this one was peachy. Being a cabby he could take time off as he pleased, visit the parks, seek out statues, and just, well, lie on the grass and drain the stiffness out of his shoulders. He was content to do this on my own, and often did, but he preferred to have a companion, and this summer he was relishing having one—Minty.

They'd been spending more and more time with each other. He found her invigorating, she made him feel younger, and she had an uncanny knack of asking questions that put him on the spot, as though she could read his mind.

He wondered though why *she* wanted to be with *him*. Perhaps it was just that he was good at getting out of the way to let people speak. He'd ferry her to a meeting, then return afterwards, take her to a park and let her offload whilst they soaked up the sun together. His earnings were taking a dip, and Michelle was fretting about their overdraft, but it was worth it, Minty was so good to be around.

On the day of the phone call he later regretted, in a gap between two of her meetings, he took her to Victoria Gardens, next to the Houses of Parliament. He wanted to show her a statue there: 'The Burghers of Calais' by Rodin.

It was blazingly hot so he was glad he'd brought some drink for them—white wine for her, chilling in a small thermos flask, elderflower cordial for himself. At the entrance to the park, she took off her shoes and stood gazing up at a different statue—the one of Emmeline Pankhurst. Personally Brian wasn't so keen on that one—he thought it made her look more like a lay preacher than the feisty determined woman she was. But Minty spent a long time studying her.

"You two have quite a lot in common." He commented after a bit.

She turned quickly, flicking round her red-streaked hair, and looked at him with her startling smile: "You're having a joke."

"No, like her you've been campaigning for equal rights. She campaigned for women to get the vote. You've been campaigning for equality in visiting the circles."

Minty looked at the ground. "Thanks Brian, I'm chuffed you think so but I hardly..."

"Well I think there's a parallel! These past few months you've done amazing things to improve people's rights."

It was true. Minty was now appearing regularly on news and chat shows, and the FCC had been astonishingly successful. First they'd won the right to free access to circles for approved adults. Then, after many protests, it got extended to all adults, then teenagers under 18, with parental consent, then even that was extended.

And their success hadn't just been in Britain. The FCC was a worldwide campaign. Barriers around circles were coming down almost everywhere, sometimes pulled down by angry crowds, more often dissembled by the state. A wind of change was blowing across the world.

Minty led the way into the park, passing Rodin's statue without a glance. "There's so much to do though, man. We've got to get more people to *use* the circles—in the west as well as the east—'cos that's what'll work best. It isn't just about us being matched with people like poorer than us and trying to help. That'd be so patronising. It's also about them being able to toggle us, so they get to compete on the level, like, with our knowledge. But if only a few people in the west end up toggling, then they've less opportunity. I'm worried not enough of us will do it, know what I mean?"

She had a point. For a few days after the circles had opened up the queues had been long, but wait time was now down to thirty minutes, less if you went at night. People were holding back.

"What about you then Minty?"

"Oh I'm doing it, for sure, as soon as I've time to be cool with it, like to digest it, Right now I'm too busy, it'd be too much."

She glanced at her watch and sat down in the shade of a large oak, curling her legs to one side, her bright blue short sleeved dress contrasting with the brownish green of the grass. Behind her the Parliament buildings loomed and off to one side a couple of students lay with their arms around each other beside a pile of unopened library books. Brian sat at an angle to Minty, as close as he thought he could get away with, and began unpacking the drinks and beakers. "But what about the people who don't want to change?" he asked, screwing her beaker into the ground and reaching for the thermos flask.

She gave him an impish look. "Talking about yourself here? You're not scared are you?"

"No!" He took a short suck of summer air. "I just wonder if everyone has to take the risk? Why can't we just be content to live as we are?" He poured her a glug of wine, recapped the thermos flask and began to get his own beaker sorted, brushing away an ant that had been climbing up the side.

"What *risk*?"

"Well, I dunno it's just…a lot of people are…"

"…What?"

He felt suddenly cornered. "…are having to cope with different…ethnic…"

Minty took a gulp from her beaker and leant backwards away from him on outstretched elbows behind her. "What d'you mean…exactly?" Her voice flat.

"Well…all I'm saying is…it could be *hard*…I'm not sure I want to risk that."

"Oh, right, whatever" she said quietly, her face drained of its usual vitality.

Brian felt a mysterious barrier had come between them as if she'd gone behind an invisible sheet of glass. He felt suddenly desolate and separated from her, the contrast jolting him into an awareness of what was really going on for him here—of what he'd only been sporadically aware of—that for weeks he'd been wanting to get closer, to somehow breach the physical gap with her, to touch her, not in passing, but to have his nose in her hair—to inhale deeply that smell of her, to ingest something from her that he couldn't quite place. And now, in a single moment, it felt like she was slipping out of reach. She hadn't said much—but her shiny lips were tight, she was closing up to him. Urgently he searched for a way of reconnecting.

"I guess you're right" he said at last. "I guess I *am* scared. There are…things…I'm frightened to let in."

She softened immediately and he was struck by how pretty she became. Sunlight shafts filtered down through the oak above them and made bright moving pools in her hair.

"Hey, Brian, that's so cool of you to admit it!" Her large eyes opened to him. "You know what? I think we're all frightened. Frightened of widening up who we're cool about, frightened of really hanging in someone else's take. Me too, for sure. Thing is though—this fear thing ends up with the whole world divvied up into us and them, over and over. It's nuts…we've a chance now to let in *just one* person, just *one* other. It's being made so easy for us. For those gutsy enough to believe…"

She was still looking at him.

"But you seem so fearless," he said, leaning towards her. "…I wish I could have just some of that."

Without losing eye contact, she moved up, off her elbows towards him until their lips almost touched. "You can, Brian."

It was then that Brian's mobile phone played its merry jingle. He stood up to get it out of his back pocket, and stared at the little screen: Mohammed. The last person he wanted to talk to, right then. He held the red button until the phone went dead then looked back towards Minty. But the spell had broken. She was standing now, looking at her watch in alarm: "I'm late for my meeting." She strode towards the park exit, calling over her shoulder: "Must rush…thanks for your company, sweet as ever."

Brian threw the remainder of her wine into the grass and packed up her beaker. Then he poured out some wine for himself and lay down in the grass, in the dappling sunlight, feeling a strange mixture of frustration and excitement. He so much wanted to understand her, to somehow reach her essence to know how she did this thing with him…

But the cynical voice inside him responded: 'It's just her body you're after.'

'No its more than that, I'm sure of it...'

He watched the shafts of light above him tickling the fluttering leaves…

The next thing he knew it was early evening and he was rubbing his eyes. He'd fallen asleep! As he packed up he remembered the phone call from Mohammed, and called him back. A voice he didn't know answered: "Hello, this is Zoro."

"Oh, I'm after Mohammed, is he there?"

The line went quiet. "Sorry, you missed him. Who is this?"

"My name's Brian, Mohammed called me, I'm returning his call."

"You're the taxi driver?"

"Yes."

Again the line was deathly quiet. "Sorry, you're too late"

"What do you mean?"

"Three hours ago, they came. He lost his case. They took him to Heathrow." Zoro's voice was cracking. "As they took him away he asked me to call you to see if you could stop them. It'll be too late now though…"

Brian felt like he'd been punched in the stomach. He'd had no contact with Mohammed since the court case. In the days after the hearing he'd thought intermittently about it, but then his life had been swept up with seeing Minty and what was happening with the circles. Now he felt suddenly guilty. He'd forgotten to keep track. At the very least he should have phoned him. And how could he possibly have been deported?

Dejectedly leaving the park he scarcely noticed Rodin's sculpture, one of his all-time favourites. It's of six bent and desolate men in flowing robes. They've just given themselves up for execution, in exchange for the release of all the inhabitants of Calais from a siege. On any other day he would have wanted to spend a decent amount of time there—marvelling at Rodin's poignant depiction of heroic self-sacrifice.

2

The months following Calvin's encounter on Pitcairn were the hardest he'd ever known. On the trip back to England his men were aloof and resentful. It had become clear that green circles didn't malfunction, the alien technology was far too advanced for that. Both the men under him knew it could have been the other that failed to keep adequate watch but privately believed that Calvin was the culprit. They'd seen how he'd been with Matilda and resented the question mark over their own innocence.

The new attitude of his men didn't help, but it hardly touched Calvin. His thoughts were all of Matilda. He hadn't a single memento of her. He searched in vain for the musky smell of her on his clothes—but it was long gone. He wished he'd taken photos, but there were none. He had no address, no phone number, no invitation to contact her, even if he could find a way. All he had was a ceaseless re-play of his memories.

He hadn't exactly been a virgin when he'd met her, but as good as. The passion she'd woken in him was beyond compare, tearing him open within just a few hours. At night as the yacht cruised on, relentlessly extending the distance between himself and her, he lay awake, replaying their love making, trying to recall every last nuance of her resonant dialect. Most of all he missed her laugh, the shine in her eyes, her playfulness and her apparently easy acceptance of him.

But these reflections were always poisoned by the sting that followed. Why had she disappeared? Why hadn't she left a note? Why didn't she attempt to meet him in the days that had followed?

Why hadn't she explained? Worst of all how: *How could she* have betrayed him?

He concluded bleakly that his feelings had never been reciprocated. She'd been a perfect actress from the start. The whole encounter had been a manipulation of his foolishness in trusting. Her laughter on the bed had been laughter at him, not with him. She'd had no feelings of her own for him. She'd been a siren luring a sailor into servitude, entrapping him in her spell. There was no escape now back to normal life, he couldn't ever trust again or find release.

And then he would recall some other flash of the magic that had happened in those few, precious, hours, and the whole poisoned progression of reflections would start up again on its one track to despair.

Back in England, he took leave and returned home to his small bedsit in Brighton. Its best feature was a veranda overlooking the sea. But now he could scarcely bear to sit out there. The busy shipping lane contrasted all too painfully with the empty seas around Pitcairn, and even when the horizon was empty, he couldn't bear to contemplate it, or even look at it. His own horizon was empty—there was nothing on it—and no longer any reason to search beyond it. In just a few hours on the island she'd begun to represent for him all that was good in life, all that was joyous, all that was playful, uninhibited. He'd placed those things in her care and then with her betrayal had lost them all, and become just an empty, grieving, shell.

A dream began his recovery. He was back there, with Matilda, in the time that they'd spent alone by the newly arrived circle. There it was again, luminous patterns in the deepening darkness. And there she was. He felt her wonderful presence next to him again, her hand holding his. And she turned to him, as before, and said gently, and with a slight shiver:

"I think ye need to enter the circle."

He woke with a start, astonished by her words. It had simply not occurred to him at the time to enter the circle. He had orders to follow, and a mission to complete and he'd been far too intoxicated with the beautiful woman sitting next to him. And now she was calling to him again, but from a dream. Calling him to trust her again.

At first he resisted and tried to ignore the dream. It was too preposterous to follow a dream, madness to trust her again. But a seed had been planted.

Although it didn't resolve his depression he reluctantly admitted to himself that his mood had shifted slightly for the better and gradually it became apparent to him that there was no other course but to trust her again. Perhaps now there could still be something to hope for. Wasn't that what these circles were supposed to offer, after all—transformation opportunities? Besides, he had nothing to lose.

He joined the queue at his nearest circle. Minutes before he was due to reach it a young man wearing a green 'I've toggled' T shirt approached him holding out his hand.

"Hi, I'm Ralph. I've come to offer you my services as a volunteer facilitator."

Calvin shook his hand "I'm Calvin—and, yes, I could do with some help."

"We strongly recommend it. It can be a bit confusing at first and it's good to have someone with you." As they moved steadily forwards Ralph told him what to expect in a low voice, recommending that he not focus initially on the green light so that they could walk, first, to a nearby debriefing shed. "Just don't give the light your undivided attention. We recommend keeping your eyes focused straight ahead at first." Calvin began to feel nervous.

Arriving at the circle he took a deep breath and walked hesitantly forwards. Just as expected a small green light appeared in his head as he touched the circle. He managed not to focus on it and walked unsteadily with Ralph to one of the make-shift sheds in a long row looking like beach cabins. He sat down on one of the two chairs in the shed.

"How're you doing Calvin, don't focus on it yet but are you aware of the green light?

"Yeah."

"Good, so before you focus on it, just remember that if you want to come back to your normal self, all you have to do is focus on the blue light. If you get into any trouble—which is very unlikely—just raise your hand and I'll tell you what to do. OK? Now first I just want you to practise a little going backwards and forwards. Alright? When I say 'go' focus on the green and when I say 'come back' focus on the blue. OK?

"I'm ready."

"Go."

Calvin focused on the green. He found himself in a mind soft and warm and strangely familiar, a feminine mind.

"OK Calvin: come back " said Ralph "Focus on the blue. Blue is back to you... Calvin, Calvin, come back! Blue is back to you. Focus on the blue."

Calvin hauled himself back. Then he bent forward, his whole body racked with convulsions.

Ralph sat patiently beside him. "You OK? It can be a bit strange at first…."

But he was sobbing too uncontrollably to answer. He was sobbing with the shock and joy of it in equal measure. The sheer enormity of it. He had been in Matilda.

"Oh my God, my God, my God," he managed at last.

"Are you still seeing a green light Calvin?"

More sobs then: "Ye-es"

"OK so I want you to stay back in you alone until you've recovered a bit."

"OK," he said in a strained voice "but will she still be there when I go back?"

Ralph smiled. "Oh yes! She's with you always now, Calvin."

"She is? My God! This is so incredible."

"Yes, it's certainly that. Who is she Calvin?"

But he hardly heard the question: "I want to go back now."

"You're sure you're ready?"

"Yes, I have to go back."

"OK, so I'll stay here for a bit while you get used to things. Just stick your hand up if you need any help."

Calvin went back into Matilda for about five minutes, emerging this time only because Ralph called him back.

"You OK?"

Calvin nodded from another world.

"OK for me to leave?"

Again he nodded, keen to return.

"OK, so I'm off to look for the next person in the queue to assist. If you get into any trouble, just press the button here. You can stay as long as you like. Nice meeting you Calvin."

Calvin toggled back and stayed in Matilda for many hours, surfacing only for short breaks to reassure himself that he could do it, and to walk briskly home.

He immersed himself in her, starting by focusing on her memories with respect to himself and the arrival of the circle. Little by little he pieced together what had happened. At first it wasn't in proper chronology, and he had to learn to direct the surfacing of her memories. But it got easier. Her mind was clear and fresh and her memory good.

He learnt that she had deceived him from the start. It had been a plot hatched by the islanders. They resented the presumption of the British authorities. Several amongst them wanted to try out the circle, whatever that meant. They didn't want to lose it after a week. Matilda agreed. Why should they be denied their own circle because of an arbitrary decision made thousands of miles away in London. It didn't seem right to her.

So they hatched a plan. They would pretend to agree. They would make it as easy as possible for the officials. They'd exaggerate their belief in the dangers, feign complete acceptance and make things easy for the officials, surrounding the area of the circle for them to demonstrate their acquiescence and deceiving them into a false confidence. Then they'd distract them away from the circle. They spoke about how they might do this and one of the islanders had suggested seduction. "There's no need for whoever it is to sleep with the man, just make him think she might, enough to lure him from his duty. For they'll likely be men, and with all the usual fantasies about us, having been at sea for a while without feminine contact..."

All could see the sense in the plan. It fitted perfectly with Pitcairn's history of mutiny and courageous deception. It also fitted with the island's rich history of misguided visitors hoping for sexual encounters. But who could do this thing for them? At this point all eyes had turned to Matilda. She was an obvious choice. She was annoyed at their suggestion and the ease with which they typecast her. "I'll think about it," she managed.

A day later she agreed. Her mother was one of those wanting to enter the circle and they'd had private discussions. She wasn't being asked to do much, after all, just lure the men away long enough for someone to open the lock with one of its other keys and touch the circle. She agreed because of her mother, and the expectations upon her, and also because she too didn't want to be robbed of this opportunity.

In the days that followed she prepared carefully. Listening to the messages of the approaching ship, she selected Calvin as her target. Finding a way to his heart would afford her maximum influence. But she didn't intend sleeping with him.

Calvin learned all this with an appalling sense of loss. Matilda's memories were far from soothing. He wondered if things could possibly get worse. He followed her memories to the point where he'd first descended into the longboat and met her.

Then things began to change. Matilda had been surprised and relieved by his youth. She'd been bracing herself for an older man. And when she looked into his face for the first time she'd found him… nice looking and all. This wouldn't be as hard as she feared. Her first smiles were smiles of relief.

Calvin saw all this and began to feel better. He began to understand that as well as relief, she was also experiencing guilt. She wasn't naturally prone to deception. And it was out of her guilt when she first saw him that she'd made a decision: if she had to deceive him then she would also compensate him. She'd give him what he wanted, as much as she could, she'd let him have his way, and she'd let herself enjoy it to the full. They'd sip from the poisoned chalice together.

As he understood this Calvin began also to get a powerful experience of her internal beauty. Cornered by events that had been unfolding, this was her best solution. She didn't want to hurt him, or anyone. She enjoyed people, she loved harmony, she loved life. It wasn't a cruel act. It was creative.

But he also learnt with alarm that there was hardly a man on the island that didn't have eyes for her, who didn't harbour his own private fantasies of time with her. He learned this because Matilda knew it from their looks, she knew it to her core, well aware of the effect she had. She'd known it all her life, from when she was a small laughing girl, sitting on her father's knee…and mostly she liked it. But also she felt blighted by it. It compromised good relationship. All her life she'd experienced the jealousy of the women around her. She'd tried to conceal her beauty, hiding in plain clothes, but it was her irrepressible joy in being alive that shone through and at puberty she abandoned the attempt to hide.

It was hard with the women but harder still with the men. It seemed impossible to get beyond their obsessional interest in her. She accepted their lopsided devotions as best she could, but secretly needed to be met in a different way. She wanted to be seen not as amazon, or goddess, but as a young woman with her own set of trials, frustrated ambitions, misgivings. She wanted someone, anyone, to reach through and see this—to take an interest in her for once, not as an object of beauty, or lust, or jealousy, but as a fellow human, on her own passage through life with her own twists and turns and secret yearnings.

Calvin learnt this with dismay. He realised that in his time with her he'd found out nothing about her. He had no knowledge of her family, her childhood, her friends, or her interests. He'd only been able to see her one way. He'd allowed her to remain a woman on a glossy page. He'd wanted that. He hadn't really had the slightest interest in her soul or her calling. Even now he was primarily only interested in how she'd related to him.

So, now it was his turn to feel guilty, and at last he was beginning to understand. The betrayal had been two-way. He too had played a part. He'd been blind to the inner lining of her beauty, to the price being paid, to her terrible loneliness, and the remarkable lightness with which she managed to hold this in the background and play her part. She'd known all along the course that events would take. She'd known it wouldn't resolve her inner dilemma. She'd also, for once, been released by this knowledge. Because of her deception there was no possibility of them having a truly meaningful closeness. Having begun with a deception it would have to remain that way. But she could at least indulge his fantasy, and join him in it, taking all the pleasure she could.

And she *had* enjoyed their encounter. That much was now clear. She'd enjoyed his attentions and, despite the deception, it had been fun. She'd enjoyed seeing his naked lust, and enjoyed indulging him, wanting him inside her, and taking what sweetness she could, knowing that her enjoyment was also part of her gift to him.

All this brought Calvin mixed feelings and some relief. He turned his attentions to the morning after. She'd not been asleep when he left her, as he had thought. She had pretended to be asleep not wanting to compound the lie by arranging further meetings. As soon as he'd left she crept out herself and walked back to her family. home, where she still lived with her mother, father, and two brothers. Nothing was said, though everyone had guessed what had happened. Her father quietly informed her that they'd used the spare key to open the gate and her cousin had been the first to touch the circle and was now having the strangest of experiences...

Calvin also began to understand why she'd elected to leave him. The job was complete. Better that she end it now, at the peak of his fantasy, than entertain the possibility of a slow deterioration culminating in the inevitable exposure of the lie. She'd known that he'd never really know her. Indeed she'd indulged his fantasy. There was no way forwards without exposing a lie that needed to be preserved.

But there was more than this. As Calvin began to enter a whole other part of Matilda's life he could see why she'd disappeared, and asked everyone to help her to do this. There was no future for their relationship because she wasn't ready yet to take *any* relationship deeper. All her encounters with men had ended similarly, with the same feeling of not having been seen that she'd felt with him. She found it difficult to fend off the attentions of men and there had been many occasions in which she'd felt under confident of her own inner consent before things had developed. She was only just acquiring the resources within herself to refuse the straight jacket that men seemed so keen to lace around her. But at least with him she'd had a reason to go along with it.

Gradually, as he stayed with her inner thoughts, Calvin realised with relief and dismay that it wasn't so much him who'd been rejected, but a way of relating that she was struggling to transcend. She knew she needed someone who understood her well, who could see beneath her surface, someone who could see the other sides to her, who'd never considered he could possibly be in relationship with her, and could be *ordinary* on account of this. And there was one such person, Gregor, a childhood friend, who was only just growing of age himself.

Initially when he'd opened up to Gregor's presence in Matilda's mind Calvin was jealous and resistant. But he began to see him through Matilda's eyes and slowly realised how right he was for her. Gregor was *innocent* with her. He was just a friend, it hadn't occurred to him that one day she might chose him and, little by little, she was unfolding her secrets to him, inching into intimacy, revealing how, despite appearances, she was lonely and self-doubting, and concerned about the consequences her looks were having for he. She could do this with *him*!

When Calvin realised that one day she would consummate her relationship with Gregor he began to grieve. They were right for each other. He knew now that any fantasy of reuniting with Matilda was just that, a fantasy. He understood why she'd left and hadn't re-contacted. He understood that her smile from the bay as the longboat drew away was laced with her own brand of grief. She was grieving too, at losing him, and also that the spell she could so easily cast was spent now inside her. She'd done her best to give him an experience he'd never forget, in the knowledge that this final moment had to come. She wanted him to know, somehow, with her presence at the tiny harbour, that she that she hadn't just manipulated him, she wasn't untouched.

Over the following months, as Calvin visited Matilda's mind, she began to marry deeply into his psyche. He developed an absorbing interest in exploring her childhood and finding out about all the other sides of her. What he'd had no appetite for, before, he could now undertake in depth. He came to know her, from every angle, as a tiny girl in her mother's arms, as a remote islander, as a woman with hopes and aspirations, fears and difficult corners. And he began to see her as a resource. Now that he'd allowed himself to be interested in her, the insights arrived.

Dimly at first, he saw a way forwards. He'd lost her in the flesh but found her within. She was part of him now. She had a miraculous enthusiasm for life, not as he'd first seen it, as a projected absolute, but rather as an orientation, a quality that she stayed in touch with, even through troubles and difficulties. He returned into her whenever he needed to remind himself. Her life enthusiasm had its roots in her innocence, and bubbling joy, as a child. Little by little he found that simple joys in his own life opened up for him. He could look again at the sea's horizon and relish a walk in the park, or a phone call with a friend. He found himself saying 'cooshoo' and 'whettles'.

His need to enter her lost its compulsive edge. She was no longer a barely attainable set of qualities outside of him, she was part of him, integrating peacefully inside, a part he could refer back to, in himself, *as himself.*

She would never know the depth, or extent, of her gift to him, and he wasn't going to risk unsettling her by contacting her now. He couldn't helpfully be in her life, nor did he need her now, externally, in his.

3

Expecting their visit he'd kept his tiny bag packed in readiness by the door.

One of the guards held him firmly whilst the other fastened the handcuffs with a detached, indifferent, expression.

Smile.

Weakly he called out to Zoro: "Help, help me please."

But Zoro was as powerless as him and stood awkward and inert by his bed as Mohammed was tugged sideways out of the door.

"Phone the taxi driver for me, *please*. Ask him to help."

Zoro nodded. Their eyes locked in a final, fierce, goodbye.

In the pressure of the moment he forgot to ask to take the bag and an hour later he looked out at Heathrow airport from the tiny window in the security van.

This is it. I'm a dead man.

They entered the airport buildings through a back entrance, then up a winding staircase. At a turn in the staircase, out of sight from the CCTV cameras, one of the guards kneed him hard from behind: "Move." He arched his back and sucked in a gulp of air. It was then that his coughing began again. Within a few steps he was doubled up, leaning forwards in a long wheezy coughing fit. They dragged him on banging his knees on the steps then down a corridor. He was still coughing when they entered a small room with a desk to one side. A smartly dressed airport official looked up as they entered. "…Mohammed Marimbey?" One of the guards nodded.

The room was evidently not for paying passengers. A row of airport personnel jackets and outdoor coats hung on a rack beside a sink, a small kettle and half a dozen unwashed mugs. A door leading off the room connected to a passenger boarding bridge and through a large window the cargo hold of a passenger aircraft was being loaded with suitcases.

Overwhelmed by his coughing and terror, Mohammed sagged to his knees on the polished stone slabs and vomited savagely, staring with bulging eyes at the taut chain between his wrists as his vomit splashed over it in a series of convulsions. The guard who'd kneed him rolled his eyes heavenwards. The airport official waited until some of his heaving had subsided, then dialled a number into a phone key pad on his desk. "Get me medical services—I've got a deportee here coughing and vomiting. We're going to need the cleaning service too." He put the phone down and looked at the guards, shaking his head slowly. "I doubt they'll let him on like this. Do you know what's up with him?"

The guards shook their heads and the airport official sighed gently. "Do you have anything on file then?" he asked, gesturing with a nod of his head towards a manila file that one of the guards had under his arm. Somewhat reluctantly the guard made a wide excursion around Mohammed's kneeling and dripping frame, brought the file over to the desk, and started thumbing through the pages: "'medical'—oh, here's a bit: 'arrived with chest infection', 'first interview got delayed so he could see a doctor', not sure what happened then—there's a later doctors report for the court. 'Early suspicion of TB *not* confirmed', but, hmm, yes, he has an asthma diagnosis, and an antibiotic prescription…."

"Have you got his medication with you?" The guards shook their heads again. The official came out from behind his desk and walked over to Mohammed and put his hand on his shoulder: "Have you got your medication with you?" Mohammed shook his head still staring at the vomit in front of him and intensely aware that some of it was still on his face and at the back of his nose. All his medication was in his bag.

“We can’t put him on a plane like this”, said the official quietly whilst the guards exchanged pained expressions.

Moments later the medical team arrived and a few hours later Mohammed was back at the detention centre where Zoro greeted him like a long lost friend. “Welcome back to the Ritz, my dear friend.”

That evening all the occupants at the deportation centre were handed official letters advising them their rights to visit a circle, in a one off opportunity.

4

In the months after he thought Mohammed had been deported a shadow descended over Brian's life. He knew it wasn't his fault he'd been deported, and Michelle told him more than once there was nothing he could have done—even if he had answered his call for help. But still he felt guilty, and somehow reduced by the turn of events. The aftermath image of Mohammed's wounds still haunted him and insisted his innocence. It wasn't possible to dismiss him as just another immigrant and living with that new truth was appalling. They'd sent him back to horror. This was not the Britain Brian thought he knew, and loved.

Summer collapsed quickly into a wet, cold autumn. All around him the buzz about the circles continued, but he felt aloof and disengaged. The world was changing in ways he couldn't have imagined and it was hard to keep up with it all. The news had little else now besides the circles and the views of those who had visited them. There was widespread talk about increasing aid, lifting trade restrictions, universal disarmament, requiring politicians to visit a circle—even world government.

It seemed the circles made people more radical, but he wasn't sure he liked those effects, whatever Minty said. He'd no intention of visiting a circle himself—he'd had quite enough change already. Until recently he'd liked to think of himself as happy-go-lucky but the events around Mohammed had thrown him off course and disrupted his equilibrium—hadn't his attitude to immigrants shifted?—why choose even more change?

Christmas came and went. That was something he usually loved, spending time with the family, seeing Rowan and Tilly's happy, expectant, faces. But though he tried to enter into the festive spirit, it was a huge effort. Everything seemed contrived and hollow, and such an effort. Michelle kept asking if anything was up so he told her it was about Mohammed. He knew there was something else though, some other malaise he couldn't quite fathom.

His gloom persisted through January and February. His whole life consumed by driving in the dark, negotiating snow and drizzle. Even keeping warm and dry was onerous. The only times his dark mood seemed to shift slightly were the ones he spent with Minty.

Then with five weeks to go before the circles were due to disappear she rang to say she was going for it.

"Brian, this is it, I'm taking the plunge, man. Can you take me to a circle?" She sounded even more excited than usual.

They chose Hyde Park, which was a mistake, because the queue was horrendous. Brian dropped her at the back and worked until she called again six hours later: "I'm through Brian, can you collect me?"

"Sure, but you sound—disappointed?"

There was a pause on the line. That was something he liked about her—for all her gung-ho attitude to life, he could always rely on her to be carefully honest in her responses. "Right Speech" she called it, a Buddhist thing, apparently.

"Yeah, man, I'm gutted. The woman I toggled—she's so sad, and stuck, its breaking me up"

"Wait right there, I'm coming now."

Half an hour later he joined her on a bench by the Serpentine lake. He didn't see her at first—she was bent forwards, crying into her handbag. He sat down beside her and put a patient arm around her heaving shoulders, keeping quiet and knowing better than to play Mr Fixit. He'd learnt that long ago. Tears need to fall, at their own pace, in their own way.

Eventually, her shoulders stopped heaving and the tears eased up. She took a deep breath and looked at him with a half-smile.

"Do you want to tell me what's going on?"

"Yeah, sure." She searched in her bag for a tissue and eventually brought out a scrunched up piece of antique loo roll. Brian passed her his handkerchief. That set her off crying again, but this time with a slight snicker. "ahch, thanks."

"Keep it, or you could overflow the lake."

Another wan smile. Another deep breath, she dabbed at the mascara rivers on her cheeks.

"…I'm toggling this…woman…from Pondicherry in southern India. Her name's Anagha, she's like a cleaner. She lives in a, kind of, slum. She didn't always. But her husband had an affair, so he threw her out." She cut off to sob again.

"*He* threw *her* out."

"…that's the way it works, man—they think if a man's unfaithful it's like his wife's fault! How unfair is that? So he keeps the house and the new woman moves in.." Minty stared down at the rainbow transfers on her nails, swallowing her sobs. "After he threw her out she tried his parents but they just beat her off *with a stick*, so she went back to her own family—but they wouldn't take her neither. They wouldn't even talk. No one wants her. And she has a three year old, right, a cute little girl. No-one would take her either. Her husband's' new wife didn't want her. So now they've nowhere to live. They're sleeping on the streets, can you believe it?"

"For something she hasn't done."

"Yeah, and you know what's worst about it?"

"What?"

"She's got no options." Minty stared at the lake "I think that's why I've been given her."

"How d'you mean?"

"She can't choose her way out of this. There's fuck all she can do. She's trapped. I've always thought you can choose your way out of stuff, and that if you're stuck that's you to blame, right?

"Hmm"

"But it isn't true. I can see that now, right? And she's isn't the only one. She knows loads of others. Like one of them killed herself with rat-poison."

Brian looked at her, appalled.

"She's working in this crazy Auroville place. She's got a cleaning job there, right, but it's kind of a weird community with over a thousand foreigners living in it, from rich countries. When her husband chucked her out she asked to live there but they refused, even though she had nowhere. Almost all the locals are refused. The people living there are like ageing hippies and they want the locals to do the work but not join the community. I think it's some kind of a religious sect, although they say it isn't. The hard part is that, like, every day she has to go there and sweep up leaves and the little red caterpillars that drop out of the thatching and to clear up the mess all the foreigners leave, *and not steal from them*. Usually she takes Parni with her, that's her daughter. It's so much stress, man, especially juggling her daughter; and she's paid a pittance—and the worst of it is she gets to see how well off they all are, right—and yet she's can hardly afford to feed Parni, let alone herself." Minty blew her nose into Brian's hanky as a kind of emphatic full stop.

Brian sat quietly, noticing that he still had his arm around her, and enjoying leaving it there. "What're you going to do now Minty?"

"Like visit her." she said, without hesitation. "To see if I can help her and…the others, they're all so *trapped*."

Brian watched a couple of swans on the lake, suddenly aware of the transience of his relationship with Minty.

"I'll miss you," he said, "I like you…" He felt clumsy saying it but for some reason she started sobbing again.

"…*What*?" he asked.

"It's just that I...*I* don't like myself much at the moment…." The tears were flowing freely now, and his hanky looked like it had just been fished out of the lake.

"Why ever not?"

"Because I've *known* about it, right,—and done precisely *nothing*." She emphasised the word 'nothing' as if lashing herself with it. I've known how lucky I am, how rich by comparison. The westerners in Auroville are no more guilty than me, it just looks worse because they're right there, holding on to their wealth alongside the poverty. But I'm just the same, and I've known it, and *still* I've done nothing."

"Until now, that is."

She looked at him with relief.

"Yeah, 'til now, thanks Brian. Now I have to act, because I can and she can't, right?"

A week later Minty invited Brian to join her at a day conference entitled 'One Month To Go'. It wasn't the sort of thing he'd have gone to himself but he was glad of the opportunity to be with her for a whole day and time was running out – she was hell bent on going to India. She looked gorgeous as ever, in a bright orange dress, shiny red shoes and about twenty thin bangles that jangled up and down her arm. 'Anagha always wears bangles.'

There were about two thousand people at the conference, They sat down, in the seats Minty had got them near the front, and watched a silent introductory video of the awe-struck faces of people touching circles for the first time.

The first session: 'The Neurology of Empathy' was led by a group of scientists from Cambridge university who'd been measuring electrical activity in people's brains in an area associated with empathy. It was extra active, they said, in people who'd visited circles. Now they were planning to develop this further –stimulating the area of people's brains responsible for pleasure whenever they empathised well. That way they hoped to help people improve their capacity.

In the next session a group of animal rights people argued the case for getting as many different animals as possible into contact with the circles. They said whoever sent the circles must have wanted animals in the mix or they wouldn't have passed on their minds so they were trying to get as many different animals in the pool before the end of the year so they could be available to all.

Zoos had been helping by taking different species to the circles. They'd even used a crane to lower a dripping whale onto a circle in California.

There were some interesting accounts of people who'd toggled animals and some of their experiences were helping zoologists. A video showed a terminally ill woman talking about how she'd entered an insect. When she first toggled she was in a cocoon and not a lot seemed to be happening. Then she gradually metamorphosed into a bright turquoise butterfly, and flew off to drink nectar in nearby flowers. She said she'd found it so useful to keep re-experiencing coming out of the cocoon and flying for the first time. There were also accounts of a Bangladeshi road sweeper who'd toggled an elephant and a member of the Dutch royal family who'd toggled a millipede. Brian had a quiet snigger at that.

The last session before lunch entitled 'Meeting Your Togglee" had accounts from people who'd managed to meet up with the person, or animal, that they'd toggled. It started with Pete Flavier—the first American to toggle. He got a standing ovation the moment he came on the stage. He talked about visiting Harvey, the dog he'd toggled, in Canada. He'd spent a whole day with him giving him the treats he knew he liked best. He told Harvey's owners what food he preferred, and where he liked being scratched inside his ears, and what he liked to do. One of his favourite activities had been dog training classes. They were a great opportunity to meet bitches and mess about! Not surprisingly his owners had stopped taking him—but Pete persuaded them to start up again—for Harvey's sake, not theirs. He also persuaded the household to stop using Old Spice Deodorant and Raspberry Rush Bubble Bath—smells that put Harvey off his food for days.

Next was a minister Pete knew, who'd toggled a chimpanzee called Whooper. He told them how he'd brought Whooper back from an animal experimentation lab, so that he could get him veterinary care and look after him properly. Whooper's leg had been broken when he was captured, and had been causing immense pain, but the scientists didn't even know. His leg was better now and he was living with the minister at his church accommodation, and rather taking it over. He had his own bed in an attic room, one side of which has been opened up to the elements, so he could jump straight out into a tall tree in the garden. The minister said he now understood chimpanzee words, and signing, and was teaching Whooper Christianity. A few things Brian had heard over this year had been hard to believe, but this took the biscuit.

After that a couple came to the stage—a man from New Zealand who had been sought out by a woman from California who'd toggled him. They'd subsequently become engaged! The man talked, rather too smugly Brian felt, about how wonderful it had been for him to know that someone knew him completely, and still accepted him. He was sure Michelle would never have agreed to marry him if she'd even glimpsed some of the murkier corners in *his* mind, beforehand.

They broke for lunch and lots of people approached to talk to Minty. Brian found himself seething at the lost opportunity – he wanted her to himself. When she finally turned and suggested eating their sandwiches outside he couldn't get her out quickly enough. But as they were leaving his phone went off. He looked at the little screen: Mohammed. Surely it couldn't be! He'd been deported. He pressed the green button: "Hello?"

"Hello, it's Zoro, Mohammed's friend, is that Mr Brian?"

"Zoro, hi, what can I do for you?"

"It's Mohammed, he's being deported again."

"What? I thought he'd already gone." His head was spinning.

"No, they brought him back last time, he was sick at the airport. Now they've just taken him again, they think he's well enough to fly. Can you help?"

"Which airport?"

"Heathrow."

"Which airline?"

"No idea, whichever one goes to Uganda, I guess."

"I'm on the case." He shouted a goodbye to Minty and barged through the crowds.

The roads to Heathrow were packed with traffic. He abandoned his usual good driving and became a bumper hugger, blaring his horn at the car in front, even when there was nowhere for it to go. If he lost his job for this, then so be it. He pressed his foot hard on the accelerator, weaving where possible in the slow moving traffic, cutting people up, oblivious to their protests. He no longer cared—fuck getting it right, fuck the police, fuck the whole fucking system.

At Heathrow he bashed on his warning lights and abandoned the cab in a bulge in the ranks. The drivers behind would just have to ride the curb. He ran through the bus area, into the airport, to an information desk. A queue of people was waiting to speak to a fresh looking young man in his early twenties. Brian pushed in front, elbowing aside an agitated looking man.

"I need to find out which flight someone is on—he's going to Uganda."

"There's a queue sir." The man had a Dutch accent, presumably he spoke many languages.

"It's an emergency. His mother is dying."

The man paused, assessing the situation for a glacial epoch. Brian was about to vault over the desk and strangle him when he said calmly: "Probably Egypt Air, via Cairo, gate 16, he looked slowly at his watch. But it's leaving soon."

"Can you make an announcement?"

"Not without some identity from you sir, and his full name and date of birth."

Brian ran out into the main concourse, racing for 'Departures'. Misjudging a gap in a check-in queue he swerved straight into a woman standing calmly beside her suitcases, reading a magazine. Her handbag flew from her arm and across the polished stone floor—sending make-up skidding in all directions. He sprinted on, ignoring shouts from behind.

In front of the neon 'Departures' sign a long queue of passengers were waiting with glazed eyes and orderly calm before the baggage check. To one side of the queuing lanes an airport official was sitting behind a desk under a notice saying 'Late

Passengers'. Without thinking, Brian sprinted along the narrow lane and straight past her, past the X-ray machines and plastic trays full of wallets and belts on stainless steel rollers, past a gaggle of officials, through the perfumed duty-free zone and on to a moving pavement heading towards gate 16. This was too easy—as his pounding feet went into overdrive he noted, absurdly, that no-one seemed to be taking any notice. He was just another passenger running to catch a flight.

He counted off the boarding gates shouting to people ahead to get out of the way—his feet alternating between bouncing on moving rubber and brief interludes of hard shiny floor. Suddenly he was there, pulling up, breathless. Gate 16. He scanned the seating area—no-one there. An air hostess stood at a desk in front of a closed door talking on a phone.

"I need to stop someone on the plane."

She looked up, clearly annoyed at the interruption: "Too late sir. The doors have closed, the plane's already on the runway. Brian pushed past her behind the desk and tried the door. It was fucking locked.

"You don't understand, this is a matter of life and death—I have to stop somebody leaving on that plane. I..."

But it was too late—guards were approaching from all directions, he was surrounded.

Three hours later Brian finally got to leave Heathrow airport after being interviewed extensively with phone calls to the criminal records bureau, to Michelle, to the taxi firm, and god knows who else. It felt like they'd checked and re-checked every orifice of his body. They'd even examined his faeces. Of course he'd explained the situation to them, as calmly as he could, and early on he begged them to get Mohammed off the plane, but they made it very clear that that was none of their business, or his. It wasn't going to happen.

Eventually, after he'd signed a long statement, they let him out, saying he'd be summoned to court.

To his astonishment the cab was exactly where he'd left it, its hazard lights flashing lamely now. Inside he rested his brow on the steering wheel unable to drive straight away. Once again he'd failed to stop Mohammed from being deported. He couldn't stop imagining him with his wounded body, sitting on the plane, thinking about what lay ahead.

Driving home dejectedly, in the cold winter fog, he impulsively took a detour to York House gardens, in Twickenham. Maybe a little time by the beautiful statues there would help—he could think things through before going home. There was a long queue of people in the park. He'd forgotten there was a circle here. Perhaps providence was conspiring by bringing him here.

5

To a passing observer Willow View would have appeared abandoned. The milk on the doorstep had separated out into stagnant bands. Unopened post lay as it had fallen, directly under the letterbox, and the front border was overwhelmed by an untidy wisteria that had raced, un-pruned for an entire year, across the curtained windows of the bottom floor, and up to the second storey where its spiralling tentacles scratched against the glass, as if searching for an occupant. In fact the house *was* still occupied. Deep in its interior Oliver sat in his semi dark study, a half drunk bottle of vodka beside him.

From the moment Marjorie had cut herself, he reflected, his life had collapsed alarmingly. And now this. He could still hardly believe that Marjorie had left him, but as the weeks had dragged into months it had slowly dawned on him that she might never return. He might have to continue coping on his own. He'd deluged her with messages, and even a massive bunch of pink roses, her favourite. But she'd remained impervious, and rarely answered the phone, or even returned his messages.

Coping with work had been hard enough, he felt disjointed from it, but the hours he spent at home were harder still. He didn't know how to boil an egg, let alone operate their state of the art washing machine, or the dish washer, or the Aga, or steam-iron. He'd been making do with Marks and Spencers' 'meals for one', now stockpiled into the freezer. They weren't too bad actually, and, though he missed her cooking, it meant he could carry on working through supper, without having to interact. He'd also been able to eat fish and chips—something she hated—which tasted better for the tiny rebellion involved. Yes, some things had been quite enjoyable at first, being able to do as he pleased. Late night surfing on the web. But as the housework piled up the attraction had faded. There must be some way to get her back.

Entering and leaving Willow View had been the hardest. Locking the front door behind him in the mornings he'd become acutely aware of the emptiness remaining mordantly behind, and when he returned in the evenings the front door unlocked again onto a house frozen, exactly as it had been left. If he left a light on, it would still be on when he returned. If he didn't clear the dishes, they'd still be there, exactly as he'd left them. Was this loneliness, this feeling, he wondered? It was certainly inconvenient.

But lately things had become a quantum leap worse. Between Willow View and his work each day he passed a park with a green circle. In recent weeks they'd posted a notice beside the road announcing the number of days remaining to visit the circle. A week ago, driving home, and seeing the notice he'd been struck by a sudden, inexplicable urge to visit. Maybe he would toggle some company. Perhaps it would be an absorbing antidote to fill his empty evenings.

He parked his BMW, and joined the queue. He must have been out of his mind! And now he had to cope with this too. It was almost unbearably difficult to curb his focus and curiosity, and to keep from toggling the green spot in his head, but when he did toggle it—it was tearing his world apart.

At first he hadn't wanted to believe the man inside him was a real person. This had to be invented. A terrible thought construction had been planted in his brain, for sure, but it was contrived. It couldn't relate to a live person.

It was the sense of dread that he found hardest. The man's body was like a sponge, saturated, not with water, but with dread. His stomach was flooded with acid, his mind raced, frantic with fear, flashing uncontrollably backwards and forwards between the indigestible horror of the past, and a count-down terror of the future.

You are a dead man, you are nothing, there is only worse to come.

It was learning the man's name, from the inside, that had first alarmed his disbelief: Mohammed Marimbey. He knew this person—though he couldn't quite place him at first. He came across so many people. But as he slowly realised who it was he began to believe that the aliens had somehow accessed the name from his own consciousness, constructing an image from his memories, then distorting it, to haunt him, transmitting it maliciously, as an invented construction, back into his brain.

For this had all the hallmarks of a nightmare—sometimes he had a sense of being out of control, of falling helplessly and interminably, from an immense height, then crashing into a blackness dark as dungeons. Or he was overwhelmed by anxiety. There was something he should have remembered, but had disastrously forgotten. How could he have forgotten? How could he? Now he was going to be punished...

The electricity...

After the first appalling toggles into Mohammed he'd tried to stop toggling altogether. But he was ever aware, of the light waiting there in his head, and his attempts to avoid it. He tried so hard not to focus on it that on occasion he accidentally toggled it on—the effort of avoidance backfiring to trip the switch. Once he was back inside it was hard to return, hard to re-connect back, out of the quicksand of Mohammed's terror.

He was also, despite himself, driven to find out more. If this was really aliens why had they constructed things this way? Almost everyone who'd toggled reported that they'd been matched in a way that somehow enhanced their lives. How could this enhance his, and why had they matched him with someone he'd met, albeit so briefly? And why had they changed things? They'd taken the man's fantasy and presented it as reality. He grew better at avoiding toggling accidentally, but there were still these unanswered questions, the green light in his head was a giant question mark.

Gradually he learnt also to toggle straight out of the worst bits. It took the utmost concentration. He needed to stay in touch with himself, Oliver, at all times. It was like unravelling a ball of string and going into the Minotaur maze. The ball of string was tied to himself, Oliver, waiting outside the maze. As long as he kept holding the string, and his connection to himself, he could haul himself back at the first glimpse of a minotaur. That was the theory, anyhow, although the minotaur had a way of appearing unexpectedly around any corner. Often it looked like Muhindo.

Move shithead! I have a very special treat for you.

The day after first toggling he'd called in sick. There was no way he could work with this torment. He knew he had to come to terms with the experience and thought that if he could find the courage to enter Mohammed enough he might somehow neutralise him so he wouldn't be so intrusive. But it was a week now since he'd worked, and it wasn't getting easier.

He focused, when he could, on Mohammed's early memories. The aliens had done an incredible job, the detail was extraordinary, right down to the smells, the vegetation, the climate, the language, the food that he ate, the conversations he'd had, the games that he'd played. There were many things Oliver had never experienced before—like eating cassava and speaking Luganda. How had they managed that?

As a boy Mohammed didn't have much contact with his father but his mother was warm and softly available, much less distant than Oliver's mother. It was bliss sitting on her lap as a small boy, and he could have stayed there for ever soaking up the smell of her, and her gentle ruffling of his hair—if he'd not also been aware of adult Mohammed in the background, undercutting the experience, nostalgic and fearful, fearful for her safety.

We will hurt your mother if you don't tell us everything.

Whenever this happened he toggled straight out and sat shaking for a while in the dark study, steeling himself to return. Vodka helped to numb the worst of the feelings, and he'd discovered an enormous supply of it in the cellar. But he had to be careful not to drink too much or it compromised his ability to negotiate Mohammed's consciousness and toggle back effectively.

Little by little he began to piece together the story before Mohammed's arrest. It was easier to focus on this period because it was less prone to intrusive interruptions. He explored his earliest memories, his early childhood, the death of his father, his coming of age.

Then he dipped into the period of his political campaigning. Mohammed was idealistic, visionary. He rightly believed how good things were in Britain and wanted Uganda to follow suit. He was a fluent speaker and spoke movingly about the changes that the FDC would make. He enjoyed being surrounded by crowds and delivering his message of freedom and resistance. At first, when Oliver surfaced out, he found this incredible. Mohammed knew the risks—his father had been killed for his political views. How did he find the courage to give these talks with such elated abandon.

Back in Mohammed the answer revealed itself. It wasn't so much that Mohammed was courageous when he gave the talks, he was oddly cut off, as if above and beyond it all. It was an intoxicating relief to be in that fearless place, oblivious to the real danger he was running and the possible consequences. And it had become like a drug. His talks drew appreciative crowds. That is until the day that the army officers had arrived…

We are taking you for questioning.

He toggled back into Oliver for another sit in Oliver's world. But his own world was now also haunted by premonitions of worse things to come. The boundary between himself and Mohammed was becoming fluid, unpredictable, their feelings were starting to overlap…

He realised with sudden alarm something that he'd known all along—that there was still an ominous scene to explore. A scene he'd been avoiding more than all the rest, because it was worse even than the encounters with Muhindo—the scene involving *himself*.

It was as if he'd just recalled it. Like Mohammed there were scenes that he, Oliver, had known were there but had been trying to hold at bay, compartmentalised. As Oliver he could scarcely remember at first what had happened that day in court and why he'd refused to grant this man asylum, but gradually some of the detail began to return. The man had smiled inanely throughout the hearing—not sufficient evidence in itself, but certainly an indication that things might not be as presented. He'd been incredibly vague about the conditions of his prison. He hadn't even tried to escape. There'd been just too much that couldn't be believed. This had been one of the easier decisions, his story totally lacked credibility.

Once he'd remembered the court case, it became impossible to let it go. He tried to stop thinking about it but he knew now he would have to return, only this time as Mohammed. It was like a damaged tooth that needed to be extracted. The pain wouldn't go away of its own accord.

He took a slug of vodka and toggled back into Mohammed, calling up his memory of the court scene. It flooded back with practised ease. Suddenly he was Mohammed answering questions put to him via the interpreter. He didn't understand why particular questions were being asked—*but he was answering with the truth*. That much was clear. He was telling it exactly as it happened. But when he risked a look at the judge, he could see plainly that he wasn't being believed—the judge's eyes were hard and unconvinced.

They will never believe.

Oliver jolted back into himself. OK, OK, now he got it! He got it at last. It wasn't an alien conspiracy. That was just his last ditched attempt to keep out the truth, a truth that had been trying to surface since before he even toggled. What he'd seen in court, experienced as Mohammed, was exactly as it had happened. The Oliver that he'd seen, as Mohammed was definitely himself. He was just too real. All the detail was too correct, too exact. His eyes would have been *hard and unconvinced.* He remembered it all now. This was the real Mohammed that he'd been toggling, and *that* meant...

That meant Mohammed had been telling the truth and he, Oliver, had made the *wrong judgement.* He should have believed him…but it had been *so obvious* he'd been lying…

For a long while Oliver sat grimly as this revelation flooded through him. It was a different feeling he was negotiating now. No longer of dread, but of overwhelming guilt. He'd been wrong to refuse this man asylum. How could he have been so blind to the truth? But the man had smiled all the way through court! And his story had seemed so implausible—there'd been mistakes in his recall of events, and the account he'd given of his escape just didn't ring true, and the explanation that followed, weeks later, had seemed like an invention to try and save his skin.

To try and save his skin! The man had been fighting for his life, not with lies but with the truth. And did it really matter if he hadn't told things exactly right? He'd certainly been tortured and imprisoned, his life had certainly been threatened. Oliver realised that now, and that meant—oh my god!

He reached for a phone. He could phone Keith. Keith was a high ranking person in the Home Office— he'd be able to find out what had happened to Mohammed. He dialled the number, got straight through and requested the information, trying to reveal as little as possible.

"I have to know what has happened to this man. It's really important he isn't sent back to Uganda—he may be in terrible danger. Please, please find out as fast as possible"

"OK, I'll phone you back in a few minutes, but we don't usually do this kind of thing, Oliver. I shouldn't really do this." Keith hung up.

Oliver went over to the window and opened the curtains for the first time in days. Light flooded the room exposing several unwashed glasses and a nearly consumed bottle of vodka. He picked up the bottle, walked shakily into the kitchen, tipped the vodka down the kitchen sink then leapt to the phone as it rang again. "Hello"

"Hi, it's Keith. Your asylum seeker—Mr Marimbey—has just been deported. Quite a co-incidence! His plane left Heathrow a few hours ago. I think he'll be in Cairo now, changing for Entebbe."

"Can you get him returned?"

"On what grounds Oliver? We have to have a reason."

"I think he's genuine."

"But on what grounds?" Keith sounded exasperated. "You were the judge who made the decision. We can't just haul him back on a whim."

Oliver felt snared by the situation, he was going to have to explain. "I...toggled him. I know he was telling the truth now. I—made a mistake. This man was genuine. And he's being sent back to—to unspeakable hell. You have to bring him back. Please Keith, he can make a fresh claim. This is new evidence."

There was a pause on the line. "You *toggled* him?

"Yes, I guess I got him because I made a mistake. Please Keith, we may not have much time."

Another pause on the line, longer this time. "Would you be willing to describe your toggling in court?"

"Yes, anything."

"Alright, I'll do it for you Oliver, but this is going to be hard to justify, there are no precedents for this kind of thing. I'll get right back to you."

Five minutes later he phoned back. "Oliver—it's too late. The plane just left Cairo for Uganda. I'm sorry."

Oliver felt his throat tighten "Can we get him back from Uganda then?"

"No, we can't do that. Once he's arrived in Uganda the authorities there have control. We won't be able to get him back."

Oliver felt his heart contract into a tight ball: "You're sure?"

He already knew the answer. Keith was right of course—and phoning the Ugandan authorities might make things worse. It would alert them to Mohammed's return.

"I'm sure Oliver."

6

Brian felt completely mad joining the queue at York House Gardens. His mind was still trying to digest the fact that he'd failed, once again, to rescue Mohammed. Why add another momentous event to an already brim-full day? But he was desperate for some release from his nagging malaise and needed a way to move forwards. Perhaps he might toggle some source of solace. It was as if he was visiting the Delphic oracle.

The complex of statues he'd come to see certainly supported the Delphic oracle fantasy, and over the hours that the queue snaked past them, he had plenty of time to look at thc eight, larger than life, white marble ladies fishing for pearls amongst the ponds and waterfalls around their aquatic horses.

Reaching the circle, he touched it firmly, then sat down on the grass by the statues and entered a new mind for the first time.

He knew immediately who he was.

Dorothy, Belgian woman, married with two children. I work as a part time teacher for a local primary school. My husband, Bertrand, works for the housing department.

He toggled back, just to check he could. Already he had a strong impression of her. It was amazing how quickly he just knew her. She was like his wife only French speaking— same capable busyness, same warm friendliness that attracted him to Michelle, all those years ago. He knew he was going to like her.

Back inside he tried to find her childhood memories. This was what people advised you to do: get the context from the past first.

Feeling high-up-happy on Dad's shoulder's. Licking cake-mix scrapings from mummy's bowl. Riding my tricycle with the other children in the road. Rubbing noses with Emile in the sandpit. Hiding all day in the sun drenched haystack. Laughing with Sophia as we keep rowing the boat into the bushes… My childhood was happy, secure, ups and downs of course…but I can't stay there. Not now. There are more important memories to think of. I have to keep reminding myself.

Brian toggled back. No amount of talking to Minty could have prepared him for this! Suddenly he was no longer just his own meandering, semi-coherent, stream of thoughts, fears, and feelings, he was also someone else's! Just like with himself she had an 'I' and a 'me' behind every thought. He was no longer the centre of things, there were two 'I's within him now. He went back inside and was pulled towards the present by her mind within him.

How could he do this? There, in his briefcase, that single note in its unfamiliar feminine hand. I was just trying to find the tickets. I wish I never had. Only a scrap of paper bit it's changed everything:

'Bertrand, my love, that was so perfect, my only wish now is to hold you again.'

I cannot bear remembering, but I know I have to. I have to be brave and grown up or I might be tempted to push it down. Just that one sentence, that's all it took to tear our lives apart. No matter which way I read it there's no avoiding the earthquake of his betrayal and its fault line slicing through my own terrible naivety. They say the first cut is the deepest. Telling the kids was hardest, never again.

He couldn't hide his eyes when he tried to deny it. But it was only when he knew he was cornered that he admitted it. I pressed him. Why did I do that? I had to. Yes he was 'in love' with Angie. He finally admitted it. It was like I was being stabbed with a sword. Perhaps he thought the truth would help, honesty might bring me round. But it was too late by then. I knew I had to divorce him.

It was the moment when I first read the note that severed my soul. I can never regain the trust and innocence I had. No use looking for it in the past, it's gone.

When he came back I could hardly stand it. His doe-eyes over-dramatically downcast as he came into the living room and saw I'd packed his things away. I could see him wondering, when he saw me so livid, if he should even ask permission to sit. That was when he said he'd made a terrible mistake and begged forgiveness. It was exactly what I'd been waiting for, but it didn't reach. I just can't. I can't trust him anymore. But it was when he said it wasn't Angie he loved at all but me that I nearly cracked...though I found the right words, I think: "Love isn't about feelings, Bertrand. Feelings come and go. Love's a verb. It's about action." That was when he crumpled and left. Perhaps I was too savage...but it's true.

Brian toggled back into himself and stared glumly at the shiny wet ladies gathering pearls in the water. As the aftermath of Dorothy's feelings flooded through him he thought of Michelle. He'd had many fears about the consequences of touching a circle, of who he might be matched with, or what the oracle might try and teach him but he hadn't dreamt of this.

Dorothy was right of course. Love *is* a verb. He'd been walking too close to the edge with Minty, crossing over even, in his mind. It was time to haul himself back.

Resolutely, he stood up, turning his back on the statues, Dorothy's thoughts continuing their work inside him: *Love is a verb, it's about action.* As he walked to the cab, aware of the strange green light in his head, the events of the last few months began to fall in perspective. He'd done what he could with Mohammed. His only real mistake had been not answering the phone when he'd called, and not keeping properly in touch with him. Regrettable, but understandable, and at least he'd been open to influence. He knew now that some asylum seekers were genuine. His crazy escapade at Heathrow—had been ridiculous from the start—*but at least he'd acted.*

No, the seam of guilt he needed to focus on was around Minty, it was because of his obsession with her that he hadn't answered

Mohammed's call, and, yes, it *was* an obsession, he knew that now, and it had brought him dangerously close to hurting Michelle.

It was time to go home.

7

Once again these metal bands around his wrists and the chain between. Once again being moved around like dead meat.

The trip to Makindye barracks, to the safe house, to the detention centre in the UK. Back and forth through the mirror, but always the same.

This time they had flooded him with medication. Just to make sure.

Forced to drink the foul smelling liquid at the safe house.

This time they'd got him onto the plane. He'd stumbled drowsily through the connecting tunnel.

This time he was being returned for sure. Two guards had come with him. He sat between them on the plane.

Jane had sat in front. She had said ***"keep your eyes looking ahead and don't look around you, and don't say anything."***

But it was all one and the same.

Africa, Cairo, changing planes. The press of thick air. The hot tarmac beneath his feet. He is the last to be boarded, at the back of the plane. It's going to Entebbe. The airport vehicles have withdrawn. Firm hands are pushing him up the steps, towards the black rectangular hole of an entrance. His cage will be air-born for a bit.

Africa, country of his birth. No joy in the recall, no longer home. Nowhere is home. He holds the railing tight. It's difficult to keep lifting his feet up the metallic steps. His feet are weary as time itself. But the guard is pressing from behind. "Move on up"

Move shithead, I have a very special treat for you.

"Move on!" He's pressing more urgently now.

Just obey, it's hopeless.

It's hopeless……

...but. He stands completely still on the steps, reckless against the needling from behind. Remember those political rallies, remember those speeches. Remember that elation….The guard is stabbing him in the back with his knuckles now. "Come on, move up."

Just obey, it's hopeless, too dangerous to resist.

"NO!" His shout is primal, a violent surge wrenched upwards from his very blood.

"**NO**!" He's turning now and toggling at the same time. He unites with the lion inside him, feeling the fur around him and his massive claws. He slams the chain between his wrists full force into the face of the human behind him. It falls backwards, headfirst down the steps, startled and screaming, its nose pumping blood. It is laid out now in a downward angle on the steps, perfect for his pounce. The other human has stepped backwards, in alarm, onto the tarmac. He flies through the air at a downward angle onto the human, smelling its man blood, his claws grip its shoulders, his teeth bear down to tear into its neck.

From the inside of his head he hears a dull crack on the outside. Now the other human is pulling him downwards, wildly he spins an unbalanced falling claw through the air, then lands disorientated on the tarmac.

He's being kicked in the stomach now.

Makindye barracks, the guard with the baton.

He starts to vomit and all goes black.

8

Oliver was sitting at the kitchen table, his head in his hands, when the phone burst into its rap ringtone—programmed by Harry, his younger son. He allowed it to play on irritatingly, then heard Marjorie's familiar up-beat message : "Hello you've got through to the Surrets. Please leave messages for Oliver and Marjorie after the beep." He must change the phone's routine.

"Oliver, it's Keith again, from the Home Office, you there?"

Oliver grabbed the phone.

"Keith, sorry, I was screening calls, what is it?"

"Your man, he's being flown back to London."

He felt suddenly hopeful. "But you told me his plane had left"

"It had left, but he wasn't on it, there was a scuffle at the airport. He got into a fight with the guards and ended up unconscious. They rushed him to hospital. Then the people in Egypt rang us to ask what they should do. Because of my phone call with you we told them to fly him back to London. So that's what they're going to do, as soon as he's well enough. Apparently he wacked a guard in the face with his handcuff chain. It might've got much worse if the other guard hadn't restrained him."

"But is he OK?"

"Not really, but he'll recover. He's got a broken nose and a bad bite on his neck. Your man nearly bit through an artery."

"No, not the guard, *Mohammed*, is he OK?"

"*Mohammed*? Oh! Yeah I think so. He came round in a few minutes. They have him sedated now in hospital.

"How come he lost consciousness?"

"Don't know, Oliver... guess the guard hit him in self-defence."

"Isn't that unusual?"

"Not really, happens all the time. Some of the people we send back are desperate. Fights at the airport are common. That's why we handcuff people. Sometimes we gag them too. Otherwise pilots won't fly with them. It's too upsetting for the customers. Your man was sedated, but it must have worn off."

Oliver stared at the table. The same table he'd cleaned of Marjorie's blood and the chopped tomatoes.

"I didn't know that."

"Really? It's common knowledge. Some asylum seekers have to be taken to the airport again and again because they kick up such a fuss. We tried to deport one nine times before he eventually won his case on appeal."

"I see," said Oliver quietly, "and lots of them do this?"

"Sure, we had one a couple of years ago who asphyxiated on the gag. You must have heard?"

"No." Suddenly he wanted to scream.

"Well...it was in the papers."

"I didn't see it. But what about Mohammed? What will happen when he comes back?"

"Well normally we'd wait until he was better, then try again. But in this case, it's a bit of a legal precedent—in view of your toggling—maybe you'll want to argue for him to stay."

"I will Keith. I'll do anything. He's innocent and his fears are real. I was...wrong." The last word came out half strangled.

"Well, at least you're admitting it."

"It's just the beginning, Keith."

"What do you mean?"

He could feel the tears welling up once more. Decades had passed without a single tear and now they were commonplace. "I...I'm starting to realise, he's not the only one. I think I've made many mistakes."

"Really?"

"Yes, I...I'm sorry...I am so terribly sorry." His face was in his hands.

"Don't apologise to me, Oliver. You're the one that has to make the decisions. The Home Office just follows through. It must be tough being a judge."

"It never felt tough—I enjoyed it, until recently. But it feels tough now." He stared down again at the table. Could he really be saying this? He felt so vulnerable, peeled open. This wasn't how a judge spoke—he shouldn't be making these admissions. But there was no going back.

"Can you help me Keith—" he whispered into the phone "I need help. When this thing with Mohammed is sorted, I need to find out what happened to the other people I refused asylum to. There have been a great many. I need to work out how many I got it wrong for and what happened to them. To make amends—if I can."

"Yy…eah…I can help with that. But hey, take it easy. Sounds like you just need a break. We all make mistakes..."

"Yes, but some of these may have been, well, huge. Look, I, need to go now. Just tell me what to do about Mohammed and I'll do it."

"Sure, I'll find out what the legal position, and, yes, there's something you could do already." It sounded like an afterthought.

"Anything."

"He gave a contact number for his next of kin in the UK. It's someone called Brian, but we don't know who that is. I wondered if you had any idea—through your toggling. If the man is suitable then maybe he can help Mr Marimbey by offering him an alternative to custody after he has been discharged from hospital in Cairo and returned here. Just while the legal process is going through of course…."

"Good idea, Keith, and I know who Brian is. He's a friendly taxi driver. He was the one person from this country Mohammed thought he could trust. He's helped him quite a bit. I'll phone him for you." Oliver was relieved at having something concrete to do.

"OK. I'll give you the number, one minute..."

"No need. Mohammed remembers his number."

9

That night Brian talked for hours with Michelle. Fortunately Tilly was out on a birthday sleepover and Rowan got himself to bed without fuss. He started by telling her about Mohammed's deportation and she got upset for him all over again. But she listened to the detail of his rescue attempt with a delicious smile on her face—and he'd thought she'd be angry about him risking his job.

Telling her about the toggling was much harder. He decided beforehand not to tell her about Bertrand's affair. It might make her suspicious, and to tell her the whole truth wouldn't serve any purpose. It would just hurt her, unnecessarily, for the sake of salving his conscience. But as soon as he started talking about Dorothy he realised he couldn't pull it off. Most of what he knew about her seemed to swivel around one scene—reading the note from Angie in Bertrand's briefcase, and Michelle kept fishing for more information. She was so bright and intuitive—it was part of what he loved about her—but it made it made it hard to hide things.

Finally, he told her about Angie's note to Bertrand. She listened, quietly, leaning back in the sofa, her eyebrows slightly raised. When he reached the end the silence was thunderous and he could sense her scrutinising him coldly.

"So why *you*, Bri?" she said, after a long pause: "Why did *you* toggle *her*?"

After that he had to tell her about Minty. He felt small and foolish. She asked a few questions, but mostly just listened in silence. He could she was hurting.

"It wasn't sexual Mich'. It's never been sexual"

"No. Though it sounds like you might have wanted that."

"No, that's not true..." It was a bare-faced lie and he knew it.

"Oh…*really*?" She got up and went to the kitchen on the pretext of making coffee. Brian felt like his heart was going to burst with shame. He listened to the sound of her bashing about for what seemed like an eternity. It reminded him of the time he'd waited at the altar for her, when they were getting married. She'd been so late he'd begun to think she'd changed her mind. It was devastating to think of life without her. Maybe she'd react like Dorothy.

Finally she returned and sat separately on the sofa, her eyes swollen. Brian wanted to hold her in his arms, but he knew better than to presume. Then she looked at him full on: "Are you telling me the *whole* truth, Brian?

He froze and whispered "I am."

"Really?" She didn't look convinced. She seemed to be able to read him like a book—just like Dorothy with Bertrand.

"I mean, I'm not." His voice was cracking. I might have wanted sex with her – it just wasn't on offer." There he'd torn it now. He looked into her beautiful eyes, trawling in vain for her forgiveness.

"I'm so ashamed…"

"You should be," she said, quiet and bitter. "How much time have you spent with her?"

"You know…some of it."

"Some of it?"

"Yes."

"How much *exactly*?"

"I…quite a bit"

"HOW MUCH?"

He was in too deep to lie now. "…several days a week."

Michelle's eyes narrowed. "So *that's* where you've been and why you've been earning less."

Brian nodded glumly. The pit he was in seemed about to engulf him completely. "But…but it wasn't sexual…"

"Except that you fancied her." She was crying now. "But it's not… *that* that bothers me so much…it's that you deceived me. For a whole year. How *could* you? How can I trust you again?"

Brian reached across a hand in the void between them. "You can trust me, Mich," he said, as sincerely as he could muster.

"Don't TOUCH me!

He pulled back his hand as if it he'd burnt it as Michelle leapt to her feet and stomped upstairs to their bedroom.

Suddenly the house felt icy cold. He'd have to camp out on the pull-out sofa.

An hour later as Brian lay tossing uncomfortably on the sofa his mobile rang—it was past midnight!

"…Hello."

"Hello, is that Mr Brian, I mean, Brian." His voice sounded upper crust, but oddly familiar.

"Yes."

"My name's Oliver Surret, I'm phoning you about Mohammed Marimbey. Sorry to phone you so late."

Memories of the court flooded back. "You're the judge, aren't you?"

"Yes, I was the judge." His voice sounded strained, it had lost the imperial quality it'd had in court. "And that's why I'm phoning you."

"But why? You already sent him back." Brian didn't want to be talking to this bastard. He'd had enough for one day, and what could he possibly want? Maybe he'd heard about the airport debacle.

"Well, that's just it. He *was* sent back but he never reached Uganda. He—put up some resistance—in Cairo. There was a fight between him and his guards, and he's ended up in hospital there. We're going to fly him back to the UK, when he's well enough. That's why I'm phoning you."

Michelle had entered the room, wearing her fluffy pink dressing gown. She must be wondering who was phoning him at this hour.

"Is he OK?"

"Yes, they think he's going to be fine. He was unconscious for a bit, but he's alright now."

Brian felt suddenly furious. "So your guys beat him until he was unconscious?

Silence on the line. Michelle was looking alarmed.

"You must be proud of yourself." He held his hand over the receiver and whispered to Michelle: "it's about Mohammed."

"…Not my guys. I'm a judge, they don't work for me. Judges are independent."

"Don't give me that shit! Who pays your salary? It was *you* who sent him back! None of this would have happened if you'd only listened."

Another silence on the line. "You're right. I am…part of the system. I made a terrible mistake."

"You're telling me!" Brian felt himself shaking with rage, but the implications of what the judge had said were starting to sink in. Mohammed was going to be returned! This was another reprieve.

"…But why are you phoning me? I hardly know him."

"You're the only person he trusts. Of all the English people he met in this country, you're the only one who believed him and has helped. He gave your name as his next of kin here. He's profoundly grateful to you."

Brian could hardly believe his ears: "Did he say that?"

"No, I..."

"What?"

"I've toggled him."

"You've *toggled* him?" This was astonishing.

"Yes…and he's only told the truth."

"Well that much was *obvious*!"

"Not to me it wasn't, but you're right. I know now. I should have known better."

"Yes. You *should* have known better." Brian agreed slowly looking up into Michelle's wide eyes. His anger subsiding.

"…But we all make mistakes," he ventured at last. He could hear deep breathing on the other end.

"Not mistakes this big, Brian. And this isn't the only one I've made. I'm sure of that now."

"You've made other mistakes?"

"Yep. Hard to tell how many. I no longer trust my own judgement."

"Well, sounds like you're learning."

"Yes, I suppose."

"But I still don't get why you've phoned?"

"Mohammed's going to need somewhere to stay. I don't want him locked up again whilst we sort out the legal side of things and the NASS accommodation is horrible. I'd let him stay with me—but I know from toggling him he'd never agree. Understandably, he can't stand me. I wondered if, perhaps, you knew someone who might help…?"

"Is that a round-about way of asking if I can put him up?"

"Well, yes! But I know it's a lot to ask."

"I'll do it."

Another quaking silence his end, then: "How come you're so generous Brian?"

Brian looked up at Michelle standing over him with her wide inquisitive eyes. "It doesn't feel like I am. I make terrible mistakes too. I just had to admit to betraying my own wife...I guess we all just have to learn from our mistakes."

"Yes, well, thank you," said Oliver slowly. "I'll phone you when I know when he's coming."

After the call Brian explained the conversation to Michelle. She seemed to soften slightly when he got to the bit where he'd allowed the judge some forgiveness. He feared she might be angry for not being consulted about putting up Mohammed, but she smiled. "Of course we have to put him up. Love's about action, remember? Not that this lets you off the hook…I'm still furious, Brian, and I want you to keep toggling Dorothy. That woman talks a lot of sense."

"I will, I will."

Michelle went quietly back up the stairs.

Brian lay awake staring at the ceiling, aware of the green dot, but not wanting to go there.

10

Marjorie hadn't intended to stop long at Willow View. It was months since she'd last visited, and there were a few things she needed to pick up. She'd timed it so that Oliver would be at work. Parking Hattie's jeep on the driveway, and taking two empty suitcases out of the boot she unlocked the front door, noticing as she did so that the wisteria had been recently pruned. Well, at least he was keeping on top of things.

The marble tiles in the porch too were brushed, and there were a pair of new begonias on display, on high stands, looking healthy. As she walked through the porch into the main entrance hall she heard the sound of a vacuum cleaner from the back of the house and froze, suddenly feeling like a burglar in her own house. He must have hired a cleaner.

Dropping the two suitcases she traced the sound to the drawing room and was shocked to discover Oliver, his back to her, vacuuming the thick pile carpet, oblivious to her presence. Briefly she considered creeping away, but something held her there, watching him from behind. She couldn't recall ever having seen him vacuuming before, but he seemed oddly at ease and absorbed with the task.

Perhaps hearing a slight sound he spun around with a start. "Marjorie! I didn't hear you!"

"No. I only came to get something quickly. I didn't know you'd be here."

"Well, welcome then." He turned off the vacuum cleaner and they looked at each other awkwardly. She couldn't quite place it, but he looked somehow *different*. Still just as manicured but less—stiff. "I thought you'd be at work."

"No, I've resigned."

"You've *what?*"

"Yes, I...oh Marjorie, it's a long story. I could tell you, but it would take time, and I don't imagine you want to stay..." This too was different—he wasn't trying to talk her into staying. Surely he hadn't finally accepted that she'd left. Come to think of it she hadn't had a message from him for at least two weeks.

"I...do want to know." Was this foolish, she wondered? He looked at her with large eyes: "OK then. Can I make you a cup of coffee?" She nodded, surprised and wondering if he had ever offered this before. Perhaps he had, when they'd first met, all those years ago.

They walked through to the kitchen. There was a pot of chicken soup simmering gently on the Aga and a new recipe book propped open at an angle on the granite work surface. The place was, well, not bad. Not quite to her standards, but surprisingly clean. She sat down on a high stool at the counter, and watched as Oliver carefully measured some coffee beans into the grinder. She waited until the grinding had finished then asked again: "So how come you resigned?"

"Because I'm not fit to be a judge." He said it with a soft, sad, voice.

"*What?*"

He looked across at her, a small container of ground coffee in one hand, momentarily paused in mid-air, and smiled broadly. She became dramatically aware that she couldn't remember the last time that she'd seen him smile like this.

"I'm not surprised you're surprised Marjorie! I've learnt a lot these past few weeks, and I've had to eat a massive helping of humble pie. I...toggled."

As he continued to make the coffee Marjorie listened as Oliver explained about Mohammed, about how he'd realised he'd made a terrible error of judgement in sending him back and feared he'd made lots of other errors of judgement as well. He explained how, at first, he'd called in sick, then gradually realised that he wasn't fit for the work. He couldn't trust his own judgement any more. "But it goes deeper than that, Marjorie, I've been remembering what you said when we went on that horrible walk, all those months ago. You know, the one by the river, when it rained so much. About the lines in the sand, and us not owning the earth, but the earth owning us… I guess I'm coming round to your view. It's not only that I don't feel fit to judge, I'm not even sure any more *how* we can make judgements." He placed two steaming mugs of coffee on the counter and sat on a stool beside her, looking over at her wistfully.

She felt a sudden wave of tenderness towards him. This wasn't the righteous, fossilised, man she'd lived with all those years. This was someone transformed. She hadn't believed such change was possible. But then again, she'd changed herself. From the moment that she'd cut her wrist she'd changed and, since Besnik had been inside her, the changes had continued to consolidate radically in her life. It was hard to overestimate the effects of toggling, of *really empathising* even with just one other being. She blew at her coffee and took a cautious sip. It tasted delicious. "So what will you do now?"

"There's so much to do Marjorie, I hardly know where to start. When I first toggled I tried to deny it at first. Then when I realised my mistake I got pretty depressed. I felt such a fool, so useless, and that my work had been hopelessly flawed. Then I realised there was other work to do, different work, and that I might be able to use what's left of my influence and, more importantly, my toggling experience, to fight to change things. I want to help change the law around asylum, to make sure asylum seekers are given time and help to recover before they're questioned, and that they're given decent solicitors, with access to sufficient legal aid; and that they're interviewed properly, with unbiased interpreters, not by a Home Office official—but sympathetically by an independent person." He seemed so animated.

"Most of all I want to help a few individuals myself. That's why I've been cleaning the house. I'm afraid I let it get into a bit of state, so I've been sorting it out. I think you were right about that too. I think we should sell it and use the money. I can't believe, in any case, how much time and effort it takes just to keep the damn place ticking over. You worked *hard*, Marjorie."

Again he was looking over at her with that new smile. She couldn't help but warm to him. "I want to use some of the money to help some of the asylum seekers I've been researching. You see I've been looking into other judgements I made and trying to find out what happened. It's been hard. I found one of the people I judged against—a nice man called Jacubu Macunu. He tried to commit suicide on the day of his hearing, the same day you cut your wrist. He took a train to Dover and jumped off a cliff there—and fell over a hundred feet. He must have been certain he was going to die. But what he hadn't realised was that it was a spring high tide and that the difference in sea level between the time he'd first seen that spot and the time when he jumped was several metres. So he landed in several metres of water and survived with two broken legs—and damage to his spine. I tracked him down to a medical facility, where he's still recovering, a year later. He's had to have a series of operations. Amazingly he agreed to see me. When I gave him a proper chance to tell his story I had to believe him. Now I'm campaigning for him to be allowed to stay on compassionate grounds. I want to help him, and others like him, to make a new start. After all it was my decision that landed him in this mess." Marjorie watched as Oliver took a large swig of coffee. He looked tired and drawn, but his face was softer than she'd ever seen it—and was that a slight watering in his eyes?

"I've been so blind Marjorie, so terribly, terribly blind."

She put her hand gently on his knee. "We both have, Oliver. We *all* have."

11

As Fergus stepped out of the Aston Martin and took stock of the park he fancied he could almost hear the sap rising, sucking up from the earth below, racing through the narrowing bark sleeves, and out into the green mist of calling tree buds.

Pete joined him and they walked to the back of the fast moving queue. He had come up the previous day, so that Pete could be with him when he finally touched a circle himself. Fergus could think of no-one that he would rather have by his side, or who was better qualified, than Pete. Over the year, the two of them had developed a firm, vibrant, friendship that they both knew was for life and Pete had readily agreed. "I'll do anything for you Fergie, you know that, I'm your brother now.

They had kept Fergus's intended visit to the circle a carefully guarded secret. Fergus didn't want to have to contend with the press on his seminal day. It had also felt appropriate to come to the same circle that Pete had descended onto by Jet Pack three hundred and sixty days previously. Pete had made history then, and there was talk of erecting a statue of him once the circles disappeared.

Fergus had spent the night in the spare bed in Pete's huge bedroom, with its ten-foot square poster of Harvey. He'd also been invited to stay with the Flaviers after touching the circle, and to wait with them as the year drew to a close. The fact that all of Pete's family were now proud togglers made it a perfect venue.

He'd left it as long as he dared—wanting to ensure that as many others as possible had had the experience before allowing himself the same. It felt a bit like being the captain of a sinking ship—needing to cater for everyone else's needs before meeting his own.

Togglers were pretty much unanimous that it was sensible to allow plenty of time afterwards for digesting and adjusting to the experience. He hadn't felt he could afford such distractions. Over the past year his life had assumed a single focus—co-ordinating the activated sites in America so as to ensure that as many people as possible could touch circles. He'd also been a significant player in a worldwide campaign to make circles as accessible as possible. This hadn't been without its challenges; there'd been continued pressure from Theo, who had regularly intruded into his life throughout the year, not just with the raid on SETI but with a range of threats and manipulative ploys designed to make him abandon his campaign. But despite all Theo's tactics and unpleasantness Fergus had, over the year, developed a grudging respect for him. Theo was using every means at his disposal to secure the outcome he felt was best, same as he was. Both of them had grasped the huge significance of what was happening around the globe and were passionate in taking responsibility for influencing how it was dealt with. The difference between them of course was that Theo feared the worst, whereas he hoped for the best. Theo saw a sinister intention behind the circles, which might only become apparent at the end of the year, whereas he saw the beneficial effects of the circles and also still hoped that there might yet be some communication with whomever, or whatever, had sent them.

It had been a huge year, but he felt he'd been largely successful. Restrictions around visiting circles had steadily lifted. Little by little the benefits of touching circles had been widely accepted. Even people with mental health problems had benefited. There were, for example, a number of cases of people with Alzheimers who had toggled themselves, thereby arresting the decay of further memories and recovering long lost memories. Those with depressive or paranoid tendencies often reported new focus and vision in their lives. By focusing on someone else or a broader issue they could lift themselves out of their own personal prisons. State policy had gradually shifted from discouraging people from using circles, to encouraging those that wanted to toggle to do it as quickly as possible, so as to avoid a mass scramble at the end. People were encouraged to keep queues moving quickly and volunteers were helping with this.

The result of all this was that around America there were now some ten million togglers and worldwide estimates ranged up to a billion. Huge numbers had taken the opportunity. But also, nonetheless, the vast majority hadn't.

As the year drew to a close Fergus had been keeping a sharp eye on queue waiting times around the country—which had been rising sharply. When he felt he could no longer risk waiting any longer he'd arranged to come and see Pete. Now, he was relieved to note, he'd timed it well—they'd only queued for eight hours and were minutes away and catching enticing glimpses of the circle's moving green surface.

"You nervous?" Pete asked.

Fergus considered: "Oh yeah, I'm nervous. I know what happens yet I'm worried it won't answer my questions."

"What questions?"

"What this is all for, who arranged it, and why?"

Pete looked at Fergus with a gentle smile: "Like questions around life really."

Fergus looked down, feeling suddenly overwhelmed. Beneath his feet, where grass had once grown, was a smooth path of packed mud, squashed down over the past few months by a continuous stream of feet.

"Yeah, you could say that: Why are we here? What happens before birth? What happens after death? Who else is out there? Can they help us understand?" The questions were deeply familiar to him, grit under his skin. "I think I've been postponing this experience partly because I've not wanted to come away with these questions still unanswered. I've waited too long for a message to come through. More than just this year."

Pete nodded slowly: "I know Fergie. I don't think I've ever met someone who seemed so profoundly…. *lost* as you. That's part of what I like about you, man. Your honesty in facing it. Most people put those questions to the back of their minds and are happier for it. They recognise that they can't be answered so they stop asking them. Some never get round to asking them in the first place—like Harvey. Those questions don't even occur to him. They're out of his range. If he was here now he'd be running excitedly around the people in the queue sniffing their butts, or racing over to that bitch by the clump of trees over there. *He* doesn't care!

Fergus looked over at the clump of trees. He could see a sleek Labrador with shining black fur, pulling on its lead. He hadn't noticed the dog before. He certainly didn't know it was a bitch.

"Contain yourself Pete! Next thing you'll be racing over there to sniff her yourself."

Pete smiled broadly "Yeah man! She does smell rather cute."

Fergus raised an eyebrow.

"Only kidding, man! But my point is—Harvey doesn't fret over the things that worry you. He just *is*." he took hold of his friend's elbow. "Maybe you'll get an animal, like me, and can ease up a bit on questions."

Fergus squinted: "But the truth is…I want more than that. I don't want to ease up on the questions, *I want some answers*."

Pete wanted to help his friend but felt concerned now at the greediness of his expectations. There was real danger he could be disappointed—quite a few togglers had been, at least initially. Not everyone got blinding flashes of insight. For some the process was much more gradual and organic. They were drip fed a new perspective. There was something jarring about how Fergus was coming across. It was almost as though his insistence in holding onto his questions was making himself out to be somehow extra special—an alien within his own species, continually bugged by questions others had abandoned.

"You're not really *that* unusual, Fergie. Aren't we all just as much in the dark, whether or not we ask the questions? Even Harvey's in the dark, he just doesn't know it." They were moving steadily forwards. Pete suddenly smiled: "Do you think we should have been born with an instructions manual, man? You know, one of those little photocopied booklets with unintelligible diagrams and tiny writing in thirty languages? Do you think that would have made us happier? I don't think so. It would just have spoiled all the mystery.

A small smile competed with the frown lines on Fergus's face. They were only a few feet away now from the circle. Officials in 'I've toggled' shirts were encouraging people to touch the circle swiftly and leading them away afterwards.

In their last few steps Pete could smell his friend's mounting anxiety "Don't worry so, man, just think of it as being like losing your virginity or travelling. You can't possibly really know what it's like until you do it—no matter how much thinking you do in advance…and you are about to do it. Good luck, my dear friend."

Fergus touched the circle. The green light appeared in his head. According to plans they'd made before-hand they walked briskly to the waiting Aston Martin and Pete drove them back to the Flavier mansion before he attempted to toggle. He wanted to do it in a calm supported environment. He'd contained his curiosity for nearly a year, a few more minutes were manageable. Back in Pete's room he lay on the beautifully soft settee and closed his eyes. Pete sat alertly nearby.

He focused on the green.

He was in the far future. He was tranquillity and silence. He was emptiness itself. An empty cup that contained all. He was a silence that could fill with voices and always remain empty. Silence.

Then a single voice said: 'Let there be music'. It was the voice of the announcements, clear, full and genderless. It was the voice of a conductor reaching back across time. It was distilled from a billion other voices and spoke for them all.

And now there was another voice—a voice at the top of a tree, honed with the savour of eons, serenading a massive red sun as it disappeared below a singed horizon. The voice of a mistle thrush. A song, effortless with practice, preserved across time, deeply familiar, repetitive, yet wonderfully varied. Each phrase an outpour of elixir. Pauses that drank the last of the day, then erupted into fresh cascades. Sound waves bounced on rocks and stirred the roots of trees.

Fergus listened, as a part of the song. He was inside the bird, he was the rising and falling breast, the rippling throat, the watchful eyes. He was both inside and outside the song. He was the ears that heard, and the trilling notes themselves.

Softly, and at first almost imperceptibly, new voices began to echo and complement the mistle thrush's lead as other birds joined in. The music was becoming diverse all around. It had the flavour of summer evenings when he used to play out in the road with the other children, subliminally aware that the sound of the birds marked the setting of the sun, and that when, at last, it all grew quiet they would all be called away, back inside.

As he listened the music continued to expand. He was now the swish of fish, the percussion of insects and frogs, the buzzing of bees. Mammals too began to be delicately present, the mating calls of deer, the chorus of wolves, and whales too—adding their range—from deep pulsing throb to scratchy cries tickling across the surface. All were echoing the opening theme of the thrush, developing it, rippling out across time. As he focused on the whales he was with them in the seas as bubbling water swirled past their barnacled leather and in the deeper throbs of the whales he could hear the chant of Tibetan monks, and then he was with them too in darkened temples, with butter lamps and incense, chanting amongst the blasting of ancient horn, the tinkle of bells, the swinging pulse of gongs. He was the young apprentice monk listening afresh to the sounds around him, he was the old abbot he became. He was the deep drone of chanting. He was an eagle outside swooping low down the hill over the tattered prayer flags, then rising over the valley, flying up into the mountains, screeching at the sky. He was the mountains he was flying over. He could go where he pleased, moving seamlessly through layers of form. He could assume any form. He was form itself, and beyond all that, swirling in the notes, immersed in melody, refining, developing. He was harmony and all its parts. He was every voice and they were singing for the setting sun, for the end of every golden day, and for this, *the last day*.

A single voice communicated through the music. It was also many voices—both a being and a non being. He searched for a name, and many came, though none was ultimately satisfactory. The naming itself was always a step removed. The word 'Gaia' surfaced as being available as a means to help him conceptualise—an approximation of the truth. Gaia—a word used to describe earth's consciousness.

And 'Gaia' communicated that the music was a farewell, a swansong for the ancestors. The poignant notes were an ending—Gaia was about to die—at least in this time frame. Two messages and some green circles were about to be sent backwards in time. The very act of doing this would change the past, and thereby eradicate the basis of an existence in this time. A communal death was coming soon, for the benefit of the ancestors and their descendants.

Gaia was about to send back a key that it was hoped would unlock new doors—a turning point for the ancestors, enabling things to evolve faster, and with more insight. The basis for a way of relating that could bypass millenniums of estrangement and difficulty, that could save extinctions, prevent wars. The green circles were the essence of what had been learnt. Not the way itself, but a pointer to the way. A purpose-built spin-off from the connecting technology that Gaia had developed—the ability to move between one consciousness and another, to unite together as one being. The circles were also a simplification of Gaian technology—allowing for only one transmission to be received by any one being. No more could be accommodated by the levels of consciousness present in humans at the point in history that had been chosen.

Gaia had decided to send back the technology it had developed as far as possible. Not so far that it would have been rejected outright or not used sufficiently, or to a time for which there were insufficient records about languages spoken, the population distribution, politics and countries, or the precise locations where circles could be placed. But far enough back in time to allow the course of history to take the significant swerve that was hoped for—away from the looming devastation, now well back in Gaia's past but from which survival had only just been achieved after appalling suffering.

The circles were designed as catalysts for change, not a final solution. Gaia had wanted to interfere as little as possible. Just enough to reach a tipping point, to accelerate a volition towards unity, and the development of a technology that would facilitate this further.

There had been many wonderings as to whether it should be done at all, was this too much about playing at God? The process of helping could so often be poisoned by the arrogance of its own endeavour.

Maybe things were better left as they'd always been.

The deciding factor had been the approaching Armageddon. The expanding sun, now huge and red had begun to engulf the charred surface of the earth with a raging storm of firey gas and radiation. It wouldn't be long now before the planet would split apart and merge. Gaia was about to die anyway.

In the face of this, life had had to change radically to survive at all. As carbon based life had become infeasible, Gaia uploaded consciousness into silicon and was now housed in a heat protected sphere deep under one of the poles.

Fergus realised that this was where he was now—inside a sphere, in a sea of terrestrial life consciousness, preserved in silicon; with new information no longer coming organically through ears and eyes or other organs but electronically through a range of mechanical receptors, on the surface of earth and from satellites and receding space ships.

He looked out through them now. Much of the information coming in was about the swirling fires of the expanding sun. But on different frequencies and from the furthest spacecraft he could look out at the wider universe. The constellations had changed, there were greater distances between the stars, and they were further away. Many had disappeared. The sky was blacker now. The universe had expanded at an accelerating rate towards a stretched out death, its very fabric splitting beyond prospect of re-connection. Entropy had prevailed.

As he looked out Fergus became aware that Gaia was still fundamentally alone. There was still no bridge in consciousness beyond the solar system. Worse, there was also a knowledge that many millions of years previously, the self-preoccupation of the human species had squandered a window of opportunity in which alien contact might have been achieved, before the distances involved became too huge to negotiate.

Gaia was alone. It was too late to complete the joining up with life outside the solar system that had long been yearned for. For millions of years Gaia had been trapped without escape. Developments in inter-stellar space travel had been outstripped by the increasing expansion of the universe. The solar system had become a prison.

The progressive inclusion of more and more life into silicon consciousness had temporarily relieved a feeling of separateness. But with an ancient exploding sun, and with stars, and whole galaxies, receding and dying out, oblivion and ultimate aloneness had seemed the inevitable destiny.

That is, until the technology to send inanimate material back through time had been developed. It remained untested for thousands of years. Gaia understood that the present couldn't be preserved if its own past was changed. It was an insoluble paradox. Any significant technology sent backwards in time would result in the immediate extinction of this present, and this consciousness. Equations were refined and reworked using many different approaches, but in the absence of any solution to the paradox, they'd never been applied.

As the sun continued to expand, however, a resolve firmed up. There was nothing to lose. Perhaps, if the mistakes in the past could be redressed, a new consciousness could be born. By sending back the circles, consciousness in the past could be given more time to reach out beyond the solar system. Gaia could start a new branch of history by helping an earlier ancestral form. It would give birth to a new, improved Gaia, and perhaps, the long wished for, *contact.* But this would also mean an end to this Gaia—the sender, the conductor, the whole diverse choir. An end to this branch of time. It would be certain death and a birth of sorts. A seed sent back from the future...

Already sent back, now being used. That future Gaia must be gone now.

Fergus understood that a record of that Gaia's future consciousness had been sent back with the circles, and this was what he was now toggling.

The music began to distil down again, the notes purifying and simplifying. He was the whales again, and the birds, and the single thrush.

The thrush stopped. He waited, expectant of the next phrase, but none came. A final phrase had run clear, across historical tree tops, to where a huge sun had set, in a boiling sunset.

The thrush had closed its beak finally to the night, *to that future.*

Fergus continued to wait expectantly in the moments that followed, his mind still echoing the music. Then, as the circles were sent, a thunderous black silence throbbed with emptiness.

He was that silence.

...and a small blue light.

Reluctantly, like a molecule of water finding its own separate vibration within a sleeping sea he toggled back into Fergus alone, opened his eyes and looked into Pete's kindly waiting face.

"How'd it go, man?"

He was unable to find words. He was still partly over the other side. He felt deeply sad, and at the same time, tranquil. Pete took his hand and waited. Eventually Fergus opened his eyes wider and sat up in the sofa, looking at his friend: "It isn't aliens that did all this."

Pete raised his eyebrows: "It isn't?"

"No, we haven't found them yet," he said quietly "that's what we have to work towards now."

12

Three days before the circles were due to disappear Brian agreed to take Minty to Heathrow. She was off to India in search of Anagha.

He said yes, without thinking, then ran it past Michelle. "If you must Brian" she said, coldly, without looking up from clearing the table. This wasn't the reaction he'd hoped for. He thought they had a frail peace. Michelle was still keeping her distance physically but at least he was back in the bedroom. Her reaction threw him into a dilemma. He didn't want to rock the boat…but then again it might be the last chance to see Minty.

He decided to go ahead. He'd stay honourable, of course, but that didn't mean he couldn't ever see other women.

The next day as he drove off to collect Minty in the family car he noticed Michelle staring at him thin-lipped from the house and almost changed his mind. He'd elected not to use the cab for once. This could be his way of saying to Minty that their relationship had become, to him at any rate, more than just a business one. They were friends. It also meant he could have her sitting next to him, rather than behind glass in the back. He hadn't seen her since the conference, and had missed her. Now he could spend one last time with her.

He helped her put her red suitcase in the boot—the same one he'd loaded when he first picked her up. It only just squeezed in, along with all the miscellaneous family items that seemed to accumulate in their boot: Tilly's glitter gloves, Rowan's cricket stuff, deck chairs, Michelle's walking boots, picnic equipment, plastic macs, a broken umbrella, and countless other items they never got around to sorting. He had to push down hard to close the boot. So much junk.

He opened the passenger door for Minty. The front of the car was clean, emptied the previous day of mud, especially for the occasion, of soggy crisps and sweet wrappers. Minty climbed in and looked immediately comfortable, as ever. She was wearing her bright yellow soft-cotton dress, probably selected for the Indian climate, and her bangles and lip gloss, and she still had that familiar smell of oranges and incense.

He drove the car slowly down the first couple of side streets, then cut to the chase, aware they didn't have much time: "I'll miss you, Minty, like I said."

She smiled her relaxed smile: "And I'll miss you…it's been such a cool year and I've felt really, like, *supported* by you."

Her reply felt insufficient. Had he just been some kind of a father figure then, a source of support? He drew up over-cautiously at an amber light, and looked across at her. Her face was eager, bursting with life. She must be excited now about the adventure ahead, he loved her easy excitement, but surely he was already a receding figure for her…

The lights turned green and he eased into first gear, aware out of the corner of his eye that she was looking at him.

"Penny for your thoughts, Brian?"

Her question caught him off-balance.

"Oh, nothing, just day-dreaming—," he stammered, clumsily.

She smiled again, full and deep, looking like she was enjoying herself. "It ain't like nothing, Brian. Something's up. I can smell it a mile off."

Gad she was perceptive. He felt cornered into making some kind of a confession.

"…it's just that I—I'm glad you found me supportive—but I, for me, I..." Goodness this was hard. "...I guess I've grown really fond of you..."

There, it was out now. He kept his eyes firmly on the road. "I don't quite understand what it is about you," He added, as a qualifier: "I've a real respect for the work you've been doing over the year. I think your passion for the cause has been incredible, I..."

"You fancy me, don't you?" she interrupted, smiling.

Brian's foot twitched alarmingly on the accelerator and the car lurched. He braked hastily, hoping the adjustment wasn't too obvious and looked at her again. This time she looked *mischievous*—her eyes crinkly and her soft shining lips parting broadly.

"Yeah, I did...do, I mean." He seemed to have stopped breathing. "How did you know…?"

She laughed: "Because it's been written in six foot high letters on a bill board for the past year."

"Has it?" his throat was suddenly dry. He felt like a small child who'd been caught stealing sweets. "I'm sorry, I didn't know it was that obvious, I..."

She put her hand over his, on the gear stick, and said gently: "Don't worry, Brian. It's cool…I feel that way too."

"*You do*?"

"Sure, from early on."

"I had no idea." he was feeling angry with himself now, and excited. This was the impossible confirmation he'd been looking for. He changed gear under her hand.

"But *why*?"

"You're not bad looking Brian, *for your age*," she laughed, "and you're cute. You've been kind to me. You've a way of putting people at ease, and you've surprisingly little ego, for a man."

"*Really*?"

"Yeah, and I like the way you listen, and respect, like when I saw how much you care about Mohammed, which reminds me—what happened, right? The last time we met you rushed off to rescue him."

Brian explained, keeping it brief, aware of the seconds ticking away and thinking all along that he didn't want to waste precious time telling her. When he'd finished she said simply: "Respect, man."

Respect. That word again. It felt jarringly formal and so overused it was drained of meaning. It was just the way she spoke. He entered Tunnel Road East, just before Heathrow. They'd be there in a couple of minutes. "Was that the basis for your interest in me then?" He asked clumsily. "*Respect?*"

She laughed again, and he felt himself stinging inside. She was mocking him now. "You need me to spell it out, don't you, Brian, even after I just told you, right?" She answered, still smiling. "Respect is like in there, but *I fancied you too!*"

This time he eased up on the accelerator and brought the car down to the slowest speed he could get away with. This felt unbelievable. "I didn't know."

"No, you're not quick like that."

"But you're half my age."

"So?" She giggled. "There's no accounting for tastes…and I like a mature man."

"But *why*? There must be younger men…"

"Sure, there are, like too many. But they don't give me space, man. They get all obsessive…possessive. 'Least you gave me space, man."

Brian thought about his own relationship with her. Had he been obsessive? Yeah probably. He just hadn't acted on it because he didn't think he had a chance.

They entered Heathrow, the scene of his recent escapade and he tried to concentrate on getting to the right terminal. He drew up in the dropping off area and turned off the ignition.

Minty looked at her watch and stayed in her seat. "We've still got over an hour before I even need to check in. Why don't you, like, park up and we can spend some quality time together?"

"Good idea." Automatically he turned the ignition back on, and drove towards the car park. He could feel a sudden rush of adrenalin.

Too many twisty ramps and manoeuvres later he negotiated the car into a small space by a concrete pillar and squeezed around to the boot which sprang open. Her shiny red suitcase rose up from the family junk.

The family junk.

He pulled the suitcase out and set it down beside Minty who was now standing close. She looked stunning in her yellow dress.

"Actually, Minty, I'm going to say goodbye now. I wish you happiness for the rest of your life. Good luck with Anagha. Good luck with everything. It's been a—great—pleasure—meeting you."

She looked puzzled, for once, without a smile. "You're leaving? *Now*?"

"Yes, think I'd better. Before I do anything I might regret." The green light was bright inside him.

"Oh." She looked crestfallen. "That was, sudden, yeah."

"Not really. Look, you know how I feel about you, and I know now, I think, part of how you feel about me. Let's leave it there, without doing anything to spoil it."

She moved even closer, and Brian found himself falling into her bright eyes. "Don't we even get to, like, *kiss*?"

He looked at her shiny inviting lips.

"No...better not."

He drove straight home, reeling from what had happened. Michelle had bloated eyes. She looked at him piercingly and asked how it had gone.

"Fine." Brian said, feigning matter of fact.

"Liar."

"What do you mean: '*liar*'?" Now he was indignant. "*Nothing* happened."

"Liar." She blew her nose. "It's no good, I can tell you're lying Brian. What really happened?"

"You're wrong. It was innocent. And she's gone now…"

"*I want the fucking truth!*"

He'd never seen her so angry. He was about to deny it again and then something stopped him. Perhaps it was the green dot in his head that he'd been managing not to toggle. Or maybe it was just that he knew, deep down, that she was right. It hadn't just been 'fine'.

So he told her, from the beginning, in detail. He told her why he'd decided to use the family car that day. He told her the whole conversation with Minty, including admitting they fancied each other. He admitted his excitement when Minty had suggested spending more time together, and about driving into the car park, and about getting her red suitcase out, and the family junk in the boot...

Which wasn't junk at all. Because every item in that boot was saturated with family memories of good times together, right down to the broken umbrella and Tilly's glitter gloves, and Michelle's walking boots and Rowan's cricket things. Because their family wasn't junk. Because it was the most important thing in his life. Because Michelle and Rowan and Tilly were more precious to him than life itself. And he'd been a blind idiot to forget it.

And he told her about the offer of a kiss, and how he'd only just managed to refuse, and the appalling loss he'd felt, pulling away.

He came to an abrupt halt, realising that he'd been talking non-stop, without looking at Michelle, and that he'd probably said far too much, and was terrified now. She'd asked for the truth and partly out of anger he'd told it in full. That much felt a relief. But now, like Bertrand, he had to take the consequences…

He looked up reluctantly, expecting rejection.

But her eyes were gentle pools.

"I believe you now Bri." She smiled.

It was then that he knew she'd forgive him. His wife was second to none.

13

"O'Donnel, what do you want?"

Fergus looked into Theo's grim frowning face on his screen. He had hoped perhaps that there might be a chink of politeness or humanity returning in the man now that the circles were about to disappear, but clearly he'd been wrong. If anything Theo looked worse than ever, dark lines scored under his eyes as if in a caricature sketch, and the brown felt shirt and Star of David pendant that he was wearing did nothing to allay the impression of driven intensity that seemed to stick to him like a coat of tar.

It had cost Fergus hugely to haul himself out of silicon consciousness and make this call, the first of many, and momentarily he regretted his decision. He'd toggled almost non-stop for 48 hours, inhabiting voice after voice and sliding through the permeable boundaries between them, revelling in the expansive transcendent realm that they all contributed to and that he now also felt a part of. But with this new experience he'd also inherited an enhanced sense of responsibility. He'd been selected for this particular toggle so that he could return to the world anew, with new vision and a capacity to influence things for the better. Now he had to follow through.

Briefly, careful to keep his voice neutral and to downplay his excitement, he told Theo about his toggling experience, concluding: "So it was Gaia in the future *as it was,* that sent the circles back to us—but it is a future that no longer exists, because of the sending back. Maybe our future will be different now—better. They've tried to help us so that one day we may be able to reach out further than they managed to, and meet with life beyond the solar system."

Theo had glared at him incredulously throughout his account, smoothing his moustache. "Convenient story O'Donnel, given your interests, and I don't believe one word of it—though I grant you it's clever because it does at least explain some of things that made no sense about an alien invasion." He paused, as if gathering his thoughts: "I suppose you've spun this yarn to try and get funding for SETI. But why on earth would we *want* to pursue alien contact?

Fergus frowned. "Why must you always be so cynical, Theo?" he asked quietly "I didn't invent anything. It's not about money for SETI. In any case, money is already flowing into SETI faster than we've ever known."

"What *do* you want then?"

Fergus smiled. "I thought it might help you to know."

"You wanted to *help* me?"

"Yes."

"I don't need any help, O'Donnel, and why would *you* want to help *me* anyway, after all I have done this past year?

"Does there have to be a why?"

"Of course."

"Perhaps I just want to help for the sake of helping."

"Get real, O'Donnel."

Fergus looked at him with a flash of irritation before his compassion returned. Theo had an acidulous persona, but it was important to see beneath that. His eyes had frozen at the suggestion of help. Deep down he was just frightened, and wasn't this one of the things that needed to change for them all: fear born of isolation? This was why he'd chosen to phone him, to help him progress through his fear. "I *am* being real Theo. I know how worried you've been, and you might be surprised to know that I'm grateful to you for worrying so much on our behalf, for trying so hard to protect us all from threats. You have one of the toughest jobs I can imagine."

Theo looked at him strangely, caught off balance for once.

"And that's why I chose to phone you" continued Fergus "*—to reassure you* that in this particular instance there's nothing to worry about. We aren't about to be invaded by aliens! Nothing terrible is about to happen. In a few days the circles will disappear and it's all going to be OK."

Theo scowled. "I still don't get it O'Donnel. After all I've done, you phone up now with this nauseating message..."

"Well I've done my part of this thing in telling you. I thought perhaps *you* might want to consider touching a circle before it's too late, to see for yourself—but it's up to you. Only you can decide whether to trust or not. All I know is that if we believe the whole universe is hostile then ultimately we wash up alone." Suddenly he felt weary. He looked into Theo's worry-grooved face one last time. "Goodbye Theo, all the best to you."

After Fergus broke contact Theo stared at the blank screen feeling angry and resentful. How dare O'Donnel be so patronising? He was no more alone than anyone else. Being alone was in any case fundamental to being alive, we kid ourselves if we think otherwise. We can never quite communicate our subjective experience accurately across our differences, so we can never be understood, completely. It was foolishness to think that there might be an end to aloneness, or a way to breach the gap, or that there is anything wrong with it. Anyhow he didn't really feel alone, he was just *unusual*, and the suggestion that he might wish to toggle, himself, was ludicrous.

But over the next couple of days he returned incessantly to his conversation with O'Donnel like a tongue returning to a sore in the mouth. O'Donnel's account was irritating. It offered an explanation, and although it was implausible he didn't have an alternative. He checked SETI's accounts—it was true, money was pouring in. So the question of motive remained baffling: *why had he bothered to call?*

On the final day of the circles he drove to work as usual. Despite the fact that it had been declared a national holiday the roads were busy and he had to go out of his way to avoid the traffic jam around his local circle. It seemed that scores of silly people were still trying to visit circles, even at this late stage, or had come to witness them disappear. The whole thing had become a kind of cult, with pressure being brought to bear on people who didn't want to touch them, who didn't want anything to do with them. He still couldn't understand why anyone would really. Didn't the fact that people wanted to 'transform' themselves mean that they were fundamentally unhappy with the way that they were. Transform. He didn't really understand what the word meant, but the whole idea was objectionable. What was wrong with just staying with how you were and learning to accept it? Why all this neurotic pressure to change?

Arriving at work he went straight to the recreation room. He had booked in an abstract board game session the previous day to overlap the period in which the circles were expected to go. He wanted to take his mind off the whole matter by doing something that demanded his full concentration. He would still be at the NCTC in case he was needed.

Briefly he greeted his usual opponent. They laid out a game of Dvonn and soon were moving columns of different coloured pieces between hexagonal cells on the lozenge shaped board.

This time he heard the buzzer and looked up to see his name. This time he paused the timer before listening to the call.

"Sir, it's Wilkins, the circles have just gone and there's another message."

"Without a word to his opponent he pounded up the stairs to the main office. Wilkins was waiting for him with a nervous smile on his face. "Only kidding, sir, there's no message."

Theo looked at him in dismay. Oddly he didn't feel angry with him; nor did he feel relieved that there wasn't another message, or that the circles had gone. He realised, with surprise, that he only felt disappointed.

14

Brian walked to the Heath arm in arm with Michelle. Tilly pounding ahead on her scooter and Rowan racing back and forth on his Christmas bike.

They found a spot overlooking the circle, and sat amongst the crowds to watch it disappear. With seconds to go people were still racing to get there in time. A few were going to miss out of course, there were just too many. He felt fortunate now that he was a toggler himself and that Michelle, Rowan and Tilly had all followed suit in last few days, with his encouragement. They'd had to camp out. So now there were three more stories in the family, taking them out of their little nuclear unit, connecting them up more deeply with the wider world.

At the expected time the circle disappeared suddenly, just as it had arrived, without fanfare, leaving a perfect black circle of flattened soil behind.

Lots of people cried when it disappeared and stood around holding hands and looking bereft—like they'd expected something else to come in its place, or a big announcement. Or something. But there was nothing. The circle just disappeared.

That evening Fergus O'Donnel was on the news. Brian had seen him before, he was from SETI. He said he was toggling the human race, far off in the future when the sun had become a red giant, and that it was them that had sent the circles, not an alien species. Brian didn't know whether or not to believe him, and in a way it didn't matter. Whatever you believe it's all a great mystery.

He'd have liked to think that he was a scrap wiser than he was, but he couldn't even be sure about that. It had been such a close thing with Minty, even with that green light in his head. Amazing how easy it was to forget other people's feelings when your own desires compete. And Minty was wrong when she said he didn't have a big ego. Of course he did. He just kept it hidden. In the past few days he'd begun to toggle regularly, reluctant at first but it was helping to keep him out of that ego prison, just a tad. Not that you needed a green light in your head to learn to empathise—it just helped give you a kick start.

They spent the whole day, after the circles had gone, getting ready for Mohammed. Rowan volunteered to let Tilly share his room, so that Mohammed could have hers. That was a big give away from both of them. Then Tilly donated Humphrey for Mohammed, saying, as she tucked him into the newly made bed, that he would probably need him more than she would and she still had Kimberly. Brian felt so proud. Given the opportunity, his kids could be so loving.

Whilst they were moving Tilly's stuff and cleaning up the room for Mohammed, Michelle was looking up Ugandan dishes, and learning simple Swahili phrases. Then she sent Brian off to an African supermarket to buy plantains and cassava and they spent the afternoon together, cooking new dishes, and lining them up for the freezer.

But after the kids had gone to bed they got an unexpected call. It was Oliver. "Brian, I'm sorry. I just heard from the Home Office. Mohammed isn't coming tomorrow after all. There's been a delay in Cairo. He's started to bleed, a lot, internally. It looks like there are complications we didn't know about. He isn't well enough to travel."

"But he's going to be alright isn't he?" Brian said, feeling horribly empty.

There was an unpleasant pause on the line. "I hope so."

15

Chinpa Dorje is on his meditation cushion in the tiny mountain cave. His mind is calm and quiet, ready for the daily Tonglen practice.

Lungrik Kechok died nine months ago. But now he has a new person to start with, perfect for the practice, and one that he is grateful to toggle.

"Muhindo, my dear brother, good morning again! I know deeply of your distress and fear, and of how much you're hurting. Here, let me ease that from you." He breathes it in, deeply, in a familiar toxic flood. My, that man has some pain. "Here, with my outbreath, take my peace. Take it, it's yours now. I give it to you freely"

And then, with the next in breath, he breathes in another dose "I know all about your sadism too, here, let me take that from you. I can manage those impulses for you. "Here, have my compassion in exchange, fill your heart with this, fill it fully, it works, it really works. It'll make you feel better.

In and out, in and out, gentle, unhurried exchanges. He spends a long time on Muhindo. Then, as ever, he spreads the practice outwards, to the monastery, the local area, to Tibet, to all countries, to all the human race and all beings, throughout time, and space. "May you all be well, may you all be happy, may you all be full of love and forgiveness—just give me your hatred, and fear, and ignorance, in exchange."

He gently brings the meditation to a close for the day, bows to the small shrine, kneels to blow out the butter lamp and begins to walk along the narrow path, back to the monastery. He is aware of the soles of his feet inside his shoes and of the leather pressing against them as his shoes alternately touch the ground. He is aware of the mist clearing on the mountains and of a single bird, singing for the dawn.

Suddenly, unexpectedly, and irreversibly, he feels his separateness dissolving into the whole.

The End

Author's disclaimer, acknowledgements, and notes.

All the characters in this novel are fictional. The stories of Mohammed, and Jacubu, however, are based (with consent) on the first-hand accounts of asylum seekers who have generously told me their stories.

Whilst specific facts in relation to the treatment and processing of asylum seekers have been simplified I have made every effort not to misrepresent, or overstate, either the sufferings that can occur in home countries or the unconscious (for the most part) institutional sadism of the Home Office and the British judiciary system with respect to asylum seekers. If anything, the cruelty has been understated—particularly the inadequacy of the system and the antiquated and Kafkaesque process of appraisal that keeps many UK asylum seekers awaiting final judgement for years, only to be sent back into danger, or to continue to live in the UK without legal status, or a viable future—and in constant fear of deportation.

The description of Pitcairn Island, its language and people is entirely fictitious. I have never been to Pitcairn, or known anyone who has, so there are liberal amounts of fantasy in the text. It hasn't been my intention to cause offence to any of the current Pitcairn Islanders, whose sheer determination and sense of adventure can only be considered extraordinary.

I'd like to thank Catherine Gundry, Pete Nicol-Harper, Cherry Mosteshar, Ruby Glasspool, Megan Kerr, the Headington Writers Group, and my wife Janet for their helpful comments on the text, and all who have encouraged me, in a range of ways, to keep on writing through countless re-drafts. Thanks are due also to Jo Renshaw, the able solicitor who finally secured legal status for the asylum seeker on whose story Mohammed's is primarily based, and to all the solicitors currently fighting against the odds to secure rights and justice for asylum seekers. Most of all thanks are due to my wife for her steadfast encouragement and faith in this book, and to both her and my son, Jordan, for putting up with long periods when I've been distracted.

Half of any profit to the author from the sale of this book will be donated to asylum causes.

Printed in Great Britain
by Amazon.co.uk, Ltd.,
Marston Gate.